The PuppetMaster

Andrew L. MacNair

Sunrise Glory Publications
Copyright May, 2013

Dedications and Gratitudes

Dedicated to the women of India who, too early in their lives, have become widows. May they be provided with the love, the kindness, and the respect that all good people on earth deserve.
Compassion for all.

I would like to thank the Department of South and Southeast Asian Language and Literature, UC Berkeley, for their patience with the author so many years ago.

I also thank Master Upadhyayi of Varanasi for his countless hours of patience with a young foreign student who sat spellbound at his feet.

And as always, I thank my wife, Lynne, whose light shines so brilliantly and continues to illuminate my path.

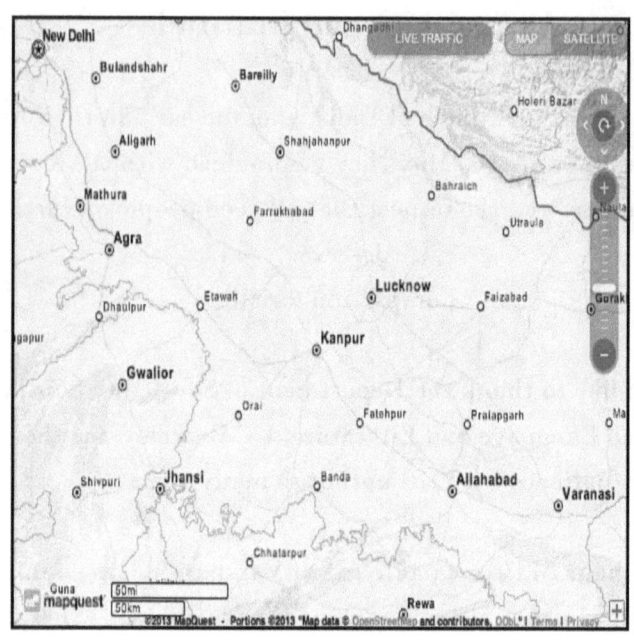

The PuppetMaster

Prologue

Varanasi, India, March 2006

Mina Rumir kissed her daughter's forehead and settled her into the linen inside the cradle next to her bed. The child, filled with its mother's milk, was sleeping now, and for a moment the young mother just looked at her infant in silence. She gazed at the rose-petal lips as they quivered from the breath or dreams that passed through them, and the sight of those lips instantly brought a fresh coursing of milk to Mina's breasts. She gazed at her baby's hands and lifted one with her own finger to study the nails, the cuticles like waning moons. With her own thumb she caressed the creases along the knuckles, because that was what Mina Rumir cherished more than anything in her world, her Surami's fingers. She could not have told anyone why she loved them so much, but the mere touch of those tiny appendages filled her with a love she could not have imagined she possessed.

For a moment she pictured an afternoon in the not too distant future when they would sit as mother and daughter on the broad swing in the garden. They would giggle and sip cane juice, and with a fine brush Mina would paint her Surami's nails in shades of vermilion and rose and smother them with kisses.

She bent once more to touch her lips to the hair on her daughter's brow, and then drawing her shawl about her head, descended the steps to the parlor. As she entered, Panchu glanced up from a thin stack of papers. "Can I assume she is asleep?"

"Yes, My Love."

"And you think it safe for me while you are gone, that she will not wake and raise the entire neighborhood with cries for her mother?"

Mina smiled. "With the milk she has drunk? She will sleep for hours, perhaps even until morning." The young husband returned his wife's smile and imagined the pleasure of them sleeping uninterrupted through an entire night. She chided playfully, "You will be fine, Panchu. I am sure you will manage our two-month old baby well enough while I am gone to temple. It is an hour only, and too many days have passed since I have been to take darshan. Perhaps afterwards I will look at the new silk that my good husband is going to purchase for me when I am thin again."

With a wave of his fingers he said, "You are thin enough, my beauty. Go. It is an evening made just for you."

The lanes that fed into to the Sankat Mochan were filled with the typical mixture of odors that evening. Fruit, incense, and the crisp aroma of trimmed carnations mingled with the foulness of sweat and excrement. Mina glided along the familiar lanes without hurry or haste, savoring the first solitary minutes she had enjoyed since Surami's birth. Her journey wound serpentine along the edge of the university and east from the district of Nagwa, and even though she felt alone as she walked, the avenues were swollen with streams of humanity. It was Tuesday, holy day--the day when the devout went to prayer, vendors plied their goods in keen expectancy, and the bare bulbs of shopkeepers glowed late into the night.

Mina paused at her favorite flower stall to select a mala of tulasi and marigolds. The vendor, recognizing the young mother, offered a fair price and inquired politely of Panchu and the baby. They chatted about each other's families and then Mina settled her shawl over her head and strolled the final distance to the Sankat Mochan.

The queue leading to the nave was shorter than she'd anticipated. It was after all the season of marriages, but only three wedding parties were gathered in the gardens, and the ceremonies had yet to begin. Mina listened to the stifled laughter and nervous whispers of the brides and their maids. Such a short time ago, she smiled, I giggled in this very place from my own nervousness.

Worshipers knelt to have their foreheads cleansed of dust and sweat and other impurities accumulated during the week. Above the nave, the statue of Hanuman rose like a tree, muscular and tall. The monkey-god was laughing, smiling at all who congregated below. Mina looked into that smile and for an instant it seemed to focus just on her. With a shy bow of her head she placed the wreath of flowers at its feet and knelt to receive darshan. The priest, pleased to see her at his altar again, lifted her chin affectionately and rinsed her forehead with holy water. Then he placed a circle of crimson in its center.

Mina gazed again at the statue and in her mind's eye the tiny fingers of her daughter's hands materialized. She stretched her own palms towards the sky. Love, she thought. That is our greatest gift. It is the blessing we are all given--each and every one of us--love, as limitless as the stars.

At that instant a bomb detonated four meters from Mina Rumir's outstretched palms. The device was calculated to kill as many worshipers as possible on that holiest day of the week. The young mother did not feel the blast; razored steel and mortar ripped through her spine and severed nerves from torso. Her outstretched hands vanished like mist in the flash, and within the minute Mina Rumir was dead. Her last thoughts were of her

Surami's fingernails painted brilliantly in vermilion and rose.

Four hundred meters to the east, from the plush safety of a dark Mercedes, Sutradharak, The PuppetMaster, twirled a silver ring on his smallest finger and smiled. He watched in dark fascination as knives of shrapnel tumbled lightly back to earth through an ascending plume of dust and smoke.

That was well placed, he concluded, a veritable model of perfection. Location and timing are so essential to this running game of diversion. Fascinating. All that death from the pressing of two small buttons.

A moment later Sutradharak detected the far-off rumble of the second explosion. The canisters at the cantonment rail station had detonated, a few seconds behind schedule, but from the sound of it, they had done precisely what they were supposed to—destroy lives, amplify fear, and generate futile searches for those responsible.

One

Varanasi, four months later

There are days that return to our memories like loop-tapes, revisit like children's rhymes, but as we move through them, they feel ordinary. Commonplace. We see them as mundane hours of little importance, but then, when we look back from some further point in time and see what they have truly brought, we realize that they moved together with the precision of a fine watch and had all the significance of our own birth.

The morning that Lalji came whimpering across the courtyard to inform me that he couldn't perform his chores for at least a fortnight was such a day. And between dawn and dusk three more seemingly innocuous events occurred that left far too many good people dead and ultimately altered the lives of millions: My teacher requested that I accompany him to the cave beyond Sarnath, Adam strolled quite casually past my front gate, and the news of the bombings in Northern India repeated itself.

I look back at those events, their seeming irrelevance, and ask myself how it was that I missed their magnitude. They should have given me some glimpse into the events of the next twenty-one days. But they didn't. Ah, but then I remind myself that that is simply the way my life has always unfolded: tiny, unanticipated events that change everything.

Let me begin with Lalji. The knuckle of his baby finger, he complained that morning in an inconsolable voice, had been cracked when a companion had struck it the previous evening during a game of cards. Lalji had been reading them prematurely, before they had all been dealt, and this being viewed as bad manners, resulted in the dealer smacking a palm sharply down upon Lalji's inconsiderate fingers. He was now displaying that cracked knuckle with puppy-like whining noises all with the hope that he wouldn't have to lift it--or any of his other extremities--to do any chores for as long as he could prolong the healing time.

I wasn't buying it.

To say that Lalji was merely lazy would be to vastly misinterpret his amazing capacity for work avoidance. He would routinely saunter back from the market, hours late, with the most creative tales of how a dozen thieves had attempted to outsmart him and steal our money—and he did refer to anything of value as ours. At first I questioned how such trickery had taken place but learned that my questioning brought lengthy descriptions of vendors attempting to pass off bad products for good ones, and thus more idle time was spent in the telling. Now I simply reminded him that I knew those vendors by name and would consult them at first opportunity as to what actually occurred.

Lalji always smelled of coconut oil and sweat, and depending upon the day of the week that odor would permeate the air in reasonable freshness or putrid rancidity.

He was so slight of build as to be called skinny. He wore a frayed purple loongi at all hours, and even though at our first meeting I had provided him money for a new one, the replacement never materialized--the rupees, I suspect, having transferred to one of his better card-playing friends. I'm not certain if Lalji even owned a shirt, which is just as well as it would have looked far too comical draped about his skinny shoulders.

So, as he stood before me that morning clutching his baby

finger and rolling his eyes as if he might faint onto the patio tiles, I wasn't fully accepting his request for a postponement of duties. First, I had fractured as many fingers as baseball catcher in my time, having enjoyed basketball, full contact sparring, softball, mountain biking, surfing and Ultimate Frisbee during various phases of my life. I knew what that finger needed. And to Lalji's dismay, I knew exactly how much it could endure once it was splinted. I told him as much.

"But Sahib…" This came out in a prolonged whine and was pronounced exactly like the European car, Saab. "It burns like the fires of the Ghats. How can I iron your shirt and pants with such pain? How can I fold them neatly the way you ask? I feel that I shall not be able to walk even the distance to the fruit-walla this morning." Feigning dizziness--quite well I might add-- he leaned against the wrought iron fence above the wall that circled the yard and let his knees sag. He cast a glance about the courtyard, ostensibly eyeing the hammock to sink his feeble body into. I stroked my chin thoughtfully and examined the knuckle with the expression of a surgeon.

"Hmm . . . Lalji, with the help of St. Thomas the Healer, I will perform a small miracle. Right now, within this very half hour, I will cure your finger." My proclamation was drawing upon his Christian beliefs, which he adhered to minimally out of respect--or fear--of his mother's sharp tongue and quick palm. "Go fetch me five cubes of ice from the freezer in the kitchen, no more, no less, because that is the precise number the cure calls for. Also, bring the drying cloth next to the sink and the white tape from the medicine cabinet." I clapped, "And do it quickly." He stared at me with obvious disappointment that I was going to so quickly eliminate the source of his evasion of duties.

I was about to add that the remedy wouldn't work if the ice melted, but then realized that such information would provide him far too convenient an excuse.

Thirty minutes later, taped and numbed with cold, Lalji's pinky was once again ready to perform his obligations as my gofer, dhobi, and watchman. That was the moment I received the request from my teacher.

I had just finished taping pinky and ring finger into a comfortable but firm union, both of us admiring the work, when the iron bell outside my gate rang softly three times. Without looking up I knew that the hand that pulled on the string was that of Soma, my teacher's young servant. She, unlike every other person who tugged on that cord, always rang the bell in a hushed, almost demure fashion, as if she were embarrassed by the rudeness of the noise.

She was hunched silently on the opposite side, hidden inside a threadbare shawl. I called out, "Namaste, Little Sister." And here, I will presume, is the appropriate place to introduce myself. My name is Martin Chandler Scott, and every person who knew me before my time in India referred to me as Marty. But in the holy city where I had lived for more than three years I was known only as Bhim--pronounced like beam, but with a whisper of aspiration. I was a linguist, more precisely, a Sanskritist of recognized skill, and my purpose for being there will be explained in due time.

I stepped from the shade of the gnarled mango, folded my hands, and affected a playful voice. In local dialect I said, "Soma, your eyes are a rather difficult to see concealed half a meter inside your sari, but I am sure they are as beautiful as the sunrise this morning." It was a good tease, one I knew she would enjoy. A visit to my courtyard and a wad of betel nut to chew on were probably the only true pleasures in her desolate life. "Are you bringing a smile for me this morning or just another trifling message from Master Devi?"

A stifled giggle. She drew the shawl back just far enough for me to see the inky curvature of her eyes. They were focused timidly on my toes. Her mouth, I saw, was already stained blood-red from her first chew of betel that morning. "I have both for you, Master Bhim." Her voice was barely audible.

"Excellent. Let's start with the smile shall we." I glanced at Lalji, who was still looking our way and still standing idly in the corner of the garden. I signaled with a thumb and a frown to get moving towards the kitchen to help his mother. Soma wouldn't raise her eyes until he had left, and as soon as he did, they rose timidly to mine. "Ah, so much better when you actually look up from the stonework, Little Sister. So, how are you today? I see you're already chewing a rather sizeable fold of betel. You will keep those pretty teeth in that beautiful smile a lot longer if you chewed less of that."

"The words you speak are true, Master Bhim." She looked at her own feet again. "But it is just a small pleasure. Such a little one." She was correct, and I mildly regretted the suggestion I had made.

The withdrawn beauty that stood before me in grimy folds of faded green, with dust-caked feet, two dozen plastic bangles, and ten toe rings, was a widow. She was also only seventeen, and this unfortunate combination foretold a long future of pain and emptiness.

Soma's husband had tumbled from the roof of a crowded train two months into their marriage. Most bodies would have survived the short fall, but the young man had had the misfortune to bounce inward. Consequently, his widow now earned a meager wage sweeping and running modest errands for my teacher and his family. She slept in the dirt of the courtyard of her obese mother-in-law and fetched uncomplainingly for everyone. Unlike Lalji and his mother, Soma spoke Bhojpuri, the rural dialect and knew of little beyond a ten mile circle. My servants, educated in the Jesuit schools, spoke decent English and knew more of the world. Soma was countryside from the rings on her toes to the black cords of her braided hair, and as a widow she was shunned by society. At seventeen she had been discarded as refuse and left to fend for herself like a starved dog.

Because of this gross inequity, and because I truly enjoyed her shy and gentle manner, I had designated her my adopted sister. Never told her such, but she knew. I taught her small things and listened as she told me through a child's vision of village life, a life that was now closed to her.

I tried to get her to smile, turned the keys to the locks on her cell, teased and complimented. Truth be known, what I secretly desired was to teach her to read, play chess, and do trigonometry in her head without benefit of pencil or paper, all of which I was certain she would do quite well given the opportunity.

Fate, however, had hidden the keys. I kept trying, and if from some lighthearted comment on the braid of her hair or the curve of her eyes, I got her to laugh, then I could laugh right back at Fate and flip him the finger.

"The betel is a tolerable habit, Soma," I replied. "Maybe one you could limit to once a day. A small chew in the evening, without tobacco, is quite sufficient." We both knew my suggestion was in vain. Soma liked her betel nut too much.

She wagged her head and raised her arm to push a strand of hair behind her ear. As her fingers moved to the side of her face, my eyes followed her forearm. The morning light glinted like water in her bangles. Hers were not silver; they were plastic, but nonetheless striking in their color. From the angle of light, the toffee-hue of skin and sparkle of soft fur, I was suddenly pierced with a sharp pain, breath shortening to gasps. In that small vision there had been an unmistakable likeness to a forearm I had known in a previous life.

"Master Bhim?" Soma had seen the shadow cross my eyes. "Are you ill?"

With an exhale I replied, "No, no, Little One, just a . . . passing twinge in the stomach. It is gone." I couldn't explain that the ache was further up, somewhere in the chambers of my heart. Gaining my breath I said, "So . . . now that you have graced me with your smile, will you tell me what Master Devi wishes?"

She affected a frown, clearly wishing to continue our discussion of her smile and minor vices, but replied obediently, "Master wishes to inform that you will be going with him on a journey to Sarnath tomorrow; more precisely, to a cave some kilometers beyond that city. I am instructed to tell you to wear your ugly shoes and clothes that will wash easily. Also, I am to tell you to bring your camera." The shoes she referred to were my prehistoric tennies. They were indeed ugly, functional for short hikes, but full of holes and scruffy beyond hope. Still, this request was a mystery.

I nodded slowly. "Well . . . if my memory is correct, tomorrow is Sunday, usually a day of rest. But if this is what Master Devi desires, then I shall be there. Did he mention where

I should meet him? And at what hour?" That detail was critical.

With some theatrics, Soma lifted the mantle from her head, liberating a braid that swung like a thick cable to her waist. We had arrived at the heart of her message, which I was certain she had painstakingly memorized. "Masterji expects you to meet him at seven AM precisely at the corner of the Grand Trunk and Chaitganj Roads. From there you will ride in an autorickshaw to your destination." She hesitated and I saw it was from embarrassment. "I am also instructed to tell you to bring exact fare for the driver. And the tip." That didn't surprise me. Generous in every other way, my teacher wouldn't impart with a single rupee, or even a few paisa, outside his home if it could be avoided. The practice of tipping was as foreign as equal rights, and as his student—his vidyarthi--it was expected that I pony up for transportation, meals, and all amenities whenever we ventured out. He rarely failed to take advantage of the custom.

"Very well,' I sighed. "Please inform Masterji that I will be there on time, with everything he requires, including my full and bottomless pockets." At which point I reached into one of those pockets and extracted a five-hundred rupee note. Taking care that no passerby or neighbor saw the transaction, I folded the bill and tucked it discretely into Soma's palm. With a wag of my finger I said, "Not for betel or new bangles. It is to be put in a safe place and saved. And if you wish, come Thursday evening and we will practice the newspaper again."

Had she not watered the dust of her mother-in-law's courtyard every night with her tears, Soma would have wept onto the stonework at my feet, but her eyes were like dry wells now—no moisture within. Instead, they shone with gratitude, and the smile, the big one that told me I'd thwarted Fate's plans, bloomed upon her face. That made my morning.

Fate, however, was taking notes, paying close attention to my silly attempts to change his plans for Soma. Within the fortnight he would alter all the features of that beautiful face and radiant smile.

Two

Twenty minutes later I was rocking in the rickety chair at my desk in the salon, watching Sahr, my housekeeper, with the usual fascination. She had just ordered Lalji to market for ingredients for the weekend meals. The list was accompanied by a stern warning that if he tarried or neglected a single duty— fractured pinky or not--she would raise sizable welts about his head that would make all his friends laugh at his condition.

Sahr was in every way a contrast to her creatively lazy son. Where he appeared thin and frail, she was filled with limitless energy and possessed a bosom so full it clearly contradicted Newton's laws of physics. The architects who designed the erotic temples at Khajuraho two hundred miles west of our city had never met my housekeeper, but if they had, her breasts would have been duplicated on the statues there.

Each day she spun about my house like a small top, sweeping, scurrying, washing, and cooking, all the while appearing as if she might topple if she tilted too far to one side. I had often glanced up from my desk and leapt to my feet from the mistaken notion that I needed to catch her before she tumbled into a corner where neither of us would be able to get her vertical again. What I eventually learned was that her center of gravity was in fact located below her navel, somewhere between her upper pubis and generous bottom. The folds of her sari mysteriously slimmed all of that lower flesh, creating the illusion of a ripe, brown pear walking illogically about on its stem.

Sahr had sharp, intelligent eyes and curved cheeks set in a moon-shaped face that made her look Nepalese. Her most prominent feature (after her bosom) was a smooth, ivory-colored birthmark that tapered from her left temple across to the center of her forehead. It stood out like a bleach-stain on a dark carpet, and I often remarked that it looked like an elephant's trunk. It appeared that way even more so when she scowled, which she did whenever she told me it was not a trunk but a swan's wing. I couldn't see it. She stated with visible pride that it was the source of her clairvoyance. That, I could see.

Sahr was an exceptional cook, frugal, and proud of all aspects of her culinary skills. In the mornings she would prepare plain American breakfasts of toast, coffee, and sliced fruit, all the while grumbling that her skills were squandered on that effortless meal, and what Master Bhim really needed was a healthy portion of samosas and pakoras for his long hours of turning pages of the large books upon his desk. I tried once, with no result, to explain that hefting those pages didn't require as many calories as she might imagine.

I took the first sip of a second cup of Nilgiri coffee and peered over the rim as she spun about the room. After sending the dust outside with a brisk warning not to return, she unhooked the sandalwood mats that hung on the window frames and leaned them against the doorjamb. With water from the garden hose she saturated them. In an hour, when the sun rose to a higher angle, the light would evaporate the moisture and cool and perfume all the front rooms of the villa--an ancient and still effective method of air conditioning.

I set my mug next to a stack of legal pads that represented six months of work--a translation one of the classical plays of the eighth century. My teacher had guided me on the project at times, but the opus was primarily mine, and one that I was proud of. It had been tedious work, and only a few people had actually heard the rendering, but I thought I'd done a decent job bringing a cast of twelve-hundred year old royals back to life.

I cleared my throat—the signal that I was announcing something of importance.

"Sahr, I will be traveling outside the city tomorrow. I won't need anything but coffee in the morning and a sandwich for the afternoon, something that won't go foul in the heat, cucumber with paneer cheese, perhaps. I will also need two Nalgenes of ice-water, a clean kerchief, my flashlight, and my camera."

Sahr normally relished these organizational chores, but a frown creased her face as soon as I'd begun. Something was amiss, and I was fairly certain I knew what it was. My trip wasn't in line with her psychic predictions.

Sahr was a clairvoyant, a seer, and everyone in Nagpur and nearby neighborhoods conceded that she was a good one. A damned good one.

Her belief system was a jumble that I could never quite figure out--baptized Jesuit, she practiced the Catholicism in a perfunctory, Hindu style manner. Portraits of Jesus, Mary, and Saint Francis sat in a small niche in her room. That's where the Christianity stopped. She performed puja to them each daybreak, lightening incense and adorning them with floral wreaths and fruit. But they took a distant backseat to a chatty green parrot, a ghost, and a pack of ornately designed astrology cards. The parrot, ghost, and cards were her tools for determining all the important decisions in her life . . . and mine, and most of the people in that part of the city. They also provided sufficient income that she probably could have done without housekeeping for me.

When I first arrived in the villa three years earlier, there had been a steady stream of clients tromping through the rear courtyard. All manner of people arrived for consultations about barren wombs, un-marriageable daughters, or aging parents. By the end of the second week I'd had to ask her to move the readings elsewhere. She did so immediately and without complaint.

Sahr leaned the last of the mats against the doorframe and rotated to face me, hands coming to rest impatiently on her hips. "And will Bhimaji be gone the entire day?" Just a hint of irritation in this.

"Well . . . yes, I would expect so, though if Master Devamukti tires too quickly, we might return earlier. I really don't know all the details. Actually, I don't know any of the details, but I assume we will be doing some research in the Sanskrit, which as you know doesn't ever seem to tire him, while I fatigue like an overworked carthorse."

"So you do not know if you will return for supper or not?"

I wasn't keen on how this was going. "No Sahr, I do not."

"And you do realize that tomorrow is the worst day of this month for Bhimaji to be traveling?" Her hand sliced the air like a knife. "The worst!"

Ah, I thought. So that's the cause of her tetchiness. She had evidently forecast my entire month cusp to cusp and the journey didn't bear good prognostications. Compound all of it with not knowing whether to prepare my dinner or leave me to forage for leftovers, and she was ill-tempered about all of it.

I knew better than to tease her much about her psychic powers, but I couldn't resist a few innocent jibes. "So, this prediction, Sahr, are you sure you have the right Bhimaji? Tall man, very neat, blond hair, twenty-seven years? Rents a nice villa near the river with a perpetually irritable cook? You're sure you have his correct birthday? That could cause some serious miscalculations you know, having the wrong birth date."

Her eyes narrowed and, with her hands still clamped like lobster claws at her hips; she pulled her shoulders back thrusting those mountains of bosom towards me. Just shy of five feet, she suddenly looked taller. "Oh yes, Sahib"—she only used that title when I was in trouble—"I have the correct man, a stubborn ferenghi who pays too little attention to matters of the heart, wades in the Ganga at the wrong hours of the night, and walks alone without a hat in the wrong hours of the day. He loses his writing pen too often from forgetfulness and doesn't send letters to his mother often enough. Yes, I have the correct Bhimaji. He is the very fortunate young sahib with a cook who sees to his every need, and that cook would weep to the end of time if he were ever hurt from his own foolishness. Oh yes...his birthday is the sixth of October."

Damn. She'd gotten it right, all of it. "Sahr, can you tell me how it will be dangerous for me to ride in an autorick with a seventy-four year old pundit, stroll through an airy cave, have a picnic, and return that afternoon?" I really hoped that was the way it would be.

She peered at me just as the sun rose above the top of the mango. Squinting, I saw her expression. She was truly troubled. "I consulted my bhuta last night, Bhimaji. The spirit told me that it is not the journey itself." Her voice trailed off. "It is what you will find on the journey that will be of danger to you." Seeing me squinting, she stepped to one side and added, "It will be of danger to you and many others. I have been told."

Not exactly a convert to her methods, I was nonetheless not a total skeptic. She had been correct on too many occasions for me to ignore it. I dropped my teasing manner.

"What sort of danger?" I also wondered how she knew of my trip a half day before Soma had come to the gate. That I chalked up to the best communication system in Uttar Pradesh--gossip, known thereabouts as gupchup.

"That is not being revealed, Bhimaji, only that your journey will bring you and others into grave danger."

"And which of your esteemed agents told you of this peril? Megadhuta the Parrot? Your cards? Tea leaves? Or maybe Durgabal, the all-seeing ghost of the Ganges?"

She didn't smile. She set her fingers upon the pulse of my wrist and looked at me anxiously. "All of them, Bhimaji. All of them"

I sighed and turned from the intensity of her gaze to stare out the window. In the street a figure passed slowly by my gate. The face turned in my direction and I recognized it. It was the face of a young man I hadn't seen for more than three years. I remembered it from the first night I entered the city, couldn't attach a name to it, but that face had left an indelible impression on me.

Habitually I reached for the thin cord that circled my neck-- my namaghanda, the name string the man had given me as he announced that I would no longer be called Martin Scott. I would be known only as Bhim. The string and the name both remained.

Absently, I tuned back into Sahr's voice. "And in case you haven't heard the latest news, there was another bombing yesterday. It is in the morning paper I set on your desk."

I glanced at the newspaper folded trimly on my desk and

squeezed my eyes shut. "Mother of God, where now?"

"A hundred miles down the rail line, outside Lucknow. The Varanasi police have pulled in people for questioning, mostly Muslims leaving the Gyanvapi Mosque. Imam Nomani is protesting it loudly, claiming it is another attempt to harass the good followers of Islam. But even worse, that fool Quereshy is ranting again, this time calling for a march down Luxa Road on Monday."

I groaned. The news of the imam's complaints didn't concern me much. His messages were, by and large peaceful, often with the goal of trying to bring Hindus and Muslims closer together. Protests were part of the expected rhetoric of a religious leader tending to the affairs his mosque. Udmir Yakoob Qereshy was another matter entirely, and his rants did concern me. He was a hothead, a Muslim cabinet member in the provincial government with enough influence to be quoted in the newspaper once a week. He could cause problems.

Neither of their reactions was as important as my next question. "How many died this time?"

"Nine," she answered quietly. Her fingers touched my wrist again. "Take caution, Bhimaji."

Three

Sutradharak, the Puppetmaster, squatted on the floor of a small loft near Beniya Park on the Lahurabir Road. The attic, located above a furniture warehouse, had a single window on the east side. It was interminably hot and coated with dust, but suited his purposes well. The building below was a disorganized mass of charpai cots, tables, and woven lamps, but normally empty of people.

The loft also had a wired Internet connection, four chairs and a table made of raw board.

He read the two lines on his laptop again, committed them to memory, and with a tap on the keypad, deleted them. The message contained no data that could connect his employers to him, no names, no subject, only a date and an amount in dollars moved into a corporate bank account in New Delhi. The planning and implementation of the next bombing, like all previous ones, would be left up to him. His employers granted full autonomy and conceded his ability carry out their objectives. Indeed, over a fourteen-month period, Sutradharak had orchestrated five bombings without detection or capture-- his most recent being the explosion the previous day that had killed nine people near Lucknow.

His employers had been pleased with the results, but the PuppetMaster considered them trifling. As always, he envisioned something larger.

His fingertips slid over the letters of the keyboard and hovered as if above a Ouija board. The message had come to him less than a minute earlier, so the details weren't even considered yet, but he had a date, and the details would come. They always did.

The Indian media, based primarily on reports provided by the intelligence agencies, declared that he was an Islamic extremist—the leader of a fundamentalist Pakistani unit operating along the rail lines between Delhi and Kolkuta. The Research and Analysis Wing—RAW—India's foremost investigative agency, issued a statement after the third bombing declaring he was the leader of Taweel Churi--The Long Knife. Many doubted this for the simple reason the group had never claimed responsibility for any of the attacks. Computer bloggers theorized he was everything from a Maoist Naxalite to an Al Quaida insurgent. One blogger even suggested he was a renegade CIA agent operating with a Special Ops team. That drew the best readership and most comments, but it was all speculation. What was clear to everyone was that he was well funded and had excellent resources. No one could describe him physically, but everyone could described his psychiatric profile correctly. He was, as they stated, an exceedingly vicious murderer. In that respect, they were all correct.

Sutradharak imagined himself differently. An masterful opportunist, geinus of disguise and diversion dwelling in the center of the flock. A bird of prey with a shadow no one saw even in the brightest sunlight.

He snapped the computer shut, disconnected the wires, and reset the baseboard that hid the high-speed connection behind the wall. Then he slid the laptop into a zip-lock, water-tight envelope and into a goatskin pouch. It appeared—for anyone caring to investigate—to contain only goat's milk. Clever design, he thought to himself.

He rose quickly from the floor and stepped to the shuttered window. The loft was vacant of furniture other than the table and chairs, decorated only with cobwebs and the ubiquitous dust. Sutradharak hated the loft, as he hated the city, the noise, the stench, and all the people that moved like cattle within it. But hatred, like money, was an acceptable, if not desirable, commodity. Hatred created purpose.

Through the slats he peered down at the crush of humanity below. A corpse wrapped in shrouds of orange floated by on a platform of shoulders, the loved ones singing dirges and spreading flower petals along the path. With a turn to the east, the funeral snaked down a lane to the Ghats and the river. The PuppetMaster sneered. Another foul procession to the pyres. He had the urge to spit, but thought better of it. The less one left behind, the less one could be traced.

Just another rotting corpse. A rare smiled etched his lips. Well, he thought, soon there will be more, hundreds, perhaps thousands.

With that thought, he placed a felt hat upon his head and a jerkin about his shoulders. He lifted the goatskin pouch and climbed down the ladder to the warehouse.

Four

I saw my teacher well before he saw me.

Master Devi was bent over a rosewood cane on the sidewalk beneath a withered acacia tree on the left side of the Grand Trunk Road. He wore a white dhoti folded into his waist to reveal two knobby knees and a pair of hideously green plastic sandals. A white kurta and a black vest, shiny from use, hung on his shoulders. Foot traffic flowed like river on the sidewalk behind him. He paid no attention. He was peering into every black and yellow autorickshaw that sputtered down the road, and as usual, he wore an expression of impatience.

Jatanaka Devamukti, Devi as I called him, had an uncanny resemblance to a bird of prey, more specifically, a vulture. His nose was large and curved like a bow from the center of his eyes to a point just above his upper lip. With bifocals, it gave him the appearance of a bespectacled condor.

His face drooped from eye sockets to his chin, all of it framed by massive ears that folded forward like a pachyderm's. Fortunately the over-sized ears and the enormous proboscis offset one another just enough to keep him from looking completely outlandish.

The inequities of his appearance, however, were quickly forgotten when one looked into his eyes; they bored into you with the disdain of the truly brilliant. He was unquestionably one of the greatest Sanskrit pundits in all of South Asia.

Bony hands and delicate fingers gave him an appearance of frailty. He wasn't. At seventy-four he had the stamina of a much younger man, and ostensibly the semen to match. Twenty-two years earlier, at the age of fifty-two, he had fathered Sukshmi. And the gods, clearly noting his features, had taken every precaution to prevent them from besmirching his daughter. She was one of the most beautiful young women in the city.

I tapped the driver of my bouncing tin can on the shoulder and motioned him towards the curb. Masterji, seeing my silhouette in the back, looked immediately at his watch. The autorick swerved left and jolted to a stop in front of his sandals. "You are late, Vidyarthi." No 'hello.' No 'how are you today,' just the reprimand.

My teacher, one learned quickly, detested modern innovation and most forms of machinery. Definitely all forms of technology. Gadgetry, he fumed, was the clearest testament the world was galloping headlong to its final days. The only post-Victorian invention he deemed worth a damn was the well-aged Timex secured to his wrist with blue plastic straps.

On occasion I had gone with him to market and watched as he slapped his cane about like a machete, clearing paths through the human jungle in front of him. He would glance impatiently at his watch and mutter nonstop about the tardiness of the merchants. His Timex, he boasted, gave the correct hour down to the second. I knew better. It was stem wound, needed adjustment every two days, and crept into the future like an H. G. Wells contraption. This kept the entire world lagging two minutes behind Masterji. My watch, being a few decades newer and of the quartz crystal variety, was a tad more accurate, but rather than contradict him as we idled in the street, I asked my driver, "Bai, what hour is it?" Drivers lived by their watches. His was hanging from a plastic garland at eye level.

With a wag of the head he pronounced, "It is six fifty-seven, Sahib." He looked with hesitation at my teacher and added, "I have set the hour this very morning when I went to temple." That added precision to his claim and a certain religious element that even my teacher couldn't dispute.

Devi wagged his head in grumpy resignation. "Humph . . . very well." Then, pitching a bundle onto my lap, he settled onto the narrow seat next to me and leaned forward to point across the young man's shoulder. "Take us by the Azamgarh Road northeast fourteen kilometers, then six more to the entrance of Imperial Mining. Do you know it, my man?" He then added that he himself knew the route and not to try anything circuitous.

"Yes, Sir. Indeed." With a wrench of the throttle the autorick lurched into the Sunday traffic, spilling us backwards and sending two cyclists swerving wildly.

I lifted my knapsack from the seat to offer more space, and as we were now rolling somewhat cheerfully along, asked, "Master, where are we headed exactly? Soma only said that we are going to a cave somewhere past Sarnath. Do you have a nice day hike planned for us?" I was joking about the hike and fishing for information.

His eyes locked onto the back of our driver's head to be sure the man was attending to the road and not our conversation. He lowered his voice to an unnecessary whisper--the coughing of motor caused enough racket to thwart any attempt at eavesdropping. Masterji also spoke in English, which our driver knew less than twenty words of. Turning to me with an odd gleam in his eyes, he said, "There has been a most fortuitous discovery, Bhimaji. It could be quite significant if it is what we think it is." I waited. That was usually good policy with my teacher; wait until things were explained in his own time and manner. "Only C.G. Chandragupta and I have had the opportunity to view it, and I only from two hasty sketches C.G. made three days ago. That is why I wanted you to accompany me today, so that we might look at it together. You have brought your camera, yes?" I nodded enthusiastically and waited for more.

He looked at the scenery.

I was excited now. Chamuk Garuda Chandragupta, shortened wisely to C.G., was one of the greatest Vedic scholars in Uttar Pradesh. He was also my teacher's closest friend and a renowned professor at Benares Hindu University. I had attended his lectures numerous times and considered him both a mentor and a friend. If these two had looked at something together and become excited, then it wouldn't take much for me to follow.

The great language had pulled me into it eight years earlier when I was a third year undergrad at the University of California, Berkeley. I had been plodding through an upper division phonetics course when a perceptive instructor tossed me a small, ragged primer on the grammar. That tattered little book was all it took. I opened the cover, saw the graceful curves of script and the romance began. During that semester I taught myself to form letters and read a few lines. In the two years that followed I signed up for every course the university had to offer—undergraduate, graduate, and then my Masters. Eventually I became adept enough to translate scripture, plays, and my favorite, classical poetry. The university hired me as an assistant professor.

But Life, as I have said, has a way of altering in tiny, unanticipated ways.

I was now eight thousand miles away, shrouded in linguistic

solitude, and had pushed that previous life where I wanted it, behind me and lost to memory.

The autorick bounced sharply as we rounded a corner, smacking my elbow against the door handle. Grasping the back of the driver's seat, I said, "This is not fair to keep me guessing like this, Master. What is going on?"

"I will explain more when we arrive, my boy, and there you may see for yourself, but" He rubbed his hands together. "C.G. and I believe we may have uncovered a small addendum to the Atharva Veda."

Now, for the average person this might not generate a great deal of exhilaration. For most, the question might arise: What the hell is an addendum to the Atharva Veda? And even more likely, why should I care? Like a botanist presenting a new species of orchid from a Central American hillside, or an astronomer announcing that an asteroid is actually a small moon, the typical person wouldn't flush with a great deal of excitement. But for a linguist? For those of us who lived our lives for such discoveries? We would salivate like Pavlov's dogs.

Sanskrit has deep roots and more branches than an acre of trees, and though no longer a living language, it is still a powerful tool for historians, philologists, anthropologists, even physicians. As the elder sister to Greek and Latin, it has many times more researchable text than those two combined. Any new finding would mean instant notoriety for the discoverers, even if only as a footnote in some arcane publication. It would be akin to discovering an additional chapter of Ulysses' return to Ithaca, an authentic piece left innocently behind in an old footlocker.

As we moved towards the outskirts of the city and the gardens of Sarnath where Buddha spoke his first sermons, the words of my housekeeper, not the Gautama, drifted back to me. 'It is not the journey, but what you will find on your journey that will be of danger to you.' It was then that the reality hit me. At the end of this unbelievably bumpy ride I was going to enter a cave. Suddenly my mouth contained less water than the Punjabi Desert.

Five

Dust. Like a vast convection oven the scorching breeze blew fine powder in layers about our rickshaw. Peering vertically through a tear in the fabric I saw shimmering blue, to the sides only muted orange. It settled into the leaves of the trees, the curves of corrugated roofs, and all the banana stalks that hung like carcasses along the way. The creases of our skin were lined with sweat . . . and dust.

There were two reasons the city was on a knife's edge that July—lack of rain and the gnawing fear of another bombing. The bombings had brought dread to those who entered crowded places, especially on the rail lines; the drought had them questioning the sanity of the gods. Rice fields had dried up, cattle had succumbed to thirst, and it seemed as if the entire province was being scorched into oblivion. People drifted like zombies, stared at the sky and shook their heads. When will the rains return? Then they looked at each other guardedly and asked, 'when will another bombing happen?'

I did my best to ignore it, lived alone, invested in a good ceiling fan, and drank lots of bottled water.

Forty minutes later our driver veered off the highway onto a secondary road of crushed rock, the change immediately taxing his skills. He snapped the handles to and fro in a futile attempt to slalom through the debris, then began tapping the gas and brakes to avoid obstacles and still maintain velocity. All of this had the affect of tossing us around like marbles in the back. I gripped a roof strut and peered through the windshield. Ahead, perhaps three kilometers distance, a high fence rose out of the flatness; chain link and circlets of razor wire stretched ominously across the horizon.

We had been motoring for two nearly hours, and I decided we had to be nearing our destination. I hoped so. The thought of uncoiling my body and stretching my wretched joints returned. My knee smacked sharply against the metal frame reminding me that we weren't there yet, and that seventy-five inches of body length was at least ten more than recommended by the manufacturers of autorickshaws.

"Devi?"

"Yes, Bhim?" He seemed less affected by our washing machine motion.

"Did I hear you say this place is in a mine?"

"No, not technically speaking. It is not within their cursed fence. The entrance to our cave is close by this mining production, you see, but outside the land this evil company has stolen and offended with their steel devices. The property we enter is owned by Mr. L. Robert Muktendra, who is a family friend. He was the first to discover the entrance two weeks ago. It was this good man who phoned C.G., who then himself came by my house last Tuesday evening with papers authorizing us solely to study what is inside."

This was the way Masterji communicated--when he wasn't grumbling. His English was spiked with dizzying rises and drops, lots of head bobbing and endearing little interjections like 'you see,' 'very well', and 'precisely so.' When he was grumpy it all condensed to terse little jabs. Inevitably there was some reference to an associate or family friend. This led me to believe that my teacher knew every person of importance in the district and most of the less notable ones as well. And being a pundit of Sanskrit, they all respected. Immensely. In that part of the world it was like averaging twenty points a game in the NBA, holding the same distinction and requiring just as much training.

"And this cave? It is large, right?" I was really hoping for an affirmative on this.

"Precisely so, you will only need to crawl a dozen or so meters from the entrance and then a short climb down." He was grinning, and I wasn't sure whether I'd received the answer I wanted.

"How far?"

The reply was another grin that curled mischievously below the colossal nose. Then I recalled that he'd never been inside the cave himself. He was enjoying a fine chuckle at my expense

It wasn't that I was claustrophobic exactly, or had an unfounded fear of the dark, but a combination of small, black spaces was not my cup of chai, especially if I happened to be trapped or lost inside one. Unfortunately, that notion had entered a few times during the ride.

My mouth had gone dry again. I reached for my canteen and checked my flashlight to make sure it was still functioning after bouncing across half the province. Another swig of water, another check of the bulb, and I was feeling more or less better.

I peered ahead again. The road was leading straight toward a very out-of-place looking steel gate. At that point it seemed to turn ninety-degree in both directions along the base of the fence. Inside the mining yard white-roofed sheds reflected waves of heat. Conveyors, crushers, and a lot of machinery I didn't recognize, zigzagged like erector set pieces. Dump trucks stood idle near the fence, and further in, there was a mound of fresh tailings and a gaping rectangle carved into a low hillside. Meter gauge tracks curved like talons into the cavity and vanished down the shaft. The entire scene had an eerie resemblance to the Morlock cave in The Time Machine--the original one with Rod Harris and Yvette Mimeau. One glance at that opening and my vision began to swim. Beads of sweat that weren't attributable to the midday heat broke across my forehead.

We drew nearer and I saw signs on the fence. Not large. They didn't, I suppose, need to be. IHI Imperial Holding International, Lucknow, India. No Entry. Six languages and a lot of sharp wire told you to turn around and drive away slowly.

To the left of the entrance there was a squat cinder-block structure with tangle of utility cables angling into it, and as we motored closer, two guards stepped out and shifted casually to either side. They were uniformed, carried binoculars, clipboards, walkie-talkies, and some serious looking assault weapons. This only added to the whole evil Morlock thing in my opinion. Instantly I wondered how they could strut around with all that mass and not melt into the dirt.

I watched them watching us. They weren't Indian. They looked more like British marines who played beach volleyball for amusement.

In my previous life I'd gone through a lot of physical training. My parents were products of an affluent Southern California life-style, runners and extreme sports enthusiasts. From my earliest years I had been pressed gently but firmly into every form of sport, martial arts, kempo karate, and even Brazilian grappling. I surfed, skied, played Ultimate Frisbee, and eventually came to appreciate any activity that didn't rely on teammates. Even though it swam up from the past I was trying to forget, I could still measure up physique with a glance. These two, standing in the heat, with handcuffs and heavy weaponry, were highly trained professionals. I didn't need to see it in their eyes or resumes; I could tell by the lightness in their step.

As we approached the gate, one of them un-shouldered his weapon, very relaxed, and drew it to the front. The other flipped through pages on his clipboard. I grinned. It looked as if he was searching through an invitation list. As it turned out, it didn't matter. Our driver, at Devi's behest, veered right ten feet before the gate and with a quick exchange of a scowl from Masterji and indifferent nods from the guards, we continued down the road.

"What was that? Those guys looked like Gurkhas preparing for an attack on their fortress. What do they mine in that place? Diamonds and platinum?"

"Yes, yes, precisely so. The local papers and government says it is bauxite, but you know how imprecise these things can be."

I looked back and saw nothing but dust from our tires.

A half a mile further, two hundred meters beyond the corner of the fence, we swerved left and jolted to a stop on a patch of parched grass. Behind us a cloud of orange rose into the air over the razor wire. I peeled myself out of the sardine can, slapped some sensation back into my legs, and looked around. The vastness of the Gangetic Plain stretched in ancient grandeur from east to west. If you ignore the fence and the rickshaw, we are in the middle of nowhere, very hot, very dry, Uttar Pradesh nowhere.

Devi was now in a positively bubbly mood. He had taken a keen liking to our driver, Rajneesh Sukkha, who, he proclaimed with a tap of the cane on the man's shoulder, had ferried us quite well to our destination. The two of them were joking like old buddies, and of course Masterji knew Rajneesh's family. He invited the young driver to join us on the hike to the cave, but not inside. Master, probably from Chandragupta's descriptions, knew of a banyan tree near the entrance. There our driver could rest and wait for our return. We would picnic, and if our driver would be so kind as to carry the cloth bundle, he could share its contents. Precisely so. This sounded better to Rajneesh than waiting in the blistering box that he spent most of his waking hours in. So, off we went looking like three chummy companions, Devi twirling his cane, Rajneesh toting the sack on his head, and I following along in nervous silence.

Six

The entrance wasn't visible from the front, and, I quickly learned, barely so from the side. The ground rose from our parking place, angled up over a quarter mile of dust and rubble, then curved upward into crags and boulders at the base of a tall cone of weathered rock. As we picked our way upward, Master began plunging his cane into the crevices with the energy of someone gigging frogs. Unexpectedly, he halted and announced, "Very well then, here it is." I didn't see anything. Behind us the Ganges glistened like a ribbon in the shimmering plain. Ox and women trudged through drying rice fields, vultures and hawks circled above. In front, the rock vaulted like a pillar. Clearly we weren't climbing that.

I helped Rajneesh open the bundle under the tree, while Masterji marched tenaciously to the left and disappeared. I followed him over a spur of jagged stones, and when I descended the opposite side I saw what had been impossible to see from the front. Two fingers of slag, side by side, concealed a narrow opening, and only by standing directly in front could one see the entrance. It was less than twice the width of my body, and immediately that scrawny entrance had me more nervous than Orpheus at the gates of Hades. I couldn't have worked up enough spit to wet a dime.

My phobia, though rather inconvenient at times, is not Jungian or involve any aversion to re-entering the womb. It has nothing to do with the tragedy that compelled me to Varanasi, either. No, my older brother is to blame for this one. On an evening when I was four he locked me in a closet. My parents were away, and he, being somewhat careless back then, conveniently forgot his obligations as baby-sitter as he watched the Chicago Bulls squeak by the L.A. Lakers in what I later learned was a classic finish at the buzzer. I pounded on the door for an hour and got so scared I wet my pants. The result is a small panic whenever I enter unlit pantries, walk-in closets, or East Indian caves.

My teacher had disappeared through the fissure, so I took a nervous gulp from my Nalgene and inhaled. Flashlight in hand, I clambered across the stones into the darkness. The beam splayed into the gloom, and I saw immediately that Devi had been teasing; I wouldn't need to crawl. The fissure expanded over a distance of eight meters and spilled into a space roughly the size and shape of a twenty-meter egg. Walnut-sized stones, black and oily-looking, littered the floor, but it was all level enough to move about easily if one treaded carefully. The ceiling appeared solid--an observation that added immensely to my ability to breathe again. It was compact but large enough to keep my anxiety at bay, and as long as no one played sound bites of Michael Jordan or Magic Johnson I would be just fine.

Ahead of me on the right, Devi was illuminated by the light of a small oil lamp. He was leaning forward on his cane, rocking excitedly as he peered at the wall near his knees. Even from that distance and in that light I knew his expression. The eyes were glistening with academic delight.

Further back the floor disappeared under a mound of the same oily rock that littered the floor. I inhaled. The air was stale but lacked mustiness. I played the beam across the curve of the walls, and there, leaping under the light, were the distinct features of thousands of tiny, recognizable faces. Script. Words. All etched into the walls in rows straight enough to make a handwriting instructor proud. The lines had been painted with some form of stain that had faded over time. Pale lotuses and red vines climbed from floor to ceiling.

"My God, It's Brahmi," I whispered. My words, even in low tones, bounced like ghosts about the cavern.

It was rare that I uttered even the most minor of blasphemies in Master's presence, but in the excitement, decorum had fled. That much script, un-translated, ancient and intact, was breathtaking. My pulse quickened. These walls had waited centuries to be read. How many? I didn't know, but it was definitely old. How much so, and what messages were hidden within, that was our puzzle to solve.

I stood with the beam flitting across the lines and knew—instinctively or intuitively--that I would be the one to free it. It felt as if a hundred voices were whispering to me. The gift is yours to solve, Bhim. Use it well.

"Precisely so, Bhimaji. Precisely so." Master was lost in the letters in front him.

To be honest, unlike my teacher who could decipher most Indo-Aryan scripts and half a dozen Dravidian ones as well, I was momentary disadvantaged. Brahmi wasn't something I had ventured into in my eight years. Sanskrit was recorded in Devanagari, 'the city of the gods.' It is India's common script and used for everything from movie billboards to documents of state. It looks like strips of silk hanging on lines in a gentle breeze. The Brahmi I was gazing so reverently at was angular, like Nordic runes, older and less familiar.

I studied a line at eye level and tugged at my memory. As my eyes adjusted to the light, so did my ability to decode the letters. Slowly, I recognized words here and there. Phalam—fruit, mamsam—flesh, dhvani—sound.

Devi called out, "Bhim, come, come. Look at this." The tip of his cane danced like a conductor's baton at a section in front of his ankles. He was careful not to touch the writing itself. I scanned the floor with my flashlight and picked my way across. "This,"--he was rocking back and forth now with excitement-- "is a prescription. Yes, yes. Look here. You see this word? Shastram. Precisely so. These are medical instructions. I'm certain of it. We are looking at a piece of the Sushrut Samhitas. Perhaps something even earlier." He looked at me with gleaming pupils. "This is it, my boy, a true find."

I glanced around. Except where it had collapsed on the left, the walls were covered in letters. Once translated, authenticated, and published, it would be hailed as a major find. Another thought came to me. If Masterji was correct and it was medical, not just linguists would take interest. That idea was a little daunting.

I dug into my pack and spent the next two minutes taking close-ups with my trusty digital Canon. Half way around, my not so trusty batteries began to run low. I swore at the oversight. I had instructed Sahr to pack everything but additional batteries. Standing close for better clarity and readability, I now, had to step back and take three wide angles to capture the rest. I could always return and photograph the remaining lines at a later time. Or so I imagined. But as I have mentioned, my life has too often unfolded with tiny, unanticipated events that change everything.

Seven

I helped Devi back into the sunlight, guiding his torso with a palm on his lower back. As we stepped through the opening, he unexpectedly seized my wrist and whispered, "Bhimaji, we must speak of this to no one. It cannot be mentioned until we have had the opportunity to study it." I wasn't certain why it was said with such intensity, but I understood his reasoning. Until it was translated and published we would need to be circumspect about its discovery.

Master was fatiguing, so it was good when we settled into the shade next to a drowsy Rajneesh. Our driver had taken it upon himself to arrange our picnic on the blanket that held the food. Then he'd dozed off for a proper nap. He'd assumed neither Master nor I would mind his touching the containers, a risky assumption as Brahmin law requires only members of their own caste touch their food. Rajneesh had guessed correctly that since he'd been asked to tote the bundle up to the tree, it was acceptable for him to open it and arrange the Tupperware.

Devamukti adhered to many, but not all, guidelines of an orthodox Brahmin. For example, he never touched leather. That meant green vinyl sandals and blue watch bands were always in vogue. Personally, I thought they were ugly as sin and added significantly to his already questionable features.

Though I saw certain aspects of my teacher as humorous, my admiration for him was immeasurably deep. For three years and four months he had forged my skills like a coppersmith, and during those months I had come to love him as a father, an irascible, miserly, but affectionate father. He'd taken me, a non-Hindu, as his vidyarthi, and in doing so had thumbed a nose at traditions and the conservative council in the city. He had recognized my passion for the language, and recognized the pain that was devouring me. A full baptismal in the language would be the best restorative. I was dunked headfirst into translation.

Rice, dal, and chapattis materialized like magician's props on our cloth. Condiments, fruit, and sweet lassis followed to wash it down. Mirabai, Devi's wife, had prepared the entire meal. She was the only person—man or woman—who could match Sahr with her cooking skills, not something I ever mentioned to my cook, however.

It was an afternoon of boyish delight. We ignored the heat and ate like rajahs, laughed at the folly of new Hindi films, sang silly tunes, and in sleepy fashion swapped stories of our youth. Rajneesh and I, being closer to that age, listened to Masterji more than we talked. He told us of times when the rajah still roamed the corridors of the great palace across the river. I attempted to engage them with anecdotes of surfing Southern California waves, but the image of ripping across roaring tubes of liquid didn't come across in Hindi quite as well as I'd hoped. Rajneesh, whose jovial company I was enjoying more and more, pumped me for information about Hollywood, especially of Julia Roberts and Angelina Jolie. I suspected he had recurring dreams about them.

At one point our driver broached the subject of the terrorist bombings that had gripped everyone along the rail lines. "This man, the one they call Sutradharak, Sirs. Do you think he really exists? He has set off another explosion near Lucknow this week. Some say he is the leader of the Taweel Churi, and others that he is a Kashmiri nationalist; my brother swears he is al-Qaeda. Personally, I think he's just another religious nut case."

I picked up enough local news from the morning paper, but

this wasn't a subject I wished to enter into.

My teacher, on the other hand, responded instantly. "This PuppetMaster, if that is his accursed name, is a murderous fiend. He leads a pack of evil rodents and is most assuredly an Islamic fanatic. I am certain that he has now scurried with all his rodent pack back to Islamabad where he is boasting to all his neighbors how many righteous Hindus he has killed in our righteous city. If I were not Brahmin, I would curse his name out loud. Let us not speak any more of this abomination." I sipped my lassi and pondered Devi's statement that the terrorists had left the region. I doubted it.

Eventually it was time to gather the containers and hike down the slope to the autorick. We climbed in and motored along the dusty strip past the guardhouse. No one emerged with clipboards or assault rifles, though I was pretty certain I saw two circular reflections follow us down the road when I glanced back.

Once we were airborne again—not a misstatement, as we undoubtedly spent more time off the ground than on it— Masterji turned to me. "Bhim, we will have busy days ahead. C.G. will join us, and together we will form a team." This image was pleasantly exciting. "Can you change your schedule to spend mornings at my house and put the Bhavabuti play on the shelf for now?" I nodded an affirmation. "We must set things in motion correctly, one step at a time, you see, and speak to no one until we know exactly what we are working with. I will discuss the same with C.G., but he also understands the need for discretion."

He peered through the spattered windshield towards the

haze of the city. "Discoveries like this bring risk, you see. In this part of the world there are those who would steal anything of value, and I believe what we have seen today is of value. Valuable bring danger." The words hung in the afternoon heat.

We delivered Devamukti to his front gate at sunset, and I watched in astonishment as he gifted Rajneesh a fifty-rupee note in magnanimous fashion. At the current exchange it amounted to one dollar and five cents. It was accompanied by a large spoonful of advice on how to spend it. Wanting to assure his safe entry into the house, I waited until he shuffled across the courtyard and through the door. His wife Mirabai greeted him and waved to me.

As the autorick rolled down Shivanan Avenue, the sky above the spires of the Durga Temple were streaked with apricot and maroon. Across the river, purple and indigo had taken hold. Varanasi, the city of light, was fading into evening.

I stood wearily at my gate. Lifting my knapsack, I asked, "Rajneesh, how many children did you say you have?" I unfolded a stack of sweat stained rupees.

"Four, Sahib, three girls and one unfortunate boy in the middle who cannot find any siblings to play soccer with."

"Yes, well he will likely become a very good cook, dress impeccably, and know exactly how much money to take to the marketplace." He laughed. "Here is your fare for the day and some extra for your family." I handed him twice our agreed upon fee.

"Sahib, you are far too generous." But the rupees were pocketed quickly. There were mouths to fill and shoes to buy. I liked my new acquaintance and inquired how I might contact him in the future. His brother, he explained, owned a cell phone, and he scribbled the number on a scrap of paper. If we were ever in need of employees . . . With a quick namaste, he throttled his rickshaw and bounced down the road towards the bridge over the Asi River.

I pushed upon my gate and the action recalled the memory of the man I'd seen walking past it the previous day. It also brought back the memory of the encounter I'd had with him three and a half years ago--the first night I entered the city. The Delhi to Kolkut train had just lumbered into the station, and I had just stepped into the human bustle of the platform. My clothes were covered with soot, my spirit covered with sadness. I wished only for the anonymity of a new life in an old city. The young man appeared from within a cluster of passengers and luggage porters, looking in all ways like a college instructor or aspiring entrepreneur. He strode towards me as if he had been waiting for me to arrive.

"My good friend, welcome," he fired off in rapid, articulate English. "Tonight you enter the perennial city of Varanasi like a newborn, and for that reason, you really must have a new name."

I stepped back uneasily, and then seeing that he was not preparing to assault me or pester me for alms, I replied, "What?"

"You need a new name, my friend, one to match your new identity." He smiled as if knowing that was my intention.

I blinked, dumbfounded. "Right . . . Okay. And what...what do you think I should be called?"

With the quickness of someone who already knew the answer, he laughed, "You shall be named Bhim, like the great Pandava brother," and without asking permission, slipped a black namaghanda about my neck and tied it. Christening me, if that verb may be used for the gift of a Hindu name, he whispered, "Bhim. Yes, yes, perfect. We shall meet again, Bhim. Be assured. Do good deeds, My Friend. It will help with the healing." I blinked again, baffled by what he had seen in me.

Then, he disappeared like vapor into the crowd.

I closed the gate and decided his reappearance the same morning I received the invitation to the cave was merely coincidence.

With a splitting yawn, I plodded into the courtyard where the only thing that greeted me was Lalji's snoring and the savory aroma of Sahr's banana fritters.

Eight

The plan for the next bombing came to Sutradharak in the small hours just beyond midnight. He rarely slept through an entire night, often suffering from prolonged bouts of insomnia, but in that sleeplessness, he was creative, his mind intensely active. Details bubbled to the surface like tar and he worked them to higher and higher levels of intricacy. Every element, every component was visited and analyzed, every contingency assessed.

At first he had rejected the idea based on redundancy. A similar event eight months earlier had gone well, but one of his rules was never to repeat events. Repetition created patterns and patterns brought traceable clues.

However, the more he considered this new design, the more he liked it. There was enough variation to it.

Ultimately, his decision to accept the plan came from the numbers. The earlier attacks required more plastique, more charges, and a larger team. This required a small team and in all likelihood, only six charges. But the numbers, the deaths it could produce . . . that was the deciding factor.

With the basic idea still twisting around in his mind, Sutradharak got out of bed and made a pot of coffee. Details always needed research, and research needed to be done in the capital. He began preparations to travel to New Delhi.

Nine

I screamed and strained every muscle against the walls of the cell, but like an animal being slowly choked into submission, no sound came out. The sphere that surrounded me, trapped me, was transparent and nauseatingly tight. I clawed and scratched at the slickness, pushed out in four directions like DaVinci's naked man. But the surface only flexed like thick, unyielding cellophane. Impenetrable. I screamed again. Silence. Colors pulsed from blue to scarlet and back again, the colors of blood. I sobbed. Beaten, I slid to my knees. With shoulders slumped, I began twisting in slow spirals. It was always slow spirals. My nightmare had returned.

I woke up drenched in sweat. The air was still cool by summer standards of Uttar Pradesh. The sun had not yet risen above bank of the river, but atop my linen, I was soaked in pools of my own perspiration.

The fan above me spun in a slow thwumping tempo, and I exhaled in panicked breaths into the draft. Three years I had suffered through my nightmare. Like a soap opera it came with variety, but always with the same theme. Over the last ten months it had receded enough that I believed it had left for good, but like a silent thief it had crept back. And the bubble, that fucking corpuscle of blood, still trapped me.

That bubble had changed my life, every facet of it. It was the tiny unforeseen event that had altered my course of life forever.

I stared at the blades of the fan. For a year now I'd been able to push her memory down, or back, or wherever we push such things--managed to keep her fragrance and eyes locked inside a vault of unwanted recollections.

The fan drew me in, and there at the center lay Lilia--where I always saw her--curled and shaking upon the carpet. She looked strangely peaceful, like a child twitching in an afternoon nap. Our pizza sat half eaten on the table, our mugs of beer half full. The air was dry and hot with the Santa Anas that had been whistling in from the Mojave.

Moments earlier we had been laughing--an exchange of childish stories that lovers do so well. She was telling me about her mother's house in Oaxaca, of eating mole poblano with her cousins on the porch. Then mid-sentence she stopped, and with a puzzled look, stared at me, and then looked at the lights as if they were too bright for the softness of her eyes. Like a priest beseeching the heavens, her eyes rolled upward. Her hand reached out to touch my face, then she leaned forward and slid most naturally from her seat, looking as if she were simply retrieving a napkin from the floor. But Lilia Garza Morales, the woman I had loved for a year and a thousand lifetimes, slid to the carpet and never got up. She died with my hands wrapped pleadingly about her head.

The doctors explained everything. They clipped images and scans onto white lights and showed me the post-aneurysm section of her brain. Pointed with sad, intelligent fingers at the bubble, and explained in practiced phrases all the reasons for how Lilia had slipped from my life.

But none of them, not a single one, could explain why.

It was September, and we were to be married in November in a ceremony of elegant simplicity on a knoll above the ocean. It was something we looked forward to more for our family and friends than for us, because Lilia and I were already joined. We knew it the moment we met--a union of a thousand lifetimes, the botanist and the linguist our friends called us, naturals together.

We had met during a dreary wait in the admissions office at the university in Berkeley. She was standing behind me swearing colorfully in Spanish and I began laughing at the creativity and turned to see who the speaker was.

Our eyes met, and we laughed, and she asked my name, but it was as if she already knew.

The next day we shared chili rellenos in a restaurant on Telegraph Avenue, and the second half of that day was spent in a library together. We were grad students after all. But it was like we were simply re-acquainting after a time apart. By the week's end we were rolling naked in a bed too small, in an apartment with one closet. We kissed chow mien from each other's lips, memorized lines from old movies, and body-surfed in cool waves. It became a single year of bliss.

For three hundred and seventy days Lilia and I were a union, studied together, and spoke the language of academicians and lovers. The future was ours, I ready to discover the roots of great poetry, she the roots of healing plants. Then the bubble, in a few short seconds, took it all. And those horrible seconds replayed far too often in my nightmares.

I spread Lilia's ashes in our favorite swimming cove the day we were to be married, and in the months that followed, friends came to me the way the doctors had, comforting me with selected words, telling me to keep her face in my memory. They wrapped consoling arms about my shoulders and said in sad intonation, 'celebrate your time together, Marty. Take the joy you shared and never forget how wonderful it was.' Fuck them. Fuck them! They didn't feel the blade that sliced into me when I saw the curve of her shoulders and hair. They didn't feel the ripping of arteries when I gazed into the eyes that no longer looked back. No, I wouldn't celebrate those memories. I couldn't, because every time I did it felt like my flesh was on fire and my soul was being charred.

So, I took the union of a thousand lifetimes and hid it. I took her face, her smell, her touch, every piece of her, and set it in a box and cast it into the closet of my past life. And I left. Some might even say I fled.

I looked at the fan again and drew a breath. I was in back in Varanasi and Lilia's face had receded once more. Sahr's coffee was calling me to splash it with milk and sip it in my wobbly chair. Read the local news. Ease into the day. There were the cave photographs to be loaded into the computer, linguistic mysteries to be solved.

"Good morning, Sahr." I entered the kitchen sheepishly, having been too exhausted the previous evening to eat much. I'd snacked only on a few fritters and gone straight to bed instead of sitting down to the meal she had prepared for me.

"Good morning, Master Bhimaji. How is the famous explorer of caves doing this fine day?" I glanced at her frown. Behind it was the faintest hint of a grin, and behind that the same worried look as the day before. The fear that my journey was going to cause some great physical harm to me, if not induce worldwide calamity, still hovered.

"I am doing quite well this morning, as you can see. I thought it might be good to eat a few of those delicious puris you prepared last night, and some pakoras too. No American toast for me today." Good way to start the conversation.

"As you wish, Sahib. I will heat them for you. The puris will likely be flat and oily since they have gone uneaten for ten hours, but the pakoras will be nearly as good as they would have been last night." I didn't miss the 'nearly' part. I was receiving Sahr's version of a slap on the wrist. I also noted her use of the title 'Sahib,' her verbal version of a frown.

I ladled out a healthy portion of compliments as I ate breakfast, and as Sahr was clearing the plate I had nearly licked clean, added one more, "You could have cooked for Radha and Krishna, Sahr. No one on the planet makes pakoras as good as yours. They are fit for the gods."

"Bhimaji is either joking with me or he wants something."

"No, it's true, they are the best, but I actually do need something of you."

"Ah, I knew it. I can read you better than my deva cards."

"Not a doubt in my mind, but I do have a request, small but important."

She waited, expecting me to add some task to her daily chores, which wouldn't have irked her in the least. She looked a tad disappointed when I said, "It's important that you tell no one that Devamukti and I traveled outside the city yesterday. No mention of caves, photographs, or a journey, nothing at all. Okay?"

In addition to all the other things Sahr did well, she understood when I was serious about a request, and unlike Lalji, I could depend upon her prudence. He was my weak link, and she--by the nature of her consultations--was quite discreet.

"As Bhimaji wishes," She looked at me as if the specters of ill fortune were still floating around my head. "and I will not ask the reason for this secrecy, though I am certain that it has something to do with the danger that Durgabal and my cards predicted."

"We are not in any danger, Sahr. It is just important no one hear that Master and I went to this place. You know how people talk about us ferenghis and what we do."

She smiled for the first time that morning. "Yes, Bhimaji. Bahut, bahut gupchup in this city."

"Well, let's make sure there isn't any gupchup about my journey." I tried to look as authoritative as possible. "And if you will be so kind as to remind Lalji of this. A firm reminder?"

"It will be my pleasure. And what would the rajah of the house wish for dinner tonight? That is assuming he will be here for dinner."

"I will definitely be here, Most Glorious One, and I will dine on your best selections. You prepare whatever delights come to mind and I will be here. How's that for an answer?"

She grinned. "That is a good answer, Master Bhim." She turned to the pantry, while I went to the salon to read the newspaper and load the photographs from the camera into the laptop.

The local news wasn't good. Followers of Yakoob Qereshy had decided a protest march wasn't a clear enough signal to send to the authorities for detaining Muslims. A police station in Jaunpur, between Lucknow and Varanasi, had been attacked and torched overnight. No one was injured, but the message of anger had been sent.

I looked out the window. Still no sign of rain.

Ten

There were two reasons I was certain no thief would attempt to steal the bicycle I left unlocked on the right side of my villa. It was so old and looked so unsafe as to be un-rideable even by Asian standards. It also had a frame with seat raised so high any thief would have toppled headlong into the first tree along the escape route. She was unsightly, shimmied unmercifully on hard right turns, and she was mine. I knew every nuance of her maneuverability, and after hours of careful consideration I'd dubbed her Ugly Bike. On better days, Miss Ugly. I loved every square centimeter of her disfigured surface. Five days a week I would swing a leg over the saddle and pump her mud-caked pedals like a log-roller to weave down Shivanan Avenue, scattering chickens, children, and dogs like a mad horseman. I was a seasoned cyclist in the streets of South Nagpur and even wily rickshaw drivers paid me homage. The image of colliding with such a large ferenghi on such an ugly bicycle put enough fear in their hearts, or sense in their heads, that they pulled prudently to the side whenever I hurtled towards them.

My home was on the southern edge of Varanasi, in a less populated neighborhood two hundred meters from The Ganges. The villa had been a fortuitous discovery a month after my arrival. All the others I had inspected were either in very crowded neighborhoods or so rundown and mildewed as to deter me from living in them. My house was spacious and clean, with a shaded courtyard, a wall with wrought iron fence and rusty blades jutting from the top. From the veranda one stepped into a large salon with comfortable, overstuffed furniture. To the side there was a bedroom complete with—praise the devas—a quiet, high-speed fan. In the back, there was a kitchen outfitted with a small oven, acres of counter space, and a large refrigerator-- Sahr's domain that I entered cautiously.

In the rear were two cottages for her and Lalji, though he usually slept in the hammock in the front. This was to demonstrate his diligence as a night watchman. I'd snuck up on him a dozen times, shaken the hammock with enough force to tumble him to the ground, where he would snuffle, roll over and slip quickly back into his dreams. So much for security.

My backpack bounced to the side as I raced down Shivanan Avenue to Sonapura and across the bridge above the Asi. Two reference books, a few leftover chapattis, and my HP laptop were wedged carefully inside. On the outside a cold Nalgene was nestled in the webbing, perspiring almost as much as I was. It was eight-fifty in the morning, and the thermometer had just topped forty degrees centigrade. Another cloudless scorcher was heating up.

On the far side of the bridge a pregnant Brahma cow glanced up at the clang of Miss Ugly's bell and shifted a lazily to the right. I breezed past her flank and swerved around two women with water pots balanced on their heads. Bicycle rickshaws, ox carts, pedi-cabs, and scurrying dogs flew behind me. I shifted into highest gear and elbowed my pack back into position.

Devi's erroneous Timex was ticking, and I was racing to beat it. Glancing at my own watch, I did some calculation. A six-minute margin. His compound was off Madanapura Road near the Raja Ghat. The first part of my route along the main avenues would be easy, but the moment I turned east into the gullies, the pedaling would be slower, if not down to walking entirely.

Varanasi, Benares, the holiest of India's cities. A thousand writers have struggled to lay descriptions of its antiquity upon their pages. Over the centuries a few have met with limited success. They have written, "It is a city so ancient that many believe it to be the oldest still in existence." But what does that say? Only that it is old. Yes, it is old, and puzzling and dark, and the deeper one ventures into its labyrinthine paths, the darker it becomes. Its original name was Kashi, The City of Light, but that luminous title referred to its spiritual side--Buddha spoke in its gardens. It certainly didn't refer to the dank gullies that twisted like a nest of snakes along its eastern half.

The central avenues are wide enough for pedestrians and the mass of carts and vehicles, but as one enters the lanes to the east there is an immediate and sudden transformation. The walls close in, the paths narrow like a constricting vascular system, squeezing into tinier and tinier spaces, the air becomes pungent with dung, cooking spices, and raw human filth. Strains of Hindustani music blare from a dozen ill-tuned radios above walls that block the light of day. Voices drift from windows where no faces ever appear. People push past each other with downcast eyes and just when the shadows grow darkest and the walls pinch to nauseating tightness, it parts. And there, like an immense, brilliant vein, the Mother Ganges spreads across to a distant and sandy shore. She sweeps by slowly, while all that confined life in the lanes spills onto her banks with visible relief.

Vaulted temples, marbled mosques, and wooden stalls have risen and crumbled on those banks from before recorded time. Layer upon layer, mortar, brick, and clay have risen and fallen to the foundations below. And no person walking there can take a step without feeling that.

The river is the center of the city set incongruously to the side, a magnificent circus of ancient ritual. Loin-clothed disciples stand in murky water chanting, "Release us from the wheel of existence." Sadhus meditate, naked to the mid-day sun. Beggars hobble with out-stretched palms. Snakes-charmers play reedy melodies. Women slap-wash cloth and men pray while the buildings rise and fall again. All of India comes to the river, as they have for six thousand years. It is a city teeming with life. And it is a city of death. People come to there to die.

I cranked Ugly Bike's wheel sharply to the right and snapped on the brakes. A bull, large enough to regard with some caution, was meandering—bulls meander in Varanasi—up the gully. I swore out loud, knowing this podgy obstruction was going to likely delay my arrival at Devi's. Jumping off, I wedged myself into a rank niche in the wall and expelled the air from my lungs. The bull clopped past with a bovine grunt, lifted its tail, defecated, and then wandered casually up the walkway.

I stepped cautiously down the slimy lane to Master's house. His, like mine, had a rear courtyard bordered by a tall, glass-encrusted wall and a thick-planked gate in the center. From the lane it was impossible to peer into the rear yard. For three years I had parked Ugly Bike just inside the gate and entered through the kitchen for afternoon lessons. An hour and a half each weekday, Master and I would sip tea, eat pakoras, and discuss conjugations, compounds, and poetic significance. I would sit cross-legged on a thin mat while he reclined in a cushioned rocker. Mirabai, his wife of fifty-six years would bustle in to serve or remove cups in decorous silence. On rare occasions I'd encounter their daughter, Sukshmi, as she moved quietly about the house. Usually she would draw her sari demurely across her face while I stammered a shy namaste. During recent months, I hadn't seen her at all as she'd been at the university in Mumbai, but gupchup had it she was now back home between semesters

And it was Sukshmi that I ran into, literally, as I burst through the kitchen door in my attempt to be seated punctually in the parlor. I sent Ugly Bike careening rider-less across the courtyard to fall where she would, ascended the steps in a single leap, and then caught my toe inelegantly on the threshold. I stumbled directly into Sukshmi's backside, which at that moment was pushed out like an offering from the fruit vendor as she searched for some object in a lower cabinet.

"Oh shit." Second mistake, I never swore in Masterji's presence, much less in the presence of his beautiful daughter. "I...I...I'm sorry. I didn't. . ." My tongue locked like a rusted gear. Three golf balls materialized in my mouth. Then I heard the most delightful sound of the week, her laugh. It gave me just enough courage to find my voice again.

"I didn't see you. Really, I'm so sorry."

She turned, and with a self-assured smile, studied the crimson in my cheeks. "Your apology is accepted, Vidyarthi, unnecessary, but accepted." I was looking into the most stunning eyes in the city, curved pools of black and emerald, and right then they were filled to the lids with amusement.

Devi's raspy voice called from the salon, "You are late, Bhim. Forty-three seconds so."

I was ready to offer my second apology of the morning when Sukshmi called out, "Oh no Papa, he has been standing on the porch telling me what a wonderful teacher you have been to him."

This was answered with a skeptical snort. "Yes? And how

long has he been in the house?" I pictured him consulting his watch, calculating.

"I have detained him for four minutes at least, asking him how he can do so much Sanskrit with you and still have time to write to his own father." Then she looked at me with eyelashes any western woman would kill for, or at least pay large sums of money to acquire. And winked.

"So, is Bhim going to join us today, or is he going to chat with my defiant daughter all morning?" I knew then that some thorny issue had come between them just before my arrival.

Leaving Sukshmi smiling in the kitchen, I stepped into the salon.

Eleven

"I'm ready to work until my fingers fall off or my eyes give out, Masterji."

"Good, because that is precisely how much we are going to do, young man. You remember C.G., yes?"

I folded my hands together, bent and touched the tiles somewhere within an acceptable distance of C.G.'s toes. Full contact wasn't necessary according to custom and definitely out of the question as far as I was concerned. Those were the ugliest appendages east of Delhi. It was, however, the customary gesture of respect for the old professor and Master's closest friend since childhood. He was also Devi's perpetual verbal sparring partner. To put it mildly, the boys liked to bicker.

I straightened up, bowed to the bald, brilliant little man and said, "It is a pleasure to see you again, Professor. I pray you have been well." Rumor had it that a weak heart and kidney stones were paining him considerably.

"Ah, Bhim, my young friend, thank you for asking. What I lack in health these days, I have in happiness. Maladies are close acquaintances of a man of my years, but with my weekly plunges in the river, I am ready to leave the great wheel whenever it is ready to release me. Devi tells me the two of you had a good visit to our secret place yesterday. Please, sit, sit. Tell us your thoughts and show us the photographs you took." He patted a large rocker next to him. That was a surprise. The mat on the floor was my customary spot. With a small flush of pride, I assumed it was because I was now the technical expert-- having the laptop and photographs in my possession. I'd been promoted.

Plugging the computer in, I pressed the start button and the drive began to boot. Master made no effort to hide his contempt for our use of a contraption newer than the plow. I realized that viewing the screen was going to present a small challenge. Being backlit, it needed to be seen at close proximity and at the proper angle. With Devi and C.G. sitting to the sides it wouldn't work. I hopped up, and without asking, retrieved the ornate tea table and set the computer on it.

"Punditjis," I said. "I think you will be able to see more clearly if you move behind me."

In a clear attempt to discredit the evil gadgetry, Masterji snorted as he raised himself. "This machine will not let us see from the side?"

"Of course not, Devi," C.G. scolded. "You would understand that if you ever graced us with your presence at the university. I use a Sharp active matrix projector and my Acer 3000 for all my lectures now. Students receive their assignments and grades by email. This is the twenty-first century we live in." I nearly bent again to touch C.G.'s toes again. Score one for the professor.

Devi, not to be bested, fired off his own shot. "That may be, Mr. C.G. Chandragupta, but I wager as soon as we start reading the script we will need an old fashioned pencil and note pad."

The boys were getting crotchety, so I plugged a one gigabyte flash drive into the USB slot, my personal filing system—neat folders on a memory stick—and clicked open to the first thumbnail. "This," I announced, "is from the wall on the right as you enter." Both men moved to stand behind me. That was unusual. Teachers don't stand while vidyarthis sit.

I blew a sigh of relief; the image was clear. In the upper left there was a small star from the reflection of the flash on wall, but it obscured two letters at most. The rest was quite readable, making me proud that I had captured it so well for our team.

Of the three of us, Chandragupta was the most learned in the ancient Vedic hymns. Like medical specialists, linguists branched into areas of preference. The professor had spent a good portion of his life studying the songs of the Rig Veda, some from as far back as 5000 BC. He was also an expert on the religious treatises of the Upanishads. He would be our quarterback.

Master had devoted himself to the dramas and poetry of the later periods, the area I also loved, though he could more than hold his own in the Vedic. He would be our tailback.

As the rookie I was hoping I wouldn't have to warm the bench too much.

C.G., flaunting his technical expertise, asked, "Is this picture made with Adobe Photoshop, Bhim?"

"No, Punditji, It's JPEG Viewer, very basic program that comes with the computer."

Behind me Master grumped. "You two will need to go back to the cave and take some better pictures. The script is too small for anyone to read."

I smiled at C.G., who was leaning over my right shoulder. He grinned back. Clicking on the zoom button I expanded the image two hundred percent. There was a muffled gasp from Devi. Casually, I asked, "How is that? Better?"

"Hmmph, I suppose so. You see, C.G.. I was correct. It begins on this side with the salutation and benediction, and moves east to west around the walls."

"Of course you are correct, Devi. You are always correct." Master let that one go.

C.G. went to reading the first few lines while I, wanting to make Masterji feel better and because I did actually need them, asked, "Master? Is there a pencil and paper close by?" As soon as he returned, our attention went to the screen.

We spent the entire morning working on the first photograph alone, and four lines into it we knew it was older than we had thought. A single reference, a benediction to the Ashvini Twins, the demigods of healing, verified it. From that reference we knew it was at least from the thirteenth century BC or older.

We settled into our individual tasks, I laboring the most, as my responsibilities, though less skilled, were more demanding. My task was to create three entries for each line of text. While Devi and C.G. bickered over word meanings and grammatical nuances, I rendered the older Brahmi script into the newer Devanagari. Then as quickly as I could, wrote the transliterations. That took the most time. Each syllable had to be depicted with a symbols from the International Phonetic Alphabet. Finally, I scribbled the English translation that the pundits did so casually in their heads. It was like creating two sets of shorthand and one of long, and by noon my vow to work until my fingers fell off was becoming a reality. For the first time in months I was happy to see Master glance at his Timex.

Three minutes later—her watch was on time-- Mirabai entered with bowls of fried dough nestled in yogurt and lentils, tamarind, and mint chutney. This was accompanied by pistachio lassis and slices of baked nan. With a click, I saved the images to the flash drive and snap closed the laptop.

Devi, through a mouthful of lentils, asked, "So C.G., it is clearly one of the early branches of the Ayur, would you not agree?"

Draining his lassi with a slurp, C.G. wagged his head "We

have only gotten to the benediction, but as strange as it feels, I must agree with you. It will be clearer tomorrow when we get into the main text, but it is undoubtedly medical, and I would agree that it is indeed much older than we thought." He turned and surprised me by asking, "Bhimaji, you are a man of the world, are there tests that will prove the age of the rock or the stain?"

I understood less than a third of the functions on my camera, so I wouldn't exactly call myself a techy. How carbon tests worked, or iridium, or whatever chemists used to determine the age of a sample of plant dye was a mystery. "I'm really not sure, Punditji. I mean, I would think so. I guess I could research it."

"Yes, yes, the age of the rock and the dye, might be helpful . . ." He paused and then said what we already knew, "but not as much as the writing style. That will tell us. We just need time with it." He paused and frowned. "I suppose a talk with Mr. Muktendra, the owner of the property, would be wise. To discuss security, you know. Then, at some point we can bring experts in with scientific equipment to verify the age." I was beginning to see that, as adept as they were in language, the pundits had never managed or secured anything like this. That made three of us.

Devi groaned. "We will do no such thing, C.G. You and I, with the help of our brilliant technical expert here, will determine the age from the language itself. And we will do the translation right here without a horde of water buffalo tramping through our cave. I will hire a guard." Brilliant? I had become brilliant. Master was correct though. The writing was the best method of determining the age.

The Ayur Veda is India's great medical treatise. Immense and old, it is divided into very detailed sections. Normally it would be easy to establish the origin by style and references. Normally. The challenge we were faced was that our discovery was closer to the trunk than the twigs—very old, uncharted territory.

While the pundits discussed security measures, I thought about how I could re-photograph the parts I'd missed when my batteries died. It would mean another trip to the cave as soon as possible.

Mirabai came in to clear our trays, and we made plans to re-convene the following morning. Besides being the official photographer, I was now conferred the weighty title of Keeper of the Notes and Photographs. Taking my new role seriously, I made a few notes about getting it all onto the computer and the jump drive correctly, then set everything into the inner pockets of my backpack.

As I stood, Master patted my hand with a thank you and instructed me to arrive punctually the following morning. The rest of the afternoon was mine to enjoy.

In the kitchen I paused to thank Mirabai--my Jewish grandmother in a sari--for lunch. Never left her house with an empty stomach. I glanced about, hoping to offer a bashful thank-you to Sukshmi, but she was nowhere to be seen, so I strolled to the courtyard where the midday heat blasted me like a shore wave.

Ugly Bike lay where I'd left her--twisted like a bull in the center of a bullring. I shouldered my pack and hefted her with a little bounce to scatter the dust from her rims. As I patted off the seat and rolled her towards the gate, I heard a whispered hiss. "Bhim!" It came from the small shack near the back corner of the wall, a hut that usually had a few tools and bags of grain for the chickens that clucked about the yard. Today the door was open just enough to see the long braid and flashing eyes of Sukshmi. I rolled Ugly Bike toward the opening with a trembling that was surely being registered on a seismograph somewhere. As I went to step onto the kickstand, from inside the house, I heard Master call out. "Sukshmi!"

Stretching out her hand, she darted past me in a bright flash of blue silk. A trace of pink drifted to the ground at my feet. I bent and picked up the folded note and slipped quietly through the wooden door in the wall.

Twelve

The joie de vivre that was torn from me when Lilia died left a void in my heart. And make no mistake; that is where the pain pitches its tent when love dies, that wheel in center of the chest. In the months following her death I ached in that space more than I thought physically possible, slept in fitful spurts, and wept at the tiniest suggestion of her departure. I wrapped my arms about that space in futile attempts to hold in a withering spirit. I whispered her name in the dark. Then, little by little, I stopped whispering. Silence stole across my spirit. Friends and family tried every method of intercession and salvation, but I only slipped further. Eventually only one option remained. To leave. I opted for an itinerary to another country and another life. It was my only choice, to seek another life. I crossed that threshold like a wraith, voiceless and alone.

But there were people on my path that refused allow me to sink further. That is the way it is in a land like India; people sustain you on your path, often done in return for nothing.

There was Sahr, who coaxed me in her incredibly hardheaded manner into talking about Lilia. She got me to smile again.

And Devamukti, who understood that I needed full baptism in the language we both loved.

There were good and erudite people along that path, a physician who saw me through fever and dysentery and recognized my deeper illness. Perceptive vendors, cabbies, and philosophers I met in the city. Tutors and healers who encouraged me to speak, when I was willing. It took time, two years worth. Most sensed that my former existence wasn't something I could discuss, so they kept it to the present.

In the final analysis, I came to see that it wasn't a process that would have worked in the West. It required a lonely cleansing and the harsh elixir of a city like Varanasi.

The fool, the ones who pressed thoughtless questions upon me--where I came from, why had I left the life of money and surf and glitter--those I turned my backside to.

In some odd way, I believe I even owed Soma's dead husband gratitude. Had the young groom not tumbled from the roof of the train and bled to death, she would not have become the banished widow she was, and I wouldn't have come to understand that others also could feel the same depth of pain. But as I began my daily lessons with Devi, I saw her sweeping the kitchen with unchecked tears, and from Mirabai I learned her story.

The irony was that we never spoke directly of our losses, Soma and I. We embarked on timid conversations about the tidbits of life, drifted like castaways on a sea of mundane. I asked her about village life, she asked me about radios. She assumed incorrectly that Master Bhim knew everything, asked how the voices sang from the front. Telling her what little I knew, I saw a curiosity and aptitude that would sprout like flax given correct nutrients. She asked about the river, the snows from which it sprang and the ocean to which it flowed. She had only seen the one, but all three she imagined beautifully. I saved my newspapers, taught her letters, and she began to read. Step by step we came to a place where we could talk in roundabout ways of ill-fortune.

In addition to everything else, Lilia's death had left me agonizingly shy with members of the opposite sex, certainly any close to my own age.

Now I stood outside Master's back gate, in a gully that

smelled of cow dung, urine and cooking oil, holding a note from the most beautiful woman in Varanasi. The paper trembled in my fingers. Somewhere down the alley, a woman's voice rose, an eerie, pitching soprano, and melded into a melody of flute and tablas. I looked at the folded paper and hesitated. The heart needs so much time to heal. With a sigh, I unfolded the scrap. In neat cursive it demanded, "HAROON'S 8:PM SHARP!!

I swore. Sukshmi had evidently picked up one annoying practice from her father. I swore again. I really didn't like Haroon's, especially at eight in the evening.

Thirteen

My ears caught the low thumping of the bass woofers three hundred meters away. Reason number one for disliking the loudest—possibly the only--night club in Varanasi, I was usually left hearing impaired for an hour after I quit the place. Decent conversation, scholarly or otherwise, during music hours was unachievable. And, under no circumstances, did I enjoy techno music. Dancing to it was the furthest thing from my mind.

Haroon's was trendy. That was another reason I avoided it. Fashionable young Indians swarmed in at dusk, drank far too much coffee or gin, smoked too much tobacco, and discussed politics ad nauseum. It was the gathering place for itinerant foreigners, and middle-class Varanasi wannabees--the aspiring young semi-wealthy who craved anything Western. You could make a fat stack of rupees selling Abercrombie blue jeans in Haroon's. There was even steak on the menu—try getting that in rural India—with the preposterous description of 'charbroiled, round-up cowboy style.' In my opinion, the place had only two redeemable features. First, it was air-conditioned, and second, Haroon himself was an astute gentleman with a delightful sense of humor.

It also happened to be where I picked up my mail once a month, sparse as it was. My mother's events-of-home letter, and a trust fund check, arrived the third Wednesday of each month. I would slip in during the early afternoon quiet hours, chat with the owner over a cold smoothie, gather my envelope, and slip discreetly out before locals and tourists arrived.

Maumed Haroon was as affable a nightclub owner as one could imagine. He memorized the names of each customer that entered his establishment, especially blond European or American girls, and called out to them in cheery fashion the instant they crossed his doorstep. For the young and trendy Varanasis who desired a modern identity, the hailing of their names was a delight that kept them coming back night after night. Haroon would spin jokes with the perfect mix of bawdiness and good timing, serve iced coffee and neon colored cocktails, while slapping large amounts of money into his two cash registers every night of the week but Tuesday.

"Bhim!!" Maumed called as I entered. I looked over to the indelible smile. It was seven fifty-five on a Monday evening and the place was already humming. The DJ, fortunately, was on a break, and I, already filled with Sahr's succulent saag pilau, wanted only a mango shake. In the semi-light of the wall sconces, I watched as he waved me over, re-set a blender, and deposited two iced gins in front of a neatly dressed young man leaning jauntily against the rail that ran the length of the bar. Haroon was demonstrating his capacity for multi-tasking with a single objective, the accumulation of money.

"And how is my favorite Sanskrit scholar this evening? It has been too long since you have visited. And not your unusual hour. So, My Friend, are you ready to publish your Bhavabuti play and make us ten thousand crore rupees?" Haroon's hand popped out at me from an embroidered silk sleeve. He wore light-gray slacks and a long-wasted salmon-colored kurta that announced both worldliness and homeland tradition--the secret to his style, displaying chic in two cultures.

I gave his hand a familiar press. "Not quite, Maumed. I'm still reworking the last scene, and pretty certain the hard-cover sales won't lift it onto a best seller list when I'm done."

He grinned. "But it has all the makings of a money-making story. Love, jealousy, death, and plenty of sex." Without taking his eyes off me, he flashed four fingers, a fist, and a V to a helper standing in front of a row of blenders. The assistant, interpreting the signals, began mixing four rum daiquiris.

"That may be, Maumed, but I don't think even the loosest poetic license will allow me to reinterpret the sex and violence our modern world seems to want these days."

He chuckled. "So, we release it as a farcical screenplay with a caste of silly characters and find a Bollywood producer to make the whole thing. Still make enough money for our Club Med vacation."

Haroon's idea of heaven on earth was a month's stay at any resort where bikini clad women actually shaved their legs. Somewhere in his office I knew he had a cache of brochures from Super Club Hedonism II, Sandals, and a dozen others. For some reason he'd decided that I was acquainted with them all and would be his spiritual guide in a quest to find the best one. I hadn't the heart to tell him otherwise.

"Believe me, Maumed, if you find a producer for this, I will happily sign the contract."

"And then we can go to Sandals?"

"Then we can go to Sandals." While Maumed personally prepared my mango shake, I looked around at the complex, and it was just that, a complex of six connected rooms of various size and shape that Haroon had acquired as his wealth had grown and his neighbor's had diminished. Eight large tables, a bar, and a disc jockey's stage formed the center. Spinning out from the hub were four smaller spaces designed for privacy and intimate conversation, though most evenings patrons had to yell like soccer fans to be heard. The largest was the last space. The dance floor.

Nearly every table was filled with young, college-aged Indians. A few ferenghis were scattered about. Two travel-weary young women with massive backpacks propped against their chairs looked my way, but no one hailed me. That was good. As inviting as it was for the hipsters of Varanasi, it made me panicky--too many people and too many decibels. I was there on the pretext of a quasi-date with a beautiful woman. The whole thing petrified me. Like the two women with the blond hair staring at me, I was carrying some hefty baggage. Mine just didn't show so much.

Haroon was offering his opinion on the most recent bombing and 'this Sutradharak fellow' when he looked over my shoulder to the door. His voice boomed, "Jatana!" I turned. And there was Sukshmi, or rather an exceedingly modified version. Dressed in a mid-length lavender crinoline skirt, purple silk blouse and ridiculously high-heeled shoes, her hair was draped in a part-up, part-down style. Heading the entire outfit was a pair of large, round, tinted sunglasses. I nearly dropped my mango shake onto Haroon's polished floor.

I hoped the light was dim enough to hide the disappointment. It often came to me when a beautiful Hindu woman embraced Western appearances. The mystique of India, delicate and old, dissipated with the shift. Too much was revealed, and like an exposed movie plot, I experienced a sense of disillusionment. Sukshmi, in modern attire, looked stunning, but . . . she was no longer the Sukshmi I peeked at shyly as she drifted furtively through the quarters of her father's house. Evidently she had learned more at University than anyone realized. I just hoped no one had taught her to smoke.

"Bhim, I am so pleased you have come, and so punctual."
Damn if she didn't look at a little pink watch on her wrist.
Behind the glasses, her eyes sparkled with amusement at my
expression. "You were perhaps expecting someone different?"

I hesitated, trying to regain a semblance of composure, and
with a tiny stutter replied, "Wwell, I guess I was wondering
what Jatana has done with Sukshmi." I shuddered. That was
the best I could come up with?

"Ah . . . Yes. Jatana. She is . . . how shall I say? The bearer of
my Nom d' Soir. I prefer her to Sukshmi when I venture out for
the evening, not unlike the way you use the name Bhim, no?"

I shook my head in mild offense. "No, not at all like Bhim.
That's my Benarsi name, my Hindu name. It's not a mask I
take off at the end of an evening at Haroon's."

She smiled, clearly enjoying the opportunity to display a bit
of repartee. "And with this name you have become a full
Hindu?"

I hesitated. "No . . . not exactly. Besides, any conversion I
might take isn't dependent upon my name. I enjoy being sort of
Hindu. At times."

"But it is temporary, something you will conveniently
jettison when you leave here? Will you not hang up your
Hinduness and toss aside your name and customs like old
shoes?"

Her questions had caught me off guard. One minute into my
first date in four years and I was on the defensive. On my arrival
in Varanasi, I had slipped easily, almost naturally, into Hindu
customs, but they were peripheral, done in my Western manner
and at my own pace. I was not a believer in any deity. That was

certain. I was merely a student who dressed in Brahmin clothes and walked in temple gardens to write poetry. Undoubtedly I wasn't religious, asking everyday how so much pain could be inflicted on someone whose only fault had been falling in love. I sure as hell didn't believe in a Supreme Being or a minor deity that dealt those cards.

Jatana-Sukshmi's eyes were daring me to enter into a discussion on faith. I dodged with, "Perhaps I won't leave. Maybe I will just live in Varanasi forever and always be known as Bhim."

She looked genuinely shocked. "You would do that? Never return to your homeland? Never take your true name again. What is that by the way, your real name?"

I felt my shield going up. "It is Martin Scott, Jatana-Sukshmi, but you shouldn't call me that. I prefer Bhim."

"Cool. Bhimaji it will be. But I for one would be very bored hanging in this stale, old city. Too few places to dance. Too many dead bodies, not enough live ones."

I laughed for the first time. She was on the mark with that. Varanasi was known for many things. Night-clubbing wasn't one of them.

"Mumbai has the tops, you know. The Blue Fox has a back-spinning DJ that cranks out the hippest cuts until three in the morning? Max styled. And on the weekends they have live bands. You should hear them. Maybe we can meet there some time." I wasn't keen on the path this conversation was taking. Religion, now dancing? Politics might be next. I wanted to talk about Sanskrit poets. How Kalidasa, described the morning sun splintering into gold and turquoise as it passed through the tails of peacocks. I wanted to tell her of snows glistening like pearls along the mountain paths, and the symphony of bees as they sipped the nectar of lotuses. She wanted to dance . . . to techno.

Maumed brought Sukshmi a cocktail concocted from no less than eight ingredients with the implausible name, Blue Mongoose. I sipped the smoothie and winced as the screech of the microphone jack pierced the air, and knew—with a clairvoyance Sahr would have been proud of—what was to follow. A simplistic, synthesized beat cranked through a bass that would knock a lighter man off his stool. I gripped the edge of the bar and waited uneasily through the two seconds it took for her say, "Come on, Bhimaji. Let's show these flat-footed clowns how to really dance." I was jerked from the relative comfort of my stool onto the parquet floor like a goat being lead to sacrifice.

Three agonizing songs later—if they can be referred to that way—and we were once again seated in front of Maumed. I was dripping with perspiration and shaking from some undetermined palsy. Our bartender set a fresh smoothie in front of me accompanied by a wink.

Sukshmi tapped the straw of her Blue Whatchamacallit, and said, "You dance well, Bhim. A bit stiff with your arms, but your feet really boogie." I looked at those feet and then at the eyes behind the tinted glasses, searching for a shred of truth in what she was saying.

"Thank you, Sukshmi, but to be honest, I love my exercise, but really don't dance much anymore, especially to . . . what did you say the name of this group is?"

"Randy Dogs."

"Of course, Randy Dogs. I prefer the older tunes, a different genre."

"Like hip-hop?"

"No, like classic rock." I saw the disappointment behind the lenses. She had enough manners not to say "Ick." I continued. "I used to dance a lot. Really. The Eagles, The Band, Allman Brothers, those sorts of groups, the ones that harmonized and had really good guitar players. Too few of them these days."

"You are far too young for those groups. They are prehistoric. So, why did you stop? You should still dance, Bhimaji. It cleanses the soul better than baths in that filthy river." Her chin jutted in the general direction of the Ganges a few hundred meters to the east.

With a sigh I answered, "I just stopped, that's all. It was like a lot of things I decided not to do anymore."

"Like using the name Martin? And what other things did you decide to stop?" It was one of those probing questions I usually avoided in some clever way, fearing a discussion of my past, but there had been a subtle shift in her voice, a tone of tenderness. As I spun on my stool to face her, I saw that she had removed her glasses and was peering at me with an expression of curious concern. Her eyes were incredible, and for a fraction of a second I wondered if Master had broken our agreement and told his defiant daughter about my past.

I took a long pull on my smoothie, set it down, and nodded. "Okay, Sukshmi, here is the deal. I will tell you why I stopped dancing, why I stopped wearing cool, Western clothes everyone in this club seems to want so much. I will tell you why I came to Varanasi to study and sit by myself all day with a pile of dusty books. Okay? The short, not-very-pretty version of my past. Then I will dance with you to one more song and we will choose other topics to talk about. Does that sound fair?"

She smiled. "That is a plumb fair deal, Bhim." I winced at that one.

"Oh yes, One more thing. I get to choose the song, otherwise no deal."

We carried our drinks to one of the back rooms, as far from the pounding speakers as possible, and in a high-backed booth I told her. I didn't offer up all the details. That would have been too hard, but at some point I described how Lilia laughed when we swam in our favorite cove and how she made the best chili rellenos north of Tijuana. I talked about her death.

Sukshmi didn't utter a word. She nodded here and there, but didn't ask a single question or offer up comment. She watched my eyes and I watched hers. The earlier games of witty responses and clever retorts were gone, and when I finished, she reached across and very simply, very gently, laced her fingers in mine. It was a warm current of friendship, and that undemanding, uncomplicated gesture was the first physical contact I'd had with a woman in four years. Then she asked me the only question I didn't feel any reluctance to answer. "How do you make chili rellenos?"

Sukshmi excused herself to go to the restroom, and I went to discuss a selection with the DJ. I had a hunch he might have what I wanted. The tune was old, but it had been part of a soundtrack in a recent movie, and if it was on a soundtrack, it could be found in Haroon's.

Sukshmi returned, dabbing a tissue at the corners of her eyes. I realized that, as much as she had veered outside her family's sphere in recent days, she still retained one of their best habits. Like her father, just below the surface was a deep well of compassion.

She slid in next to me and with a frown, whispered, "He wants to arrange my marriage, you know."

I wasn't totally certain what she meant but had a pretty good idea. "Who?"

She flicked her fingernail against the empty glass. "Father, of course. He wants me to marry a young, well-to-do Brahmin from Delhi. Some perfectly boring clerk who works in a perfectly boring bank, has perfectly boring parents, and probably hasn't danced once in his entire boring life. While I've been away at university, Father has been writing the boy's parents, whom he already seems to know quite well. It is a horrible abuse of old tradition and the modern postal system if anyone asks me, but no one does. No one asks me anything at all. They just all agree that it will be a right fine union. Like prized cattle—a most desirable match. Everyone agrees except the bride-to-be." She looked at me and blinked back tears, and for the first time I saw the real Sukshmi— beautiful, intelligent, and petrified of a cage she was being goaded into. She had wanted to tell me earlier but had run headlong into the tale of Martin and his flight to India.

I took her hand, and this time I lead us to the parquet floor.

The song started slowly and stayed that way all the way through. It had all the classical features: a ripping, bluesy guitar, Joe Cocker's unmistakable voice, and the soul-baring lyrics of Eric Burdon. We danced slowly, hand in hand, not too close. I mouthed the lyrics "Baby do you understand me now? . . . I'm just a soul whose intentions are good. Oh Lord, please don't let me be misunderstood."

With that, my first date in a very long time was brought to an end.

I saw Sukshmi safely to an autorick and we promised to do it again sometime soon. She squeezed my hand and waved as the cab trundled across the cracked roadway. I took a deep breath. The air had cooled. A half moon and a glistening web of stars sparkled down. It was a perfect night for a poet's walk along the river back to the villa. I crossed the street towards the Ghats.

Behind me a light leapt along the pavement from Haroon's front door. The two blond women I had seen earlier stepped across the threshold burdened like pack mules. The taller one that had been watching me converse with Haroon and Sukshmi halted, the other continued on. For a moment I thought the tall one was going to ask for directions, or worse, cross the street and initiate a conversation, but she merely placed her palms together, bowed, and whispered in a distinctly accented voice, "Namaste, Good Friend. Namaste." Northern European. She smiled, spun on a heel, and with all that weight on her back, trotted with seeming ease to catch up to her companion.

Fourteen

My stroll back to the villa took me along the banks above the river. The Ganges, north of Varanasi, veers westward in a huge curve, like an enormous well-shaped breast. Seen from the air, that is precisely how it appears, but from the lowly bank of the river it takes on the more modest shape of a bay. The Ghats themselves are marvels of masonry, over-sized steps that descend steeply to the river's edge. With no rhyme or reason they are fractioned by turreted temples and jutting blocks of stone and soaring walls. Faded yellow script names each Ghat in English and Hindi, though there is no other discernible difference. Well before dawn it springs to life with humanity. Boats stack against each other like logs in the river, and by daybreak it is a raucous amphitheater of fakirs, musicians, hawkers, and every purveyor of service from dentistry to phrenology. Holy men, holier women, poets, and orators sing to a thousand gods, and everyone has a talent.

Nighttime, however, was the time I walked the river. At that hour I could hear the current and actually feel whichever of Sahr's spirits pervaded the water, and when the moon was up it was the most quixotic venue a lover of poetry could imagine. That was the time I drafted my own verse and let Lilia's spirit separate molecule by ethereal molecule from my own.

From Haroon's door I skipped down an inky, but familiar, gully and emerged at Scindia Ghat. I always enjoyed that starting point because it never failed to bring a smile. A temple dedicated to Shiva sat skewed at the river's edge, submerged like a warthog in the mud. Over centuries it had sunk into the sludge from its own weight, and that irony--an over-weighted shrine sinking into the muck--struck me as rather funny.

I turned southwest along the bank feeling strangely content. A woman, a beautiful one at that, had conversed with me. I had danced and spoken without coloring more than six shades. For the first time, other than Soma and my housekeeper, I had spoken to a woman about Lilia. In addition, I was now The Keeper of Notes and Photographs and ready--no, chomping at the bit--to solve the linguistic puzzles of the cave. It was a fine evening.

After a short distance I descended to the water, purposefully avoiding the next Ghat, Manikarnika. I steered around it because it was a place of death, constant death--the ancient venue of cremations. A flame burned there continually since Varanasi's birth, and that, as has been noted, is a long time indeed. The air was thick and perpetually orange with the flames of oil, and timber, and human flesh. The stench and weeping of mourners reminded me that the reaper really didn't give a shit how much you loved. It destroyed you and whatever you cherished, whenever it pleased. That evening I wasn't going anywhere near Manikarnika.

I picked up my pace and set a healthy kilometer between the pyres and myself. Gradually I began humming and swinging my arms in childlike motions. Rhythm, syncopation, Kalidasa's opening verses to The Birth of Kumar came to me. Uttarasyam dishi devatatma . . . to the north, the great god of the mountains . . . I skipped across the Washing Ghats, and listened the echoing drumbeats of cloth slapping against rock, all faded with the light, but I heard it still. Suddenly, a tingling apprehension gripped me and my tempo was shattered. Someone was watching me. Glancing over my shoulder, at the top of the moonlit embankment, I saw a glowing ember. A shadowed face with a burning cigarette was turned in my direction—no features, no mouth, just an unrecognizable oval and a speck of orange—but I knew with certainty that those eyes were following me. With a shiver I turned and trotted the last few kilometers home.

Fifteen

Sutradharak never handled explosives, timers, or wires, or any other instruments of mass destruction for that matter. As his name suggested, he merely pulled the strings--and pushed the buttons--to bring about the death. The more, the better.

After his basic blueprint had arrived in the middle of the night he had stayed awake for two more hours planning. Then he had slept deeply and woken up invigorated. Immediately he drove to the loft in the center of the city and transmitted a text message that initiated an appointment with two men in a small vegetarian cafe in a decaying section of the city. At noon he arrived in his merchant disguise and entered the Peshawar Cafe. Even though the two men he was meeting were loyal lieutenants, they did not know his identity. They had never seen him in clothes other than those he was wearing. To them he was a purveyor of goat products--milk, hide, and cheese. He wore heavy, dark lenses and carried business cards with embossed lettering in the name of Akhmed Jamil. But the two also knew that he was also the same man that orchestrated bombings that terrified millions. Wisely, they didn't ask questions.

Sutradharak, as usual, would not discuss details at their first meeting. He sipped tea and merely began pulling strings, spelling out a few of his needs--a team of four, the same that he had been on the bombing event of the train outside Agra a year earlier. He did not discuss dates or time, only some of the materials that would be necessary.

The first lieutenant assured him that sufficient quantities of the most critical element could be made available. "Yes Sir. HBX-3, more powerful than the C4 plastique. It is a mix of RDX, TNT, powdered aluminum, and D-2 wax, and can be easily shaped and to fit inside any ordinary container."

Sutradharak halted the man with a wave of his fingers. "That is less important for this event. Tell me this? Can it be detonated underwater in the same way as the C-4? And with the cell phones?"

"Using the proper wiring and detonators, yes Sir, but obviously the receiving phones can not be submerged. They will need dry locations with wires leading down or up to the HBX."

The goat merchant nodded. "That is adequate. Good. And all the items can be delivered by car to a location I will speak of later? No public transportation."

"Yes, Sir. If you wish to tell me where and when . . ."

With another wave of the hand he silenced the man. "You will be contacted."

The second man provided information about the two drivers needed to complete the team. Sutradharak wanted no names, only their curriculum vitae and assurance that they understood what would happened if they were apprehended. Or if didn't follow his instructions in every way.

The subordinate squirmed. "Yes sir. They understand the consequences. There will be no problems."

After a dessert of coconut flan and mint tea, Sutradharak pushed envelopes of washed rupees across the table and the three of them slipped quietly back into the slums.

A second meeting was convened two days later, this time in the loft, and this time Sutradharak presented his plan in full. Every detail was discussed. Maps, schedules, and structures were analyzed a dozen ways. Afterwards, as they had on previous occasions, the men lit a small fire in a brass bowl on the wooden table and incinerated all their notes into fine ash. With a few drops of water they blended it into a gray paste and smeared three horizontal stripes on the two men's foreheads. As devotees of Shiva, they left the loft, and the Puppetmaster remained.

Sixteen

"Lalji! Laljiiiii!" I was leaning against the front of my gate rattling the chain and hinges in mounting frustration, screaming at the sleeping, obviously deaf, figure snoring in the rear. He had padlocked the chain through the bars as he was supposed to when I was safely inside. The problem was; I wasn't safely inside. I was screaming like Fred Flintstone outside. Lights were popping on in the nearby villas. I stopped yelling.

In the back, under the mango, I heard his contented buzzing.

I looked for a pebble in the darkness and found something better, a hefty clod of dirt. My left-handed hook-shot, honed over the years as I had driven the lane against equal or taller opponents, arched over the fence in a perfect rainbow. It bounced with a thud off Lalji's naked chest, resulting in a shriek and another light to come on somewhere up the street.

"Lalji, open the goddamned gate."

"Saab?" The frightened, sleepy voice approached. "What are you doing out there?"

I took a breath and counted to four before pointing out that he had set the chain, settled into the hammock, and forgotten to check if I was actually inside before drifting off. He stared at me in confusion, and then offered the feeble excuse, "But Saab never goes out so late at night, even when he walks by the river, it is always early."

"Yes, well not tonight." He stared at me. With a sigh I asked, "Lalji?"

"Yes, Saab?"

"Do you have the key?"

As if finally awake and realizing that I was still on the opposite side, he proudly drew the key from around his waist and held it up for me to see. "Indeed, Saab. I have it with me all the time."

"Then I suggest you put it in the lock and let me in." He quickly—as rapidly as possible for him—opened the gate and issued me into the courtyard. "Thank you. Now you may lock it and go to your hammock, but do try to remember that you are a night watchman. Sleep with one eye open from now on."

"Yes, Saab, I will do that, one ear open also."

I sighed and as I made my way up the steps to the veranda, thought to ask, "Are there any messages?"

Lalji looked puzzled for a moment, digging through the memory of the last six hours. "Oh yes. Master Mejanand came to the gate this evening. I told him you were not in."

I stared at Lalji with such ferocity that he slowly arrived at his own conclusion. I hadn't been inside when he'd delivered that message and hadn't been inside all evening.

"Did he say what he wanted?" Mej Whiton coming to my gate was not unusual. As far as I knew he didn't even own a cell phone and his preferred method of conveying messages was to just drop by unannounced. I was certain of the reason for his visit anyway.

"He asked if Saab wishes to play with the flying platters tomorrow. Sunrise is best he said, because he is traveling to the capital by the morning train."

I nodded, thinking out loud. "I suppose I could work on my notes before he arrives and play for an hour before going to Master's. Did he say if he was coming here, or am I to meet him at the fields?"

Lalji patted off the remains of the dirt missile that powdered his chest. "He says that he will come here before sunrise with two new platters."

I smiled, and with a final reminder to sharpen his duties as night watchman, plodded sleepily to my room.

Seventeen

Nearly every person in Varanasi created and offered opinions of the bombings. Two had been set in the heart of the city and four more along the rail line between us and New Delhi. Sixty-nine people had been murdered, including the most recent near Lucknow, and during the previous fourteen months the attacks had been the topic over most cups of chai and evening meals. Most considered themselves informed enough to declare the guilty party as Taweel Churi, a terrorist group based out of Pakistan, but operating in northern India. An interrogation of the only captured suspect provided intelligence agencies with a name, Sutradharak, The PuppetMaster. Nothing else came from that interrogation but the name and the mysterious death of the prisoner two days later. The media picked up on the title and used it persistently to drive up readership. But no more arrests came. No one knew for certain if Taweel Churi or Sutradharak truly existed, but logic dictated that whoever was responsible had a nasty agenda. Murdering innocent people in a temple was a profanity no one could imagine. Thirty-seven had died in the Sankat Mochan blast in March. Hindus were clamoring for retaliation, though against whom, they were not certain. Muslims walked about in larger groups. Hindus whispered that the mosque leader, Imam Nomani, or more likely the crazed Cabinet Minister Qereshy, were channeling funds to the terrorists. Now, both were under surveillance by the intelligence agencies. Conspiracy theorists whispered at tea stalls, and every cult in every religion in every neighborhood was nervous.

Blistering heat and a sky devoid of rain added to the tension.

The only person besides me that didn't offer opinions was Mejanand Whiton. As far as I could determine Mej didn't care about anybody but himself. If he did, it certainly wasn't expressed or shown. I cared about all of the victims in my own quiet way, and certainly felt the agony the loved-ones left behind, but like the pyres at Manikarnika, I sidestepped any opinions.

Mej had no desire to chat about worldly events. He preferred to fire off truly offensive jokes in a raspy Cockney accent, while chortling non-stop at his own vulgarities. He usually had me smiling or chuckling within minutes. This was one of the reasons I rather enjoyed his company—albeit for very short periods of time--he never asked where I came from or why I lived alone. I reciprocated by not asking anything of him.

Our association was based on a single passion. Freestyle Frisbee. Mej, like me, even in my self-imposed monasticism, liked to stay in shape, a challenge in the crowded confines of Varanasi. Being creative, we'd discovered a unique way to burn off the calories of rice and butter-based dishes, and together we'd found the only place it could be done--the marigold and henna fields south of the city. Marigolds and carnations adorned every holy object, especially dead bodies and lingum and yoni alters. The henna was made into dye for hair and body art. Fortunately the fields were just a short walk from where I lived. They provided the raw materials for the ritual of Varanasi, and provided us a place to exercise.

The fields weren't perfect, being rock-strewn and often covered with thatch, but as sections were rotated in and out, we discovered that we could romp across them for our fun and sweat.

Mej Whiton was English NRI--Non-Resident Indian-- and that was the extent of what I knew of him. He had a rough East

End inflection and a coffee-complexioned features that, to put it nicely, were plain. His pajama pants and loose shirts were always clean, and he seemed to know the ways of Varanasi as well as I did. He spoke fluent Hindi, which I took to be an endowment of his English Indian parents.

We had met the previous year at a fruit stall in the central market in the Chowk district. I happened upon him one afternoon as he was juggling five sweet-limes, chatting to an expanding audience in his version of English that had no Hs. He hailed me with a friendly 'ello, mate,' and after his performance we struck up a conversation where he got me quickly smiling. According to extensive research—his own--it was a proven fact that long, firm bananas were the fruit of choice of local brides after only six months of marriage. He gave me a lurid description of their use and in short time we discovered that we shared a passion for Frisbee.

Mej stood on the far side of the gate grinning at me like a winning jockey. Two new discs, a blue one on his left index finger, and a green one on his right, spun in smooth silence. With a soft flick he sent them aloft where they crossed and resettled on opposite fingers. "Crickey, now that was foocking good one, eh Bheemster."

I grinned. The trick was better than average. I pushed a mug of steaming coffee through the bars. "Yep, you're the well oiled machine, Mej."

I set my mug on the bricks and stepped to Lalji's hammock— the snoring hadn't changed since the previous the night. I tugged on the key and as I unfastened it from his waist, my vigilant watchman rolled over with a girlish giggle and resettled into the folds of his cocoon.

"'Appy you got me message. Been a shame to waste this part o' the day."

With mugs of coffee we strolled down Ramnagar Road towards the pontoon bridge that spanned the river. The water was wide and sluggish there as it exited the bosomy curve in the north. A kilometer away, on the opposite bank, the dilapidated fort of the Raja rose in the shimmering light of the new day.

Mej launched into his first joke. "So, Pope John Paul and 'enry Kissinger walk into a barber shop."

I groaned, "Jesus, Mej."

"Nah, e's in the next one. He didn't want the 'aircut."

I shook my head in disbelief. "What do you do? Save these just for me?"

"Nah, store up 'em up for the birdies. Good sense of 'umor will snook ya more quim than your mug or talking up the size of your knob. I should know, mate. Me face doesn't get me pussy, jokes do. So, whot do a tornado in Texas, a flood in Mississippi, and a divorce in Utah, 'ave in common."

Before I could even picture the first of these oddities, he laughed in a Cockney-Loosiana drawl, "Some poor arsehole's gonna lose a double-wide."

I groaned. "Gimmee a disc." He spun it at eye level just within reach. I snatched it, and in a single motion spun like a ballerina and sent it rocketing ninety feet up where it leveled like a gyroscope, drifted languidly and then angled straight back down. He leapt, caught it behind his back, and flipped it into the breeze again before his feet touched the earth.

It had begun.

The art of the dance, that's what we called it. Salsa, Rumba, and ballet with two vinyl discs, and once it started, we didn't stop until an hour had passed. We jumped, caught, flipped, and launched ourselves like acrobats. There was a competitive element that seeped in naturally, a machismo desire to outdo each other. The discs flew. We dashed, leapt, and snatched them between our legs, heads, or backs. Mej perfected the toe- kick; I mastered the index flip. We knew every trick, every move, and by the end of sixty minutes we had pushed ourselves to a very sweaty fatigue.

And always it passed without question or chatter.

An hour later we stood drenched, watching boats poling against the current. The sun had risen above the far bank. I took a pull from the Nalgene and offered it to him. He gulped down half the bottle and slapped my back. "Sweet session, Mate. Ya made me sweat like a Shivdas whore. Sorry I've got to flake out on ya so quick, but I'm on the eight fifteen to Delhi. " He spun the green disc in front of me, and I tapped it back to him. We started jogging back towards my house, and he grinned and asked, "So, whot's the difference 'tween a moose and a Maine 'ousewife?"

I knew this one from somewhere in the past, and before he could beat me to it, I blurted out, "Bout twenty pounds and a red flannel shirt, I reckon." I'd answered in a respectable New England accent, which got him laughing.

"Well bugger me, Marty. I never took you for a fooking Mainer. Always figured yous a West Coast boy, a SoCal surfer type."

It was the first time he'd pried even gently at my history, an innocent remark meant as an opener if I wished to take it. I didn't, but still answered, "I grew up there. In San Diego, so you figured pretty well."

He nodded. "So 'ow'd you get into all this bloody Sanskrit shite?"

That surprised me a little. First, it was another probe. Second, it was an acknowledgment that he knew what I did all day long. It wasn't as if it was a secret; everyone in the city seemed to know I was Devi's student, but it surprised me that he'd asked. As if reading my thoughts, he added, "A lot of folks say you're one of the best, Mate. I think that's the dog's ollocks, you know, being able to read all them fookin' words. I mean, it's soooo old."

"I've been working at it for a long time, Mej. It's like a huge set of word puzzles to me. History, law, politics, it's all written in the mother tongue. And to be honest, I just like the sound of it." I decided it was my turn to ask something. "So how'd you learn Hindi so well? I mean, it was like going from Latin to Italian for me after knowing the Sanskrit. How'd you learn it?"

He looked at his fingernails and answered quickly, "Me Mum taught me mostly. It was 'er first language, not mine, so I sort of picked it up 'ere and there. I figured I needed to improve on it when I got 'ere, so I bought meself a teach yourself book last year."

As we reached my gate he asked, "So whatcha working on now, Bro? Any juicy shite? They say that Kama Sutra can give you a right fine woody." It sounded a little boring when I told him I was translating a play about a monarch with family problems, but he told me quickly that he wanted to hear more about it when he returned from Delhi. We set a time to meet in a few days, and then I watched as he bounced buoyantly down Sonapura Road towards the Asi River. Just before the bridge he turned and grinned back at me.

Eighteen

I pushed Ugly Bike through Devi's gate with a cushy six-minute margin. My backpack contained my HP Pavilion laptop, the flash drive with our photographs, and the previous day's notes scanned with my portable DocuPen scanner and saved on a file. I'd arrived early, hoping to chat with Sukshmi about her marriage predicament. Instead I found Soma.

She was squatting in the space behind the right side of the tool shed and the wall, and I could tell from the way her shoulders slumped forward and her hands shook that she was crying. I leaned Miss Ugly against the wall and squatted next to her in the dust. Her hands moved up to hide her face, but as I lowered myself with a groan from the morning's exercise, her fingers spread into a childish vee. Between her dusty knuckles I saw a smear of black kohl and tears. One eye peeked at me.

Suspecting her mother-in-law as the cause, I asked, "So, Little Sister, is your Sas angry with you again? You mustn't listen to her puffing, you know. She grumbles at you from jealousy because you are young and beautiful and she is a fat camel with foul breath."

Soma sniffled wretchedly and mumbled through her fingers, "Oh Bhimaji, Sas always grumbles at me, but it no longer bothers me."

"So what is causing all these tears to fall from those pretty eyes this morning?"

She drew in a choppy breath and in an uneven voice, whispered, "It is Sri Ralki. He..." She broke into a fresh round of sobbing.

I inhaled sharply, that name typically having that effect upon me. Madru Ralki was a first inspector and assistant to the

Varanasi Chief of Police. He was a fat weasel, and a purported
spy for the Cabinet Minister Qereshy, which did not make him
particularly popular within his own Hindu community. He
denied being a turncoat, but not vehemently enough to convince
me or anyone else. Unfortunately, he was also the first in a line
of bureaucrats I had to speak with to renew my visa every six
months. Those encounters were inevitably uncomfortable unions
of oil and flame. In my slightly biased opinion, he was a pudgy
bit of pomposity with far too much time and power at his
disposal. His office reeked of beedees, the pungent eucalyptus
cigarettes that he smoked incessantly. Always, by the time I had
gotten the stamp for six more months of stay in Varanasi, I
prayed that one of his little cigarettes would ignite the grease
that coated his outstretched palm. What his business with Soma
was, I couldn't imagine.

"Madru Ralki? What does he have to do with you? You've
committed no crime," other than being a beautiful, young,
outcaste.

She lowered her hands and wrapped them around folded
knees. What I saw in her eyes sent a bolt of anger through me.
Fear—coming from something Ralki had said. Or done.

"He just asked me some questions, Bhimaji. Just a few."

"Questions? What questions? He has no business asking
anything of you."

She hesitated, confirming to me that he'd threatened her.
That would have been his way--intimidation for silence. What
he didn't understand was that Soma was more like a sister to
me, and I a brother to her, than true siblings. What she might
withhold from someone else, she wouldn't withhold from me.

"First he asked me what I do for Master Devi all day, who I talk to, what my jobs are. He said they are searching for suspects in the bombings and all the people of Varanasi are being questioned. I told him I only talk to Master Devi, Mirabai, and my mother-in-law, because they are the ones who tell me what to do." The simple truth of this statement stung me. There were few, besides me, who spoke to Soma. Why would Ralki be asking questions of a husbandless, second-hand sweeper girl?

"He asked you that, nothing else?"

Soma's chin came to rest on her kneecaps. A long hesitation. "He asked me about you."

I sucked in a lungful of hot dust and almost swore. Slowly I asked, "What did he ask about me, Little Pearl? Tell me the truth, every question. I will not let him harm you. I promise."

She looked sideways at me, trust shimmering in her pupils. "He asked me what you study with Master Devi."

"And you told him that I am a student of Sanskrit?"

"He knew that already. Everyone knows that, Bhimaji. He asked me what you are doing now."

This time I did swear out loud. Even in English, the word 'fuck' brought a flash of smile to Soma's lips. "Bhimaji swears."

"Yes, I did swear, and it's a bad swear because it's no business of Ralki's what I do at all, especially what I work on with Master Devi. If I thought it would do an ounce of good I would march into his smelly little office and tell him so." The image of the ember-lit face staring at me the night before returned. Had it been Ralki? I hadn't even considered who might have been watching me because it seemed inconsequential at the time. Now I wasn't so sure.

Instantly the fear returned. "No, Bhimaji," she pleaded. "Please, you must not do that. He would know that I have spoken to you and send for me again." There was something in her voice—a quiver--that told me Ralki had gone beyond a mere warning. He had intimidated her with something else.

"Soma, tell me the truth. Did he do anything else? Did he hurt you?"

She stared solemnly at her toe rings and dug them into the dust. Lips trembled as she whispered, "No, Bhimaji, he did not hurt me."

Inside the house I heard Devi's voice grumble, "Where is our fine young Keeper of Notes and Photographs, eh? Late again." Then a calm, but unintelligible, answer from C.G.

With a boiling that rose from deep inside, I asked again, "Did he hurt you?"

She replied in a reticent whisper, "He pushed his hand under my chola and squeezed me there. It did not hurt. But he . . . said that he would throw me into the streets with just my bangles to cover me if I spoke to anyone about it."

I made a mental note to break at least nine of Ralki's fingers for that grope of my little sister's breast. Then I would sit back and watch him try to smoke one his fucking little beedees with just a thumb.

Stroking the back of Soma's hand, I said, "He will need to go through a very large, very strong, ferenghi to do that, Little One. You go now and wash that pretty face. Mirabai will be asking for you. And Soma?"

"Yes, Master Bhim."

"It is probably best that you do not talk to anyone about this."

With the smile that always made me forget my aches, she sniffled and rose gracefully from the dust. "Just to you,

Bhimaji," she answered.

Nineteen

I wasn't that late. Three minutes by my Casio, six by Master's Timex. Later than ever before, but being the Keeper of Notes and Photographs provided legitimate excuses.

"Good Morning, Punditjis. I pray that you are both feeling very well this morning." I entered the parlor with a broad smile and purposeful stride. "And I assume you are wondering why I am a few minutes late." Before Master could even inhale, I went on. "Yesterday I found the perfect program for us. It has allowed me to rework all of our notes into Devanagari on the computer. And now it all typed and safeguarded onto this." I held up the memory stick for emphasis. "I finished just before I left this morning, and now . . . we are ready for our second day of research." That was my first fib. I had scanned the notes the previous afternoon. The second was that I had been using the optical character recognition program for three months.

While Devi made disapproving clucks and scowls at the innocuous, but technical, flash drive, C.G. coughed a soggy burst of phlegm into a handkerchief and said, "Do not be concerned over a few seconds of tardiness, Bhim. You have done well. A good OCR program with Hindi script? Which one? It must be Letter Box East. My students tell me that has the best Asian fonts."

C.G.'s praise of the gadget rustled Devi's feathers. He grumbled impatiently, "If the two of you have finished with your pleasantries, I believe it would be good to actually look at some of that fonze and continue the work from yesterday." And being linguists, that is precisely what we did.

Before Mirabai arrived with our first mugs of chai, we knew the text was something not only old, but far more compelling than we could have imagined.

It took C.G.'s translation of the first seven lines of the second photo. Borrowing my pencil, he scribbled and asked, "What does this sound like to you?

'When the man's self thins the like a reeds in a summer sun;

And his waters pour out like a swollen stream,

And none replenished will slake his thirst;

When his water is sweet as the juice of the cane,

 And yields a fragrance as sweet.

Then the man's self lightens and pales like the moon,

And in the dawn the self thereupon dies.'

Devi and I looked at each other, puzzled, while C.G. tossed me the notepad. "Make something up, my boy, anything that comes to mind. One young mango is better than two old melons." He grinned at that.

I thought out loud, "Well . . . sounds like a high fever, perspiration, something to do with cane juice. Whatever that means."

Devi added absentmindedly, "Precisely so, precisely so. You see, C.G., I told you it was a shastram. It is definitely one of the old Ayurvedic treatments." After a moment of silence, we began looking at the screen like schoolboys over new set of puzzles.

A cure of some sort. But for what?

C.G. and I then spent an hour organizing it into sequenced thumbnails--snapshots we could look at six at a time and expand with double-clicks. I labeled each by lines: 1-12—Benediction/Salutation. 13-41—Description of Symptoms. As I typed the words sweating, emaciation, and slow death, I wondered. Cholera? Yellow fever? Were those the symptoms?

We moved on, and the next fourteen brought us to the

beginning of third photograph and elaborate instructions for cremation of the corpse. These, I assumed, were necessary when the cure hadn't worked. I kept going until my fingers felt like they had run a marathon.

Lunch arrived--trays of chapattis, rice, dal, and bowls of condiments. I saved the file to the flash drive, so excited I didn't want the session to end, even for one of Mirabai's feasts.

We dined cross-legged on the floor and I listened silently as the boys talked in short, giddy exchanges.

"It is one of the cures, Devi. That is certain."

"Indeed, C.G.. All the earmarks. Tomorrow we will encounter some of the old plants. Do you not agree?"

Chandragupta wheezed, "Most certainly, Devi. Herbs and mixtures. That is always the way, a lot of damned flowers and pastes that we linguists know nothing about. Probably need to find a pharmacist from four thousand years ago."

They both giggled.

"Precisely, C.G.. And you have such a person in mind, no doubt?"

"Hmm, yes. That could pose a problem, a four thousand year old herbologist.

Masterji beamed like a drunken condor. "I believe, C.G., the correct term is herbalist."

"Yes, yes, herbalist." C.G. patted his friend's knee and asked, "And what about our security, Devi. You have found someone, yes?"

Master chortled, "Yes indeed, we now have a young security fellow posted at the entrance to our cave. Rajneesh, the taxi driver, has a younger brother with a cell phone. He will be our watchman and sleep there. Instructed to call your office at any sign of trouble." I suspected this arrangement had been made the previous afternoon using Soma to find Rajneesh, who then hired his brother. I also suspected it had cost Devi the least amount of rupees possible.

After another moment or two more, I cleared my throat. "Excuse me, Punditjis."

Both sets of eyes swung in my direction, silence followed.

I looked from one to the other. "I have a small question. Do these ancient cures ever actually work?" The look I received from both of them gave me my answer.

We just needed to find a doctor to verify it, and I had just the person in mind.

Twenty

From Master's back porch I saw immediately that Ugly Bike had a flat, her deflated tube drooping like a squashed cobra below her spokes. The moment I saw that disheartening sight I entertained the idea of kicking something, but then thought better of it. There was no purpose in expending that kind of energy at that time of day, or in injuring my toe, so I sent a good string of cuss words in her general direction instead.

It was the hour between noon and one, the hour made famous by the expression "mad dogs and Englishmen." Those happened to be the only two things stupid enough--or in the case of the canine, insane enough—to venture outside. During the Varanasi summer, stores were shuttered, autoricks disappeared, and the city dozed to hold its breath until a cooler part of the day. Nothing moved. I, however, had to.

Deciding to leave her at Devi's, I gave Miss Ugly a fond pat on the seat—with an apology for my cussing--shouldered my pack and trudged up the lane.

My trip might have been shorter had I taken a direct route home, but I didn't. Curiosity spurred me to swing by the scene of my first date in four years. It wasn't the thought of Sukshmi or the conundrum of her forced marriage that changed my path. It was the voice that kept oddly repeating in my head--the voice of the backpacker who had wished me a good night. There had been a puzzling, rather pleasant, accent, Scandinavian my trained ears told me. Swedish or possibly Danish, and being in the business of language, it had piqued my curiosity. I thought on it when I woke that morning, and at most moments when I wasn't too occupied with the project.

It would have been a shorter along the Ghats, being less

serpentine and a smaller curve--like on the inside of a racetrack, but I chose to walk through the gullies for a different reason. They were shaded. I plodded up Madanapura Road, sweat dripping into my sandals, turned right on Luxa and into the overshadowed lanes that took me past the Vishwanath Temple-- another famous Varanasi edifice. In addition to being a survivor of a dozen assaults by mogul emperors, and that many reconstructions, the current interior was crafted from nearly a ton of pure gold. Not that anyone would have thought to chip any off. A cadre of devout guards stood watch even during that hour when only mad dogs and Englishmen strolled about.

I arrived at Haroon's just as my gregarious friend was shuttering his doors and pocketing his keys. He turned at my approach. "Bhim!" The friendly smile was followed by a bewildered look. "A second visit in two days? What a delight." Noticing the sweat streaming down my neck, he asked," My good fellow, what are you doing traipsing around in this god- awful heat? This is when devils sit and laugh as we melt like candles. I hope you are not coming to talk about your play or politics." He jingled his keys. "I am just now leaving for my house where the air conditioner is working. Alas, here it is not, but the workers promise that it will be ready for our evening's happiest hour. You are welcome to join me if you wish." With an inspired look he added, "We can make our travel plans to Cancun and Puerto Vallarta."

Shaking his outstretched hand I replied, "Maumed, I would truly enjoy that, especially to be out of this heat, but I'm afraid I cannot. I have my own work this afternoon. Actually. . .I was hoping to see if. . ." My speech faltered. He stared and waited. "I was wondering if by chance you might know anything of the two ferenghi women, the ones with the big backpacks who sat near Jatana and me last evening."

A wicked grin crept across his face. "Ah, Bhimaji. You are a sly fox. One beautiful Benarsi woman is not enough for the likes of you, eh. You need three to please. You are a god amongst us."

"Nothing of the sort, Maumed. I am only interested in who they are. Just curious is all."

Disappointment erased the grin. "Ah. . . Well, in that case, I know for a fact they are staying at The Riverview Lodge. That establishment is owned by my brother-in-law, so my bartender recommends it to the patrons, you see."

"Uh huh. Well, not to offend, Haroon, but your brother-in-law runs a grade-D fleabag. I know it well. Anything else?"

"The taller, pretty one talked for both. The plump one never smiles and talks little. She referred to the pretty one as Uliana. My barman said that they are from some country in the north of Europe that he could not remember. But it is certainly a place too cold for women to wear bikinis much. Quite unfortunate."

I shook his hand again. "Maumed, you're a good friend and a fine gentleman. Maybe later this week we can sip smoothies and really plan your vacation to the great resorts of the world."

"Our vacation, Bhim."

"My mistake, Maumed. Our vacation."

Twenty-One

Instead of trundling over to Haroon's brother-in-law's fleabag hotel, I ended up walking home by way of the Ghats again. Shyness, or some such fear, prevented me from striding like James Bond up to the desk at The Riverview and asking if a tall blond named Uliana had recently signed the register. My curiosity didn't need to be satisfied that much. Instead, I found a favorite cheese vendor, his stall still un-shuttered to the mid-day warmth, and purchased a kilo of fresh—guaranteed refrigerated—goat cheese. With my purchase wrapped in moist banana leaves and string, I curved my way through the gullies and out to the river.

The Ganges, unlike the slumbering city above it, was not shut down during that part of the day. The river flowed at its same pace and only the people at its edge drifted more slowly. Most had surrendered to the shade of umbrellas or the overhangs of temples or vending stalls, but it was still crowded. Here and there half-dressed mendicants cleansed their souls as dhobis smacked clothes against the rocks a few feet away. I, feeling the affects of it all, the heat, the morning's mental and physical challenges, dreamed only of a glass of cold lager and my bed beneath the fan.

I never got that cold lager.

As I plodded down to the water's edge and around the pyres of Manikarnika, I instinctively felt eyes following me again. Glancing up at the small temple that housed the eternal flame, I saw a strange sight. Below it, seated in the shade of a shala, a large palm hut, was a young man. Even more strangely, it was the same man who had met me at the train station, bestowed my Hindu name, and passed by my gate two days earlier. At his feet were the two blond backpackers and four foreigners, two of whom I knew. All of them at that moment were looking directly at me.

There are moments we come to understand as crossroads, times of decision. Unlike the unanticipated events that alter our lives without warning, these are moments we have some power over. Sometimes we see them for what they are; sometimes we understand later. The moment I saw that unusual congregation, I knew I had arrived at a crossroad. I could have fluttered a non-committal wave and shuffled off to the coolness of my fan and that tumbler of ale. I was a recluse, a bookworm, and any number of excuses would have sufficed-- hunger, thirst, or the forbidding heat of the Indian sun. No one would have considered it discourteous had I kept on my path. But I didn't; I took a deep breath, and trying to look casual for the benefit of the watching eyes, turned and climbed the steps.

As I neared the top, the young man gestured with his fingers to a woven mat at the edge of the circle. In rapid English he called out, "Bhim, my good friend. It has been far too long since we have been in each other's company. Come, take advantage of our shade and, as we often say in these parts, have a Fanta." He chuckled at that, flipped opened a battered ice chest, and without waiting for an answer, produced an orange soda. He snapped the cap with a rusty opener on the side of the box and thrust it toward me. There was nothing to do but accept the drink and the camaraderie of the group.

With a traditional palm-to-palm thank you, I took the Fanta and sat in the only space left, on the mat between the only people that I knew in the group. I'd chatted with them on occasion through years and referred to them as The Sadhu

Wannabees, Petey and Shawn.

They were English, and the focus of a lot of jokes around the local merchant stalls. For a few obvious reasons. They were overtly gay, dressed in orange loincloths, and never once wore shirts. They anointed themselves with gray ash and red paste and had the longest, filthiest, dreadlocks in human history. Their feet made C.G.'s look attractive. Naturally, they were the subject of some humorous comment. The amount of holy beads alone that dangled from their necks was enough to start most laughing.

In their quest for spiritual enlightenment, Petey and Shawn smoked no less than ten chillums of hashish a day, drank a lot of sharab, and ate balls of black opium in the afternoon to enhance their dreams. To put it mildly, they liked to get messed up. It brought them closer to nirvana.

Like all year-round ferenghis, you eventually crossed paths. We had chatted enough at the Ghats or fruit stalls for me to realize that they were harmless and more interested in brain altering substances and each other's penises than who I was. That was fine by me.

Shawn, whose dreads were coiled into a wooly beehive, whispered as I sat down, "Bhimaji Man, it is righteous good to see your light amongst us again." I hadn't thought it had left, but whispered amiably, "Good to see you too, Shawn. You guys still staying at the Hodge Podge?" The Hodge Podge Lodge was a few notches lower on the rating scale than The Riverview. A true dive.

"Yeah, but me and Petey are in a better space now, Man. We got a shower." That must've been an exciting improvement, but by the looks of it, neither of them had yet to avail themselves of it. I took a long pull on my Fanta.

Our host seemed to be wrapping up some sort of discourse on the physics of the river below us. "And so, good friends, our little molecule of oxygen and hydrogen, two gases drawn into mysterious partnership of liquid, flows with no fanfare whatsoever from this very spot in front of us down to the vastness of the ocean." He chuckled. "And in my opinion, a journey of such perseverance and length deserves more recognition. A toast. To The Process of Light Energy." He raised his own bottle. His was grape. I took that moment to study him.

The first word that came to my mind was--eccentric. Then I changed that. Eccentric from Latin eccentricus and Greek ekkentros, meant outside the center. He wasn't outside, he was right in the middle. Then the word 'quirky' came to mind. That seemed appropriate. He was Indian, but had the look of wealth and education, perhaps an affluent Vaishya family— the merchant caste. He had handsome features, like a Punjabi, was medium height, and wore comfortable pajama-pants and a loose-fitting green kurta the color of unripe mangoes. His hair, brushed straight back, had none of the oil-slick worn by most of the young men in the region. I suspected he was Oxford-educated because he had retained just enough of that accent for my ear to detect. He had a straight nose and eyes that were exceptional; they danced and absorbed everything around him with humor, a lot of humor. They were also the most intelligent eyes I had seen since the university at Berkeley, but without the haughtiness of the academicians I had met there. Even with all those refined features, the word that still came to me was. . . 'quirky.'

His eyes focused on me. "So, Bhim, we meet again. I told you we would, did I not? Let's see, you already know Shawn and Peter. Uliana and Jitka you have seen but haven't formally met." I glance shyly in their direction, wondering how our host knew this. "Marley and Frederick you don't know from Archie and Betty. Okay everyone; this is Bhim, a great Sanskritist in our fair city. There, now we all know each other." I glanced shyly at the other's faces. The blond-haired Uliana, at that distance and full light, was simply stunning.

If the rapid-fire introductions hadn't sounded so odd, I might have felt uncomfortable, as it was, I nearly started laughing.

I screwed up enough courage to state the obvious, "Not quite all. . . I don't know you."

He laughed as if that were outrageously funny. "Yes, yes, we have met, but you are quite correct. You do not know my name. I was once known as Sharmalal Dijna. Years ago. Now I'm Adam."

Okay, I'd expected something like Bhapu or Gopal, something a tad more indigenous. Adam didn't fit. Not yet.

He looked inquisitively at my wrapped package, but I had the distinct impression he knew what was inside. He validated my suspicions by asking, "Feta?" I nodded. He held out his hand, and thinking he meant to feel its weight, I handed it to him. Then I turned to Shawn and Petey on the pretext of asking if the shower was actually working in their new room. I wanted to steal another glance at Uliana and Jitka. Uliana had deep-ocean eyes, high cheekbones, and full lips. Michelle Pfeifer from Oslo. Jitka was plumper, and wore a travel-weary expression that told you to back away slowly lest your testicles be at risk.

Suddenly, Adam's voice called out loudly, startling me. "Ao, Bacchi, ao. Come Children, come." I turned as a swarm of riverbank urchins scurried across the steps. A dozen soiled hands of various dimension, stretched towards Adam. Skinny bodies, festering sores, and sunken eyes surrounded us. Half my feta sat in front of Adam neatly cubed on the section of the leaf that had wrapped it, a small folding knife next to it. The other half of my cheese was divided into two parts, fourths of my original kilo. He handed the green plate of cubes to the largest of the children with a stern directive to share it equally. Then, with a wave of his fingers he sent them scampering away. My mouth dropped, and as quickly as he had handed me the Fanta, pushed a remaining fourth in my direction. The final cube he divided for our group. With pleasant thank-yous, everyone popped their feta, correction, my feta, into their mouths.

Twenty-Two

We're supposed to gain a lot from first impressions. That's what they say anyway. That singular event below the temple at Manikarnika returns to me more often than I would have imagined. I sat looking at my remaining quarter kilo, totally baffled by Sharmalal, or Adam, or whatever he called himself. That first impression bounced around from quirky orator, to devious thief, to generous benefactor. He didn't clarify it much when he hopped to his feet with a hasty good-bye and left the seven of us staring at each other. Other than The Sadhu Wannabees, I had absolutely no idea what the others were thinking or why they were even there. My English buddies were pretty easy to read.

Petey, in falso-soprano and exaggerated esses, broke the silence with, "Well, that was the cutest thing since Prince Andrew, wouldn't you agree, Shawney. I can so picture those molecules hooking up like little drag queens to float down the river together."

Shawn, holding out his hand in a cue that it was time to head back to the Hodge Podge for an afternoon nap, responded, "Cute as William and Andrew combined, Sweets. Come on, let's go fire up a tube of Bombay Boogey with a pinch of dream maker in it." With a toodle-oo and a finger wave they sashayed up the steps to indulge in their mix of hashish and opium. Five of us remained.

Marley and Frederick introduced themselves first. Pleasant couple, mid-thirties, from Toronto, having a wonderful time riding first class rail to all the holy sites listed in Frommer's. She had carrot hair and a complexion too freckled to be out in the Uttar Pradesh sun. He looked like an insurance salesman with wire frame glasses. It was easy to see that they had money, nice cameras and safari hats with small air conditioners in them. Truly, little battery-operated coolers in the headbands that guaranteed you wouldn't get heatstroke. Unless your batteries died. They inquired how long I'd been in Varanasi and whistled in low unison when I told them. I caught a new look of appraisal from Uliana and the same tough-ass look from Jitka

After a second round of questions I learned the blond women were from Tönder, Denmark, which I also learned was in the southern part of the country, just over the border from Germany. In brave or foolhardy fashion they had hitchhiked nineteen days to Turkey and then flown across the less tourist-friendly regions of Iraq and Iran. From Bombay they had set off on a tour of the North. That had been a month ago.

I assumed—which was not something I did with frequency—that they were on a spiritual quest more than the typical tourist trek. Uliana anyway. She bore that out when she replied in a silky Danish accent to a question from Frederick about sites they had seen in Agra. "Ya, we toured the Red Fort und the Taj Mahal, und then stayed for fifteen days in an ashram for the Hatha yoga. It was the best time we've had on our trip so far." I saw Jitka scowl.

Marley's face, even with her refrigerated hat, was flushing to beet. "Why did you leave?" She asked.

Uliana smiled and blushed. "The food was not very good for our stomachs." Light gutturals swirled into her speech like honey.

Jitka, spoke for the first time, her voice sounding more like a German rock-crusher. "We had the runs the entire goddamned time, Uli, and the yoga master kept trying to get you into positions that I've never seen in any yoga book. He was a horny little veasel with b o and we were both happy as hens to get the hell out of there." I decided right then that I liked Jitka.

Uliana looked at me, and I saw something in her eyes I hadn't noticed before—dispiritedness in the blue. "Achh...it wasn't that bad, but maybe less pleasant than I describe." She hesitated and asked me, "Und how is it you came by the name Bhim? It is one of Arjuna's brothers from the Mahabharata is it not? The big, strong one?"

That was impressive; few Westerners knew the intricacies of India's two massive epics, certainly not the details of the minor characters. The Mahabharata is the longest poem ever written, and nestled like a diamond in its center is the Bhagavad-Gita, The Song of God. Beautiful reading for any tourist, and required literature for any student of Hinduism, but few went beyond its boundaries to the surrounding story.

"You have a . . . good memory," I stammered. "He is one of Arjuna's brothers, a giant who does a lot of Paul Bunyan tricks, like tossing boulders and snapping trees." Marley and Frederick nodded. Being Canadian I guess they knew who Paul Bunyan was. Uliana's expression told me she didn't, so I explained.

With a quick smile she asked, "So, you chose this giant's name for yourself?"

I touched the name-string at my neck. "No, actually our friend, Adam who just shared three-fourths of my goat-cheese with the world, gave me the name three years ago. It sort of stuck. This is the first encounter I've had with him since." They all stared at me again. The subject then shifted to how they had been drawn to where we stood. Adam, I learned, had been lecturing to no one, just sermonizing to the air about electrons

and molecules. He had gone on and on while people passed by
unheeding. That was understandable. He'd been orating in
English, which narrowed the audience, and sermons along the
Ghats were as common as funerals. Somehow though, what he
was saying, or how he was saying it, had caught the attention of
the members of our small group.

I listened taciturnly as they chatted about hotels. The
Chapens, Marley and Frederick, were quartered in the Radisson
and were mildly disappointed by the clicking of the air
conditioner, but the mini-bar and continental breakfasts were
decent. Jitka growled that The Riverview was a stinking sweatbox that pigs shouldn't sleep in. I thought that an accurate
assessment.

I stifled a sleepy yawn. Eight hours earlier I had tossed a lot
of Frisbee, and in between had worked on a translation for a
cure for some unknown disease. Not bad for a single day. I was
now dreaming of tossing Lalji out of his hammock for an
afternoon snooze.

The Chapens departed for the clicking coolness of their room,
and then there were three of us. I watched nervously, as Uliana
gave Jitka a pleasant go for a walk' signal. Stretching her spine
and patting her ribcage, Miss Congeniality snarled, "Right,
Svester. I'll go alone to our little sheisahole with the roaches in
the faucets und bedbugs. Und I'll wait for you, but not long.
Lunch was supposed to be an hour ago, und I vill find a ham and
a rye sandwich in this stinkhole if it kills me, und potato chips
too." Svester, Jitka was her sister. She tromped up the steps,
and I was once more awkwardly facing a beautiful woman my
own age.

Uliana Hadersen, meet the inhibited, bashful, and

stammering Sanskrit hermit with two names. Please to meet
you. I hoped she was capable of carrying on a conversation by
herself, because I was having a hard time swallowing, much less
vocalizing.

She asked if I wouldn't mind sitting for a moment. That
simple question was another crossroad, one I wasn't sure I was
ready to veer onto, even just to sit and chat idly by the river.
But of course, I did.

She wore a simple, tan blouse and a long cotton skirt printed
with sea horses and curled eel grass. This she raised tactfully to
her knees as we sat down. No earrings, no necklaces, no make-
up, and not a hint of a tattoo. Perhaps there is a small one, I
thought, a rose, or a butterfly, in some hidden spot.

She glanced up the steps that Jitka had just ascended and
offered, "My sister is really quite kind when you get to know her,
but cautious of strangers. She watches out for both of us, but
has a very kind heart."

I took a deep breath, hoping to settle the pounding in my
ears. "I can understand that, being protective of someone like
you. Is she older?" Someone like you? God, did I really say
that?

Uli let out a breezy laugh. "No, I am the older, but she thinks
she is the tougher, so she believes it is her duty. I am called Uli,
by the way."

Yes, I supposed. It would be a good thing, protecting
someone like you. I asked the only numb question I could think
of. "So Uli, have you enjoyed India so far? I mean, other than
the ashram and sour stomach."

"Oh yes, very much. Especially the people; they always want
to help." She smiled and added, "Everyone offers food and asks

us to come to their homes for meals. Though I expect they don't have so much for themselves. The train from Delhi was long, but the rice fields and ox and women planting barefoot--it made me feel like I was . . . really seeing it for the first time. Does that sound silly?"

"No, not at all. The villages are the soul of the country. Very little changes in them, and when you see them up close, you are seeing the real India. Trains are a great way to take it in."

She gazed absently at the river and continued. "Ya, but I think I wish for a . . ."

I finished her thought. "a deeper experience?" I had seen it in her eyes earlier. I'd also heard it from a hundred ferenghis who had come the city searching for personal epiphanies. Eventually they moved on.

"Yes. Something like that. How did you know?"

I looked to the river also. "A lot of people come here for those kinds of reasons. India draws them, Varanasi holds them. For a short while anyway. Hindus believe it is because their souls lived here in previous lives."

"Is that what you believe? Is that why you came here?" It was asked with such innocence that my usual defenses remained lowered.

"I'm . . . not sure what I believe anymore. I came here to study poetry, and it may sound exaggerated when I say it, but it makes me shiver from its beauty. I think it's why I'm here, really, to work in the verse. Well, mostly in a way." I was struggling, trying to verbalize one half of why I was here. Then our eyes met and I saw that she was listening, so I kept on. "It's a blend of sounds and mathematics. A concerto, like the best Elizabethan sonnets set in this incredible song that resonates the strings of the heart like sitars." I had rambled a bit and blushed from of it.

"That doesn't sound exaggerated. It sounds beautiful."

"It is." Curious, I asked, "So, Uli . . . how do you know the names of characters in the Mahabharata?"

"Ach, I read it last year. I wanted to learn about the country und thought it was a good place to start."

"The whole thing!" I was stunned. A few thousand pages of couplets could send anyone scurrying for a cheap suspense novel.

"Ya, a condensed one, but I read it and The Ramayana before I left Tonder. It was good practice for my English, and the stories were amazing, plots inside plots. Great love stories, too."

Incredible. A woman who read the epics, the Great Poetry? "You enjoyed the tale of Rama and Sita?"

"Yes of course, very much. Who could not? Rama searching the entire earth for his wife. Such pain and devotion, nothing could stop him. He went to war to bring her into his arms. That is love. And Hanuman, he is my favorite ever. How could a woman not love someone with a heart of gold and the face of a monkey." I smiled and shooed away two curious boys who had come to stare at us.

For a few minutes we said nothing, just watched the throngs of people drifting along the banks. There was, I supposed, an unspoken understanding that we would ask each other's deeper stories later.

A hundred meters south, a pair of men began arguing heatedly, their voices lost in the din of the ghats. A Hindu and a Muslim. The Hindu was in simple garb, but I noticed the Muslim wore the Nehru-style jacket of the followers of Yakoob

Qereshy—ridiculous attire in this heat. A small crowd gathered around them, and then—I didn't see from whom, a fist flew. Pushing, shoving ensued, and with difficulty the crowd pulled the two apart. It was a forewarning that I didn't pay enough attention to.

Uliana cringed visibly.

In the vacuum that followed, the sounds of the city settled around us. Horns and bells echoed through the gullies above. A high-octave flute warbled a movie theme from a radio somewhere, and from the mosque to the north the muezzin rose above the din. Allah Akbar, Allah Akbar. Allah is most great. Come to prayer.

Curious again about the disparate nature of the gathering around Adam, I asked, "Uli, how did you end up here today? It was . . . an unusual group."

Her eyes scrunched into a charming frown. "A bit strange, ya? Jitka und I were on a walking tour of the temples. I had a map of the best ones to visit, and I saw those two monks, or sadhus, or whatever they call themselves with all those beads und hair."

"Petey and Shawn, the English guys?"

"Yes, those two. Und they were swaying und spinning like Dervishes, so I look und there is this young man giving a sermon that no one is listening to. It was so odd that we decided to see what it was about. We came und listened, und even Jitka admitted that his speech was fascinating. You walk along this river und you don't hear too many lectures on chemistry."

She had that right. I looked at the river and we grew quiet again.

"Bhim?"

"Yes?"

"You know this city well, ya?"

I nodded. "I suppose. I've been here longer than most."

Her voice got strangely quiet and sad. "Would you take me on a tour sometime? I believe you would be a better guide than anyone I could pay. I would like to go the place where Buddha gave his sermons, maybe some of the temples und parks where people pray. I would pay you for your time."

With more courage in my voice than I felt in the base of my spine, I replied, "I would be happy to be your guide, Uliana Hadersen. And no payment will be required. But there is a condition. By the way, I do know the gardens and temple of the city well enough to guide you without a map." I managed that without a single stutter.

Her lips curled into a knowing smile. "And what condition is that, Bhimaji of Varanasi?"

It came out in a rush, but at least it came out. "I will take you on every path of this old city if you will do me the honor of having dinner with me tomorrow evening."

Twenty-Three

I never got that nap or my glass of lager. Another of those unforeseen events that explode into my life got in the way.

As I stepped through the gate into the courtyard, Sahr came bolting out the door and down the steps wailing, "Bhimaji, Bhimaji. Something awful, an accident. Horrible. Horrible! I knew it. Durgabal is never wrong. Never!" She was moaning and wringing the end of her sari. I set my hands on her shoulders, suddenly anxious; Sahr didn't lose composure often, and when she did, something dire had happened.

"What in heaven's name is wrong? Is it Lalji? Is he hurt?" If anyone could get hurt from some foolishness, it was he.

"No, Bhimaji, he is fine. It is Jotilal Sukkha. He cannot be found and they believe he has been crushed under the stone."

Sahr's words were coming too rapidly, and making no sense. Who was Jotilal? Then it struck me. Rajneesh Sukkha--my rickwalla buddy. Jotilal was his brother with the cell phone, our newly hired guard. Blood pulsed in my temples. "Sahr, please listen. Look at me." Her locked on mine. "I need you to tell me slowly what has happened? Take a deep breath and first tell me who told you this." The rumor mill spun efficiently in our neighborhood, but was often laced with inaccuracies. The first order was to know the source.

With one name she eliminated the possibility of misinformation.

"Professor Chandragupta." Blood pounded behind my eyes. "He came in his car an hour ago and called at the gate, demanding to talk to you. He yelled at Lalji and said he would talk to no one else. Quite out of character. He was so upset, but when I came to see what the fuss was all about, he calmed down and told me." I understood then. The professor had approached her for psychic advice in the past, and like all her customers, he trusted her. "He told me that your cave has collapsed."

"Collapsed. Oh God! And Jotilal?" But, I already knew the answer.

"Missing. They think he is buried inside." Before I could ask another question, she started sobbing again. "His brother, Rajneesh, drove out with food and more bedding in the morning, but when he arrived, there was only rock. He tried, but could not find a way through."

"He only slept there one night." The thought astounded me, and for a selfish instant I saw myself standing inside that chamber three days earlier. It had felt safe. Now it was a tomb. Something vile rose in my throat. "What did Rajneesh do?"

With each question Sahr was gaining more self-control. "He drove to the professor's cottage at the University. The professor called the police and then came here." I suddenly pictured an investigation with uncomfortable questions. What was in the cave that needed to be guarded? What had been discovered? And why hadn't we told the authorities about it? I took a deep breath.

Handing her my backpack I said, "Please put these away and fetch my cell phone and something cool to drink." Both of us knew that small chores were the best way to keep her from shredding her entire sari with nervous fingers.

I lowered myself into the rocking chair on the veranda, emotions running like gazelles. I'd never met Jotilal Sukkha, but knew he had a wife and children and a brother that loved him. I was heartsick. Then anger came over me, though I wasn't even sure what I was angry at. Fate? God? Allah? Vishnu? I'd been angry at all of them for years now. Never changed a thing. All the cuss words I knew—English, Hindi, and the Spanish ones I learned from Lilia--poured out. Then a calmer thought took over. We had the photographs, and the pundits were so respected in the district that nobody, certainly not any Hindus, would question their need for a guard at the entrance of a cave. The tragedy would be seen as just that. I dropped my face into sweaty palms and drew my fingers through my hair.

The iced coffee Sahr handed me was rich and sugared, but didn't clear the foulness from my mouth particularly well. I took another sip and scrolled through the three numbers stored in my cell phone.

C.G. coughed after the second ring, "Bhim. You have heard?"

"Yes, Punditji, just now. How is Rajneesh holding up?" I imagined my rickshaw friend scrambling frantically over the boulders near our picnic spot, clawing desperately at the rubble where his brother lay.

"Not very well, I'm afraid. He blames himself, saying that he should have arrived earlier, or that he shouldn't have allowed Joti to stay alone. It is nonsense, of course. No one could have foreseen this. Devi and I are going to their family house this afternoon." Guessing my next question, he asked, "Will you go to the cave in our stead? Mr. Muktendra and First Inspector Singh have asked to meet us there at four. There will likely be some official questions." I'm sure there would be, and C. G. was asking me to answer them. It was the last thing I wanted to do. The clock on my phone blinked twenty after two. In an autorick I couldn't possibly get there until five. With a car I might make it.

"I need to hire a car, and I don't think I can get there until five at least."

"Do not be concerned, Dear Boy. I will send my driver straightaway in the GC, and call the inspector and tell him to meet you there at five. Devi and I can taxi to the Sukkha house. It is quite close, you see."

A little confused, I asked, "Punditji, what is a GC?"

"Of course, Bhim. You don't know. GC is my Grand Cherokee. Quite new. I named him G.C., sort of a flip-flop of C.G., you see. And he is at your disposal."

Twenty-Four

GC, complete with air-conditioning, Dolby sound, liquid suspension, and a driver named Ram, arrived at my gate ten minutes later. Lalji, who hadn't shown his face the entire afternoon, and who I was certain had heard every word of my conversations, appeared out of nowhere. He stood proudly next to the SUV when it arrived, and from his stance, I knew that he was hoping his buddies were watching. Around the card table the exaggerations would expand like carnival balloons. Yes, of course the Cherokee was ours. And of course he drove it. Every day for Master Bhim.

I told Sahr of the dinner plans for the following evening and watched as a warm smile rippled up to her birthmark. Yes, Sahr, with a young woman, tomorrow evening. No, it is not a date. Well maybe, I heard myself say.

I warned Lalji that if he smeared the SUV's windshield one more time with his oily fingers I was going to crack one of his un-splinted ones. I would be back after sunset, I said. Lock up and wait up for me. Sahr left for the market with a long list and a tall stack of rupees. Tragedy or not, I was going to entertain with fresh flowers, good wine, and the best meal my housekeeper could dream up.

Ram knew how to drive that beast. He rumbled out of the city, weaving through afternoon traffic like an F1 driver. He blasted the horn authoritatively and forced everything out of our path. Once we were beyond the congestion, I slid a CD into the player, reclined the seat and tried to take my mind off the sorrow with Sibelius. In the meantime, Ram revved up the eight cylinders and sped us northwest on NH56 and across the rock dust of the access road. At five minutes to five we turned sharply in front of the Imperial Holding gate and spewed some gravel in the general direction of the polished boots of two new guards.

Ram didn't park next to the ancient Maruti automobile parked on the grass. With a touch of a button, he shifted us into four-wheel and bounced up the boulder field to the bottom of the incline. From there I hiked the final hundred meters and arrived one minute ahead of schedule. Master would have been proud.

As I mentioned, during my year with Lilia she had taught me to swear in Spanish. I had been pretty fluent in it before, but she taught me how to really curse. I muttered every ugly word I knew when I saw the two men standing just below the cone of rock. Inspector Gupta Singh wasn't there. Madru Ralki was, cupping a match to light a beedee. He looked sweaty, bored, and generally irritated that he had to be standing in the middle of god-awful nowhere in the afternoon heat. Robert Muktendra, the owner of the property, was fidgeting nervously at his side.

Instantly, I pictured Ralki's hand groping Soma's breast and entertained the idea of kicking him very solidly in the groin when I got within three feet.

Muktendra I had met once. He was a moderately wealthy cloth merchant with shops in Agra and Varanasi. The prices were fair, silks of good quality, and his clerks always served good tea to their customers. Using profits and family inheritance, he'd purchased a house and parcels of land on both sides of the river. Why he owned this piece in the middle of nowhere, I couldn't guess. Whether he owned the mining company's land, was also a guess.

Muktendra had helped me select the right color of sari to send to my mother. He was fidgety-nervous then and more so now.

The two of them looked like Mutt and Jeff at the top of the rise--total opposites. Muktendra was tall and thin, with clothes that hung loosely on his shoulders. His eyes twitched from me to his companion. Ralki was short, fat, and wore the condescending expression of authority--eyes showing the compassion of a dead carp in the fish market. Neither of them looked overly pleased to see me.

Ralki took a deep pull on his beedee, sent the smoke billowing in my direction, and in nasally English said, "Ah, Mr. Scott, I was not expecting you. The pundits Devamukti and Chandragupta will not be joining us today?"

I held out my hand to Muktendra for a quick shake and replied, "I really wasn't expecting you either, Ralki. I was told your boss, Gupta Singh, would be here. The pundits apologize, but they thought it best to visit the Sukha family. I'm sure you understand."

"Yes, I see. Well, I suppose we will have to make do with you. Let us get to this quickly then. Mr. Muktendra," He nodded at his companion. "tells me that he leased this property to your friends, and that this man . . ." He glanced at a notepad to jog his memory. "Jotilal Sukkha was guarding it. For what purpose did you hire the guard? There seems to be nothing but dust and bird shit out here."

I was good at this game. Years of avoiding questions about my past had taught me how to dodge like a prizefighter. In a casual tone I replied, "As Muktendra has also undoubtedly told you, there is a cave just on the opposite side of that rock." I pointed to my left. "and the pundits thought it might contain some writing in the old language. Jotilal Sukkha had been hired in case it did."

"And did it?"

"Did it what?"

Ralki looked perturbed that I wasn't following his bored line of questioning. "Did the cave have anything inside it?" Curveball number one.

"Well. . . I was told there was some writing, but no one thought it overly important." Ralki nodded slowly. The fish-eyes didn't reveal if he believed me or not.

"So you have not been inside yourself then?" Curveball number two.

"No, I came here with Master Devamukti on Sunday, but I waited at the entrance while he went in."

"Why?"

"Why what?" I faked that one just to chaff him. It had the desired effect.

In a flash of anger he said, "Why didn't you go inside with him, Mr. Scott?"

"Bhim."

"I'm sorry?"

"Bhim. Everyone in the city calls me Bhim, Ralki. You know it and I know it, so let's use my Benarsi name instead of the ferenghi Mr. Scott. I didn't go inside because I really don't like caves very much. Devi told me there were a few lines of script on the walls, nothing too important. He hired the guard until we could examine it further and preserve it for posterity, though he didn't believe it was particularly valuable or important." I looked right at him, daring him to doubt me.

While Ralki and I jousted, Muktendra fingered a mala of prayer beads at his side, eyes blinking incessantly. I suspected that he had never drawn up an authentic lease and now might feel some obligation to pay the dead man's family a stipend. He finally joined in the fray. "Fellows, this sounds like simple and tragic accident. Let us see what we can do to help the poor man's family and be done with this sad event." With that lift of the carpet, he whisked everything neatly under.

Ralki was pinching the end of his beedee like a pot roach. Taking a last oily puff, he flicked it indifferently to the side, and turned angrily toward the rock spur. I watched the orange ember arc and bounce to the side of the path. I followed him over the outcropping, and when I came to the entrance, I pulled up with a jolt. The channel, opening, and cave were gone, filled with fifteen feet of shard. A hill of crumbled rock stood guard now. Immediately I thought of the man crushed underneath.

Ralki nonchalantly bent and picked up a fist-sized chunk of the same oily stone I had seen inside. He tossed it a few inches into the air, hefting its weight, letting it fall back into his palm. He observed it for a moment, as if its color or shape might provide a clue as to how it had managed to entomb a man whose name he couldn't remember. He dropped it quickly and stared at the boulders. "Well . . . I don't believe there is anything more to be done here. Even if this man were still alive inside that mess, he would be quite dead by the time we had gone to the trouble to dig him out. Simply bad timing for the poor chap." With a sneer in my direction he dismissed the entire affair with, "Probably angered some god by pissing in the wrong direction or shitting too close to a holy shrine. Right, Mr. Scott? My report will be to the point. Stupid bastard chooses stupid place to nap, unfortunate accident results in one dead low caste. Another minor tragedy of karma."

I prickled. It was an ugly remark, none of which felt right. Ralki was snapping this shut faster than the cave-in itself, swatting it away like an annoying gnat so everyone could return to searching for mythical terrorists. I remembered that he was rumored to be one of Qereshy's spies and wondered again if it was he that had followed me the night before. Why me? I thought of Soma and the fact that he questioned her with such ferocity, asking what Devi and I were working on. He dug hard for those details, but now didn't care to investigate the death of the man inside the cave? The entire thing smelled worse than a latrine gulley.

Dusting his hands off on the sides of his pants, he spat on a scorched weed and turned from the outcropping. I followed. Muktendra was shifting from foot to foot in the same spot, still flipping prayer beads.

Ralki wiped the sweat from his neck onto his sleeve and looked at me. "Well Bhim, I suppose I will have the pleasure of seeing you in three months again when you are Martin Scott, seeking his semi-annual visa. Good day." With nothing else, he spun and left.

Muktendra looked as if he wanted to at least shake my hand or offer a conciliatory word, but with a shrug and a half-hearted namaste, he turned and followed his companion down the path. I stood and fumed as Ralki climbed into the Maruti. Somehow, I needed to find a way to cut that fat, little bureaucrat down to size. Nothing immediately came to mind.

Alone in the shadow of Jotilal Sukkha's grave, I watched the sun slip behind the spur of jagged stone, the setting rays bathing our picnic tree in orange light. I thought sadly of the man under the stones. He'd died alone. I'd wondered if he had gone quickly with little pain. I hoped so. I hoped he had gotten to live a few of the right dreams in his life, hoped he had been given the chance to love deeply and been loved in return. That was important.

I picked up a small handful of rouge earth and tossed it into the evening breeze. As the motes drifted, I whispered a short requiem, May you be released from the wheel of all suffering, Jotilal Sukkha. May you find loving peace wherever you are now. It was the best my agnostic spirit could come up with.

As I slapped my palms together to cleanse the dust, I glanced at the ground where I had scooped the dirt. A meter away, lying in a shallow depression, was the burnt tip of Madru Ralki's beedee. It wasn't the cigarette that drew my attention, however, it was where it lay. That little cone of eucalyptus and tobacco had landed right in the center of a footprint, a vibram sole, deep-heeled, military-style, boot print.

Twenty-Five

Ram walked me from the Cherokee to my doorstep and sped off into the night. My body and brain were telling me it had been a month since I had sipped coffee at my gate and gone to the marigold fields to play Frisbee with Mej. My Casio told me it had been fourteen hours.

I dragged myself into the kitchen and dined on masala dosas, cheese sandwiches, and mango ice cream with coconut cookies. Sahr set everything out silently, not pressing any questions on me, though I knew she was ready to launch a salvo if I offered an opening. I didn't. I needed to sort my thoughts.

The cave hadn't collapsed like a card house. I knew that from checking the ceiling, and even though I wasn't a geologist, it had looked solid enough for me to stand below it.

I also came to the conclusion, sadly enough, that the pundits and I had been naive. If the boot print suggested what I thought it did, we had underestimated an opponent, one I couldn't set a face or motive to. That was a mistake I didn't like admitting. It came from a few lessons when I was eight in my first karate class. Never underestimate your adversary. Someone had taken note of our entry into the cave and done what they needed to keep us out. But why?

Other pieces nagged at me. Ralki's intimidation of Soma and the questions about what I was working on. The quick dismissal of the cave's collapse. Then there was the boot print. A visit by one of the guards from Imperial Holding? I couldn't be certain of it. Perhaps someone had merely wandered over to investigate why our rickshaw was parked so close to the mining operation. Or perhaps, as I was beginning to suspect, it portended something more sinister.

I knew why Ralki had chosen Soma to question--part of the five thousand-year-old social pyramid. She was low caste and female, and as a widow, easily manipulated. The pundits, on the other hand, as feeble as they might appear, were far more powerful than Ralki and his superiors. He had selected an easier prey to question. But why?

My eyes were drooping as I licked the last of the ice cream from my spoon. Sahr carried my bowl to the sink with the expression of a lolling puppy. Handing her the spoon, I said, "It was an accident, Sahr. The roof caved in, and there is no sign of Jotilal, and no way to get through. The authorities are going to say he died while he slept. Devi and C.G. will see to his family the best they can."

She nodded, and rather than quoting from some Christian or Hindu scripture about his soul resting in eternal peace, she set her hand on my wrist and said, "Bhim, this afternoon I have thanked all the gods that it was not you in that place. I know it is not right to be thankful when someone has died, but I am. The gods must follow the laws of the constellations and my cards mirrors those laws. They are rarely wrong. There are no accidents. The gods tumbled that rock when the stars and planets directed them to. And even though I am sad for this man's life being taken, I am also happy it was not you inside."

I smiled weakly, though my thoughts were telling me that something other than meddling deities had killed the man. With a brain feeling like day-old pudding, I decided not to enter into a discussion about cause and affect. Besides, Sahr's beliefs were unchangeable. Or so I thought.

Before I rose to stretch out in complete nakedness below the coolness of my ceiling fan, she announced that tomorrow evening she was going to prepare a feast all the gods would be jealous of.

Twenty-Six

It took less than ten seconds for the lingering sweetness of my dream to be shattered the following morning. I had been strolling in the loveliest of gardens--streams of cool water percolated over round stones, periwinkle, and clover. A fine mist permeated the air. I followed the water down a gentle slope to the ocean, and before me a wide cove spread out with waves curling around a rocky point. Perched like a small tree in the sand, a new surfboard stood waxed and ready. I loved surfing dreams. They always beat the hell out of the other ones, the ones with the bloody bubble.

Above the murmur of the surf, I began to hear yelling, arguing, and an odd moaning. I woke and touched the droplets of mist still sprinkled upon my cheeks. Coming fully awake, I realized the mist was perspiration and the fan above my bed was idle, no electricity--a common occurrence in our part of the city. Sahr was moaning in the salon, an indication something else had gone wrong.

Wrapping a loongi around my middle, I rubbed the sleep from my eyes, the sweat from my face, and stepped into the salon.

"Aiyeee. . ." She was yowling and clutching the edges of her sari again. Seeing me, it increased.

I had to almost yell to make myself heard. "What on earth is the matter?" I glanced out the front window, and not seeing Lalji in his hammock, began worrying again that he'd gotten himself into some sort of trouble.

"It is gone, Bhim. Gone! It was here, right here yesterday when I went to the market. I set it on the desk right after you left in the big car. I plugged the wire into the back exactly the way you taught me, and now it is gone."

The coolness of my dream splintered into a flash of dread. "The laptop?"

"Yes, Saab. It is gone." She started to wail again and I cut her short.

"Sahr, stop." Her moaning ceased abruptly and in the silence that followed, we just looked at each other. Then I looked at the empty rectangle amid the papers upon my desk. "First," I said as calmly as I could, "it is only a computer, not a family heirloom. It can be replaced. I will have a new one sent by train from Delhi in three days. Second, no one has been hurt. Where is Lalji, by the way?"

With a hiss she said, "He is hiding from Saab."

"Uh huh. And did he mention before he went into hiding why he was not guarding the house when somebody broke in." I was rising from a slow simmer to a full boil.

"After I helped his feeble memory with the palm of my hand, he admitted that he had strolled over to Ramuna's to boast about driving that car he has never set foot in." Ramuna was a young beauty, the daughter of my tailor, who lived three streets to the north. Lalji had been trying for months to woo her with stories of bravery and wealth. She, being of sound wit and good vision had measured up his courage and finances accurately, and spurned his advances.

Worried that I was going to receive yet another unpleasant answer, I asked, "And what about the backpack? Was it taken as well?" The camera, notes, and jump drive were in the inner pocket. They held the only remaining images of the cave.

"No, Bhimaji. I set it in the kitchen last night to get your canteen ready. It was still there this morning."

The thief, whoever he or she was, had slipped in through the front, snatched the most valuable object in sight and exited the same way. Considering all that had happened, I couldn't help wondering if it was a random theft or something planned.

"Well, I suppose we can thank those friendly constellations of yours that my backpack happened to be in the kitchen." She smiled for the first time that morning. Not a big smile, but it expanded when I asked, "Do you think you could brew some of that Nilgiri dark roast and a rustle up a few goolabjamins? Also, fetch me the phone and the largest knife we have in the kitchen. Then have someone go fetch Lalji to me."

Understanding my intentions, she smiled a bit wickedly. I was going to make certain my watchman never left his post unguarded again.

Twenty-Seven

Before that morning, Varanasi had been somewhat of a cloak
for me. I'd moved about its avenues and gullies, wandered alone
along the Ghats, and pulled that covering around me in relaxed
anonymity. Big cities do that for people. It had been a shawl
shielding me from the pain of memory and the memory of pain.
Now it had been yanked from my shoulders and I felt exposed.
Theft does that to people.

I stood on the corner of Sonapura Road attempting to hail a
rickshaw to take me to Devi's and felt a dozen eyes watching
me. More than at any time, I was aware of being a foot taller
than anyone on that road. Looking in both directions, I realized
was the only blond one as well.

My driver and I didn't exchange more than three words
during the journey to Devi's. Just before the turn to Raja Ghat
and the lane to the back gate, I had him stop in front of a
bicycle-walla. Miss Ugly needed some repairs, and I didn't want
to be burdened with walking her up through the alley to have
her fixed.

With a rapid namaskar and less of a smile than usual, I gave
the walla—a scrawny teen who looked capable and owned a
decent set of patching materials—some very clear instructions
regarding my needs. Half the price up front, the balance when I
returned. She would be parked inside Master's unlocked gate,
and he would need to fetch her, patch her, and more
importantly, treat her with the respect due an aged lady.

I had phoned Chandragupta earlier and left a message.
Whether he received it or not, and had been able to accomplish
what I suggested, was unknown. If he hadn't, it would be a
short morning for all of us.

I pushed open the gate, leaned my miserable looking bicycle against the wall and closed the door. Turning around I found myself staring directly into the dazzling, but shaded, eyes of Sukshmi. A thoroughly traditional Hindu shawl was drawn about her head.

"Bhim, this is so awful," she said. She reached out to give my hand a gentle press. "This poor man had two children, a wife, and his mother to feed. It is so sad."

"What did he do for work?" I asked. "I mean, before he started with us?"

"Father says he was a brass shaper, made pots and bells and candleholders, but his shop had shut down from competition. It is a hard business in the slums. The tourists buy on the Ghats, never in the poor sections. But, father says his family will be seen to. I think he and C.G have put something in place. A few of the neighbors have also donated."

"I'm glad people are helping, Sukshmi." I sighed. "It was an awful death."

"There is too much death in this city, Bhim; too much death and old ritual." She stared in the direction of the river. I understood more of what she wasn't saying than what she was. The same feeling had come over me that morning. Varanasi felt less like home and more menacing now. She had grown up in the gardens and been taught the traditions. Now her father wanted to employ another—the selection of a proper husband. Like a bird sensing a capturing hand above its wings, she wanted to fly.

With a sigh, I said, "There is sadness and death everywhere, Sukshmi."

"Yes, I suppose there is, but there is more here." Her eyes sparkled again. "You know, BhimajiMartinScott, I did enjoy myself the other night. You really are a good dancer, even though you like stodgy music." I winced. Where had that word come from?

For the second time in two days, I boasted to a woman. Two different women, but nonetheless, a spark of self-assurance—a small spark—seemed to have been re-ignited. "Well, if you like the way my feet move to techno, you should see them dance to Frisbee sometime."

"Frisbee? Is that a British group?"

I didn't have time to explain. As I leapt up the steps to the kitchen, she called out, "Bhimaji?"

"Yes?"

"Have you seen Soma this morning? She didn't show up to sweep."

With a tingling uneasiness, I replied that I hadn't.

Twenty-Eight

"There is nothing left for us but to use the photographs on your little jumping driver? You have saved them carefully, yes?" Devi was asking me this. The walls about his tower of aversion to things technical were beginning to show hairline fractures.

"Yes, I copied it all from the computer onto the jump drive yesterday. They're also still on the camera." I patted the backpack.

The two of us were sitting in rocking chairs in the front parlor waiting for an uncharacteristically tardy C.G.. Over a cup of sugared Darjeeling, Master described how Jotilal Sukkha's family would receive a modest income for a decade. A collection was being done this morning, he explained. Calls were being made, chips cashed in, and two revered, old pundits had tugged on strings. With what was raised and what they had added, an annuity would provide some relief.

"It is very strange, this business of the cave collapsing, Bhim. You saw the rock. Did it look weak to you, because it did not look that way to me?"

I hesitated, not yet fully convinced that the rock had been brought down deliberately, though the idea was growing stronger. My hypothesis was built on clues that were too flimsy and I wasn't sure my teacher should hear those. Being crotchety and distinguished didn't always ensure being prudent. With Devi it usually meant the opposite. He could easily start launching scatter-shot accusations around town. I took the chance, however, because I felt he had a right to know. "Master, I don't know how to say this any other way, but a few things happened yesterday afternoon that you should know about."

I described the meeting with Ralki and Muktendra, and he bristled at the mention of the inspector's name. "That boy has been a number-one trouble-maker since he was born. I had the honor of blessing his mother and father's marriage, you see, and over the years I wish I had not blessed it so well that they had four sons, because the fourth has turned out to be a very sour fruit on a good tree. He has aligned himself with that fool Qereshy and stained his family's good Hindu name."

The description of the boot print sent him into a rage that made him sound like a ham character in a Hindi film. "I knew it! I have suspected this accursed mining company has been up to no good all along. Do you believe that they had a hand in this foul deed?"

"I'm not certain, but it does seem suspicious. Someone wearing boots was walking near the entrance, and now it's a pile of tumbled rock."

He scowled. "Precisely, with a poor dead man inside, and who better to tumble rock than a mining company?"

I let the matter drop and also omitted Ralki's episode with Soma. She had confided those ugly details in trust, and if she wanted to tell Master about it, that it was up to her. I wondered uneasily again where she was.

Looking over the top of the front wall, I saw C.G's sparkling SUV slide to a stop in front of the gate. Ram must have polish it twice a day.

Extracting himself slowly, he puffed up the steps. His complexion was florid, but with the usual cheerfulness. I saw immediately that he'd received my message. Tucked under his arm was a black computer case, his Acer 3000. We were back in business.

He gave a short bow and wheezed, "Apologies, my friends, but unusual circumstances demand unusual schedules, and this sad business has made for unusual circumstances. Bhim, I have brought this for our use." He handed me the computer.

"Tut, tut."--Devi actually said tut, tut-- "It is of no consequence. We are all feeling the effects of yesterday's grief. Let us be thankful that we are all still here ourselves." Patting me on the knee he continued, "and our boy has saved the day by cooking all our pictures onto his little jumping driver."

"Burning, Devi. The term is burning." C.G. winked at me.

Master's smile disintegrated. "That is the same thing."

"If cooking and burning are the same thing, Mr. Devamukti, then I do not wish for you to prepare me dinner anytime soon." The boys were off to a rapid start.

"Punditjis," I interrupted. "Shall we continue on C.G.'s computer?" It was the best way to keep us off the fact that we couldn't enter the cave for an undetermined time.

They nodded, and within minutes we had three steaming cups of chai and the next photograph expanding on the screen. I breathed a sigh. Other than the same flash blemish in the upper corner, nearly every letter was readable. Then a detail I had missed earlier became apparent. I opened the next photograph to verify it. The last three pictures were from further away, and as the wall circled left towards the collapsed portion, the script was more difficult to read. The rock must have been softer there, because the etching was shallow and faint.

I swore silently.

C.G. noticed it also. He frowned and then started into the translation. Devi followed, and soon my pencil began to buzz along once more.

Fourth photograph, which I labeled Remedy, Part One.

Straightaway we were plunged into anatomy and the central feature of the writing. It was also the most complex and technical part yet.

While the pundits conjugated, I scribbled like a mad stenographer: Thirty six lines described precise points on the body, eighteen pairs of points called bastis with lesser partners called urvi. It was a type of acupressure. The width of fingers and the creases of the knuckles were used as measurements to locate them. I realized it was a simple, but ingenious, method; a person's own body became the measuring device, so the smaller the body, the smaller the measuring units. Custom made. And by the time we had finished translating the thirty-six lines, I was ready to run out and find a set of anatomical charts.

The next section dealt with plants, just as the pundits had predicted. They were beaming, and after a few I-told-you-sos, were tossed back and forth, C.G. announced, "It seems to be a list of nine, each with a silly adjective in front of it. See these? Delicate, passionate, delightful, etc. Clearly nonsense. The first three plants are Nimba, Medhika, and Haridra--neem, fenugreek, and turmeric in English. Add butter and onions and we have a fine batch of curry." He chuckled.

Devi responded with, "I know the Neem plant. It's an astringent. All of these are. They are blood purifiers."

Ignoring the medical opinion, C.G. forged on. "The next three are amalaki, emblic myrobalan, and kino—cousins we could find in any of the old apothecary shops. And this one," he pointed to the screen, "is Guggula, the British called it beddelum. These are all still used today. Fairly common."

Common to him, I thought.

Then C.G. hesitated, looked stared at the screen and frowned. "Hmmm . . . that is a rather sticky compound. Wouldn't you agree, Devi?"

Master stared at the screen. "Indeed." The boys, it appeared, were stumped—not by the words in front of them, but by the name of the plant itself.

"Spreckledtounguespoonsoftpinkconchshell. Unusual name for an plant, eh C.G?"

I, being the rookie, could ask dumb questions and get away with it. "So, is that a description? I mean, it sounds like a compound describing what it looks like."

They both stared at me, verifying that it was a dumb question.

"My Dear Boy," C.G. answered tenderly—father to two-year-old. "That is of course what it is. You have encountered these compounds in your poetry?" I had indeed. Classical Sanskrit was full of them, long combinations of smaller words. English has short, closed ones like lawnmower, and longer hyphenated ones, like mother-in-law. German employs them, but Sanskrit connects them like boxcars on a freight train. "Well," C.G. went on, "This is a fine example. We can read the words, but we still don't know what the actual plant is, only that a part is spreckled and shaped like a spoon, and another part pink and soft."

I mused out loud, "Well, it sounds to me like a pink flower shaped like a conch shell. The pistil or stamen, which I think they are calling the tongue here, is spreckled and looks like a spoon. Sort of sounds like an orchid or bromeliad." Lilia's botany lessons hadn't been entirely lost on me.

The boys stared at me again; this time I guess I hadn't sounded dumb. Without a word, Devi hustled away and returned with six over-sized books. We each took two, and forty minutes later his old condor eyes found it. With a stab of a finger on the page he declared, "It's the orchis mascula, the Salep orchid." He held up the book. A black tongue stuck out at us from a pink flower.

We were nearing lunch and had identified eight of the nine plants, or herbs, or spices, or whatever they were. It was a decent fraction, but not complete. I was ready to push on, but when Devi called for a break, I didn't object. It gave me the opportunity to ask what had been buzzing in my brain. Not wanting to sound ignorant again, I treaded carefully, "So . . . is this . . .are we supposed to combine these pressure points with these plants somehow." That didn't come out sounding quite as smart as I hoped.

Being our Vedic leader, C.G. answered. "The old cures could be quite complex. Fancy sacrifices that could go on for years. Some had very odd treatments, like hanging upside down over a smoky fire for a month. Pure fancy. But this is a rather straightforward Ayurvedic remedy. These pressure points energize something, maybe like those little pins the Chinese use. The herbs get mixed into a potion. And there you have it, your cure." He paused and added, "for whatever the sickness is."

It was all a little too vague for my Western brain. "Okay, that sounds . . . reasonable, but how would a person know how much of the herbs to use? Don't you ned amounts? And what order do you press the basti and urvi points?" Both of them frowned and neither looked at me like that was a dumb question.

The last plant didn't have a fancy name. In Sanskrit it was called Shilajit, Mineral Pitch. What it had, though, was the oddest adjective in the entire list—Sweat-drenched Shilajit. C.G.

again was adamant that they were nonsense. Little did we know how important those nonsense adjectives would become.

Nine of nine from the list. We were shooting a hundred percent, batting a thousand, and had just performed the equivalent of a linguistic hat trick. For me it was only over-shadowed by the images of Jotilal's crushed body and Soma weeping in the dust of the courtyard.

Twenty-Nine

There were too many chores on my list that afternoon. I needed to be in three places at once, and Miss Ugly had better be ready or one young bike-wallah was going to be very sorry he hadn't patched her tire.

I slipped out the back gate noticing that my bicycle, Sukshmi, and Soma, were not there. One of those concerned me.

My eye caught the first hint of a sparkle as I entered the final curve of the gully. Encouraged by the thought that maybe, just maybe, my bicycle boy had followed my instructions. I picked up my pace. Twenty meters further and I saw her in her entirety, and she looked like a queen in a wedding. Her rims shone like circular mirrors, her frame like a show car. Even her dented little bell was reshaped and had reflection that you could floss your teeth with. The young boy, my new friend, Charup, the under-aged bicycle-walla, stood next to her with a soft rag and a bottle of Armor-all. Damn, even her chain looked like something out of a BMW catalogue.

Charup--at the age of fourteen--was a master. He had no shoes, eight fingers, and fewer teeth, but he was an artisan. And because he was a harijan, an untouchable, he would have to love his work. It would be his calling until he died.

Ugly Bike was tuned and polished to perfection, no softness in her brakes, no squeak in her pedals, and she now had three gears that flowed like quicksilver. "Is it to your liking, Sahib?" He asked as I wheeled to a stop after my test run.

"Charup, this is the best she has ever looked or felt, and I will be the proudest ferenghi in the city sitting on her. She's a rejuvenated lady, my friend. There is only one small problem."

He looked crestfallen. "There is a problem, Sahib?"

"Yes. Now that she is the finest bicycle in Uttar Pradesh, I will need to give her a new name and purchase a thick chain to keep her safe." Relieved that it wasn't his fine work that was being called to question, he told me where I might locate the chain and lock for a decent price—a shop owned by his uncle. The re-christening he had no suggestions for.

I paid him the agreed upon balance and added enough tip to buy at least one of the shoes for his feet. With a promise that he would be my number one bicycle maintenance engineer for as long as I owned her, I swung my leg over her frame and pedaled proudly towards the Sigra section of the city. I had business with the police.

By the time the new wheels were clicking smoothly in third gear, I'd decided that the eight-fingered Charup deserved the tip for the second shoe. Missy Ugly rode like a dream. I weaved smoothly up Madanapura Road to Luxa and Vidhyapeeth Avenues. The sour feeling that had gripped me that morning departed with every click of the chain. Twenty minutes later I cruised into the neighborhood of Sigra and slipped unctuously back into low gear. The Mother India Temple, with its impressive gardens, rose in front of me, but that wasn't my destination, the mildewed Sigra Police Station was.

I pushed through the door with my bicycle in my right hand and my backpack in the other. The Sikh sitting behind the desk, with red turban, neat beard, and sweat-stained armpits rose immediately to command in 'veddy crisp English' that my bike would need to remain outside and my backpack searched. No problem with the bag, I replied, but Miss Ugly stayed inside. I asked Mr. Singh—all Sikhs have that name—if he would fancy leaving his wristwatch outside on her seat. He got the point, especially when I told him I was there to report a theft.

"What kind of theft would that be, Sir?" he inquired as he plopped himself back into his chair and stroked a pair of handlebars on his mustache that were longer than Ugly's.

"My computer was stolen yesterday . . . from my home."

"Ah…" He began flipping through a file cabinet next to his desk. "That is a valuable item. Would you estimate that it was worth more than one hundred dollars American, Sir?"

"Yes, about ten times that amount."

He lifted a folder and dropped it in front of him. The weight of Indian bureaucracy thudded heavily onto the desk. "Ah Yes. Well, let us see. Here it is. You will need to fill this out, Sir. And this one as well." Two forms from the previous century were turned towards me.

For the next half an hour I wended my way through a maze of ludicrous questions. In the twenty-ninth minute I was wondering if my sense of humor could still be intact. Assuring me the form was correct, Mr. Singh assisted me with such queries as: Will you be selling this item in Uttar Pradesh? Or, Would you consider the purloined item to be an heirloom?

As I gratefully arrived at the signature line, I had a thought. I mentioned casually that I was an acquaintance of Assistant Chief Inspector Madru Ralki, and had information regarding the death of Jotilal Sukkha."

"ACI Ralki does not work in this office, Sir."

"Yes, I realize that, but could you inform him of something important? Send a message to the head office, perhaps."

Morbid curiosity is a wonderful motivator. Mr. Singh would be more than pleased to send a message. His pen poised expectantly over his note pad.

"Would you be so kind as to tell him that evidence has come to light indicating that the accident near the Imperial Holding was not an accident." The pen scratched and came to a stop with a little jab. He waited.

"Nothing else, Sir? Do you not wish to explain more?"

"That's all. No, wait. Add this: As you are probably aware, this evidence is incontrovertible." I helped him spell it. Hopefully Ralki would sweat a drop or two over the contents and have to consult his dictionary. It was a jab, a small feint to stir things up. I thanked Mr. Singh in my veddy own crispest English and rolled Miss Ugly out the door.

Thirty

I arrived at Manikarnika by way of Dashvamedha Ghat, the most popular tourist site on the river. It was always crowded. Foreigners, sadhus, artisans, and beggars, were scattered across the steps, and like Manikarnika, it was a spiritual center-- sacrifices had been performed there since before recorded time. They also sold precisely what I needed in the shops above the embankment.

With my gifts, I made my way out to the river.

Besides my packages, I was also holding the horns of a dilemma--the handlebars of my bicycle. I couldn't leave Ugly unattended, so I would have to roll her, or carry her, along the riverfront. Had the Ghats any uniformity to them, that might have been a simple enough task, but the stairways were a like a stack of demented Legos, frustratingly difficult to traverse. From Dashvamedha they went in rational fashion and could be crossed easily, but soon obstacles reared up that forced me to the river's edge. Boat's prows pushed across my path like jousting lances, tents, stalls, vendor's blankets, and the ever-present mob of worshippers reared before me like a maze. I was also sure Miss Ugly had gained a kilo of weight with her new layers of polish and oil. Liquid began to course through my pores, along my skin, and into my kurta. So much for looking cool.

Approaching Manikarnika, I saw a gathering under the shala. More than twenty listeners were pressing under the overhang, some, for lack of space, stood uncomfortably in the afternoon sun or sat on the steps below.

At the center of the audience, Sharmalal-Adam reclined in a folding sports chair, legs crossed casually at the ankles. In light-gray slacks and a white short-sleeve shirt, he looked like a CPA checking for last minute deductions. A clear thermos of what appeared to be iced coffee rested at his elbow. Petey and Shawn were standing behind him looking beatifically stoned.

I searched for Uli and spotted Jitka. Miss Congeniality had positioned herself to the right of Adam, elbows splayed like an offensive lineman lest anyone enter her hallowed space. I could just make out the waving blondness of Uli's hair behind her.

Adam's rapid fire speech sharpened as I trudged up the steps.

"The seeds of hostility, those minute germs of hatred and vehemence are sown early into the soil of our lives, My Friends. They are watered and fed by those who want us to hate. They point out dissimilarities. He is Brahmin, she is Harijan. My color is correct, yours is not. He is a brown Musselman, she is an ivory Catholic princess with ADD and too much make-up. Did you see the color of that Buddhist's robe? How could he wear those sandals with that saffron? Maybe with a red purse it would have worked, but they were totally wrong with that yellow. And that hairstyle. Oh my Gaaawd." This last part was sung in a Valley Girl accent that had me shaking my head with laughter and bewilderment. Where had he picked that up?

As humorous as his accent was, his message was clear.

"Seeds of aggression are cultivated by ten thousand years of separation. Be different from them you are taught. Lessons that are, how shall we say, erroneous, false, incorrect, and full of more cow dung than the bleak gullies of this fair city. Commandments to violence have been woven like fine silk into the fabric of our lives, and we continue to carry them. Now we stand with our backs set firmly against crumbling walls and gather larger stones to fling at our perceived enemies--enemies that we do not need to search very far into the past to recognize as our own family." He uncrossed his legs and stared down at me as I lugged my bicycle up the steps.

"Ah, Bhim, my thirsty friend. How are you this fair, but sizzling afternoon?" And with that peculiar greeting, he leapt from his chair, down the space between us, and lifted Miss Ugly from my arms and up to the shala with athletic ease.

Twenty people turned to stare at me as sweat poured unimpeded from my hairline into my eyes. I forced a weak smile and noticed Jitka frowning. But Uli...she was smiling at me like I was her favorite knight. Suddenly, I didn't care who stared.

After I assured myself that Adam wasn't preparing to divide Miss Ugly's tires between the destitute of the riverfront, she was given a place of honor in the shade. I thanked him and edged as close to Uli as I could without subjecting my ribs to Jitka's elbows.

Settling back into his folding chair, Adam pulled another Fanta from his cooler, popped the cap, and thrust it towards me. He studied my face and then the faces of those around him. His eyes swept across us like beacons in a dark sky and his tempo slowed.

"We will change, my brethren, for good reasons, not the least of which is that we must. It is not written this way in any holy book. We will not change because scripture tells us to, or because some invisible deity is directing us. We will change because it is correct to do so and we have no choice. Our survival depends upon it. We will demand that the politicians, the clerics, and all the so-called leaders of humanity change as well. We must force them to revise their creeds, and if they continue to adhere to violence, they will be rejected. If their words set blind conviction above common sense and compassion, they will be rejected. And do you know what will be our greatest challenge in this quest to adapt and survive?" Without waiting, he surged on. "Admitting mistakes. Ten millennia worth, my brothers and sisters. But that, as we say, is another story." He grinned at me. "One for tomorrow."

I realized with regret that I had again arrived at the end of Adam's speech. As he rose to fold his chair and tote his cooler up the steps I noticed two things: He didn't place his hands together in the traditional namaskar, and second, I was thirsty, not for another Fanta, but for more of his message. His phrases, few and simple, were a draft of freshness and I found myself desiring more. I knew why. They rang true.

Varanasi was a center of ritual, and its steps were soapboxes for a thousand orators. Sermons were intoned at every corner, temple, and tea stall, and scripture flowed like river water. Opinions sprouted as commonly as grains of rice. But those sermons, as time-honored as they were, had always been coated with the same rhetoric for me--stale as week old chapattis. They bounced straight off my non-believing ears. Adam's message was different, and for that reason I was fairly certain the gathering beneath his shala would continue to grow. Different, however, wasn't always embraced in the old city.

The crowd drifted away, and I looked at the remaining. Other than the Chapens, we were the same group as the day before, with a few additional faces: three Australians—a tall woman and two men with thick accents and short crew-cuts--and four English-speaking Hindus. It was a diverse group, especially with Shawn and Petey, who always added a healthy dollop of diversity. All of them seemed to still be languishing in Adam's words.

Petey and Shawn, since the previous afternoon, had acquired some fancy designs of henna on the backs of their hands and forearms. A talented mehndi artist had decorated their skin with mandalas and vines. Leaves snaked into the dirt between their fingers and spread up their arms to their elbows. Shawn, whose beehive hairdo now had gray mud caked into it, twisted his decorated arms together and wrapped his legs around each other. It made him look like a four year-old needing to pee. Garudasana—the eagle pose. From this ungainly stance he managed to bow without toppling over and chirped, "That was the most amazingly beautiful thing I've ever heard. His words were like totally unreal. Bom shakti."

Petey, who had struck his own pretzel pose, concurred. "Even more beautiful than yesterday's, Shawny. Ethereal it was, like the clear light of samadhi bottled in the prettiest speech ever spoken." I couldn't have stated it better myself. For a few seconds we drifted back into our own thoughts, and then the English boys ambled northward to find a bhang lassi--a yogurt smoothie with enough cannabis in it to keep them brain altered for a day and a half.

While Uliana and Jitka asked the Australian trio where they were staying, I shifted closer to Uli. This didn't go unnoticed by Jitka, who scowled. I suspected that she wasn't too keen on the prospect of having to search for bratwurst and pumpernickel on her own while Uliana dined with me.

I struck up a conversation with one of the Hindus who had been listening to Adam. "Aap Hindi bolte hain?" Do you speak Hindi?

His head bobbed. "Oh yes, Sir, that it is indeed my native tongue, but I much prefer the speaking of English. I am called

Bijram Nataratri, and you are Bhim who studies Sanskrit with Master Devamukti, yes?" Damn, did everyone know that? He wagged his head again, while I let out a small groan. How many times did I have these exchanges, one where I wanted to converse in Hindi and my counterpart need to practice his English? I usually caved.

"Okay, English it shall be. Do you live in the city, Bijram?" This was the standard opener that would eventually segue into some prediction about the rains. His buddies gathered around. Close. Clearly I was good post-sermon entertainment, and if Bijram happened to drop the conversational ball, they would be right there to scoop it up.

"Oh certainly, Sir. We are all from Kotwali beyond the Alamqir Mosque, though I am born in the red-light. And you? What is your native place?" I did some quick translation. The red-light was an infamous warren of prostitution. Bijram apparently called that his birthplace.

"I live in Nagpur, south of the Asi," was all I offered. I had learned not to tender much information about where I lived.

Over Bijram's shoulder I watched a funeral pyre being readied at the top of the rise. The deceased, I could tell, was from wealth, the pyre constructed from an ample supply of wood. Good wood meant good money. Partially consumed body parts of the poor often floated downstream where I liked to wade and cool my legs. That tended to keep me from dunking my head too much into the loving arms of Mata Ganga.

Bijram was rambling on about the heat, the topic of rain clearly approaching. I listened inattentively and peered over his shoulder as the priests circled the pyre, saturating the cadaver with oil. The cries of loved ones drifted down with the heat of the afternoon breeze, while hand gongs tolled softly into the air. From the tirtha, the eternal fire, the flame was lit. The ceremony was nearing its climax, and I felt compelled to turn my head and avert my eyes. But I didn't. The cremations tortured me, yet like beggars, they demanded just enough attention to pay them heed.

Five doms, the untouchables given the grisly task of lifting corpses to their place on the pyre, set themselves in a circle about the body. The corps was obese, another sign of affluence, and a sixth dom slide into position near the belly. I gasped-- audibly enough that Uli halted mid-sentence to look at me. The untouchable squatting to lift the corpse was wearing light gray slacks and a white short-sleeved shirt. Adam! He was sliding his hands under the mid-section of the corpse.

I looked at Uliana. She followed my gaze up the pyre and looked puzzled. I knew she didn't grasp the significance. Adam was a harijan, an untouchable. It was as unlikely as snow in the afternoon.

They heaved the body, as respectfully as its weight would allow, onto the wood. The priests ladled it with more oil, the kindling caught and flames swelled. I was grateful that we stood enough distance away to avoid the stench. I had smelled that foulness at a close distance once. It would linger indelibly. In the haze, Adam receded. A harijan? How could he be a achut, one that handled corpses? It was the lowest position, next to shit-sweeping, that a person could be assigned in life.

I turned back to Bijram, who had just predictably predicted rain in two days. In whispered Hindi, I asked, "Brother Bijram, do you know much of this Sharmalal, where he comes from? His education?"

He replied in equally quiet Hindi, "This Adam? Very little, that is a fact, Sri Bhimaji. I do know that he has no varna. He is a harijan, and I have heard that he is also a gifted nipuda. The rumors say that he was orphaned and taken in by an instructor at BHU, but schooled in the U.K. He used to speak at the railway station, but now he speaks here, and the priests pay him enough respect to keep the shala open during this hour of the day. Many young people listen, but they are the ones who do not care that he is a achut."

"And you . . . why do you listen to him if he is untouchable?"

Bijram wagged his head like a hula doll in the rear of a Chevrolet. "Because. . . I like his words. My friends and I are engineers, alas, currently unemployed clerks of the government office, but we are learned in the sciences, and his words make sense. They come back to stay inside here. Always" He tapped the side of his head. His buddies wagged in unified agreement.

I looked at the spires of the Alamqir Mosque towering above. Bijram noticed where I was looking and whispered. "The Imam does not like the words of Adam, and it is said the Cabinet Minister also is very displeased."

"Qereshy?"

"Yes."

"Between us, Bijram. Qereshy is an asshole." He grinned and everyone wagged their heads at that one.

With assurances that we would see each other again, the boys moved off to find other entertainment. The Australians departed, and Uli, Jitka and I were alone once more.

For three breaths we stood looking at each other, and then I reached into my pack. "Jitka, here are two gifts for you," I stammered. "Small, but given as thanks for graciously allowing your sister to join me for dinner." I fixed her with my best 'truce be with us' smile. Her scowl stayed, but when she opened the pink carton and saw the squares of pistachio, milk, sugar, and egg confections, it disintegrated. "I also know of a cafe, if you are interested, where you can find the best Chinese stir fry in Uttar Pradesh. Beef or chicken, and I thought perhaps, while Uliana and I discuss the poetry of the Ramayana, you might like to try it." I hesitated for a minute as she eyed the candy, and then added, "I would have invited you also, but my housekeeper would object to my bringing two beautiful women to dine. She is traditional."

I had taken her unawares, sideswiped her armor with sweet-talk and confections. With a smile that looked as it might crack both cheeks from the effort, she replied in brusque gutturals, "That is very thoughtful. I am . . . grateful for both."

"Well, they're the least I can offer. I know what it is like to be in a strange city on one's own, but I can assure you that, other than a few neighborhoods, it is quite safe here, even at night." Not that I believed anyone would assault her. The chain mail was too thick.

She grunted. "Thank you," She hesitated, not feeling comfortable saying my name, I suppose. "Uli likes this place more than me. I don't like the smell, but if they have beef stir fry . . that would be gut."

From my pack I retrieved a writing pad and for the next two minutes drew the most detailed map possible, one that would bring her safely to Johnny Chang's House of Mandarin Cuisine. It would also take her through the sweets vendor lanes, which might change her mind about the smells. It usually did.

With the handshake of a blacksmith as a gesture of a newly

formed armistice, and a kiss on the cheek for her sister, Jitka departed.

"That was very kind of you, Bhim. Und wise. You won over my sister with gifts that she wouldn't refuse." Uliana smiled playfully and sat on one of the cracked blocks that bordered the staircase. Her hair was braided with teal ribbons in tight pig-tails that, with her Nordic features, gave her a Swiss Miss look. Heidi of India. Her skirt was a blue-green with a silk border that resembled a sari. Her blouse was a loose kurta of the same shade as the ribbons. Simple, beautiful, and with just enough Indian style that she wouldn't draw undue attention.

I tried with questionable success to breathe deeply enough to slow the racing of my pulse. "Well, I did feel badly about not inviting her, and also to give her a better path. If she follows my directions, she will walk past some of the better smells in the city. You just have to know where to find them."

She looked at me with cobalt eyes and pigtails and asked, "Will you take me there as well?"

I gave a short bow. "This very evening Uliana Hadersen. I will pick you up at five-thirty, if that's acceptable, and show you some of the sights before dinner."

Her smile came easily, relaxed but with the earlier sadness I couldn't fathom. "I look forward to it. It will be like Rama showing Sita the countryside from their flying chariot."

I was stunned again. "My God, you know that part of the epic?"

"Of course, they were some of the most beautiful lines I'd ever read. I even memorized a few of them"

With a new rhythm in my heart, I took hold of Ugly's handlebars and told Uli that I would see her at the Riverview at five-thirty sharp.

Nodding at the bright spokes, she laughed. "And does your shiny chariot have a name?"

Without thinking I answered, "Surya."

"Surya, I like that name," she replied. "The sun god."

Thirty-One

Sutradharak desired to create the greatest amount of carnage possible with the smallest team and the least amount of plastique possible, and he felt certain he had designed an event to do just that. The scale of devastation it would create would be greater than anything he had previously unleashed. Fear would spread like cholera. The intelligence agencies would scour the cities in a dozen new places, all of them wrong. And that was precisely his intention, or rather the intention of his employers.

His employers also wanted an event that would trigger a reaction that went beyond the standard political response and intensified investigations. They wanted something that would raise the threat of war regionally, something that would really get sabers rattling.

Sutradharak believed he had designed an event that would do that as well.

The media continued to speculate he was a Pakistani extremist. Appropriately so, as his targets had been primarily Hindus traveling along the rail lines. Computer theorists did the same. He smiled to himself, because they were all so mistaken. His motivations weren't religious. They weren't even nationalistic or patriotic. He really didn't give a flying fuck which of the two countries occupied that frozen piece of shit between them. 'The bosses', as he referred to them, wanted Delhi and Islamabad to square off and march down paths of folly to the brink of armed conflict. Escalation on a massive scale. But diversion, at this point, was their topmost priority.

Sutradharak only wanted to bring about and watch the death. And, in an almost childish way, he delighted in the explosions that made it all happen. It was like a grand fireworks show that he held a front seat ticket to view.

So, he had his plan now, and a date. What he didn't have was the location.

Studying a topographical map for the seventh time that morning, he twirled the ring on his left hand. The entire map south of the Himalayas was spread out in front of him. Geophysical played a big part this time. After a few minutes, with a rare smile, he deftly stabbed the tip of his knife to a place just above the name of a city. *Exactly*, he mused. *A perfect location. Now the only the schedule needs to be set.*

Thirty-Two

I had a great deal to ponder, puzzles my cloistered, scholarly existence hadn't really prepared me to do. Five days earlier my priorities had been fairly simple, finish the Bhavabuti play, make sure Sahr and Lalji had provisions for the villa, and get to Devi's before his Timex snitched on me. Now I owned a different set of priorities.

Living as a foreigner in a holy city could be like being in an enormous paint ball game or a carnival ride. Surprises of ever sort popped up just when you were feeling complacent. I needed answers. Haroon might have some, so I pedaled from the river up to his club.

I rolled my newly christened bicycle through the door. The sign said business was closed for two more hours, but he was there and called my name as soon as Ugly was across the threshold.

"Bhim. You have come to finally plan our vacation. For that you I will fix you the best smoothie on the menu. On the house."

"Sorry, Maumed. No planning quite yet, I have other concerns to discuss. Important ones."

He frowned, but then patted the bar. "Okay. Sit, my friend. The smoothie will still be free. What are we talking of today? No, don't tell me. You need advice on how to handle all the new women in your life, and I am the man to give it."

I purposefully chose a seat at one end of the bar, wanting to be out of earshot of the bartenders stocking at the other. "Not that either. I need to get information about a mining company, what they are doing, and whether they are operating legally. My guess is they are not. I also need find a way to get some information about a crooked policeman."

He ordered one of his barmen to fetch two smoothies and some nuts, and then took the seat next to me. "An illegal mining operation you say? Something close by?" I nodded. "Mmm . . . That requires the use of two things, a new law enacted last year, and a healthy dose of caution."

"I'm fairly practiced at being cautious, Maumed, but I know next to nothing about law, especially here. What are you referring to?"

The blender leapt to life and he waited until it stopped. "Last year our less than expeditious congress created something called the Right to Information Act. It took them over four decades to get it enacted, but now citizens can demand information about what companies are doing in their neighborhoods. Very slowly it is being used to check activities that used to go unmonitored."

"Four decades? That is moving slowly."

"It started after the Union Carbide gas leak that killed three-thousand people in Bhopal in 1984."

"And it is just now becoming law?"

He nodded.

"So, why do you say a lot of caution is needed?"

Our smoothies and peanuts arrived, and Maumed waited until the bartender left. "Some investigators have dug too deeply and demanded to know about too many high–level operations. They paid the ultimate price to obtain it."

"Murdered?"

"Quite. It's the first time these businesses have been subjected to any scrutiny, and many aren't keen on the idea. A lot of them are run by powerful people with political connections who don't want the little people meddling. Bhopal was a very ugly example."

"Ummm . . . you make it sound as if it isn't the wisest thing to cite this law. Can I assume a ferenghi with a temporary visa probably wouldn't be able to?"

He took a long sip of his smoothie and smiled. "Good assumption, my friend, though a well-connected dance club owner might."

I wrote down two names on a napkin. I slid the paper across the bar. As I did so, I realized I was probably creating a debt that meant I would be going to Sandals after all.

Lalji had left the gate unlocked and the courtyard unguarded again, but with Surya in my possession there was little a thief would covet in the courtyard, unless ripe mangoes were on his list.

I chained Surya to the tree with a new lock the size of a grapefruit and called out to Sahr as I entered the salon. Her hello was followed by a directive to keep my fat ferenghi nose out of her kitchen. She was up to culinary secretiveness. Fine, I said. I have things to work on. Don't worry about me.

I checked my phone messages. One. Mej would be returning from Delhi on the late train and would see me at my gate in the morning. He also had a surprise gift for me, he said. Wonderful. Surprises from Mej could range from practical office equipment to blow-up dolls named Cindy with life-like openings.

I opened C.G.'s Acer and slid the jump drive into the USB slot. As I clicked through the photographs, I wondered, could this really be more than just medical folklore? An actual cure for something? The pundits believed it was. What if the authors had discovered some workable combination of plants and pressure points? Not likely, I decided, but it wasn't totally out of the question. They had obviously deemed it important enough to carve into very hard rock and decorate it with some nice stain.

Lilia had once told me that one of the fastest growing fields of pharmacology was ethno-botany, the study of regional medicines and remedies. Pharma companies were spending large sums of money to research indigenous cures in remote areas of the world. Plants and their recipes were being studied from the Kalahari to the Andes. Maybe this was the same type of thing, just ancient and long forgotten.

I finished scanning our notes and looked at the list of plants again. The nonsense adjectives that C.G. had sworn were junk jumped out at me. Unlike the professor, I wasn't totally convinced of that. Otherwise, why had the original writers gone to the effort to record them? It seemed like too much work for something useless.

During my academic time, I'd read and translated a lot of metric language, miles of it. Sanskrit, like Elizabethan, was based on syllables. The patterns had devilish, if not ingenious, designs--long and short vowels in exact mathematical sequences. Truth be known, Shakespeare's own conventions rose in roundabout fashion from earlier Sanskrit roots.

The list stared at me. I jotted the nine adjectives onto a fresh sheet, and next to them, the nouns they were modifying--the plants and herbs. Something was wrong--a hard and fast rule was being broken. Nouns and adjectives have to agree. It is a chief grammatical rule--number, gender, and person must match. The endings for the adjectives and nouns were supposed to be the same They weren't. Quickly, I divided them into syllables, marking the long and short vowels. And then, like Archimedes stepping ever so gingerly into his steaming bath and seeing the water rise, I knew the answer. At least I was fairly certain I did. It would need to be verified, but I knew why those strange little adjectives had been used.

They were ratios.

Sahr hustled in to see what was wrong with her Bhimaji, why he was hooting like a drunken hyena at his desk, and finding that he was just fine, returned to the succulent aromas of her kitchen.

Thirty-Three

Being a tour guide in Varanasi is not simple. There are too many sights to choose from, rituals to demystify, and too many sensual assaults to filter. Like setting onto a jungle trail, or an Internet search, without a clear sense of direction one becomes rapidly lost. A calculated plan is essential. I, however, being a veteran of the lonelier paths of the city, had that sense of direction. I knew the precise moment the sun's rays kissed the Durga Temple and bathed her in bashful scarlet, or the best spot to hear the supplications of the holy men at the river. I knew the secret corners of the temple gardens and the purple shadows of the gullies. Guiding was an art form, and though I had never shown anyone else my paths, I was well prepared to reveal the finer distinctions of my Varanasi.

I picked up Uliana from the Riverview three minutes ahead of schedule, in an autorick that was cleaner and quieter than most. She was standing patiently in the doorway as a hundred Benarsis a minute filed past. A few slowed to stare, because she stood like a princess outside the quarters of the raja's palace. Her hair was covered by a long silk purple scarf draped in front and behind to her waist. Below that, a pale-green kurta, sheer enough to reveal just a bit more than was acceptable by local standards, hung in diaphanous folds. She had burnt orange pajama pants tapered to the ankles in the Punjabi women's style Thin-strapped sandals with tiny green sequins graced her feet, and on her arm twenty silver bangles jingled like light rain as I helped her into the backseat.

The language of dating was obscured under a lot of layers for me. It had been a long time since I had spoken carefully selected words to a woman. I had done it for myself in scraps of poetry, translated plays and regaled in the results. But openly to a woman? I was frightfully out of practice and agonizingly nervous. It turned out not to matter.

After mutual complements on each other's appearance—I in my handsomest royal-blue, embroidered kurta —we settled into the relative comfort of the autorick. My driver waited as I turned to Uli. "I thought, if you would like I mean, that we could see a few of the sights you don't usually see in Varanasi." Then I added, "We only have forty minutes, and my cook will get grumpy if we aren't at her table on time."

She loosened the knotted scarf, and with a modest smile, slipped it from her head. Her hair glistened like water and smelled of peach and lavender. "You are the guide, Bhimaji of Varanasi. Lead on." With instructions not to go too quickly, I told my driver in Hindi where we were going.

We slid into the afternoon tide of bicycles and carts.

"You speak this language quite fluently. It is Hindi, isn't it?"

I nodded. "It's a local vernacular called Bhojpuri, a little

different from what you hear in the movies, but similar enough."
Seeing that she was interested, I continued. "There're a lot of
dialects here, two hundred and twenty-five if you believe a
census from the 1930s. A farmer speaks differently from a shop
owner in New Delhi. Enough changes in pronunciation and
spelling to call them dialects. It makes it hard to get people to
concur on things, but nearly everyone understands Carte Bole,
standard Hindi, so the country can still function."

"Und you enjoy this learning, ya? Like other languages?"

"I do. I'm a long way from total fluency." I laughed shyly.
"When I was younger my father said I spoke a completely
different language because I surfed."

"Und surfers in your town speak another language?" Her
mouth pursed in a curious smile, and I realized how at ease I felt
in the backseat of an autorick with Uliana Hadersen of Tönder,
Denmark.

"It's like a totally one-to-one dialogue with a righteous set of
tubes. Radical, like ripping the lip off a folding section, grabbing
a rail, and getting a mountain of air." I grinned and added,
"Babe."

She patted the back of my hand. "I understood more of the
Bhojpuri."

"That's understandable."

Uli had a most endearing feature in her own speech that my
ear caught at our first meeting. When she was excited, she would
inhale with a tiny gasp that a phonetician might call a guttural
implosion. That sounded too much like a digestive problem, so I
re-named it Uli's Delightful Squeak.

Our driver deposited us outside the Gyanvapi Mosque and
closed down his motor to wait. As I helped her out, I explained

that it was also called The Great Mosque of Arungzeb, constructed atop an enormous Hindu temple. As a characteristically feisty Moghul Emperor, he had felt obliged to knock it to the ground in the mid-sixteen hundreds. Now it was the place where Imam Nomani led prayer five times a day and bristled as the police rounded up his followers for questioning.

"If you look carefully, you can see where his architects copied from the original." I pointed to the columns and the odd mixture of materials and styles. "Arungzeb had a heart like a glacier. Skewered his brothers and imprisoned his father in a cell at the top of the Red Fort in Agra. Not a particularly sweet guy."

She nodded. "I remember that from our visit there. His father watched the reflection of the Taj Mahal in a piece of glass from his prison. I didn't like the story. Too much sword fighting and beheading."

I glanced up. The sun was almost into position. "Come quickly." I jogged across the avenue opposite the mosque and felt Uli's arm slid inside mine.

"Are you going to make me run much on our tour, Bhim?" A gentle squeeze on my forearm.

"Uh . . . just this once." We halted near a curved coconut palm. "Now, stand right here," I turned her shoulders gently, "and look through the minaret."

The spire is its finest feature. Dominant, it shoots seventy-one meters skyward like an alabaster needle, and at that moment, the sun's rays were slipping through its eye--the window of the minaret--to bathe us in a warm afternoon light. Uli drew in a quick breath, and I knew she had seen it. "Mein Gott, It looks like a candle, all orange und yellow with the dust."

"Right. You have to squint to see it, but it sort of looks like a huge popsickle stick."

She glanced at me and then back at the minaret. "What is a popsickle?" After I explained, we both laughed at how delicious they sounded in the late afternoon warmth.

She turned from staring at the mosque to look at me. "How did you discover this?"

I shrugged. "Walking home from the University one afternoon, I saw the shadow and the light going the room at the top. I moved to where it came down and did it the next day at a better time. It was a week's puzzle figuring out where to be and at what time, because each day it changed."

We walked to the rickshaw and this time she didn't slip her arm inside my elbow, her hand found mine--innocently, without much intention or suggestion.

Our driver was growing accustomed to my directions and seemed to be enjoying the routine and easy money. I told him our next stop and we chugged through the crowds to the Mata Bharat Temple. He parked on one of the shaded side streets, and Uli and I walked through the gates. Couples and people in prayer moved along the lane. I un-strapped my sandals, and she did the same. As I took hers, I said, "This is one of my favorite places this time of the day."

"Und why is that?" She looked at the flowered plants and I knew she assumed it was because of the landscaping.

"Two minutes and you will understand."

I lead us to a quiet grove where we wouldn't be disturbed by the passing curious. We sat off the path on a patch of thick, well-watered lawn. "Okay," I said. "Close your eyes and listen. Breathe slowly and just listen to it."

She looked at me questioningly, but with trust, and without a word closed her eyes. After a time I saw her chest begin to rise in slow repetitions. Then I whispered, "Now, listen just to the cows."

I'd done this often, so I didn't need to close my eyes and let the sound wash over me as I had before. I just watched Uli's contented smile grow. It came from those deep places found only when the mind releases and the breath takes over. She was hearing it.

I'd chanced upon it my first year in the city, in the same garden, on a different patch of lawn—but that didn't matter. It happened as I was drifting in a bit of poetic ardor, one of those moments when the brain ceases to crackle. The lowing of all the cows in the city at the hour when they sought stalls and warm hands to relieve them of milk. I had dubbed it simply 'the enormous moo,' and in moments like this, it could absorb all the other sounds of the city, the motors and horns and rhythmic chants of the sadhus. It could draw the rhythms into it like a great river until it dominated every space inside the mind. And if you waited long enough, and listened carefully enough, it vibrated all the neutrons and electrons of your corporal being. Or so I am told.

Unfortunately, we had a schedule to follow; otherwise I think Uli might have listened for a longer time. I didn't care to face Sahr's cold stares if we were a microsecond tardy. I looked at the sun again. Right on time.

Uli didn't say anything as she slipped sequined sandals back over her hand painted toenails. I don't suppose they're ever machine painted, but they were damn pretty to me.

"Next stop, Durga Temple," I announced as we settled into

the backseat. She didn't respond immediately, just laced her fingers inside mine. Electricity, more reliable than current that flowed in the cables of South Nagpur, surged through my hand.

"Bhim?"

"Hmm?"

"That sound . . . I don't think I can describe it. It's not something you put into words very well is it?"

"No, you're right about that, it isn't. I knew that the first time I heard it, because I had a hard time describing it in any language."

She looked at me and squeezed my fingers. "Then I definitely heard it." She fixed me with a sly expression. "So who else have you taken to see this popsicle halo and hear this song?"

"You heard a song?"

"Well . . . maybe a humming."

I looked ahead to make certain our driver was on course and replied, "No one."

"No one? Seriously? You have shared these beautiful things with no one? You are fibbink with me?" A quick grin.

It was an admission of my lonely existence when I replied, "Not a single person but you, Uliana." She looked at me curiously.

Our driver dropped us at the foot of the lane and repeated my instructions to pick us up on the other side. I reached for Uli's hand, an easier motion now, and whispered, "You will have to close your eyes again and trust me."

"Easy on both accounts."

I lead her slowly and evenly up the crowded street, guiding her with gentles tugs, while clearing pedestrians from our path. Less mobile objects I veered around. With a squeeze of her hand

I whispered, "This time just use your nose, and if someone bumps into you, it's okay. I'm right here." The lane was famous-- stalls of flowers and sweets lined both sides, nothing else, no foods to confuse the airs, no spices, or soaps, or perfumes, just confections and flowers, lots of them. It was even better than the one I had sent Jitka to on her way to Johnny Chang's.

At one point, two children approached, palms outstretched for alms. My expression and rebuke in Hindi sent them scattering. I told them I was leading a blind holy woman and to leave us alone.

I glanced back to see if Uli was okay. She was walking tall, neck raised; nostrils flaring like a colt's. At some point, near the end of our stroll, I heard what was clearly a groan of pleasure that set my spine tingling.

Our driver grinned from ear to ear as we approached the top of the street. He was clearly enjoying my version of a tour of Varanasi. Uli just sighed as we clambered into the back.

A short distance from the house, she turned to me. "This afternoon, when we were on the Ghats, your face got very dark when you were watching that cremation. Are they difficult for you to watch?"

She didn't miss much.

"Yes . . . I don't enjoy the ceremony much. I've seen it too often, I think, but it wasn't the cremation that shook me, it was Adam. He was one carrying the body, and that is very, very strange."

"I know. I saw him also. Is this a bad thing?"

I took a breath. "No, not really bad, I guess, but what it means is, he's harijan, an untouchable, and that's surprising. I would have sworn on a stack of manuscripts he was a high caste.

Certainly not untouchable. He's well dressed, well educated and, in his odd way, rather influential. It's like this. People here look at your feet to see what shoes or sandals you're wearing--a little measure of who you are. His were very nice, and it's a contradiction that makes no sense. The young Hindu I was talking with afterwards told me that Adam was orphaned. Being orphaned and harijan, that's a couple of heavy strikes against you in this place."

"I heard that man use the word a nipuda. What does that mean?" Now I was positive she didn't miss anything. Her eyes searched mine.

"Well, a literal translation would be savant, a genius."

"Well," she smiled. "Is that wrong, being a genius und untouchable?" I smiled and shook my head, because couldn't answer that.

We turned onto Shivanan as the sun slipped below a sea of spires, domes, and corrugated roofs. I paid our driver and tipped him well. As I handed him the folded notes, I bid him health and wealth for himself and his family. He looked at Uliana, then me, and with a little grin, returned the blessing.

She had pulled the purple scarf back across her hair, eyes shining like polished lapis beneath the shawl. "So Bhimaji of South Nagpur. You have shown me these amazing sights, sounds, und smells of your city. But I seem to remember that there are five senses, six if you count a woman's intuition. What about the sense of touch?" Shyly, but with growing confidence, I took her hand in mine and gave it a gentle squeeze. Electricity, when it is so reliable, is a marvelous thing.

She grinned. "Okay, so that just leaves the sense of taste."

"I have, as we say, saved the best for last," and with a hand on her shoulder, I guided her to the dining nook between the kitchen and salon.

Thirty-Four

I nearly burst out laughing as I entered the room. Lalji was wearing a shirt--a white one, two sizes too large for his bony frame. It had a ruffled collar, puffy sleeves, and good assortment of noticeable stains. But, what really put me into stitches were the gloves. He stood like a mannequin in the corner with his hands folded across his crotch. The hands were covered with small, white waiter's gloves. Thank god he still wore his purple loongi, otherwise I might have mistaken him for an Oberoi Hotel doorman, or Mickey Mouse. With the gloves, the resemblance was uncanny.

"Would Saab and his premika enjoy a cocktail or a glass of wine before the dinner?" He stepped to pull out Uli's chair and I bumped him out of the way with my hip. That was my job.

I replied quickly, "A glass of U.B. for me, and the premika would like...?"

Uli, understanding that she was the premika, asked uncertainly, "Red wine with ice?"

"Very good, Maam." And Lalji, of recent broken pinky fame, hustled with all seriousness into the kitchen to fetch my lager and Uli's Cabernet.

I whispered, "Dinner isn't usually like this."

"He's sweet. What's his name?"

"Lalji, and yes, he is sweet, in a lazy, undependable, lethargic, sort of way." I looked at the table. Sahr had pulled out all the stops on her table-setting organ. Two pink candles flickered in low brass holders. Carnations and lilies floated in ceramic bowls in the center of a linen-covered table. Somehow she had gotten one of her housekeeping friends, or perhaps one of her wealthier clients, to loan her two china place settings replete with real silverware and crystal water glasses. We were in a five star bistro.

Lalji re-emerged with a tall, frosty glass of United Brewery Lager and a full glass of Cabernet on cracked ice. His tray was trembling so much that I thought it prudent to stand and help him set it down. We didn't need a disaster before the first course.

Pakoras stuffed with lamb, peas, and cheese arrived with a small tray of salted cashews and macadamias. Our first course saw us through a second glass of lager and iced wine, and a lot of laughter. Uliana couldn't stop describing the events of the afternoon as simple and sanctified as they were. Sahr peeped out to say hello at one point and announced that my ferenghi nose was still not allowed inside her kitchen.

Lalji kept astonishing me with how well he'd grasped the teachings of some crash course from his buddies. He displayed a decent talent for waiting tables, with the one exception of a palsied hand when carried liquids. I rose to help him set the bowls of spiced pumpkin soup in place. The second course surpassed the first.

As Lalji lifted our empty bowls, Uli confided that she thought she knew why I loved the classical poetry so much. People usually asked me first why I liked it, followed by standard comment that it must have been hard to learn the language. She skipped all that and went right to what inspired me. "The sound," she said. "Und because the themes are mostly about love."

After some encouragement, I recited some of my favorite lines from Meghaduta, Kalidasa's The Cloud Messenger. It had the same name as Sahr's parrot, and to a novice it is like hearing a

Brahms sonata for the first time.

When I finished, she said exactly what I'd hoped to hear. "I never knew it was so . . . melodic. What does it mean?"

With shyness, I took a sip of lager and replied, "Well . . . my translation still needs work, but I think I've gotten the idea of it. 'On the ascending paths of mountain snow, where elephants amble on a yearly course, the pearls from the claws of lions stay." I translated the second verse and the third, watching her eyes as I explained the deeper meanings. Her face was an oil lamp glowing brighter.

She took a sip of Cabernet and said dreamily, "Your verses are like a gateau cake. You know this pastry? Ten layers and all of them filled with flavor. Your voice makes it even more delicious." That reaction, so unorthodox, delighted me.

For the third course, Sahr had prepared one of my favorites-- cucumbers and chopped currants in dill, parsley, and fresh yogurt. Uli, by this time, was beginning to undulate, rippling back and forth with each bite. When she began emitting little chirps of pleasure, it had a profound affect on my groin, and had I wished to really embarrass myself, all I would have had to do was stand up.

With a light laugh, she asked if a rubber scraper came with the meal. I told her it was an accepted, if not an expected, custom in South Nagpur to lick one's salad plate.

Sahr came out to present the main course herself--a dish she had dubbed Chicken Bhiryani for Sri Bhimaji and His Fair Premika.

She chatted with Uli for a time, explaining all the important functions of being an oracle and a godmother to Master Bhim. The two of them bonded immediately, as I'd expected they

would, Uli taking Sahr's side on everything, including the shape
of the ivory birthmark. With an 'I told you so' glance at me,
Sahr returned to her kitchen.

Uli whispered, "What an amazing woman. She is rather . . .
full . . ."

"Bosomed?" I finished for her.

"Yes, that is the word for it."

We lingered over the Bhiryani, Sahr's piece de resistance—
perfectly proportioned spices, each bite brimming with a dozen
flavors, none of which overwhelmed the other. Tamarind,
saffron, curry, sharp mango chutney, and succulent chicken.
Another glass of wine and lager arrived.

Our conversation shifted into the spheres of literature,
history, and art. I learned that she had mastered in geology in
Copenhagen and that she loved to ski and hike in the mountains
near her home. As we were nearing our final bites, she suddenly
asked, "So, what does this word premika mean?"

I turned three shades of crimson as I stammered that it
meant girlfriend. She nodded silently and stared with traces of
wine and melancholy at the candle. "I'm sorry," I moaned. "I
didn't mean to embarrass you," Lowering my voice, I added,
"Sahr is like a worried mother with an aging son that won't
leave the house. She would like to see me . . . have more stability
in my life."

"You mean have a girlfriend, und it isn't you that needs to be
sorry. It is me, I have..." She hesitated, stared at me, and then
looked away. A fleeting shadow, not a result of the candlelight,
crossed between us. Suddenly, I was filled with all the old
apprehensions. Had I said something wrong?

It took a moment to respond to her unfinished statement,

and it still came out stilted. "Uli, it's alright. You don't have to explain a thing to me. It was . . . a silly word misused by my overly-protective housekeeper."

She moved the candles that had melted to three-inch stubs to reach across the carnations for my hand. My fear began to melt like the wax at my elbow. "Sometime, not now, not tonight with all this bliss, we can tell each other our stories." She traced a fingertip along the edge of my hand. "You know, I watched you that evening in Haroon's, and it is easy to admit that I watched because you fascinated me. What was a tall, handsome American, speaking Hindi, doing in a disco bar with a beautiful Indian woman? It intrigued to me." She paused. "But there was something else. You were talking und dancing with one of the most beautiful women in the city—we women recognize these things--und I could see that you didn't want to be there. I saw it in your eyes und the language of your body." She smiled and squeezed my fingers. "Ach, I'm glad I don't see that in this light."

"Uliana, I can truly say there is not a place on earth I would rather be than here. And with no other person. To be honest, I rarely go to Haroon's. I'm not really the social type, and that happened to be the first date I've been on in four years. Disco is also not my kind of music." I looked shyly at her. "So, is that why you said namaste to me? Because, that fascinated me."

A coy smile touched her lips. "Ya...und the fact that you were the cutest thing I'd seen since Tönder. How could a woman not say hello to cute and fascinating?"

"Cute? Do you still think so after being yanked all over Varanasi listening and smelling all sorts of odd things?"

She just looked at me with the same teasing smile.

Fruit compote in Varanasi is the best dessert one can offer a favored guest, with the possible exception of mango pie, which would have been too rich after the Bhiryani. It's the assortment, and Sahr had found the sweetest and ripest selections in the market.

Uli declined coffee or tea, and we took our dessert cups into the salon.

She went to stand in front of my desk, and I followed. "So what does it look like, this magical poetry of yours?"

I opened an over-sized book, Shakuntala and the Ring of Recognition, a love story as powerful as Romeo and Juliet. It was illustrated with large, glossy plates, and as her fingertips drifted across the script, I saw the look of fascination, the absorption into the curves and shapes that reminded me of myself many years ago. Our bodies touched as we leaned over the desk to study the lines. She turned to an illustration near the end--Shakuntala and Dusyanta wrapped like forest vines in a lover's embrace. Whatever reluctance Indians had in showing eroticism in modern film, they certainly didn't mind in their ancient art. With a giggle that I could only describe as unique to her, she pointed to a random verse.

"Can you read this one?"

"With pleasure."

I read the couplet, the syllables tumbling like mountain water, and Uli, with a small clearing of her throat, read the faintly penciled translation in the margin. "Shall I employ the wetted lotus-leaf to fan away your weariness, your grief? Or take your lily feet upon my knee and rub them till you rest more easily?" She nudged my ribs with her elbow. "So her lover wants to give her a foot rub, ya? I like this. Much better than sword-fighting. Is it sad or happy?"

"A little of both, but it's happy in the end. I think you would enjoy it, no sword-fighting at all." We stood looking at the page, neither of us inclined to leave our places.

"So it is a good love story then?"

"One of the greatest."

She turned and the space between our eyes and lips narrowed. "Then I shall read it," she whispered. A pause ensued where we looked at each other. I smelled mango and cabernet on her breath. Then the moment evaporated like mist. She looked at my legal pad and notes on the cave writing, and seeing the angular Brahmi said, "This looks different, more like our Nordic runes."

"It is. Same language, but earlier script, something I've been working on for about a week."

I think she was expecting it to be like the play we had been reading, because she giggled and asked, "And do the lovers snuggle und kiss und rub each other's feet like in the other?"

"Not exactly, it's a list of plants and anatomical descriptions. No kissing at all." For a brief moment I wanted to share with the fascinating woman next to me. I wanted to tell her about the discoveries, the etchings, the possibilities, but Devi's voice whispered, "What we have found today is of value, and valuable means dangerous." A voice told me that a man had been crushed under a mound of rock two days earlier. I decided if I told her, it would be later. Nothing would tarnish this evening.

We took our compotes and sat on the sofa where she drew her legs under her thighs and onto the pillows. Our knees touched lightly as we talked about the city and its history.

"Und your poetry und language has been at the center of all

of it, ya?"

"Pretty much. Almost everything of importance is written in it. If you study yoga, or dance, or law, or anything like it, you need to know some of the language."

"Like Latin und Greek for Westerners?"

"Exactly, but even more so here. The three are actually close sisters and share a lot of grammar and vocabulary."

"Like all that amo, amas, amat we had to memorize in school?" Her nose scrunched. "It wasn't my best subject."

"Honestly, it wasn't mine either until I found this. It just clicked. But all those repetitions we had to learn in Latin are nearly the same in Sanskrit."

A piece of mango slid smoothly from her spoon through her lips. "So who figured out the languages were sisters?"

"A very bright young English gentleman named Sir William Jones was the first. He spoke thirteen languages by the time he was twenty, so The East India Company figured he was the right candidate to hire to master the grammar. They sent him here to learn more about the original laws so they could create better ways to make money. Sir William mastered the language in a flash and wrote a paper that he sent back to London. That little paper shook up the entire Empire."

"Why?"

"Well, what he discovered was that Sanskrit, Latin, and Greek were identical. The structure was the same, declensions, conjugations, all of it. There were lots of cognates--similar words. It meant the people who spoke them were from the same linguistic roots. It's like this. People carry language around like suitcases, and William's paper proved that all three languages were closely related. Aristotle, Plato, and all the kings and queens were relatives of Kapila, Ramanuja, and the Brahmin priests. The subjects the British were trying to civilize were not only close relatives, but quite a bit older in terms of civilization."

She flashed a sparkly grin. "So those stuffy old Britishers were really cousins to the Rajahs. I like that story."

"I've always liked it too. Good example of irony. This place has a lot of stories like that." I wanted to tell her how the city felt so transitory, how people came and went while I remained. At one point I realized that she hadn't asked me once why I, Bhim the Linguist, lived alone in the oldest city in the world. But then, I hadn't asked her about her past either.

As we nibbled on the last of our fruit, I said cautiously. "You know, I don't give advice often. Honestly, I hand it out about as rarely as a hamburger around here, but I think you and Jitka could find better accommodations than The Riverview. That spot is a bit run-down."

"Run down? Mein Gott, you should hear Jitka. The air turns blue over her head with her cursing about how filthy it is. The beds sag like rotten hammocks, the water is the color of tea, und when I asked the desk clerk why they call it the Riverview when you can't see the river, he said you used to be able to see it back in the thirties."

"He probably meant the 1830's." I hesitated and then rushed through my hastily drafted speech. "Well. . . if you would like, I could help you find a better place. My tailor has a two bedroom flat that is comfortable and available. It's upstairs from where he lives, but it has its own entrance and a balcony where you can see the north section of the river. There's a kitchen, and I'm sure I could get you a decent price. You would just need to pay the first and last month's rent and the electric."

Her smile told me that my suit of armor was lustrous shiny and that my white stallion was the noblest in Uttar Pradesh. "Oh Bhim, we would love that. Where is this wonderful upstairs flat with the balcony und view of the river?"

"Uh . . . about four streets east of here."

Almost desperately I wanted to escort her back to the stinky hotel with the foul water and view of a dung-covered wall, but she wouldn't have it. With a cabernet glow, she laughed, "Nein, I vill take a rickshaw, and be fine, though I do like the idea of being with you in the back of a little cab. That would be sweeter than the fruit dessert. But it is late, and you must find me an apartment tomorrow and continue with all of that important work over there." Her arm swung in a graceful arc towards my desk, bangles jingling like tiny bells.

From the kitchen I heard giggling. Lalji and Sahr had finished the dishes and were peeking at us through the crack in the doorjamb. They'd seen too many American films where the man and woman kissed during this part. Suddenly, I was nervous, differently than before, but still nervous. I called for an autorick on my cell and walked her to the courtyard. The fragrance of gardenias and jasmine drifted to us on the breeze. The air felt different, and I knew why. Looking at the moon, I saw a cloud draw like a cape across its face.

"The rains will be coming soon," I whispered. "The season of marriages will end and the season of honeymoons will begin." I looked at her. "The rains will be very welcome this year."

She smiled and took my hand. "There are no words to describe this afternoon, Bhimaji of Varanasi. And this night too." A rickshaw chugged to a stop at the gate. "No words." She placed a silencing finger to my lips and stood on her toes to kiss me—a warm, moist kiss, not too long, but not a peck either. She turned and with all that beauty and jingling, stepped into the darkness of the cab, and my second date in a very long time was brought to an end.

Thirty-Five

As much as I wanted to, I couldn't sleep in the following morning. I was trying to re-insert myself into a dream where Uliana Hadersen and I were hovering like Superman and Lois Lane somewhere over the Himalayas. Nice dream, but my alarm rudely reminded me that Mej was arriving at my gate in half an hour with Frisbees and some form of gift.

Extracting my weary body and reluctant psyche off the top sheet, I plodded into the kitchen. There I found a very cheerful Sahr and the best cup of coffee I'd had in a month. "And how is the handsome Bhimaji with the beautiful girlfriend and soon-to-be wife and mother of his children, doing this fine morning? Don't forget that it is going to rain this afternoon, so you will need to take your umbrella today."

I bolstered my strength with three sips before answering. "You mustn't say things like that Sahr. She is a good friend and that is all."

"Hah, good friends don't kiss like that, besides, I have seen it in my cards."

I groaned. "You were spying on me, and that isn't nice, or good manners." I took another gulp. "But you are forgiven, because you're the best cook in all of Northern India and I probably wouldn't have gotten that kiss if it weren't for the incredible dinner last night. Thank you for every delicious bite. By the way, where did you get all those extras? Lalji's serving gloves were a nice touch."

"Thank you, big boss ferenghi. I do have my connections."

"An understatement if there ever was one. Listen, I will be off to Master Devi's right after Mej and I get some exercise. Would you mind saving me a few left-overs for tonight?"

"They will all be here, hot, and ready." The bell rang raucously at the gate, reminding me of another concern. "Sahr, could you also ask quietly of the whereabouts of the young widow, Soma. No one's seen her since yesterday morning. Perhaps one of the neighbors has heard something. You know, gup-chup."

"I will ask, Bhimaji." Her expression became serious. "I can consult my bhuta if you wish. He see more than any of these rumor-mongers."

"I know, Sahr. But let's wait on that. She is probably just feeling ill and doesn't want to be at her mother-in-law's. Not surprising. I expect she'll turn up at Master's this morning."

I pulled on my ugly tennis, trotted out to meet Mej, and was immediately relieved that tucked under his arm wasn't a life-size doll, but two leather-bound books. "Nanu-nanu, Bheemster. Greetings from planet Delhi." Two pairs of forked fingers thrust into a Vulcan salute in front of Mej's homely visage.

"Nanu, nanu back atcha, Brother Mej. How was planet Delhi?"

"God-awful, worst city in the 'ole fucking world, Bhim, especially driving, not that I ever do that. I 'ire taxis. Largest, fookin' tanks I can find, and my cabbies are instructed to push all those little farting tuk-tuks out of our way. It was also 'otter than a gigolo's pecker in that fucking 'ole. I did manage to score you a couple of gifts though."

I opened the gate and the books popped through first. I took them and read the titles--The Kama Sutra and The Arthashastra. Finely bound editions, printed on a quality, cream paper in both languages, and as puzzling as could be. Before I could thank him he chirped in rich cockney, "I know, I know. I

didn't 'ave a foocking clue what I was getting. I mean, I know
the Kama Sutra, read it eighteen times meeself, memorized most
them positions. Practice makes perfect, right?" He went to slap
me on the back, but I spun and held up the books in a defensive
move. "I got 'em because the covers were right cool. Cool
pictures inside, too. The Arthawhatever is way over my 'ead,
'istory, politics, wars with a lot of army shite, but I figured you
know all that stuff. 'Ell, you can use them for door stops if you
fookin' want. Books ain't my gig. I once gave a girl a book called
Candy thinking it was about chocolates. That one didn't last too
long. Anyway, I know 'ow much you like adding to your library,
and the sex manual might come in 'andy."

"No, they're great. Really. Both of them. Thank you." I
thumbed through the Arthashastra. Sketches of cavalry and
foot soldiers in fine detail stared back, a good research book to
add to my library.

I ran them inside and called to Sahr to make sure Lalji
attended to duties while I was gone. When I returned to the
porch, Mej was already trotting towards the fields.

It is said, or perhaps written somewhere, that to truly see
India one must view a sunrise in Varanasi and a sunset in Goa.
Whoever said that knew his or her guidebook to some degree.
The sunrises over the river are magical, but they are not just to
be seen. One must, like all things Indian, open all the senses.

They arrive through the dusty haze of the Gangetic Plain,
accompanied by the intonations of priests calling to the gods in a
dozen tongues. The smoke of morning fires, fried dough, and
temple incense drifts like fog. Bells chime and voices swell in
chants. Colors cling along the shore in muted layers of crimson

and salmon above a smooth river where poling guides steer drifting boats. Women glide barefoot in saris with urns balanced on their heads, buttocks swaying like elephants, and for the patient observer, there is an undeniable connection to a very deep past. One feels the greed of monarchs lusting over the realms, and listening carefully, one hears the feet of a million soldiers and a billion slaves. The life and death of a thousand battles arrives with the first rays. The sunrises along the river are not just the heralds of a new day; they are the portals to five thousand years of history.

I'm not sure if Mej saw them quite that way, but he always took the time to watch them, and that morning the arrival was spectacular. The rays shot upward into shifting clouds-- gathering plumes that held a promise of moisture. The breeze tasted sweet and foretold of rain. There would be dancing in the streets that afternoon, and that morning we would dance with the Frisbee in the marigold fields. I sprinted across the dirt, turned and leapt. The disc met my hand in perfect timing.

On our return Mej ripped off a couple of tasteless jokes involving blondes, George Bush, and Osama Bin Laden. As sweat continued to roll down my chest, I laughed "Typically crude. You pick those up in one of your Delhi brothels?"

"Nope, not this trip, not enough hours to visit any of my favorite whores or add to my jokes. I had to work." He said it casually.

"Work? No, no. You're employed?" I thought he'd been joking and was ribbing him, but when he answered, I realized he was serious.

"Yeah, had to bugger a pair of big-arse shears cross a bloody fat wad of red tape, I did. Two fookin' days of it."

I didn't say anything until we turned down my street. Curiosity tugged at me. "So, what kind of tape? Bureaucratic stuff?"

"Naw, You could call it import-export 'assles, little money-makers I dabble in. And it isn't drugs, if that's whot you're thinking. Anyway, I gotta run. Enjoy the books. Check out the birdie on page two-fourteen in the Kama Sutra. I think she's me next year's prom date. See if you can get me 'er phone number." He lit off down the avenue leaving me amused and puzzled.

Inside, I collected my notes and the Acer, and then on an odd hunch did a simple experiment. I set the Kama Sutra upright on the desk on its spine and let the covers drop equally. Eight out of ten times it opened to the same page. Mej was right; the woman in the illustration was a contortionist of exceptional skill. As Mej would have said, "right cool picture, Mate"

I let the Arthashastra fall the same way, but it dropped to the side as if it had never been opened.

Thirty-Six

Soma had not returned to Devi's. Mirabai had dispatched Sukshmi with a container of rice and dal to the mother-in-law's house in the hopes the young girl was just feeling ill. Such remedies usually helped, but Soma's mother-in-law snapped that the lazy girl had not been seen for two days, and she had needed to light the morning fire all by herself. However, if Sukshmi wished to leave the food . . .

Concern was spreading through the household, and I felt like someone was taking sandpaper to my skin. Could Ralki have been so insidious as to harm her? The question returned throughout the morning session.

We gathered in the front salon as usual, and as soon as the computer was whirring and the old boys were bickering, I attempted to explain my new theory.

"Masterjis, I think I know why the adjectives are used to describe the plants."

I waited for some encouragement, a short round of applause, but C.G. merely patted my knee and wheezed, "They are rubbish, my boy. Pure nonsense, you must know that." Pointing to the legal pad he shook his head and said, "Even the gender and case do not match."

I let it fly in a burst, "Exactly, they don't match. That's the whole idea. It's written that way on purpose as a signal. It's nothing to do with the denominations or declensions at all. They're numbers. Fractions! The number of syllables gives the ratio in the mixture. Look, eight syllables means eight parts of neem, nine parts of kino, seven parts fenugreek. They're directions for a pharmacist, and it even tells which herbs are supplementary and which are primary. There's no other answer, and I would bet my very shiny bicycle that we will find a similar pattern for the pressure points. We know the locations, but there has to be more. What order they're supposed to pressed. I'm sure of it." I was out of breath.

Outside, a bicycle bell clanged with a Doppler sound as it zipped past the house. Inside there was silence.

"The syllables you say?" They both stared at me, unblinking.

"Yes, look." I pointed at the calculations. They studied my notes.

"Well," Devi conceded slowly, "it seems to make sense. The boy may be onto something you know, C.G."

"Of course he is onto something, Devi. I told you how smart our Bhimaji is. You really should listen more carefully."

Before that one could escalate, I tossed another item onto the table, "And there are also patterns with the long and short syllables. Look. This one is used three times. I think it tells which part of the plant we are supposed to use. Two longs, a short, a long means the bark or resin is to be used. At least I think that's what it is."

"Well," C.G. replied. "I believe you are correct again, Bhimaji. It is the bark of the Kino that is used to make dragon's blood."

"Exactly," I blurted out, "and this adjective for the neem bark has the same pattern. It's a work of genius."

"Precisely so, Bhim. Precisely so." Masterji accolade resonated with hollowness.

I knew why.

We had come, by laborious and exhilarating steps, to the time when we would have to relinquish our discovery to the world. We might have done it earlier, brought them in at the start, archeologists and others, but we wanted our time with it first. Now it was clear that others would need to take the fruits of our labor and bake the pies and tarts from it.

There was another concern that I had. The discovery of the text, like additional threads in the great linguistic tapestry, was one thing to publish, but a medical discovery, that was a gift to be shared cautiously.

I understood enough about the control of medical knowledge, the malicious competition and staggering regulatory processes. Lilia had talked about it often. I had also been in close proximity to some very ugly diseases over the last three years. In a place like Varanasi death swept with casual indifference through the city's neighborhoods. Infections and viruses, from AIDS to hepatitis, sliced like scythes through the destitute sections, always the destitute sections. Some survived, many did not, but those who had the medicine always had better odds, and that came down to money. And control.

I was too guarded, or stubborn, to allow some corporate goliath snatch away our four thousand year old gift. The voices in the cave reminded me that profit wasn't the reason they had preserved it. "It was a gift to us, it is a gift to you. Let it remain that way," they whispered.

Before leaving for the day, I showed Master and C.G. the final photograph of the partially crumbled section of wall. The letters sank to illegibility under the rock.

"Oh my," Chandragupta coughed. "I can barely make out the lines," His fingers trembled as they slid across the top of the screen. "We will need to guess at some of the parts." He sighed. "It appears as if it is discussing varnas, or colors, but I don't think that is the full intent."

Devamukti leaned across to study the screen, and then nodded. "You are correct, C.G., but look at these two words, dosha and vayu. Those are references to diet. And look, this is another list." His finger tapped the left corner where the text disappeared. "It is a list of foods." He sighed. "Tragic that we cannot get inside to see it."

Hell, I thought, nothing that a sixteen ton back-hoe couldn't remedy. I closed the computer. I had my own list of things to do.

Thirty-Seven

Three months after I'd settled into my villa, I'd fallen ill. Very much so. It hadn't been the typical alimentary cleansing from overly-spiced curry. It had been longer and much worse. Poisons excreted from every pore and orifice of my body, and after six days of unintended weight loss, Sahr came to my aid. I weakly attempted to shoo her away with a wave of my fingers, thinking to outlast it on my own. Her head proved to be harder than mine, as it usually did. First she spoon-fed me green apple skin scrapings. Then she sent for Dr. Satnam Kangri.

Kangri knew a great deal more than his fluffy mustache and dimpled smile suggested. With piercing eyes and a warm smile he prescribed tea that tasted like lacquer and settled my insides instantly. But he didn't stop there; he probed the deeper wounds. For a week and a day he came to my house at sunrise, sat by my bed, and plied me with delving questions. I, being a weak and captive audience, mumbled answers as he massaged my muscles and tendons with adroit fingers. Then there was a rubbing of my feet and questions about my childhood. It seemed to be mixture of foot reflexology and psychoanalysis. I told him of being raised in seaside luxury and wealth. That part was easy. But as we neared the episode of Lilia's death and my tumble into my own personal abyss, it became more and more painful. My wounds were still fresh and Kangri sensed it. Still he demanded in his gentle manner that I tell him what I would.

Slowly, as I returned to a place where Sahr's cooking was appealing again, I learned about him—an unusual medical practitioner to say the least. He was a specialist in two systems. Following an internship in Los Angeles, he had trained as a cardiac electrophysiologist at UCSD Medical Center. That happened to be in my hometown, so it somewhat validated his Western credentials for me. But equally as important, he had trained under the best Ayurvedic teachers in Northern India. Kangri knew the body, mind, and spirit from two cultures and two systems.

It was he who encouraged me to talk with Sahr, patting my hand and stating in articulate English, "You need to rid yourself of these contaminants, my boy. Pain coats your heart like patina and the despair is polluting you. Remove it if you wish to live in good health. And talk to Sahr. She knows more of these things than you might think." Then with a grin he added, "and eat more bananas, small greens ones will do the trick nicely."

From Master's back veranda I punched the buttons of my cell to call Satnam. He answered immediately and agreed to meet me in his office in twenty minutes. I was just pressing the end button when Sukshmi stepped from the kitchen, wearing a sari of deep plum and maroon that magnified the black kohl around her eyes. Her bodice was a rich betel nut red, but it was her hair that shocked me--sheared to just above her shoulders in a style I knew must have infuriated her father. The whole effect was one of sultry attractiveness. And determined resistance. Seeing my hands on Surya's handlebars she frowned. "You are skipping out again, Bhimaji, and not stopping to shoot the breeze with your dance partner? Are you avoiding me?" I winced. Twice. I had been avoiding her and 'shoot the breeze' was one another of those catchy phrases that grated on my ears.

"I'm not avoiding you, Sukshmi." I whispered. "I've just been a little too busy with . . . things recently. I've had my laptop stolen, a man's death to discuss with the police, and a mountain of translation to finish with your father and C.G." I decided prudently to leave Uliana's name out.

"And you have no time now to chill and make chit-chat, or dance any cool tunes with me?" If we had not been below her father's back veranda I believe she would have tried to tickle me. She did like to tease.

"I always have time for you," Sukshmi, I said, feigning offence in my voice. "Dancing is another matter, and it's not that I didn't enjoy myself the other night; I'm just feeling like everything in my life has . . . begun moving so quickly. I hardly have time to look at the clouds in the sky or a sunset over the plains. I haven't written a line of my own poetry in two weeks, or even read a good book lately. Anyway...once it settles down again, maybe we can meet at Haroon's again."

The teasing smile faded. With a nod she said, "You know, Bhim, I believe you are more Hindu, or perhaps more Indian than me or most of my friends. These things you desire are what a proper Hindu would prefer to do on most days." Her eyes met mine and looked as they had when she exited the restroom at Haroon's—pained and stripped of defenses. "It makes me like you more, you know. But it also lets me know we are quite different from each other." She sighed.

I wanted to stay, because I sensed that she needed to talk, needed to tell me that being forced to marry a man she'd never met was perfectly detestable. I wanted to sit in a quiet pastry shop and listen, and I suspected I might have been the only person besides a girlfriend or two that she had confided this to. Young, modern, and educated, with the cords of tradition strangling her. It was an all too common dilemma in modern India. I wanted to stay and listen...but I couldn't. Satnam Kangri was waiting.

Offering a convincing smile, I whispered, "You and I are alike in more ways than you might imagine. I like to think that you will listen, and remind me to keep my dancing feet moving. That's a generous attribute in any culture. You set a time and place and I'll be a better listener. I promise. Maybe we can even dance to a few more of Randy Dogs' tunes."

"That is a pleasant thought, Bhim. I will wait." She glanced at Surya and the teasing grin returned. "Your bicycle has had a face-lift, yes?"

I glanced at her hairstyle. "Actually, more like a total make-over."

"And what do you call her now that she has this special look?"

I wiped a speck from the chrome bell and answered proudly, "She used to be named Ugly Bike, but now I call her Surya."

As I rolled through the back gate with a second promise to listen, Sukshmi called out, "You know, Bhim, you might have called her Jatana with all those new features. She does not look like she used to at all." I left her comment drift into the heat of the afternoon.

Satnam's office was west of the Alamgir Mosque on the Kabir Chaura, a mile from Master's back gate. Barring large herds of cows, carts, or funeral processions, and I would make it to his waiting room punctually. What I didn't count on was a large group of migrating clouds.

I had just wheeled onto the Chaitganj Road when the skies cracked open with a single slap of thunder. It was as if a giant creature of myth had stepped in and struck a colossal drum announcing the end of the dry season. Seconds later the rain began to fall, large scattered drops that bounced and smacked against the tarmac in dark circlets. Then it thickened and came with determination. The paths that bordered the road, previously of fine rouge, transformed to lanes of pink ooze.

That first downpour of the year—though less than an hour in total length--obliged all but the most infirm Varanasis to celebrate. The drought had felt interminable, but the relief, instant. The air cooled, the sun disappeared, and people poured into the streets eyes turned upward with gratitude. In seconds there was dancing, clapping, twirling, and jumping. Bodies of every age and size leapt and spun until they were soaked to the skin in a festival of innocent jubilation. The men, as a single entity, decided that shirts were superfluous and bared their chests like polished shields to the drops. The women, in an uncommon display of immodesty, loosed the braids of their hair and began twirling like maple seeds, palms aloft. Saris, soaked and sheer, clung sensuously to every breast and buttock. No one paid attention to anything but the savoring of moisture. Children ran with mouths turned skyward, and everyone, without exception, laughed and sang to the glory of the gift.

It made me twenty minutes late, and I cared not. Kangri, of all people, would understand.

"Bhim! These welcome rains arrive at the same moment as my most cherished patient. What a delight. Let me look at you." He took my hand in both of his and studied my pupils and some facet of my face.

We stood in the front parlor of one his medical offices, white-washed stucco with wooden benches portioned along the perimeter. It was an old room with a curious blend of odors--spices, medicines, and mold--empty and silent, but from beyond the door the music of rain and singing filtered in.

I stood, embarrassed that I was dripping so much water onto the tiles.

After a moment he took my hands warmly and said, "You look well, my boy, clearly better than the first time we met. That was a messy week, eh?"

"Messy is the right word for it, Satnam. Not my best appearance, but I have you to thank for getting me through it. You and Sahr."

He raised a bushy eyebrow. "I see your pain has grown less, a great deal so. That is good. There is evenness in the eyes. Even a bit of softness now. Hmmm..." He chuckled, as if at an inside joke. "This heart is smiling quite a bit more. Quite a bit. . He grasped my shoulder with, "You have not become a sadhu, I assume." I shook my head, and with a small squeeze he released it. "Countenance is strong, heart smiling, so, what can this curious doctor do for you today?"

I trusted Kangri on the same level I trusted Sahr, both seeing to my well-being far beyond what was customary. That develops trust. I knew he would not divulge what I was about to show him. I also knew he could give me more answers about it than anyone in the province.

Tentatively I explained, "I'd like you to look at something. But I can't tell you where it comes from, or why I have it. I know that's not exactly fair, but if you could look at it and tell me what you think, I would be even further in your debt."

He glanced at my bag and nodded quickly. "There is no debt. Let me see what you have."

Half a minute later the jump drive was open to my notes. Tilting the angle of screen for his eyes, I said, "Just read and tell

me what you think, your best medical opinion." I paused and
added, "Perhaps your western opinions would be better for the
moment, but…" He hushed me with a wave of his hand, having
already read the references to the basti and urvi pressure points.

For a long time I sat on a bench and listened to the rain clap
against the windows. A few streets over tablas and a wooden
flute had been added to the rhythm of the dancers. Soft rumbles
of thunder added to the symphony. I thought of Soma and
hoped she was celebrating somewhere, bare feet and green sari
soaked and cleansed by the rain. I hoped she was spinning
happily like all the others, hair loose and splayed like a fan.

The storm pushed to the north over the plains toward the
Himalayas. Inside it was silent as a cemetery. Kangri read on,
then re-read. Still he said nothing. Finally he pinched the bridge
of his nose and straightened up. "So . . . you want me to tell you
what this could be, eh? You want me to offer my medical
opinion of these pressure points, the plants, all of it?"

I nodded. "I don't know any other way to say it . . . but I
trust your judgment more than anyone. I need to know whether
it's even remotely legitimate."

He pursed his lips. "Whew . . . well it is, I'm sure you realize,
an amazing work, a true masterpiece of the ancient cures. But is
it legitimate? Yes and no."

I arched an eyebrow. "That doesn't help much."

"No, I suppose not. But, bear with me. Let us say you
present this to the medical societies of Europe and the United
States, maybe via a carefully written article. There is nothing to
validate it, no trials, no clinical tests or assays to support the
findings. Active elements are not isolated, which by the way,
would reduces their efficacy, like taking kernels of fresh corn and

making Fritos. There are no data to identify which nerves are stimulated by these acupressure points, and so on and so on. Most would huff and puff and dismiss it before they had read five lines. Medical purists are the world's worst skeptics, you see--officious, self-important, nonbelievers of every curiosity that falls outside the realm of understanding and methodology. But that is just my objective opinion." He tapped a dimple.

"But here, in this country where such things are accepted because they have a six thousand year history, it might be viewed with less cynicism."

"But do you think that it is . . . ?"

Satnam cut me off. "In my opinion, my boy, this is not merely a preventative or a stay of the symptoms. This is designed to be a cure." He let that hang for an instant before adding, "but one requires a more time and effort than eating a few nicely colored pills and taking a ten minute nap in a machine. It is a holistic approach, you see, designed to augment a lifestyle. These for instance," He pointed at the pairs of basti and urvi pressure points, "are meant to stimulate the Isles of Langerhans and pancreas, but meant to be done over a period of months, not days. That leads me to certain conclusions about the disease itself. But, I'm not willing to share that with you quite yet."

I was preparing to protest when he added, "Because you will likely discover it yourself. Is this all of it?"

I was anxious to hear what he thought the disease might be, but replied, "For now, yes. It's all we can get our hands on." He didn't seem bothered by my holding back, his mind leaping a step ahead.

"I ask because there is usually more. The Ayur often

prescribed complimentary guides for diet, mind-set, and a host of external influences. This is from early Ayur, is it not?"

"Yes, we think it is from the Sushrut Samhitas, perhaps earlier. There are some pieces missing, parts that are inaccessible right now. That's all I can tell you . . . really." He nodded and I unplugged the memory stick to begin repacking the computer.

He nodded toward the screen. "I can make a fairly good guess about the cure, but I'd rather wait until we all have more time to study it. Will you do me the favor of showing me the last of it when you get it? I would enjoy studying it more thoroughly."

"Satnam, you have my word that it will be the first person I contact."

"Good, because to answer your most important question, it is legitimate."

I stared at him and he nodded again. "Yes, legitimate."

As we moved to the door he said, "Think about this. Two-thirds of the plants made into modern medicines came to the attention of pharmaceutical companies from how they were used in traditional ways. And most of those came from developing countries." I tried to grasp the implications of that.

Outside, the rains had slowed. Random streaks of sunlight were beginning to slant through the front windows. Satnam took my hand and reminded me to call him soon. As I wrapped Surya's chain beneath her seat, he laid a palm against my chest and smiled. "You know, this chakra is healing better than any of the others, still tender, but definitely healing. She must be beautiful, this potion of yours."

I swung my leg over the seat, and with a shy grin and a push on the pedal, replied, "Yes, Satnam. She is."

Thirty-Eight

It took me longer to locate Uli and the ever-present Jitka than expected. The crowd surrounding Adam's chair had multiplied six-fold from the previous day, and locating the sisters, even with their distinctive features was not easy. People stood in concentric rings ten meters out from the shala. Children in tattered shorts scampered about, searching for unguarded items to pilfer. Vendors, entertainers, and two policemen were positioned on the upper ledges. I even saw the Chapins, Frederick and Marley with their battery-operated hats, standing at the outer edge. I had expected an increasing number of listeners for the sermons—they had the magnetic quality of loadstone--but this was taking on the air of a carnival.

I noticed a few spectators that I didn't want to see. Standing near the wall below the mosque in an easily identifiable robe and turban was the Imam Nomani. Further back was Yakoob Qereshy and a small cadre of his jacketed followers.

Adam had just had just offered a welcome and asked everyone to join him in three deep breaths of rain-washed air. I was pleased; this time I hadn't missed a word.

I lifted Surya down through phantoms of steam floating up from the moistened stone. Standing to the side, three Benarsi women were translating into Urdu, Hindi, and Farsi. There was a feeling of organization to it all, all new.

He closed his eyes and momentarily seemed to mentally depart the place where he stood. When he opened them, his voice rang out strong and clear. "The ancient metaphors of our universe, my brothers and sisters, carry with them outdated ideas, pictures and myths that have been painted for far too long. A flat earth, flaming chariots, or bearded gods with bolts of lightening, they are obsolete, incorrect, and must be abandoned. Our survival depends upon it. God is not a he or a she, does not sport a mustache, beard, or freckles. Jehovah, Vishnu, Allah, and Shiva don't wear sandals or sport rivers of blood in their hair. There are no gnashing teeth or burning cauldrons.

The hour has arrived when we must create new names and new descriptions with no likeness to humans. The energy we attempt to so vainly define has no gender, no recognizable shape, and certainly no resemblance to us, none whatsoever, even though it might comfort us to think so. We are simply another form of life standing at the peak of a vast array of complex organisms that have risen from this energy. If, in our need to do so, we feel compelled to give a shape to this universal force, then let us say it has closer resemblance to humming strands of wet spaghetti than anything else." There was a considerable and understandable wave of murmured confusion at this. "Like the taut strings of a sitar, subatomic strands of light give rise to particles of matter—miniscule strands of energy that begets matter and forms our entire universe. They just happen to look like Barelli pasta. That energy is creation, my friends. Always in motion, ever-changing, with absolutely no human attributes."

I listened as I edged my way around the crowd. I could no longer see Adam at that level, being now a part of the throng, but I could observe, and feel, the sentiment. More than a few were bewildered—the spaghetti metaphor still baffling. Most nodded in agreement, but here and there, anger was shaping on faces.

Adam's voice called out firmly. "But, friends, does this mean we should love this energy one iota less? No, no, no. Quite the opposite. We are a species of compassion and should love this energy even more. Loving it means loving all. Repeat that to yourselves." That request appeared to ease a few of the concerned expressions.

"Today I offer you The Simple Plan." And as this was said, I watched in embarrassment as the crowd in front of me parted like a hairline. The fingers of Adam's left hand were motioning for people to move to each side. In his right, a cold bottle of Fanta beckoned. To me. I was being given an invitation to the inner circle, and suddenly felt like I was trudging slowly up the aisle to my third grade teacher's desk to receive a Child of the Day sticker. Surya and I rolled sheepishly forward.

Handing me the icy bottle, Adam winked and continued, "The Simple Plan is a union of three thoughts and actions, three means, each dependent upon the other, none more, none less important than the other two. A blend of Absolute Compassion, Pure Science, and Common Sense. Though how common common sense is these days might be in question." Without warning, Adam hopped from his chair and turned slowly to focus on everyone within his vision. His pupils bored into the crowd that had now swelled from the upper part of the Ghats to the moored boats of the river. Bathers turned, children stopped scampering, and a hush seemed to descend on the bank. "ABSOLUTE COMPASSION, PURE SCIENCE, and INTELLIGENT COMMON SENSE." His words shot into the throng like gravel. "they are the heart of The Plan, friends . . . and from them all good will come." He took a deep breath and exhaled. "Right. And when we have cultivated this compassion for our human family, for our air, water, food; when we love the great energy with all our strength, then we create only good.

Love for the energy begets greater love. And, like molecules of water entering the ocean, we will merge, and the entire human family will be lifted." He paused and took a short pull on his Fanta. I did the same.

"We are bound by universal responsibility to take The Simple Plan and use it. In every action, every deed and thought, we must ask, 'is this done with compassion, common sense, and right science? Ask it in everything, but be aware that we will make mistakes, but we will learn, and with new intelligence and compassion, we will repair the errors and move forward together."

It was at that moment that I spotted Jitka, and incredibly, she was smiling and nodding her head. Beyond her bobbing forehead, I saw the glistening curves of Uli's hair, and immediately the taste of our ephemeral kiss returned. The chakra that Satnam had touched suddenly warmed like a glowing ember.

"Imagine hundreds of projects; the world's nations working together--distillation and irrigation systems pulsing water into the deserts, oxygen pumped into a wounded atmosphere, poisonous gases decreased. Imagine the sick being cured, the hungry being fed, and the suffering of billions eased. Imagine the cessation of violence and hatred. These are not as difficult as we might think. And the doubters? The ones who say it is trapped in complication and cannot be done? They are mistaken. It can be. It will be. We have only to let go of our obsolescence and accept The Simple Plan."

I looked around and saw that the multitude was separating like clarified butter and cream. Small clots of orthodox Hindus, Muslims, and Christians--in the only vein they'd been in agreement on for an eon--were muttering angrily. Terse words hissed arbitrarily from the crowd—'blasphemy, sacrilege.' Then from somewhere near the upper steps the ugly, but predictable, 'achut, achut. He is nothing but a filthy harijan.' It was spit like venom. The larger group, those who had been in agreement with Adam's words, had been nodding peacefully until that moment. Someone in their midst yelled angrily back.

One thing was certain; there wasn't a drop of lethargy in the returning heat.

I looked up the embankment toward the mosque. Imam Nomani still stood with a small congregation. Qereshy's group had slipped away.

Adam's words poured out for an hour. At times they drifted like fine ash, at others they shot into the crowd. He described ways to merge with the energy through breath, music, meditation, and movement. He elaborated on its nature, all the while setting forth his plan to transform a violent world to one of functioning unity. At moments it made us laugh, at others cry. "Oh sure, my friends, a pack of bearded, grumpy clerics interpret a few lines of scripture penned fourteen hundred years ago and tell us that God not only allows but commands a gullible child to step aboard a crowded bus wearing a vest of dynamite? Kill yourself, kill others and you will become divine? This is common sense? This is compassionate? We will shout with a single voice that it is not. A group of celibate old men in designer robes dictate that contraceptives are sinful in a world that is exploding with starving children. This makes sense? Shout that it does not." He pointed to the river and all eyes followed his outstretched finger. "We douse our healthy children in this water so full of microbes that we might walk on it, and are told that by doing so they will pass go and never have to roll the dice of the living again. Do not be so deceived." At that, a ripple coursed through the predominantly Hindu section.

Adam held nothing back. He struck out at every government, religion, or ideology that condoned violence, ignorance, or intolerance. He swept aside the illogical like fine talc and replaced it with new visions.

Ignoring any reaction from his audience, he finished with, "And then, my brothers and sisters, imagine dying. It isn't so hard or frightening. We are made of the great energy after all, composed of it. We don't disappear at death or get wrapped into a fatherly embrace on a couch of puffy clouds, nor do we get to frolic with a bevy of shapely virgins. False pictures from old books, and they are wrong. Death, if we may employ the metaphor, is a melting of salt crystals into the ocean. That is death, energy into energy, light into light. The brilliance of a billion suns growing a fraction brighter, neither terrifying, nor permanent, only a transformation of energy, the greatest, purest compassion there is. Universal bliss." Adam's arms stretched out to the crowd in a parental embrace. "Absolute compassion, my friends, pure science, and common sense—very simple." His arms dropped slowly to his sides. There was no folding of hands, no wave of good-bye; merely a folding of his canvass chair and it was done.

For the first time since I had been attending his lectures—admittedly only three--there was an ovation. Perhaps two hundred of the Benarsis in attendance began clapping while vendors and entertainers circulated quickly to ply their merchandise. The disgruntled drifted away in small groups. Others turned to glare at the speaker and his followers.

For some time, I couldn't say how long, I stood in the shade of the palm as if in a dream. It felt like a time when I was very young and my parents had set me on a blanket in a park above the ocean. I drowsed to the sound of the waves, at peace. There were no bruises in my world, no bandaged knees, only goodness. It had been a long time since I had felt that. Satnam's words echoed back. "In my opinion, my boy, this is not merely a preventative or a temporary stay of the symptoms. It is a cure." A cure. Good deeds would be done, and I had a part to offer. I looked up to see Uliana Hadersen recently of Tönder, Denmark smiling at me.

Adam, appearing almost child-like, ascended the steps above me. As he moved away he whispered, "Enjoy it, Bhim, all of it, but do not tarry. You are an impetus." Puzzled by this odd statement, I wondered how much he knew. And how? Damn!

Uli's voice sparkled behind me, "Svester, the best guide in Varanasi is taking us to our new home today." I felt her arm slip inside mine, her hand wrapping warmly about the base of my thumb. I turned from Adam's retreating back to the blueness of her eyes. "He tells me it even has a real view of the river und a kitchen with an oven."

I believe she was already moved in.

Jitka's granite voice restated her sentiments of the day before. "It could be a schwein pond und it would be better than where we are, Uli. Gott, my back feels like twisted bread."

At that moment I felt dreadfully shy. It was the doubt that always follows a first date. I hoped the feeling at the end of our evening together was genuine. It had been true, hadn't it?

Uli, squeezing my thumb, whispered in my ear, "It was the most beautiful date I've ever been on. Ever. When can we go again?" I wondered if she heard my sigh of relief.

"Thank you," I murmured. "Choose the time and I will make a new tour."

Jitka seemed to be gradually accepting the notion that I wasn't preparing to kidnap her sister and sell her into slavery. I guess she'd also found the stir-fry at Johnny Chang's to her liking, so I could be trusted, to guide her to good food sources at any rate.

The crowd was thinning, drifting away to other distractions. Men and women in semi-clothed wetness returned to the river's edge. The water had changed, and not just in my imagination. A dusky, yellowish-gray stained the surface. The effluence from the gullies had washed into the rainwater, cleansing the lanes, but staining the current with additional filth. Suddenly, I wanted to move south, away from the shala.

"Are either of you hungry?" I asked optimistically.

Jitka grinned and nudged me with an elbow. "I could eat one of those damned cows standing up there. You know a place with bratwurst und spatzel?"

"Might be hard to find in this section of town . . . but I do know an Afghani cafe with kabobs and pilaf that might measure up. We can get lunch and then I'll show you the flat and introduce you to the landlord. If it looks right we can move your belongings this afternoon."

Then I became nervous that I was directing too much.

Uli, who still hadn't released my arm, smiled slyly and said, "Lead on Macduff." And into the slickened gullies I did.

Lunch was a success all around. Jitka, I soon discovered, became a tamer and rather humorous beast when fed sumptuous quantities of lamb accompanied by nan, currants, and pilaf. We sat cross-legged on a dais layered with plush carpets as a studious-looking Afghan brought us appetizers and milkshakes. The air was heavy with drafts of water pipe tobacco, baked bread, and Hindustani music.

As the cucumber and yogurt soup arrived, the conversation turned to Adam's extraordinary speech.

"Ist klar, what he says," Jitka rumbled through lumps of nan. "Science will pull us out of the mess humans have brought the world to. Bestimmt!" Three crumbs shot capriciously towards my tea cup.

Perhaps I was less hopeful of science being a panacea, but added that I thought the world in general could use a dash more common sense.

It was Uli who delicately reminded us, "It must be all three. It is as he said, none more, none less than the others. A way of love, science, and good judgment." I felt her toes edge against the side of my foot and a current of electricity shivered up my leg. "It is strange, but I believe I could remember every word he said. It stays here," she tapped her temple. "like it is printed." I knew what she meant. The words returned easily.

We ended our meal with pistachio dessert and more dialogue. Harmony and good deeds were pleasant thoughts. Jitka kept us amused with jokes about projects involving stinky methane and soybean diesel. It was clear she had a solid foundation in physics and chemistry. "You know," she rumbled, "He knows his quantum physics, this Adam. He understands string theory, und that is saying something. You know, the little spaghetti pieces?"

I nodded distractedly. Since his discourse, a nagging

uneasiness had begun hopping gnome-like in the back of my mind. I'd observed the mood of some in the crowd—the negative and sour. People don't embrace change so easily, especially when it involves faith, and especially in a city like Varanasi.

The bill arrived on a small silver tray surrounded by cardamom seeds, the local after dinner mint. I wanted to treat, but was firmly outvoted. They would pay. After all, I was the guide and apartment finder. As they buckled their sandals and I laced my worn tennies, I voiced my apprehension. "You know, sometimes in a city like this, with all its old traditions, new ideas aren't accepted so easily. I hope Adam is . . . careful how he . . . expresses himself."

Uli glanced up and said, "It proves again how dangerous it is to be good." I must have looked puzzled trying to remember where I'd heard the quote before. "George Bernard Shaw when he was told that Mahatma Gandhi had been assassinated," she said.

Thirty-Nine

The tip of Sutrdharak's knife nicked a miniature hole in the large map in front of him. Five lines converged at the tiny perforation he had made, but the lines didn't captivate his interest, only the place where they joined.

He frowned at his indiscretion. The chart was still essential in the planning and couldn't be reduced to ash quite yet, and now there was a tiny clue for anyone who cared to study it. The chart was topographical and highly detailed. Sutradharak calculated the curved lines around the nick again, and since the map was already marred, took a blue pen and drew a series of small lines on either side. Next to those, he penciled numbers. Satisfied with his calculations, he allowed himself a rare smile. Location, undoubtedly the most essential factor to the success of battle. He touched the lines with a finger. *Sufficient height and depth, and at the correct time of year. It will suit our purposes well.*

The team he had assembled wasn't large, and that pleased him. Four to place the detonators and run the ire, a fifth as a communications specialist. There was also a back-up driver if the situation became necessary. Each of them were highly trained, held valid documents of residency, and were totally disassociated. There were no connections, physically, financially, or otherwise to himself or the employers.

The cell phones, RDX, wire, and blasting caps had been sealed inside cloth bound copies of the Islamic Hadith. They, in turn, had been posted to a non-existent madrasa religious school in Delhi. The address was real, the school was not. The PuppetMaster delighted in the irony—instruments of death inside holy books, and any interception would only add further confusion for the intelligence agencies and media.

He folded the map into a tight square, sealed it in plastic, and pushed it into the recess near the high-speed cable behind the baseboard.

Now only a few details remained—the most critical being correctly positioning himself for the detonation. He realized this was his one act of vanity, and admitted that it came from two things, pleasure and ego. But unless the explosions were simultaneous, like the temple and rail station in Varanasi, he always bore the responsibility of pressing the buttons. Watching the fireworks display, and the instantaneous or lingering death, was his reward.

Just as he was closing the laptop, a window popped onto the screen announcing a new message. That's odd, he thought.

He opened the message and read it with a combination of mild irritation and tingling excitement. His employers desired a small change in plans. Their schedule had changed, which meant his would change. They needed an additional event, something small, but enough to attract attention.

Sutradharak transmitted an assenting response and spun the ring on his smallest finger. This would require swift planning and implementation. That was not always sensible; he liked thorough, meticulous preparations with sufficient time. Rushing led to mistakes.

Pondering this change of schedule, he donned his hat and jerkin and once more transformed into a purveyor of goat products.

Forty

"Bhim, It's perfect. Absolutely perfect."

It wasn't really perfect, but it was pretty hard not to like it; the flat was airy-fresh with a good view of the river. When the haze lifted you could see the palace on the far bank. There were two small bedrooms with single beds of reasonable firmness, a fan, kitchenette, and water that flowed with a semblance of clarity. When I led them to the rooftop with the water tank and an even better view, they were ready to move in.

Trying to polish my champion image, I added, "With some scrubbing and bit of fixing up we can make it work. I've got tools for the leaky faucet and oil for the doors and windows, and I'm pretty sure Lalji has hidden a couple of old paintbrushes somewhere."

As Uli began arranging scarves around window frames and lit sticks of incense, all culled from her magical handbag, I went below to speak to the landlord.

I wanted a local's rate and was prepared to squabble for it, but he agreed to my price quickly when it was discovered I was one of his brother's most loyal customers. He also knew Sahr and Devi, neither of which surprised me.

When I returned, Uli offered Jitka a proposal, "Bhim and I will fetch our bags und you can do a bit of cleaning. Ist good ya, Jitka?"

Jitka stopped bouncing on the mattress long enough to say, "Ya, ya, ya! Go, und fetch them and I will have our meitshaus shining like spiegals when you return."

Against an oddly gnawing apprehension, I let Uli to lead us back to the hotel by way of the river. She wanted to go along the water, she said, and return to the flat by taxi. Surya was stowed safely under the steps at the flat, but an inexplicable unease still nibbled at me. At first I thought it was the nervousness of being alone again with Uliana, but I knew that wasn't it. She made it all so easy.

Eventually, I pinpointed the source, and oddly enough, it was from the color gray. I had seen it in the river right after the rains, gray from the slime and gray in the scowls on some of the faces in the crowd. The clouds had reassembled in dark shades of gray. Sahr would undoubtedly have said it was some invisible bhuta whispering to me, and only when Uli reached out to take my hand did the apprehension recede. "Come on," She smiled. "You can recite to me more poetry, and I will be the guide. I want to hear how the lovers wrap like vines und rub each other's feet again." From that simple request my fear dissolved, and I realized something deeply significant, Uliana Hadersen wanted to be with me for reasons I hadn't fully understood before. She didn't pity me, or regard me as some temporary novelty in a strange city, or even as a decent tour guide. She wanted to be with the peculiar fellow who walked alone and wrote poetry and joked with his housekeeper, the one that saw the loveliness in the sunrise and made small talk with shopkeepers. A wall tumbled and I knew I would never be nervous next to her again. And somehow, in some strange way, I was certain Lilia was smiling at my revelation and nodding with approval.

My hand slid like a coil of pearls into hers.

While Uli threaded us a path along the Ghats, I told her stories about the old fort across the way and some of the intrigues of the rajah's court in the waning years. She led us over steps, around shore temples, and down to the boats, and all I could think of was sliding my fingers through her hair. I watched her skirt and blouse swell and ripple in the breeze. A burnt-orange scarf, draped about her shoulders, fluttered as if pulled by tiny strings. Un-polished poetry rose. Like unfurling petals folded and the yielding of speckled shells. Like sun on wings of dragonflies and mist in mountain springs—you touch me. Sensing my thoughts, she squeezed my hand and stopped abruptly to look straight into my eyes. "Me too," she whispered. Nothing else.

Kissing is not done in public in India. In Varanasi there might even be a law against it. Not wishing to break that arcane commandment, I felt a compelling urge to jog, possibly sprint, to a private place or shaded room. I ached for the woman standing in front of me at the river's edge. I wanted her mouth on mine, her hair and skin touching me, our bodies wrapped like forest vines. But we didn't sprint; we walked far too slowly towards the one of the foulest hotels in the city, The Riverview.

Near the Chauki Ghat, at the deepest curve in the bosom of the stream, I noticed a gathering--men, women, and children standing knee deep at the river's edge. None were making the customary praying or bathing motions. That was unusual. They were bent over an object, not touching it. Two men started waving frantically to those further up, more people descended and finally the khaki and red of a police uniform trotted down.

The policeman waded authoritatively into the water in shorts and sandals as the crowd parted. Between the knees and hips of the curious I finally saw the object of their focus, and it took two full breaths to comprehend what I was seeing. My knees sagged and my hand slipped from Uli's into an agonized fist. I whimpered softly, "No." Faded green cotton, dark now with saturation, drifted about a bloated corpse. Plastic bangles and a sweetly familiar braid floated in the gray current. I screamed, "Soma!!" and leapt down the final steps to the water's edge. Uli, frightened and confused, followed.

A second policeman trotted down the embankment as I pushed through the crowd. Beggars, children, and old women stared with morbid curiosity at Soma's body. They'd all seen corpses; it was impossible not to on the river, but few had seen a murdered woman, and when the second policeman turned Soma over, everyone knew that she had been. Her chola had been torn from her chest, leaving her half naked. Her neck had been sliced in a jagged crescent from ear lobe to ear lobe. A patchwork of gray bruises mottled the once gentle face.

I dropped to my knees in the shallows, and pleaded in English, "No, no, no, not her. She didn't know anything. She didn't know." I moaned and tried to wrap the cowl of her sari across her exposed breasts.

Above me a brusque voice asked, "Do you know this woman, Sir?"

I managed to pull a single fold of cotton across her front, but the fingers of the current tore it away. I couldn't seem to get a breath. "Yes." I answered slowly.

A strong hand gripped my upper arm and lifted me firmly from my knees. I stared at the officer who held my arm. He was young and imperious-looking. Through a fog of tears I saw I was being regarded with suspicion. I looked around. Others in the crowd were assessing me the same way, and I understood. I was a ferenghi, a foreigner, and this was a low caste woman, young and pretty, half naked in the river. The authorities had seen these types of crime before, usually in the red light district of

Shivdaspur, but there was no doubt in anyone's mind. She was a prostitute and I was an overly aggressive client.

The young officer asked cockily, "And how might you know such a woman?"

Through a choking anger I snapped in Hindi, "Her name is Soma. She is the servant of my teacher, you moron, and I've known her for three years. She works for Master Jatanaka Devamukti of the Chowk District. I am the master's vidyarthi and his close friend. And this woman that you insult so easily is my bahina." Two dozen startled looks followed my outburst. I had just called the dead girl my sister, replied rapidly in the local dialect, and announced that I was studying under the most revered pundit in the city. None of those was anticipated. The policeman looked stunned, then mortified. Slowly he said simply, "was."

"What?"

"Was, Sir. She was your bahina, and I am very sorry for your loss. I apologize. I did not realize. Perhaps we could ask a few questions of you? At the station?" He nodded in the general direction of the city and added contritely, "If it would be a convenient time, Sir."

The policeman's use of the past tense was a cold slap. Soma, my sweet, shy sister was dead. Her light, as Adam had so recently put it, had merged into the light of the universe. But she had merged that way from someone else's hand. Brutally. My anger surged. I looked at the body in the river, not from a desire to see her face, but too burn the image in my mind. Then I squeezed my eyes shut.

Turning to the policeman I said, "No, it would not be a convenient time. You may take a statement here, or do whatever you do in such cases, but I will not be going to the station today."

I shuffled wearily up the embankment behind the officer, while others lifted Soma from the water. They wrapped her in a thick, oily cloth, and I wondered absently if the cloth had been used for the same purpose on other occasions. It looked as if it had. We stood near the top on a stone ledge below stained wall, and the young man asked me routine questions. Name and address. How long had I known her? He paused to bark at the curious who had gathered to stare. They withdrew and then proceeded to tell the new arrivals to do the same. Uli pushed through and found me, and without speaking or touching, stood close enough that I could feel her warmth and the rippling of her scarf. The policeman didn't ask who she was, and my expression warned him not to.

As we neared the end of his inquiries, Soma's body was carried past us, not on anyone's shoulders, but low like a scarred steamer trunk. And suddenly, it seemed so minimized, like the disposal of some unwanted refuse. She had lived seventeen years and now, like a leaf of autumn, she would be burned with the other inconsequential leaves that had fallen.

I felt Uli's shoulder rub against the muscles of my upper arm. The policeman had just asked me a question that I couldn't answer. I wanted to. Desperately, but I couldn't.

I didn't know Soma's last name.

"Wait!" Uli walked rapidly, almost at a trot, up the steps. The crowd parted and the two officers carrying Soma's body turned and halted. She lifted the long orange scarf and drew the stained sheet from Soma's face. She lifted Soma's head with one hand, and with the other, slipped the scarf under the neck and across her face. In a final act of veneration, she crossed it over Soma's breasts.

The policemen began their ascent again and I barked, "It stays right there. Do you understand? Right where it is." They nodded firmly. The silk would not be removed.

Forty-One

"She was your sister?" Her fingers rose unpretentiously to tuck a length of wet hair behind my ear and then to linger at the side of my face.

It took a long time before I could reply. "She was . . . my teacher's servant, a sweeper girl with a batch of luck no one on earth should ever have. Young and widowed. Her husband fell from a train just before I came here. She was fourteen and treated like a street dog by everyone but my master and his family, so I sort of adopted her . . . for a while anyway. I never really told her, but she knew. It was like a game we played."

Uliana and I stood just inside the threshold of the hotel room. The door was open, the room, tiny and dingy, smelled strongly of hashish and urine. I wanted to grab the backpacks and be out the door and into a cab. Not an open rickshaw where all the world's eyes could peer in, but a large, darkened sedan. I wanted to shut the city out, and for the first time since entering it, I wanted to leave and be completely away. I needed one of the most treasured commodities one could have in a country of a billion people. Privacy.

She closed the door and her soft accent pulled me back. "What was she like?"

I ached, grasping for words. They came slowly, then bumpy and swiftly, like a stream through a gorge. "Soma? She . . . was shy, and sweet, and intelligent in her way. But sadness held her, penned her in, and she chewed betel nut too much. Her smile was like moonbeams through the clouds. We came to be like . . . old people talking about early parts of our lives, undemanding, effortless stuff. I wanted to teach her to read, because she deserved. . . something better than being kicked around for being a goddamned widow." I winced at what I had said. "And she was tough in ways I don't think I could ever be. Never once wore the white saris or shaved head widows are supposed to. And she trusted me." My chest pinched. "God, she was only seventeen, Uli. How could anyone. . .?" My words slowed and suddenly my hands and neck felt sticky. I smelled the rankness of the river in my clothes and had a burning desire to brush my teeth and scrub my body with strong soap.

She sat on the corner of the bed and leaned forward onto her elbows. "Would it help if you told me what it is about, Bhim? I'm not asking you to, only asking if it would help."

I looked at her and Master's words returned. "Valuable means dangerous." Too many loved people in my life seemed to die. The cherished were gone. I couldn't lose another. I wanted Uli with me, sitting across from me at restaurants. I wanted her next to me, wrapped in my arms. And for those reasons, as strange as it sounds, I knew I had to tell her.

I sat and asked if she really wanted to hear it, and added that it might be dangerous. She did, so I described the cave and the walls of words written so many centuries ago. I told her about the pundits, and what Kangri had said about a cure for something not yet known. I told her how Jotilal Sukkha had been crushed, and my encounter with Ralki, and his cruelty toward Soma.

She listened without comment, question, or judgment.

The darkness of evening crept in and Uli stood to switch on the bulb that hung naked from the ceiling, and when she sat back down, in that fetid light, in that foul room, I told her about Lilia. Part way through, I began to weep. I explained how she died, and I wept. I described our apartment, how we lived together, how her hair drifted and spread as we swam in the waves, and how her lips felt on mine. I wept and sadness flowed out like water from a shattered vase.

Eventually, nothing was left. Emptied. Uli's arms folded about me. The drone of the city's noises drifted in and filled our silence.

Softly, she said, "She was very fortunate to have had you, Bhim. They both were. So lucky to have been loved by you. A minute of love is eternity if it is pure."

With a strained voice, I answered, "It's just so empty where she was. . . inside me."

"But she is still there. You feel it, the light inside you. It isn't empty. Everything you see and touch, she is in it. It is as Adam said, now she is the energy in you."

She pulled my head onto her thighs and stroked my face and neck, and after a time I whispered, "I disappeared, you know, when she died. Just fell out of touch with it all and ran."

"Und was that wrong? Losing such love would make any of us want to be somewhere else. But . . . you have come through to the other side now."

I wanted her to know what it had been like for me, why I had fled. "For over a year all I could feel was anger. Not at people, just anger at whatever had taken her away."

"But your anger has gone now?"

"A long time ago, I think." I sighed, wanting to remain where I was, my head in her lap. There we were in one the dingiest, foulest space imaginable, and I didn't want to move. But Adam's words kept returning. "Remember, you are an impetus. Don't tarry."

We needed to go.

As I stood and wiped my face with my hands, she whispered, "And do not forget Bhimaji Martin Scott, I am here . . . if you wish me to be. Right here." She touched my lips with her fingers and I lifted the packs.

Forty-Two

Uli and I settled for a small taxi back to the flat, but the
streets were dark now and few people were passing along the
avenues. No one took notice of us. We didn't talk as we passed
through the center of the city and into the more spacious
outskirts. I watched the shuttered store fronts slide by and felt
her closeness, her touch offered without shyness. That contact
lifted my spirit slightly from the horrors of the afternoon.

She understood completely now who I was in the rawest of
terms, and she still wanted to stay. I'd beset her with the pain of
Martin, the deaths of Lilia and Soma, had made clear the perils
that had leapt into my life, and still she erased my fear that she
would disappear the way she had entered. In a place as transient
as Varanasi, where foreigners always had ancillary destinations,
where corpses became ash, and the river and death were the only
truly permanent fixtures, the feeling was unreal. It was if she
had appeared just for the purpose of being with me. Three days,
one date, a single kiss, and it felt as if she wanted to be next to
me as much as I with her. I had to know.

Nearing the Asi bridge, I turned to face her. "Uli?"

She smiled in her knowing way. "You are going to ask me
why, aren't you? Why it is you und me?"

I nodded, beyond understanding how she could divine my
thought.

"Has there ever been something that you knew was made just
for you, something you knew was chosen for you, but with no
reason you could understand when it arrived?"

I thought of the time I opened that Sanskrit primer at
Berkeley, the first time I heard Lilia cursing behind me in the
admissions office. I thought of the script in the cave, and the

first time I saw Adam. I thought of a thousand perfect waves that had been created just for me. None were coincidental, they were designed. "Yes. They were the most important, the most wonderful moments of my life."

She set fingertips against my cheek, rose on sandstone, and I closed my eyes. They slipped lightly across my lips, along my jaw to a place below my earlobes, and as we slowed to cross the bridge at the river she kissed me deeply, with every part of herself.

When her eyes drew back, they were smiling. "You are the gift given to me. We are given to each other."

"Not to point out the obvious, but you hardly know me."

"Ya, but I want nothing more than to learn who you are."

This time, I kissed her. Slowly. I felt her back arch with a small shudder, her legs push softly against mine. Both of us realized, as we turned onto her new street, that small Indian taxis weren't manufactured for physical romance. With a soft smile, I asked, "And at what point did all this need to know me come to you Ms. Hadersen? No, let me guess. When I led you up the street with all the flowers and sweets? When your eyes were closed? That was it, wasn't it?"

"No. Actually I knew the moment I saw you take a sip of your smoothie in Haroon's."

That caught me by surprise. "Really? Rather early on wouldn't you say, since you hadn't met me or even heard my voice. I could have talked like Mickey Mouse."

The little squeak of pleasure that was uniquely Uli came out. "It was your lips, Schnuki. The way they wrapped themselves around that straw. Gott. It made me wish I was standing in the middle of that glass instead of it."

What lips could resist such a compliment? I kissed hers.

We entered the flat and Jitka looked like she wanted to shred something into small, ragged strips, most likely me. Hunger seemed to have that affect on her. But Uli sent her a sharp look and the message was sent through the language of sisterhood that something dreadful had happened.

The flat was already glistening from the positive effects of Jitka's strong hands. Broom, soap, and cloth had been put to good use and there was a noticeable to sparkle to it all.

We were a ravenous trio, so I trotted alone to a tea stall to purchase rice, masala dosas, pakoras, and enough sweets and drinks to call it dinner.

When I returned Jitka looked softer, more sympathetic.

We dined on the masala dosas at the kitchenette table, the chili in the crepes causing tears and smiles to come to our eyes. Uli lit candles and turned it into a pastoral banquet.

No one spoke of Soma or death, the conversation instead turning to the cycle of the rains and the paradox of Varanasi, the opulent grandeur next to grim impoverishment. At one point, through a mist of fatigue, I explained how I viewed it, "It's contrasts and opposites living side by side on equal terms. The whole country is that way really. Anything you can see or feel has an opposite waiting around the corner. Modern and old, bland and spicy, rural and urban. Polytheism next to monotheism and no one bothered by it. Calm or chaotic. Hindus see it as the union of opposites, like night entering day."

Uli's knee rested against mine under the table. With a twinkling smile she added, "Like that phallic stone you see everywhere. The lingum and yoni?"

Jitka summed it up with, "Ya, I vondered why there were so many pecker und pussies everywhere."

I couldn't much to add to that.

Standing at the sink, drying the dishes, I thought about the difficulty of finding a late hour taxi to my villa. I could walk the four blocks if need be, but the weariness in my limbs made the idea unattractive.

Jitka said goodnight with hugs for both of us, and Uli took my hand and led me to the small porch above the yard. She pulled me close and her hips rolling into mine. Tiredness began to slip away as I said, "My world has shifted so quickly, Uli. Pieces of it feel so right. You especially. What Adam talks about; they feel . . . so clear." She didn't say anything, just kissed my neck and slipped her hand under my kurta, along my chest, and down along the flat of my stomach. With her head against my chest, she listened. "The work with my teacher, it's good. Voices tell me it is important. But, there is so much I don't understand, scary things. Soma was murdered, and I have no idea why. The worst part is, I don't even know who to trust or what to do."

She looked thoughtful for a moment, gave a small, very out-of-place giggle and lifted the front of my shirt to nibble on the muscle above my nipple. She bit the skin just hard enough to make me wince. With mischief in her eyes, she said, "Three things my Bhim needs to do, maybe not in this order. But they should be done. First, talk with Sahr und hear her advice. She knows this city und the people. She can help. Second, take me home with you und let me shampoo you. You smell like old river water und sadness. Und third, and most important, make love to me. Tonight."

Forty-Three

Memory is a mysterious entity, receding into shadowed places just when we need it most. Far too often it re-enters an hour after our need for it is gone. It hovers unwanted when we wish nothing more than for it to leave us in peace. But sometimes, sometimes it enters right on cue.

I had forgotten the sensations of cool water and long fingers in my hair, of chamomile soaps and scented shampoos lathered by someone else, of tenderness and love scrubbed along my body. I hadn't kept the memories of loving hands sliding along my thighs, my legs, and the souls of my feet, because I had waged a battle to banish them and won. But when Uliana bathed me that night by candlelight, they all returned like well rehearsed actors--entering right on cue. Every sensation.

We made love in air cooled and freshened by new rains. I touched her with tentative hands at first, and she drew me into her gently and slowly like estuary water. Our rhythms quickened and surged in unison and we rose to a sweet and tumultuous climax.

In the quiet moments and receding waves, as she nestled into my arms, I felt a luscious sense of healing. It increased tenfold when she propped herself on her elbows, looked directly at me and said, "I am here, Bhim, und won't leave until you tell me to."

"That won't happen."

"Good, because I would get very petulant if you do."

"I'll bet you're very pretty when you're petulant."

Squeezing my thigh between hers, she whispered, "You don't want to find out."

I fetched us mint tea and pastries from the kitchen, and

afterwards we made love again, longer, more transcendent, love. As we slipped from wakefulness towards sleep where no nightmares waited, she giggled dreamily, "Ach, I knew I was right. The moment I saw those lips, I knew they would taste like powdered sugar."

The only person reasonably close to being as happy as Uli and me the next morning was Sahr. She had never aligned herself with local mores, preferring to live by her own set of values, and the occasion of my tryst with Uli didn't bother her one bit. Quite the opposite, she couldn't stop smiling. First at Uli, then at me. Even the pall of Soma's death couldn't subdue the lightness in the kitchen that morning.

"Would Memsahib like the incredibly delicious Uttar Pradesh breakfast, or the bland white toast Master Bhim forces me to fix?"

"That was evenly stated, Sahr. No prejudice there," I mumbled into my coffee.

"Sahr, you may fix me whatever you wish," Uli replied, "und please, I mustn't be a memsahib. I think you must have at least thirty years before that title can be used. I am Uliana, Uli to friends, und since we are now friends . . ." She rose to retrieve the carafe of coffee and Sahr waved her back down.

With an undisguised frown in my direction-- the elephant's trunk rearing feistily--Sahr announced, "I will prepare Miss Uli parathas, samosas, dahi, and jalebis, and you, O Great Rajah, get toast."

"Is there any orange marmalade to go with it?"

"Oh yes, that will spice it up nicely."

As she set the steaming bowls in the center of the table in

hopes that I would partake of some of it, Sahr's eyes rested sadly on mine. "I am so sorry about the young widow, Bhimaji. I know she warmed your heart, and you did much for her that will come back to you. It is a horrible custom, this shunning of widows, especially the young ones that might have a chance of re-marrying."

I noticed Uli listening carefully to the conversation. "Thank you. She was warm in my heart, still is. I will miss her greatly, especially her smile."

Sahr clenched her fist. "Such an ugly custom it is. I remember not so far in the past when we widows were expected to put on our best white saris and leap like hysterical fools onto our husband's funeral pyres. Can you imagine such foolishness? In my case, I would have fried next to a sot who was unconscious from sharab before every sunset. Drank himself to death before he was thirty. Pay homage to that drunkard and bake myself like a chapatti for him? Hah, not in this life."

I knew it had been difficult for Sahr when her husband died—more from financial hardship than grief. Her clairvoyance had been her only means of revenue, and in the beginning it was a pittance, but word spread, and eventually it provided well for her and Lalji. She also spoke English, and that made the difference.

Two years after her husband died, she found employment with an elderly British couple who took tea punctually at three, dressed in post-Regency attire, and read Lord Byron and E. M. Forester to each other in the evenings. They adored Sahr. The 'Colonel' and Glinnis were remnants of the British Raj, properly refined and proud. They had been the toast of society in their day. Now their society was each other. The others had all passed. A few years before my arrival, on the 'Colonel's' eighty-fifth birthday, Sahr returned from market to find them both dead from a self-administered poison. It had been in their three-o'clock tea.

Dipping a samosa into fresh yogurt, and smacking my lips loud enough so she would hear, I announced, "Breakfast of the gods, Sahr, and, oh yes, something else. I think I need your advice. Change that, I know I need it."

Instantly she set the honeyed jalebis on the table and sat down. "Advice I have, Bhimaji, especially for you." She winked at Uli.

"Well, I need your prophetic talents to peer into events of the past few days. A card reading with Meghaduta, maybe a séance with your river bhuta."

She looked immediately disappointed, almost crestfallen, which surprised me as I assumed my request would have been well received. Uli noticed the look also and added, "Sahr, Bhim has no one to turn to. There was no sense to Soma's murder und corrupt officials may be involved. He needs your help."

Sahr squeezed Uli's hand and replied, "No, Memsahib, do not misunderstand my look. There is nothing that I would rather do than help my Bhimaji and his premika with the beautiful hair of gold, but you are asking me to look into the past."

Then it hit me—the little fact she had mentioned years ago. My housekeeper looked into the future. "The past is the wrong side of the stars for me," she sighed. "I'm not permitted to ask there. But there are those who see the past as well as I see the future."

"So you do know someone, another nabi, who might be able help? Someone you trust?"

She stared out the window, then at Uli, and the birthmark rumpled deeply. In her eyes I saw hesitancy, then fear. It was odd. Before uttering a word she took our hands, ostensibly to form some barrier against a nosey bhuta that might be floating over our kitchen counters. Her voice dropped. "There is one, and she is no charlatan, but she is . . . " More hesitation.

"Expensive?" I asked.

"No, no. She's less interested in coins than the counterfeits along the river that pocket rupees and roll bones in the dirt. No, this one is very skilled and very powerful. But sometimes she demands payment in strange ways . . . and she isn't one you would care to be indebted to."

Uli smiled, then began frowning, thinking, I believe, that the payment might involve sexual favors. None of it made sense. "What kinds of payment?" I asked.

She answered slowly, "Sometimes she likes to search deeper into one's past than one likes. That is what is said, anyway. We would need to be cautious."

At that instant the bell clanged sharply at the gate. "Tell the teacher we're surfin'. Surfin' USA." Mej's Cockney voice, horribly off-key, blared with the subtlety of a diesel truck horn, and I recalled with a groan that I had committed to a session with him that morning. I looked at Uli. She stared questioningly back. "A friend. Excuse me, this should only take a minute." I rose from the table, breaking the bonds of our triangular. Then, feeling a need to explain more, I said, "It's someone I throw Frisbee with. I forgot that I was supposed to exercise with him this morning."

"Und now you don't want to? You don't want to exercise

anymore? Your legs are broken? You want to become plump und wheeze like an old man when you climb the stairs to my flat? Why? Not because of me, BhimajiMartinScott. I want you strong. Go und play."

With that endearing reprimand all I could think of was sending Sahr off to market and carrying Uli back to bed with me. "No, Ms. Hadersen, it is nothing of the sort. And I believe I have had enough exercise over the last twelve hours to stay in fairly decent shape." She flushed enough to brighten her cheeks nicely. I went to postpone my appointment with Mej.

"Well that's a fooking shame, Bhimster. I was 'oping you and me could burn off the three liters of ale I sucked down last night. Pisspond Brewery of Greater Pukestan. Marvelous shite if you 'aven't tasted it yet."

I pushed open the gate with, "No Mej, really. . . any other time. You know I don't like missing the game, but it's been kind of rough around here lately, and I . . . didn't sleep well last night."

He whistled. "Right-o, Mate. I 'eard about that shite. Locals are all yackin' about it. You know that widow girl well, did you? Bloody nasty way to go." He drew a finger across his throat.

I couldn't recall how many times Mej had seen Soma. I was trying to recall if I'd ever introduced them, when Uli stepped onto the veranda. She had dressed hurriedly but still looked like Danish royalty. Descending the steps, she extended her hand with a curt, "Halo, I'm Uliana Hadersen, an acquaintance of Bhim's."

For the briefest moment Mej looked like he'd been touched by a live wire, but just as quickly regained his comic routine. "Sir

Mejanand Whiton, Milady, and a friend of Bheemer's 'ere is a friend of mine. Especially a friend with eyes like yours. Knock me flat, they could. And definitely, call me Mej." He grinned with a lechery that chaffed me.

"Pleasure to meet you, Mej. I was actually coming to tell Bhim that I think it would be good for him to exercise with you this morning."

"Well, I was just trying to convince 'im of that one meself. See, we already 'ave things in common."

"Yes, I suppose we do." Her voice sounded hollow and, to my ear, frosty.

I cleared my throat. "Well, I'd love to comply with each of you, but I'm not up to it and also have a list of chores to attend to. Tell you what Mej, toss me the blue one and I'll send you on a route into the next cantonment. Day after tomorrow. Sunrise. Okay?"

"Right-o, Mate. But I'm 'olding you to it. No excuses about being blown out from not sleeping." Another look of lechery in Uli's direction. He spun the disc in front of me and sprinted away calling back, "'ey did you 'ear about the skeleton that walked into the bar and ordered a beer and a mop?" For Uli's benefit, I leapt higher than necessary, snatched the disc behind my back and sailed it into an eighty meter arc. Mej jumped spread-legged and caught it flat against his ass. I did miss the dance.

"Show-off," she whispered. Not caring who watched, I slipped my fingers into moistness at the nape of her neck and kissed her.

With the impish smile that I was beginning to recognize, she murmured, "We could go back to the Riverview. It's a little smelly, but the room is paid until this afternoon."

"And miss all the mysteries heating up around here. I'd love to." As I closed the gate I thought of Soma's delicate fingers tugging on the tassel. "But. . ."

"I know, Love. I know," she whispered softly.

Forty-Four

There was no work that morning. C.G. phoned to tell me the obvious; Master and his family were too distraught over Soma's death. Grief had settled on the compound in real and traditional ways. Devi had contacted the authorities to have Soma's body moved to a parlor in preparation for cremation. Clean muslin was sent to join Uli's scarf. Wood and oil was purchased. The right and good things were done for her funeral. Soma's mother-in-law wanted none of the expense and had no reservation in telling any and all how she regarded her dead daughter-in-law. The way she saw it, the girl had had bad karma, and it was better that she was dead.

Uli and I returned to the flat to spend the better part of the morning cleaning and scrubbing-- a form of catharsis for me.

Jitka seemed genuinely happy for her sister and me and announced that she had prepared breakfast from the leftovers of the previous evening. By eleven, however, she was rattling her cage again--food, and it had better come quickly. Uli and I decided that a trip to the central market was in order. Solitude and snuggling were also the list, so I hailed a taxi with tinted windows.

"So, My Handsome Guide, you are taking me to the big market, und I suppose you know all the merchants und they give you the best prices?"

"As a matter of fact, I do. I have privileges. So what would my fair premika like today?"

A note pad appeared from within her over-sized handbag. "Let's see . . . we'll start with mangoes, which in case you are wondering, are my favorite. Then leechees, bananas, papayas. . ." It continued for a minute. "und cheese, milk, und fresh brown eggs." She finished with, "Und I believe a piece of silk would be nice. Something purple."

"That shouldn't take us more than a week."

"Mmm, well, we could still send an errand boy to fetch it und sneak back to the Riverview." She expression got serious. "Bhim, your English friend, have you known him long?"

"Mej? Not that long. Ten or eleven months, I guess. I could tell you didn't find him particularly charming. He can be rather . . . coarse. I didn't like how he spoke around you today." I felt an odd need to apologize for his behavior, but she stopped me.

"That doesn't bother me. It was the way he looked at you that I didn't like."

"Oh?" I laughed. "That's funny, I wasn't really keen on how he looked at you."

We were going into the Chowk district--central and extremely crowded, Varanasi—down the Asi Road to Sonapura, past my villa, and then on for two miles into the city. With each meter it would become more congested. "Uli?"

"Hmmm?" She had settled into my arms to nibble my jaw.

"It will be crowded where we are going. I want you to stay close to me."

"Closer than this." Her tongue found some reflexive part of my ear that sent shivers into my groin.

"No. . .yes. Aah!" Laughing, I managed to say, "Just make certain we don't get separated."

"Never, I want to be loving you too much tonight. What are you making your premika for dinner by the way?"

As we passed my villa I tapped on the partition and motioned our driver to pull to the side. "I need to see what Sahr has found out."

"Do you want me to come with you?"

With a kiss I said, "No, I'll be right back."

Through one of her baffling methods, Sahr had made an appointment for a darshan, a meeting with the nabi. It was supposed to include just Sahr and me, but that wasn't how it turned out.

"She wants both of us to come this sunset. With Uliana," she said.

"What? That is totally out of the question. First of all, it's too soon, and how does she even know who Uli is? Did she ask for her by name?" I knew Sahr was too discreet to have revealed it.

She was fidgeting with the end of her sari, a patent sign of nervousness. "Best not to ask how she knows, but she does. She asked for all three of us. And no, she didn't ask for Miss Uli by name, just asked for the blond woman."

I lay my hand on her jittery fingers. "Okay, send an acceptance message back, however you do that. Where is her place, by the way,?"

Sahr's finger twitched faster. "Near the center of Shivdaspur.

"Oh God, no," I moaned. The last place I wanted to go with Uliana or Sahr was into the heart of the infested squalor of the whore's district. One and a half square kilometers with twelve thousand people, the vast percentage of whom were involved in the flesh trade.

In the taxi I tried politely to explain our dilemma. "I don't think we'll be able to do a lot of shopping for silk this afternoon, and dinner may be a later." There was a rare moment when she couldn't read my thoughts. "And why is that, Liebchen? My shopping list isn't that long."

I had to tell her sooner than later. "We have to go to Shivdaspur, the red light district, this evening. The prostitute's quarters?"

She grinned, but seeing the seriousness of my expression, decided against joking. "Und this red light district, it is like the boring one we have in Copenhagen? Everyone thinks is such eine grose und it is nothing."

"Uli, listen. Shivdas a very ugly, unpleasant part of town. I walked through it once from curiosity and swore I'd never return. I would have gone with Sahr alone, but this . . . woman asked for you also. How she knows about us, I can't guess."

With another grin, she asked, "Do you think she looked into a crystal ball to watch our love-making? That would have been an eyeful."

As we drove up the main road towards the market, a river of humanity began to close in determined waves about us. Hundreds, then thousands, of men in shortened loongis and women in saris, crowded against our doors. The under-fed, the barefoot, the wealthy, and the affluent. Pedi-cabs and autoricks came within inches of our taxi. Dust choked the air. Finally our driver slid the partition open to announce, "Saab, I believe there is funeral or a parade ahead. Possibly it is a political rally. Do you wish that I continue?" Through the windshield I saw what appeared to be a dense mob of Hindus of various sects--unusual enough in itself. Devotees of Shiva and other deities were moving in a semi-organized fashion up the avenue. It wasn't political, it was religious. That was good. Religious processions in Varanasi were usually benign and non-threatening. Usually. Then I heard chanting, and down a side street I saw Muslim protestors, followers of the firebrand Qereshy, marching in a parallel line to the first group. That wasn't good.

I handed our driver fare and a tip and helped Uli from the backseat into the crowd. "Hold my hand and stay close," I whispered. "We'll go down the side lanes to the market. It's close. Keep your hand around your bag."

Avoiding the parades, which had piqued my curiosity, we entered one of the paths feeding into the market. Trays of okra, squash, and rice rested on dazzling fabric on the ground. Purveyors called out, "Saab, bahut acha deal, Memsaab! Sau rupee kilo ke liye." Ignoring the hawkers, I guided us into the main market.

As we emerged, Uli squeezed my hand with delight. The prismatic vitality of it was stunning for me even after a hundred visits. Fruits, vegetables, and legumes were piled in wooden carts and semi-permanent stalls. Urns of milk, cheese, and yogurt stood waist-high next to stacks of clay pots and moistened banana leaves—Varanasi's version of recyclable packaging. The market spread out in a grand, sloppy rectangle. Brasswares, silks, cottons, betel, teas, coffees, and the ever-present beedis and cigarettes, ran in formless sections. Fruits and vegetables of every imaginable shape, size, and color were stacked in tenuous pyramids. Music and a cacophony of bartering surged around us.

We spent an hour and a goodly amount of rupees. My cloth sack filled up first, then the one I purchased for Uli--the first of many small gifts. She, on the other hand, only bought a single gift for me. Just as we were preparing to leave, she asked me to find her a kilo of the best coffee in the bazaar. She was on a mission, she said. I pointed to the exact spot where I would wait nervously until she returned. When she did, it was with the most beautiful fire opal I had seen outside a museum.

"It wouldn't hurt to wear a single piece of jewelry, would it?" she asked as she tugged the strings on the pouch and slid a stone onto my palm. I was overwhelmed. An opal, a flame of vibrant blue surrounded by a teardrop of filigreed gold, hung on a strong chain.

"My god. It's exquisite. You shouldn't have spent so much."

"Yes, I should. I saw it as we passed the gem shop." Fastening it around my neck, beneath the namaghanda, she whispered lustily, "For our passion, Bhim."

Knowing the answer already, I asked, "And how did you know it was my birthstone?"

"How do you think?" She laid her hand across my heart.

"Sahr?"

She just smiled.

Large, dense crowds in Varanasi, you simply learned to accept their inevitability. In my three plus years there I had taken great pleasure in their anonymity. I had also learned to dread them. It depended on their mood, not mine. The multitudes in the bazaars and train stations were marvelous to melt into on normal days. I would retire to a shaded bench and watch as families parted, workers toiled, and merchants bartered. Most days it felt safe, and offered a peek at the great cross-section of Indian existence. Most days, but occasionally the crowds transformed into frightening, undisciplined monsters.

With bags overflowing, I led us back down the side street to the main avenue to hail a taxi. It was getting late, and we were hungry and ready to wash off the dust of the day. I envisioned a naked, fragrant shower with Uli, and a quick meal before taxiing to Shivdaspur for a meeting with the nabi whose name I did not know. But as we turned from the market lanes, we came straight up, face to face with a cordon of forty policemen armed with lathees, bamboo truncheons. The wore uncompromising expressions on their faces, and by the looks of it, they were preparing to launch themselves into the procession of religious devotees we had seen earlier. That parade that was no longer a peaceful group of Hindu devotees, it was an angry mob of Hindus and Muslims together. I pulled Uli quickly back into the obscurity of the side street just as a fusillade of stone and brick flew across the opening. Shouting and cursing exploded, and then, with a single blast of a whistle, the police attacked.

Complete chaos erupted. More whistles shrieked, debris arched and shattered on the road.

With the police charging, the crowd splintered north, and we were suddenly on the south side with everyone scrambling in the opposite direction. It was our opportunity. I tugged on her wrist, and she looked at me with terror, as if rioting mobs were the nascence of her worst nightmares. She froze, and I yelled, "Hold my hand and run."

I had to yank on her wrist to get her moving. We dashed up the avenue as quickly as our over-laden bags would allow, and moments later were enough distance away to stop and catch our breath. I guided us into a nook between an empty vegetable cart and a steel-shuttered building. She was trembling violently. "I hate it. I hate the riots!" Her breath came in gasps, eyes terrified and focused far away.

With my free arm I pulled her close and whispered, "We're safe now, Uli. Safe. It was just a rowdy party of over-zealous merry-makers." I kissed her cheeks and smoothed her hair. "It's okay now. We can go home."

It took a long time for her to calm, which puzzled me. The scene had startled us, but it had been relatively small, and we had been enough distance from it.

I caressed her cheek again, feeling the mannish pride of protection. I liked it almost as much as being a guide and a lover. Then I hailed a taxi.

Jitka greeted us with a sour look until she saw Uli's expression and the cornucopia of food in our sacks. Uli went to shower while I made a salad and heated up some nan and barley soup. Jitka stowed the groceries and set the table, being pleasant enough toward me, though not too talkative. I sensed she was happy for her sister's blossoming relationship with me, and I considered asking a question or two about Uli, but then decided against it. Those were discoveries I wanted to make on my own.

I gave her a condensed, less dramatic, version of the afternoon's events.

Uli appeared from the shower toweling her hair. She had wrapped herself in a man's loongi that just covered her breasts and fell in diaphanous folds to a delicious place along her thighs. Suddenly, I wanted to be closer than that silk, and must have sighed audibly, because she came and kissed me.

"Und I suppose I will again be sleeping here tonight alone?" Jitka tried to look disgruntled, but her expression gave way to an impish smile.

"Svester, Bhim und I have a date tonight, und time only enough for an appetizer. We will eat later und we don't know if we will come back or stay at Bhim's."

"You said so already, Uli. So what is this big appointment?"

"It seems my guide is taking me to the red light district tonight. We are going to the whore's town. Quite exciting, ya?"

Jitka didn't look particularly thrilled that I was taking her sister to the prostitute's neighborhood.

I tried to explain it without painting too unsavory a picture. "We are going to see. . .a fortune-teller tonight. She just happens to live in that part of town."

"A fortune-teller? You two want to know your future when you don't even know where you want to sleep? Maybe she can tell you. Ach. Go. I am happy for you und will be fine. Now let's eat."

I gulped my soup and took a piece nan to the shower with me. Uli came in to help me towel off. "I wanted to see you wearing just the opal," she cooed, "something for me to think about during our date." The loongi slipped to the floor. "Und something for you to think about, too." We laced fingers, eyes lingering for a moment on what we would share later that evening.

When we slid apart, she stood in front of me unabashed. I reached for her hand again. "You are so beautiful, Uliana, like Radha or Parvati. I never. . ."

"Shhh, don't say anything. Just promise to hold me like you did this afternoon and write poetry about us." She kissed me again. "Just that."

"I promise. Lovers will read about us a thousand years from now." I took a deep breath. "We need to go."

Forty-Five

A taxi large enough for the three of us to sit comfortably was on the list of requisites, one with a driver that could get swiftly through evening traffic. We got lucky. As soon as Uli and I stepped onto Asi Road, a gregarious, green-turbaned Sikh hailed us from the window of his cab. "Hallo, Sahib, Memsahib. I am most reverently at your service. Where may I take you this glorious evening? Vinduram Singh I am called, Vin by my good customers." This was all announced in English, through the window before the car had pulled to the curb.

"Namaskar, Brother Vin," I said cheerily. "You may take us down Shivanan Avenue to South Nagpur, There we will pick up one more. Then you may take us to Shivdaspur as quickly as your fine car can get us there."

"All this is I can do with pleasure, Sahib. And I will not venture to ask why you wish to go to such a section of the city at this time of the day." His eyes met mine in the mirror.

"That is good, Vin. Because I would not venture to tell you."

Vin was good to his word. He moved us quickly down the avenue, detoured around two blocks of thickening traffic, and brought us to my gate punctually. As I entered, Lalji approached. His normally infectious grin was missing, replaced by a melancholy I'd rarely seen before.

"Lalji? Is everything all right?"

"Saab. . .I. . ." Words caught in his throat. "It is . . . so horrible about the widow. She was so pretty, and should not have died. She . . . She just needed someone good."

Suddenly I understood, and it astounded me. Lalji had had feelings for Soma, and in all our time together, I had failed to notice. He'd not spoken a single word to her, and it had me wondering if was from shyness or the fact that she was a widow.

The rims of his eyes filled and he blinked back tears and croaked, "I am sorry, Saab. I do not know what has happened to me." A fleck of grin returned and his shoulders drooped just enough for me to notice. "Perhaps I am coming down with illness and need a day of rest to regain my strength."

Sahr entered just then from the side of the villa and Lalji's shoulders straightened like one of the Queen's Guard. She eyed him skeptically.

Her sari was a shade of pale ivory, the shawl drawn over freshly washed hair. There wasn't a single piece of jewelry, make-up, or tilaka powder. I noticed she was breathing in a deep, even rhythm, which I assumed was part of a calming routine. Whether it was for meeting with the nabi or for simply entering into Shivdaspur, I didn't know.

She set her hands on her hips and spoke quickly to Lalji. "You will lock these doors, leave the kitchen and salon lights on, lock the gate and sit on that middle step until our return." A small, but menacing finger wagged at him. "And you will not, under any circumstances roll your scrawny legs into that hammock." Her finger swiveled toward the hanging bed. "Lalji?"

His head wagged in perfect time with her finger. "No sleeping, Maam. Only my best duties as night watchman."

"That is the answer I wish to hear, and I don't need to remind what will happen should you forget."

The bandaged pinky that desperately needed re-dressing, flew instinctively to the side of his head. "No, Maam. I know what would happen."

Vin opened the door in a chivalrous motion, asking if Sahr wished to sit in the front. "I have a fine working radio for the music," he added as an incentive. With an stern nod she settled herself onto the vinyl.

I slid in next to Uli with the ridiculous feeling that I was going on a double date. I lay my head back onto her shoulder and drifted into the scent of her patchouli and perfume.

Vin chattered like a mynah, green turban bobbing with every word. Sahr stared silently through the windshield. "You know, I grew up in this city," he chirped. "Born here, raised here, apprenticed in the fine art of taxiing here, but it has changed so. Look at these streets, so crowded they are now. How can a driver be expected to make six trips a day in a car like this, much less the twenty he needs to feed a family. Not that I have a family. I am unmarried, you know. And you bahina, you are Benarsi?" The turban rotated jovially towards Sahr. I couldn't see her birthmark from the back seat, but I knew it had scrunched into a warning scowl. Without answering, she turned and continued staring out the windshield.

After a few more unsuccessful attempts to engage her in some form, any form, of conversation, Vin caught my gaze in the mirror. "Yes, Sahib. Most definitely this city is changing. Why just this afternoon I am taking a rather obese fellow, who tipped quite miserably I might add, to the Chowk Market and a riot springs up in right front of my bumper. Folliticians and holy men it was. Imagine, holy men in a holy city, rioting."

I felt Uli tense.

"We saw them also," I replied evenly. "What was it about? It looked like Hindu and Muslim sects together."

"Oh yes, Sahib. Even Christians. All different groups, it was.

But it was the hooligans in the mix who got everyone riled up over some chap talking on the Ghats. Foolishness."

Uli leaned forward. "What man talking on the Ghats."

Vin glanced to see if Sahr was paying heed to his ability to be so well informed. "Some man has been making lectures, you know, and the priests organized a walk in support of traditional Hindu beliefs, or some such nonsense. Then the cabinet minister Qereshy called for his Muslims to object to something. Trouble-makers joined in and riots start. Those young fools are always the first to pick up a rock when the police arrive."

We had missed Adam's sermon that afternoon, but I had to assume it was as inflammatory as the previous day. It worried me. Small riots had a way of magnifying. "Do you know what this man talked about?" I asked.

The turban wagged assertively. "My customers tell me he is selling a new religion." Our eyes connected again in the mirror. "But perhaps new religion is not a bad thing. The old-timers would disagree, but not me."

Uli replied, "We know this man, und he is not talking about religion. It is about making our world better. That can't be wrong." I could tell she was irritated, or maybe frustrated. I was just concerned.

We snaked our way through a maze of narrow cobblestoned lanes until Vin found a space wide enough to open the passenger doors fully. Faster than I imagined possible, he had Sahr's open and a hand extended to help her out. To my surprise, she took it. As I was settling the fare, she asked rather icily, "Mr. Vinduram Singh, It is said that a proper Sikh does not imbibe alcohol or swear. Is that true for you?"

Vin glanced at me for help. My look told him to tread

carefully. "Ah . . .well, I have been known to sip a glass of wine on the rare occasion, Maam. But that was in my ill-spent youth. Now, I am much too busy for such frivolity. Clean as Himalayan snows I am now." He tapped his chest to illustrate that purity.

"Then a bright light will shine upon your future, Mr. Singh." And with a perceptible sparkle in her smile, she turned towards the darkness of Shivdaspur. Uli and I followed as the last of the sun's rays disappeared behind a layer of clouds on the horizon We were right on time.

Forty-Six

The dominant first impression was the color of lips. Red. Entering from the side street, we were immediately struck by the vibrancy and variation of red. Fire engine, cherry, flame, and grenadine, all moistened with hungry tongues. Then you saw the eyes, vacant like street dogs, and you looked quickly down to the cobbled stone and gray puddles before your feet.

I took Uli's hand.

At first it was just women. Along the outer lanes the jaded veterans casually sized up our disparate trio. Some stood with hands set casually on hips, others sat sullenly under bare bulbs in the doorways of musty two-story hovels. Their cheeks were dusted with bright circles of rouge--orange or crimson. I had to assume we didn't present ourselves as customers, but from habit they called quietly, seductively to us, and it didn't seem to matter that Uli and Sahr were women. One lifted her chola to expose wilted breasts, another the hem of her sari. Every debauchment was offered, prices were cheap.

Then you noticed the smell. Rancid garbage and excrement assailed the nostrils.

Pimps, soiled and grimy, approached with whispers and dodging looks. Sahr backed them away with a cold stare.

We moved deeper into the jumble of tin-roofed shacks.

A ghostly melody from a sitar drifted from a radio or music player in one of the larger buildings, and below the resonation of strings I could make out animal gruntings and the rhythmic slapping of skin upon skin. Uliana's fingers laced into mine. I could hear her breathing, shallow but distinct.

As we stepped around an oil splattered puddle, I thought, What in God's name am doing bringing her here? Do I truly think some old hag is going to look at my palm and tell me what happened to Soma? It isn't going to happen, Bhim. You're fooling yourself. I sighed and kept walking forward.

We passed into the heart of the quarter and an eerie variation began to grow like mold. Girls of indeterminable age sat on low stools with legs splayed, drugged and shivering with dread. Boys, arrayed in garish skirts and faces painted in clown-like colors, mumbled fees and services. Drugged voices. I wrapped my arm about Uliana, thankful that she couldn't understand the language. "Mein Gott, Bhim," was all she said.

And everywhere, if you dared to look, you saw emptiness in the windows of their souls. The eyes, even in the young, were vacuous and hungry.

As we walked, Sahr was the only one that looked directly at the prostitutes. She had removed the shawl from her head—it's white radiating against the gloom of the doorways—and kept repeating an odd Hindustani mantra. "The light in your heart is the love of God. The light in your heart is the love of God."

Then she abruptly halted at a dingy wall with a small door set crookedly on the right side. She spoke in rapid dialect to a haughty-looking woman smoking a beedee against the wall. "Is this the place of Kaliduna, the nabi of Shivdas?"

The woman took a long pull on her cigarette and flicked it onto the stones at our feet. I saw her triceps flex and knew instantly she wasn't a woman. She was male. "What do you want of the nabi bitch, old woman? She doesn't sell spells to cow dung like you."

Sahr, with surprising speed, landed an open palm squarely on the transvestite's ear. I had seen her clip Lalji before, but nothing like this. Clearly she had anticipated the response. I also knew from my years of sparring that she had likely just perforated the man's eardrum. He howled and fell to the ground to pull painfully at his lobe.

"That was a simple question I posed, Child. Answer it with respect or feel the force of my own spells." I saw him glance up from his hunched position with venom. He saw me step closer and the meaning of Sahrs' warning began to sink in. Menacing intention flickered out.

"Perhaps the nabi witch lives here. How would I know?"

"You know, boy, and unless you find your memory quickly you will feel the pain of this nabi."

The transvestite, still holding his ear, looked more carefully, saw her birthmark and the cold stare in her eyes, and understood that he had miscalculated. It was ill-considered to cross a nabi, but crossing a powerful one was simply stupid.

"Ji han, Mata. She lives here." He crooked his thumb towards the door behind him and stepped submissively to the side and back into the shadows.

Sahr tapped on the wooden panel. "That is good, Child, because we are expected."

Uliana was frightened. The reality of where we were and the uncertainty of what we were entering made her tremble visibly. She shrank away as the door opened. "Bhim, it doesn't feel right. I, I don't know if I can do this." The ingress was nearly pitch-black, illuminated only by a flickering of unseen candles further in.

A voice, raspy with age, commanded, "Enter and close the door."

Trying to lighten her mood. "Guess I'm being a pretty lousy

tour guide tonight. How about dinner and a movie when we're done?"

Her tiny smile flickered as we stepped inside.

Forty-Seven

Kaliduna, the Nabi of Shivdaspur, looked exactly like what I expected. I'd painted a good picture of her in my head and needed to retouch only a few details when I saw her in the flesh. She appeared to be as old as Varanasi itself, with strands of sparse hair that hung like gray corn silk to her waist. As my eyes adjusted to the muted light, I saw Uliana looking with horror at the woman's fingernails--seven inches of curled yellow grime. I squeezed Uli's hand tightly and whispered, "It's okay."

Hearing my voice, the woman hissed, "Nahin." I pressed my lips together.

The room was stifling, a sweatbox of scraps of paper and rotted fruit peelings. An obscene odor, like burnt hair, hung in the air. Jars of powders and translucent liquids leaned haphazardly in the corners and below the cot against the back wall. The only space that had any semblance of perspicuity was about the wooden table in the center of the room. Four chairs beckoned from each side.

Sahr said something to the nabi in what I was knew was Farsi, a language I understood only fragments of. The old woman answered her in biting, negative monosyllables. Sahr persisted and the old woman responded in the same demanding tone. Unexpectedly, the witch hissed and rattled off a string of invectives in Farsi again. Her use of the language made me wonder if she were Pakistani or Afghani. Sahr began arguing vehemently, to which the old woman flashed her nails like a puma and grunted a reluctant agreement. The rupees I had handed Sahr at the villa were pressed into the woman's hand; the nails curled like spider legs around them.

For some inexplicable reason the nabi then looked directly at me. Her eyes were clouded with thick cataracts-- sightless orbs that didn't blink. But when she looked at Uliana, the way she stared gave me the peculiar feeling that she was seeing precisely what she wished to see. Maybe she possessed a form of alternate vision, or maybe she just sensed Uli's untainted beauty so out of place in her hideous lair. It unnerved me enough that I shifted closer to Uli.

"Baitho!" Sit! Back to commands in Hindi. I quickly pulled out two chairs to do the old woman's bidding. She shuffled off to her jars and began selecting liquids. Holding them one by one close to her milky eyes. She squinted and grunted at the refracted light passing through them. Then she began measuring and ladling with small tin cups.

Once the three of us were seated, Sahr smiled and explained in English, "You may breathe now, talk if you wish. There was a tense moment between us, a small battle of wills, but it is done now. She demanded that I join in the vision rendering, and that would not do at all. Very unwise for me to be in her sway even for a short time. She could drain me like a vampire and suck my powers into hers. It is a typical, nasty trick played upon the inexperienced, but when she realized I was onto her, she backed down. I asked her to do a reading of the past with her cards, but she refused. It is too bad. I would have liked to see how it is done. They say it is backwards and upside down from mine. Anyway, tonight she will use the taralakala, the black liquid." That did little to reassure Uli or me.

She grasped our hands and smiled, "I've given her your questions, Bhimaji, without telling the reasons. I wish I could tell you how this tarakala works, but the old hag reveals nothing." A tender squeeze. "So, my children, are ready?"

I shook my head. "Honestly, Sahr, probably not. In English there a good word for this. Creepy. The whole thing makes gives me the creeps, but if she can shed details about Soma, or the cave, or even what pawn shop my computer might be in, then I guess I can handle it."

I glanced at Uli, who looked even more nervous in the candlelight. She asked, "Why does she want me here? Is she going to ask me about the past?" The fear in her voice upset me enough to consider packing the whole thing in and leaving. The money I had handed over was a pittance and meant nothing. I said as much.

"No. Bhim," Uli whispered. "We can't do that. You need to know,"

The nabi, after much selecting, measuring and stirring, parsed by occasional grunts of satisfaction, placed a large shallow bowl in the center of the table. The mixture was viscous with just enough fluidity to call it liquid. It looked like coagulating gelatin, and she must have culled every disgusting object in her collection into the recipe. Twigs and leaves clung to bits of fur and bone, and in the dim light I swore I saw a shred of white flesh. "Fingers," she hissed in Farsi, pointing. "Fingers in the middle, and do not touch the sides with the palms." Sahr translated the nabi's instructions into English. Uliana and I reluctantly obeyed. "Close your eyes. Now!"

Like a liquid Ouija board, I smiled reassuringly at Uli, who looked petrified as her nails disappeared under the surface next to the nabi's claws. I slid closer so our forearms might touch and closed my eyes.

The old woman began slowly, chanting a litany, ostensibly to summon the paranormal forces. Her mantra sounded like nonsense, but as when Sahr rendered her own visions, I kept an open mind--a skeptic waiting to be converted.

The skepticism vanished when the liquid began to warm.

The old woman moaned. From pain or pleasure? I felt Uli stirring uneasily next to me. "From the blackness of the liquor let her rise. Let her rise and enter. Give way guardians and let her speak." Sahr's whispered translations trailed the nabi's like echos. The witch repeated the request a second and third time. "Let her rise. . ." The gelatin was now heated almost to a level of discomfort, and then to my astonishment the bowl began to quiver, the table trembled. "Give way guardians and let her speak."

There was a vibration and a rumble like thunder coiled around us. It felt as if the entire room was struggling under compressed air. "Ssssst. . . I come" A voice, not Sahr's nor the Kaliduna's, nor even human, spoke. And in the center of my inner sight, with my eyes closed firmly, an enormous serpent--a flared cobra--rose like a massive cable. Its hood pushed to the horizons; its presence in my mind, in my vision, was as real as the heat in the room. Uli moaned and I knew it had appeared to her too.

The nabi spoke in Farsi with a tone of timid reverence. Sahr translated, "Let the Bhujanga speak. Let her tell of the days beyond, hours that have come and gone. Let her speak of the man they call Bhim, the vidyarthi of Jatanaka Devamukti."

Then, like thundering waterfall inside my head, a woman's voice hissed in English, "Ssssst. . ..ssssadness. Death. Sssadness and death." I tensed, fearing what I felt was impending, a forced viewing of Lilia or Soma dying. "Ghosts, the ghosts of two women, their years only forty, they whisper of blood and death."

"The younger one, how did she die, Bhujanga? Speak to us."

The hood flared and the eyes of the beast penetrated my vision. "By the blade and fists of stone. By the talons of evil."

"Speak of the knife, Bhujanga. Tell us of it."

"Sharp as the sickle, cold as the moon. Breath and life it sliced like wheat. Death's face washed by rain."

"What hand held the knife, Bhujanga? Who's face?"

"Bird of prey, the hunter at night. He with the talons of death. The lover of confusion and the thick-witted wielder of chaos."

" Bhujanga. Speak. Tell us the name of the bird of prey."

"Sssst. . ." The hood spread, filling to the horizons of my inner world. In that moment only the serpent and I existed. "The master of puppets. The master of diversion. The PuppetMaster"

My breath was sucked away. The PuppetMaster, not Ralki? It wasn't possible. My mind spun.

"There is a cave in the rock beyond Sarnath. How did it fall, Bhujanga?"

I barely heard the answer, my mind still reeking from the previous answer. The PuppetMaster! How could Soma's murderer be a faceless name in the periodicals, a supposition of the media and intelligence agencies? It made no sense? She was light-years from the disputes of nations or ideologies.

"All is not as it seems. The earth trembled from within, from a chasm deep." That answer drew me back into the vision.

"Was the rock made to fall? Done by the hands of men?"

"Yes, but they did not wish it so. Like a string plucked to hard, the vibration swelled and could not be controlled. The ringed finger of the PuppetMaster guided it."

Questions and answers were assailing me too quickly. Riddles drifted like dandelion seed.

Then the voice halted abruptly, and I heard Sahr hiss emphatically, "You cannot ask it."

The nabi taunted, "It it is our agreement, Dasa. I will ask what I will."

"I am not your slave old woman," Sahr snapped. "And you will not ask."

In Hindi I heard, "Bhujanga, what of the woman they call Uliana?" Sahr fell silent at the question and then began translating, hesitating on each word,

"Serpent, tell us of the woman called Uliana."

Uli moaned, "No!"

"Ssssst. . .sticks. Sticks thrust into the nests of a million hornets. The twelve faces of Mohammad. It was she that stirred them, she that beckoned the flood and the tide of death. She, the yeast that made the poison rise." At the uttered name of Mohammad I felt Uliana go limp.

Good God, I thought. What the hell is this?

Uli's arm slumped, her hand slipped from mine. There was a crash of wood and stone. I screamed, "Enough!" Instantly the enormous hood folded like a curtain upon itself and the serpent disappeared. My eyes jerked open to see Uli lying on the floor.

My heart froze, brain pounded in confusion--too much like Lilia curled on a carpet below another table a lifetime ago.

For a breath I sat paralyzed, unable to wrench myself completely from the spell of the snake. Then I dropped to the floor and cradled her into my arms and held her against my chest. "Uli, please, please." I kissed her hair, her eyelids, her mouth. Then a soft moan issued from her lips. I kissed them again and spoke softly in her ear. "I'm here, Uli. Bhim is here. Come back to me."

One eye opened, her chin drooped for a heartbeat, then both pupils focused on me. With a weak smile, she asked, "Can we go home now?"

Forty-Eight

I was angry enough to strangle the Kaliduna, or at least snap a few of her ancient joints. Sahr placed a hand on my chest to provide a measure of common sense. I cooled, though still angry enough to snarl, "You crossed the line old witch. You didn't need to look there and ask that."

The nabi sat hunched in one of her wooden chairs looking less witch-like and merely wrinkled and old. Her chalky eyes rested on mine. "You sought your answers, Vidyarthi. The bhuta doesn't care whether you like the answers or not. Leave my place and go back to your own nest, little bird."

I glared a final time ate her and pulled Uli and Sahr through the door and out into a pounding rain.

Our walk back out of Shivdaspur was done in near complete silence. Everything reeled from the eeriness of the séance, the puzzles, and the ugly climax. None of us had the strength to verbally compete with the downpour. We walked slowly, with heaviness. Even Sahr's indomitable spirit was down. I think she felt terrible about setting it up and taking us to the den of the nabi. Twice she inquired as to our well-being, and I answered that we were still alive and would talk later about what had happened. After that she fell silent. I pulled a listless Uli close to me under the umbrella and guided her through the lanes. Her warmth, the wetness in her hair, revived my spirits some, but the passage was still somber.

Because of the downpour, the lanes were mostly deserted, but at each curve I felt strangers' eyes peering at us through shuttered windows and cracked doors. Once I spun and thought I saw, far back, deep in the dark-gray, a smoking a beedee, and a pair of painted lips grinning wickedly.

Exiting Shivdaspur felt like the lifting of clouds, and in truth, by the time we arrived at the Chaitganj crossing, the stars were sparkling, and the rain had ceased.

Sahr kissed Uli's cheek. "I am so sorry, Child. I should not have agreed to the Kaliduna's demands. It was my mistake."

I answered, "No, Sahr. It was my mistake. I shouldn't have let any of it happen."

Uli kissed Sahr's cheek in return and said, "There was no mistake. The truth of the past came out."

I was exhausted and famished and wished only for a quiet dinner with Uli. I went to hail an autorick to take Sahr home, and before I could lift my hand, a large, suspiciously familiar taxi rolled to the curb from the opposite direction. Vinduram Singh's green turban poked out the window. "I am at your service, Sahib. The day meter is still running for you, your memsahib, and of course for the regal lady with the sari the color of fresh cream."

I looked at Sahr whose arched eyebrows said, 'why not.'

Vinduram offered Sahr the front seat again but she plopped herself stubbornly in the back. With a reminder to me that her best almond kheer dessert was waiting in the refrigerator, she and Vinduram disappeared down the avenue.

"Do you know what is the Jyllands-Posten?" Uli asked me in a cheerless voice. We were sitting in the back of a small Bengali restaurant sharing a dish of Panaspatu Curry. I chose the cafe less for the menu than the tall booths that provided privacy. I needed to feel her body touching mine and hear what she needed to say.

It had taken an appetizer, a second glass of house wine, and some baked-cheese nan before she had the strength or courage to begin.

"No," I answered, though it sounded vaguely familiar.

The sadness in her accent shook me. "It is a newspaper, Bhim, the biggest in Denmark. My father has worked for Jyllands-Posten for thirty years." Her fingers slid nervously around her wineglass. "He is a, how do you call it? A caricaturist. A political cartoonist." I must have looked confused, because she said, "Do you remember the events of last September?"

Remembering headlines wasn't my strong point. I had barricaded myself from world events, preferring my books and a bit of local news from the morning paper. September, I remember, hadn't been a kind month for many. Hurricane Katrina had torn a few million lives apart. On my side of the world, an outbreak of encephalitis had killed seven-hundred in one of the destitute sections of Varanasi. Islamic riots had swept through almost all the northern provinces in September, and Yakoob Qereshy, had offered fifty-one crore rupees, eleven million dollars, for the beheading of any cartoonists from . . . It slammed into me. The twelve faces of Muhammad—twelve cartoons that had sparked Muslim riots around the world. They had been published by the newspaper Jyllands-Posten.

"Your father? He works. . .?"

"for the paper." She answered without looking up from her wine. "His drawing was one of the twelve."

"Oh my God, Uli." Now I understood the implications. "How are you. . . connected? Besides being his daughter?

"I helped him design it . . . No, that is not the best way to say it. He asked me for my ideas one morning und I was feeling humorous. We made silly jokes at breakfast and laughed. An idea of mine seemed especially funny to him; it became his drawing and Jylands accepted it. Does that make sense? Was it such a bad thing to do, Bhim?" Her eyes began to fill with tears.

"Yes, it makes sense, Uli, and no, it wasn't a bad thing." I kissed a tear rolling down her cheek. "A daughter's laughter with her father is a good thing. Honestly, I think the reaction was just a lot of overly-sensitive types convincing themselves that they had to be offended." I brushed away another tear.

"So now you know." She said.

I smiled. "Right. Now I know, and it doesn't matter or keep me from wanting you a fraction less." I kissed her knuckles and looked into the ocean-blue of her eyes. "But . . . it does frighten me. Why . . . how did you decide to come here, to this part of the world? I mean, I am really, really glad you did, but why here? It isn't the safest place you could have chosen."

Her eyes misted with more pain. "You, more than anyone else, may be able to understand. After the riots, I was so tormented and sad that I had caused hurt. I knew in my head I wasn't to blame really, but my whole life I've seen myself as a good person and thought of myself as . . . kind. I liked reading about those who gave of themselves, Christ, and Buddha, and Gandhi. I tried to walk a good path. Coming here seemed like it might be a way to take away some of the pain, or guilt, whatever it was. I don't know. At times I think I just needed to say I was sorry and maybe do something good. I knew I had to leave Tönder, because it felt like every person in the city was watching me." Her sentences were flowing rapidly. She was correct. I understood how she felt about leaving.

"But you knew how dangerous it could be?"

"I don't know. Maybe I was naïve, but once we were out of Tönder, I actually felt safer. Just another nomad with an over-stuffed backpack and a protective sister. No one knew me or what I had done. Not until tonight."

That thought disturbed me greatly. Someone did know.

I knew then the cause of her sadness and what I had seen in her eyes at times, why the riots that afternoon had terrified her so. I knew the reason for the sporadic despondency, and I was going to try to make it right. "No one will know of it, Uli. I'll be here to make sure of that, and every day will get better."

She smiled for the first time since we had left the flat. "When you say things like that, Lover, I understand the reason I am here. I was supposed to find you, und finding you must be right, because it feels so damned good. What did you say this dish is called?"

"Panaspatu Curry, and it does feel good, Uli."

Remembering Sahr's almond kheer at home, we declined dessert and only took demitasses of thick coffee after the meal. That was when we spoke of the details of the nabi's vision.

"That creature, whatever it was, felt so real, Bhim. Gott, it terrified me, like it was grabbing me inside."

"I felt that way too. Up to now I've been more a skeptic than believer in Sahr's spirit world. Maybe I believed a little bit of it. I mean, being around her, I've sort of had to. But tonight was . . . real. When we were coming out of Shivdaspur in the rain I toyed with the idea that it had been hypnotism, but I know it wasn't."

She took a sip of coffee. "Can you remember it all?"

"Most of it, if I think hard enough. It got crazy confusing at the end, and I don't understand that part about Soma being killed by the PuppetMaster. That doesn't make any sense. I've spent two days pinning this on Madru Ralki or one of his hoodlums. Now I'm being told it's a phantom they write about in the media."

She stared into the swirling coffee between her fingers. "What did she . . . it was a she, wasn't it? What did she mean when she talked about a bird of prey?"

I tried to recall the exact words. "Let's see. First, a bhujanga is a cobra, and I heard a woman's voice too, so I would say that it was a female cobra talking to us . . . as weird as that sounds." Uli nodded. "And I'm pretty certain she was talking about an owl."

She straightened. "An owl? Why an owl?"

"Two reasons. The bhujanga said the bird hunted at night and was the 'thick-witted servant of chaos."

"I thought owls were supposed to be wise."

"Not here. In most of the myths they're portrayed more like jack-asses. A little on the stupid side, if you know what I mean. I don't think this Sutradharak is stupid, though, just sadistic."

She nodded. "And the cave-in?"

"That was another big surprise. If I heard it correctly, it was unintentional, started somewhere deeper down. How did she describe it? Like a . . ."

Uli finished the quote, "like the plucked string, the vibrations could not be controlled. That sounds like an accident, but she said the PuppetMaster guided it."

I agreed, but it didn't make it any clearer.

Both of us sensed it was time to put it to rest, to stop

thinking of riots and Shivdaspur and petulant transvestites with beedies. Still, she asked the final question, "So, Lover, did you think they are somehow connected? Soma's death, the PuppetMaster, and the cave-in?"

"Before tonight, Madru Ralki was sitting in the middle of it in my mind. Now I have to think differently. I would have scoffed at this darshan business, the voice of the cobra, but the damn thing knew details that only you or I could know. . ."

She daintily licked the last drop of her coffee and looked at me sadly. "I was going to tell you, you know, tonight actually."

"About your father?"

"Um hmm. And my part in it, because there couldn't be such a big piece unknown between us. You told me who Martin was; I wanted you to know who Uliana is."

I took her hand and nibbled on a finger. "I already know who Uliana is. And both Martin and Bhim want her."

The impish smile rose back up through the sadness. "Und which one of those cute lilliputs wishes to carry me back to his villa and make love to me until the sun rises?"

The taxi ride back was all that I could wish for--cozy, safe, and with a driver completely unconcerned with his two amorous passengers in the back. Darkened temples and clapboard hovels in silence as Uli and I touched and kissed with renewed tenderness. A new understanding of who we were had been formed, and without a word spoken, we reassured each other that we were still right there in each other's lives.

Lalji hadn't moved. He was sitting on the same bottom step repeating to himself that he really was a diligent night watchman. He ushered us through the gate solemnly and added another surprise to the evening.

Sahr hadn't returned.

"No Saab, Maam has not returned to our house. I have been waiting this whole time for my supper, and you see, I have not moved from my post. Do you wish for me to go look for her? Just say the word and I will have fifteen strong men searching house by house."

I knew Lalji's friends. The only one that I might use that adjective for was the one that had cracked his pinky. "No, I think she is fine. She may even be out enjoying herself for once. If she doesn't return by midnight, we'll call on your search party. Go get your supper, and I'll lock up the front. Sahr can come through the back with her own key."

As he shuffled towards the path along the side of the house, I suddenly felt rather sorry for my watchman. He really did need someone in his life.

Uli and I ate the almond kheer and sipped cups of green tea. She had recovered well enough from the evening's ordeals to sit on my lap and smear the almond paste and cream onto my lip and nibble her way downward. Just about the time I was ready to recite my finest romantic doggerel and dance us off to bed, she surprised me with an unexpected question. "So, My Sukkerlips, you told me about the cave und the cures with the plants und litle points." She nibbled an earlobe. "But you never told me what it is for."

Shivering in my groin, I slipped my hands up the back of her blouse to cup her shoulder blades. "That's because we still don't know *what* it is."

She painted the end of my nose with the last of the kheer and licked it off. "Und why not? Three brilliant pundits like yourselves. Tell me the clues. I'll figure it out."

"Is it the almond kheer that is making you so feisty?"

"It's making me more than that."

"Alright, let me think. This is from memory, so give me a dew seconds." I'd recited the lines in Sanskrit enough to have them committed. It just needed our team's best translation.

'When the man's self thins the like reeds in a summer sun;

And his waters pour out like a swollen stream,

And none replenished will slake his thirst;

When his water is sweet as the juice of the cane,

 And yields a fragrance as sweet.

Then the man's self lightens and pales like the moon,

And in the dawn the self thereupon dies.'

She asked me to repeat it, and then asked, "This word 'self', what does it mean exactly? Is it his soul?"

"We aren't entirely sure. The original text used the word 'atman,' which can have a few different meanings, but it usually translates as soul or spirit. Why?"

"Could it mean his physical body?"

I frowned. "I suppose so. It's a stretch from the usual meaning."

"Und when it talks about water, could that mean his urine?"

"Another small stretch. We were thinking more along the lines of perspiration, like a fever, but we've encountered stranger metaphors. What's your idea?"

"Well, I think about it this way. His body gets thin und his urine comes out smelling sweet. He gets thirstier, paler und thinner, und then dies. My grandfather had that. It's diabetes.

Ketosis makes the urine smell like syrup while the body gets eaten away."

If she hadn't been perched on my lap I would have leapt around the counters and swung from the light fixture. "Damn, damn, damn!"

"You're repeating yourself, Lover."

"My God, that's it. It's got to be, and I'll bet Kangri knew it, too. He just wanted me to discover it for myself. Damn. Can you imagine if we've really found something authentic. I need to call Masterji and C.G. And Kangri. This is incredible. You're incredible."

"Yes. I am." She wrapped her arms around my neck. "Happy to be of assistance, My Handsome Guide, but it's too late to make calls. I have a better idea. Carry me to your room, lay me down beneath the fan, und show me how much you really appreciate me."

I lifted her into my arms.

It had been a long day of riots, and fear, and revelations—a day of dispiriting ugliness and sad stories of the past. Uli had said during our dinner that fate had drawn us together. That sounded rather like Sahr's constellations. I wasn't certain, but whatever it was, it felt right. Those strange events of that day ended with lips smeared of almond kheer, and sweet kisses, and as all such evenings should end, it faded gently into undiluted passion.

Forty-Nine

The PuppetMaster gathered information like a squirrel in autumn—every item gleaned from a cadre of shiftless, faceless informants. Intelligence was transmitted to him via a vast network of carefully compensated individuals totally unaware of the source of their stipends—taxi spies, stall merchants, mendicants at the river, boat handlers. Most were malefactors from the dregs of the city—thieves, addicts, and pimps who knew how to avoid authority and melt into the cracks unseen. They garnered tidbits, trivial or vital, and passed them upward to superiors, who passed them along to until they reached the three trusted associates of the Puppetmaster. From them he learned all he needed of the region.

It was in this cumulate manner that he first began to hear reports of the holy man at the river. Initial reports made him out to be the Madman of Manikarnika--a common lunatic spewing nonsense, and there were certainly plenty of those in that loathsome place. He ignored the news as unreliable drivel. But the reports continued and began to shift in ways that intrigued him. This lunatic was, it seemed, drawing larger crowds, and perhaps he wasn't such a lunatic. Sutradharak learned that the man possessed a level of intelligence higher than originally assumed. And if he knew how to draw a crowd, he was not totally useless to the PuppetMaster's plans.

Then, and unexpected order came from above. His superiors needed an additional, unscheduled event, and Sutradharak had to devise something quickly, to improvise. It wasn't in his nature to do things quickly, but he knew better than to refuse his employers. His thoughts came around to this speaker at the Ghats. Perhaps he could be a catalyst. With this in mind, the

PuppetMaster dressed once again as Ahkmed Jamil, goat-products merchant.

Basic principals. To survive in his shifting, tenuous world he needed to follow basics principals to the letter. Disguise wasn't merely a matter of dabbing on make-up and changing attire; it required creating an entire persona, every detail perfected, every voice inflection, accent, mannerism, and history. In this way, he had given birth to two people, completely separate and each with its own purpose. One allowed him to blend into city and conduct the intricate business of terror; the other was an escape hatch that also allowed him to travel freely through the country. When he wished to blend in, he became the goat's milk merchant, a character so commonplace no one would think twice about who he was.

The only risk came in the very unlikely possibility that someone might recognize him as both, connecting the two. The numerical probability of that, he decided, was far too low for concern.

As the merchant Ahkmed, he set off for the Ghats to see for himself what this "holy man" was all about. With him were a bloated hide bag, and an umbrella to shield his face from sun, rain, and scrutiny. Dark glasses obscured his eyes, a felt cap concealed his hair, and the umbrella was angled expressly across his face.

From a carefully selected position on the upper bank of Manikarnika, Sutradharak listened with a curious smile. He made no comments about the sermon to those around him, and conversed only casually with a few others to gather information. The most cogent fact he learned was that the speaker was a harijan. He was also a genius, or something close to it.

Sutradharak saw this quickly, and also noted the man's influence on the crowd. This orator, with all his idealistic pig-shit, just might be a useful. If the timing coincides, a small diversion.

From his remote viewing place he witnessed a most amusing sight; a ferenghi with a shiny bicycle arrived and was summoned like a houseguest up to the harijan's inner circle. It almost started him laughing. It was oddly humorous after all.

Moments after the speech, as he was moving up the path through the gullies to the loft, the unthinkable happened—an event of the slimmest of chances, that should never have occurred. But it did. As he was crossing the gulley behind the Golden Temple, in the tightest quarters of the lane, he bumped against a young woman and continued on. He had been looking down and had not seen her face. But she had seen his. Then he heard his name—his other name. It was called out in a puzzled manner, as if the speaker wasn't altogether certain of his identity. The woman called a second time, and he made the disastrous mistake of turning. He was recognized by the woman and knew immediately that it was a monumental blunder. It took him, however, less than the time to eat a small meal to repair the damage. With a quick decision, and a quicker smile, he offered a few hastily manufactured words of explanation. He lured the woman to a secluded boathouse and without warning spun like a pit viper and sliced her larynx. The only sound that issued from her was an indistinct gurgle. She looked at him with the astonishment of someone who realizes she has just crossed paths with death, then she slumped to the boards of the boathouse. He quickly added contusions, torn garments, and some more knife work, all of which would send the authorities searching down false paths.

Regrettable, he thought as he leaned over the planks to rinse the blood from his blade. With his foot he rolled the corpse into the fetid water and then partially opened the outer portal to the river. With another push, she drifted out.

That afternoon Sutradharak began putting to use the information he'd gathered about the speaker. He sent messages to his lieutenants, who in turn sent orders that rumors should be circulated, all slandering the harijan. A call was placed to the office of Yakoob Qereshy and a small, but exceptionally active riot took place the following day.

As he planned for the unscheduled bombing, his thoughts passed indifferently over the woman again. Too bad really. Fate, bad timing, or a rare error in judgment. Who can say?

Fifty

I woke next to Uliana for the second time in my life, and it was indescribably more delicious than the first. I curled into her back, drifted into her scented hair, and kissed her shoulder. She sighed and pulled my hand up to feel the morning rhythm of her heart. As I slipped back into honeyed sleep, I heard her say, "Let's stay like this forever."

When I awoke again I was alone and warm. The electricity had disappeared again, leaving the fan above me hanging idle. Voices drifted in from the kitchen, light laughter and whispers. I slipped on my pajama bottoms and searched around for my top.

"Who paid for it?" I heard Uli asking.

"Him, I told him it was his responsibility if he wanted me to go anywhere with him. And I made him buy coconut dessert, too." More giggles.

I padded through the dining nook to see Sahr and Uli sitting at the kitchen table, mugs of coffee steaming merrily in their hands. Sahr was smiling, but looking less energetic than normal. Uli sat in my pajama top and nothing else.

"What's a man have to do to get a cup of coffee around here?" I joked.

Sahr began pushing away from the table and I motioned her to stay put. I could get my own coffee this morning. I was more than a little curious to hear about her evening and arched my eyebrow to say, 'Do please continue.'

"Well. . . then he drove across the pontoon bridge to the sand beach south of the palace. Such a fine taxi he has. We walked barefoot in the water. I haven't acted so silly since I was twelve."

Uli patted Sahr's fingers. "Silly is good if it makes you feel young, Sahr. Did he try to kiss you?"

I had forgotten that women enjoyed getting to the core of things rapidly in regards to men. Sahr looked relieved when I said, "It's okay, O Great One, just pretend I'm not here."

"No, but I let him carry my shoes. I think he wanted to hold my hand, but I would not allow it. It was a first date."

It was my turn. "And is there a second date in the works?"

Mild embarrassment showed in her smile. "There was some talk of it, Saab. He wants me to meet his mother and sister."

"Meet his mother? And his sister? My God, that sounds positively serious. We'd better start saving for the wedding. And by the way, you called me Saab. Are you're upset with me?"

"Oh no, Bhimaji. Far from it, I've never been happier with you. You are the wisest man I know." She touched Uli's hand this time.

"Well, every now and then I think I make a few good decisions. So what can I fix you two for breakfast?"

The morning session at Devi's was a combination of poignant recollections of Soma's short life and a celebration that our cure might be for something I'd identified. Me, The Keeper of Notes and Photographs.

Before I left my villa I made the decision not to mention the nabi's séance with the pundits. It just wasn't the sort of news I wanted to divulge, or the questioning I wanted to face. I packed my backpack while Uli and I made plans to meet at the Afghani cafe for lunch. Jitka, whom both of us were feeling guilty about leaving alone so much, would join us, and afterwards the three of us would go down to hear Adam's discourse.

Master announced over the first cup of chai, "The police came to speak with me yesterday. They first believed Soma might have been a victim of a crime of passion and that she was violated. But now they say there is no evidence that she was. She was murdered without reason." He stared across the front wall at some movement along the avenue. "Who could do such a thing to a child?"

I closed my eyes. Yes, I thought, who could kill an innocent. A monster perhaps. "Do the police have any idea when she was killed? Or where?"

"Not precisely. They believe she was not in the water very long, so it is likely she was killed that same afternoon."

If that's true, I thought, then she must have been hiding somewhere for a day before she was murdered.

We all assured ourselves that the police would do their best to find her killer, though without it being mentioned, we knew they wouldn't. A low-caste widow didn't generate much expense or energy. C.G. again offered to establish a source of money for her relatives, but we all arrived at the same sad conclusion. There were no relatives to receive it. As the two of them discussed the details for her cremation, I learned a final item. Her last name was Tarahansa. Devi, seeing my sadness, said, "She will have a fine cremation, Bhim. We will see to it."

After a moment of quiet, I made my announcement and concealed my excitement in studied casualness. "By the way, Punditjis, I think I may have figured out what our disease is."

Tea cups almost cracked as they were set down. "Brilliant, I told you he was brilliant didn't I, Devi."

"Let him continue please, C.G." Master looked at me with obvious pride.

"Diabetes. We've been translating two words incorrectly.

Change 'self' to 'body' and 'water' to 'urine' and the whole thing fits."

After reading my new notes, they chuckled and began patting me jubilantly on each knee. "It does indeed, my boy. How did you figure it out?"

I had told no one about Uliana. Satnam Kangri had guessed, and Sahr knew, of course, but no one in Master's house knew about the confluence of Uli and Bhim. Lack of opportunity or some other excuse had held me back. Explaining to Sukshmi that we wouldn't be dancing to Randy Dogs again would be an interesting conversation. Without thinking I said, "A friend helped me solve it."

"A friend! Oh My. Is that prudent, Bhim? To reveal our project to another after all this violence?"

I defended the decision. "It's someone I can trust. She won't say a word."

They both stared at me silently. Then the pin that everyone can hear, dropped. C.G. coughed into his handkerchief "She?"

Master focused his condor eyes on mine and nodded slowly, then patted my knee one last time. "Good for you, My Boy. Good for you. I'm happy indeed. And I suppose this is the reason you are not having your regular lunch with us today?" I just returned his smile.

After a moment, I added Satnam Kangri's observations. "He knew the plants and the pressure points, and believes the combinations show great promise as a cure. Tests need to be done, of course."

"Kangri, eh? If there was ever a physician's opinion to be trusted, it would be his. Top shelf reputation." Master obviously felt the same way about the doctor that I did.

C.G. fell into another racking coughing spell and looked at me with a melancholy that perplexed me. "Satnam? He understands his subject only too well." With a fold of his hands, he asked, "So, my friends, is it time to tell the world about our discovery?"

I hesitated. "Punditjis, I am. . . only your student, The Keeper of Notes and Photographs, but I have some concerns about *how* we're going to tell the world. If we publish that we've found an addition to the Samhitas, the world of Sanskrit will take notice." I paused. "But if we announce that it involves a possible cure for diabetes, the entire world will take notice. Meddling people will swarm in, many of them greedy. There could be battles, and companies with a lot of money will use all sorts of tricks, bribing officials, filing injunctions, that sort of thing. I worry about this being misused or becoming legally entangled."

They hadn't anticipated that. But perhaps I'd underestimated Jatanaka Devamukti's understanding of the machinations of the world, because it was he that came up with the best solution for presenting our findings. He announced that he would see that our work was published in the Ayurvedic medical journals first. That was, after all, where it had come from. He then laid out the second part of the strategy.

Fifty-One

Jitka dropped a small bomb on us at lunch. It was an announcement both of us should have seen coming, but raw passion seems to affect one's vision. I was gazing at the curves of Uli's neck, thinking, how could I be so fortunate? when it hit.

We had ordered chicken kebabs with currants and carrot pilaf and were listening to the hollow bubbling of hookahs in the next stall, when Jitka announced, "Svester, I am flying home Tuesday. While you love pigeons went to the market yesterday, I went to a computer cafe and purchased my ticket. Cheap, non-stop to Coopenhagen. You wait to the last minute und they drop that price right down."

Uli, I could tell, was set to argue, but then thought better of it. "This is something you are sure of, Jit?"

"Ya, I am. Last week a two-ton bull couldn't have moved me from your side. But now it is different."

Suddenly I felt bad. Varanasi was a long way to hitchhike to have a stranger wedge himself between you and your sister. "Jitka, I don't want you to leave because of me. I've taken too much of your time together. It's not right."

Uli frowned, but Jitka laughed, a deep belly laugh. "Und here I was just thinking how you were so smart, Mr. Knucklehead. It is because of you that I can leave."

"Excuse me?"

She reached out and touched Uli's face with her palm. "Mein Gott, look at this girl. The sweetest eyes in the entire universe, and for half a year they've been filled with nothing but sadness. Now look at them. The hurt is gone. Goodbye. Farvel. Auf wiedersehen. What do you see there now? Happiness like Christmas to a five-year-old. Did I do that? No, Mr.

Knucklehead, you did. I'm going because I want to und I can. It
has been four months of travelling, and I am ready for feather
beds, real toilets, frikadeller und pandekager."

I looked to Uli who silently mouthed, "Meatballs and
pancakes."

"My Uli has never been so happy, Bhim." I was grateful I
wasn't Knucklehead this go-round. "Und it is because of you. All
of it. I must hand it to you, you must have some big, stiff
schlanger there. Whew."

"Jitka!" Uli grabbed the palm from her cheek and bit it.

"You two need time to learn about each other, und I see that
it is good learning. Me? I'm going back to Tönder to find a well
hung Danish boy who loves his mother, studies physics, and
knows how to cook."

"And you will, Jitka. I have no doubt," I laughed. "But
we've still got three days. Let's make the best of them. What
airport do you fly out of?"

"Indira Gandhi in Delhi on Tuesday night."

Uli squeezed my hand. "Bhim, can we see her off? All of us
take the train together?"

I thought for a moment and was hard-pressed to come up
with enough reasons we couldn't. The research team had a
blueprint to reveal its discovery. There was little I could do in
regards to Soma's death, the investigation, or the cave-in. It had
been a long time since I'd left Varanasi on anything other than
short excursions. The idea of time outside the city felt agreeable.

"I guess so. Sure, why not? We can take the train over on
Monday night, get first-class sleepers and arrive on Tuesday
midday. If we aren't too tired we can see some of the Delhi sites
and get to the airport with plenty of time. I might even

purchase a new laptop."

Thinking of the computer inspired me to do some research on a certain mining company later that afternoon.

Right now we had a date to hear Adam.

We enjoyed two servings of coconut pudding with three spoons, but afterwards, as we were slipping on our sandals, Uli's earlier quote came back. 'It proves once more how dangerous it is to be good.' A tingling apprehension passed through me.

I told both of them that I wanted us to stay close on the Ghats. Uli stood and put her hand lightly on the opal that hung over my heart. "Schnuki, I am always going to be close. By the way . . . the bunks on the trains, are they big enough for my tall man und his big, stiff schlanger?" I started laughing so hard I choked.

"Just barely, Premika. But we make do."

"Und will there be enough room for this long-legged Danish girl?"

I kissed her. "Just barely, but I'm sure we'll make do with that too."

"So where does it go, our love train?"

"What do you mean? From here? Well, we'll go through Jaunpur, Sultanpur, Lucknow, Sitapur, Shajahanpur,"

"There are a lot of pores here."

"Puras, anyway, we'll roll along the Ramganga River to one of my favorite spots on the Kolkuta-Delhi line.

"And what place is that, Mein Schatzki?"

"Okay, can you translate that one for me?"

She tapped the opal again. "It means 'my treasure.' Und the city?"

"Ah . . . Bareilly Junction. There's an exquisite temple near the station and a long ride over the bridge when you leave."

"A long bridge ride. Mmm . . . you, me, und our bouncy friend on a long bridge clicking und clacking along. Sounds exciting."

I looked beyond her mischievous eyes to a flurry of movement outside. Later I would ask what the source of my foreboding had been, the commotion beyond the window or something else?

Fifty-Two

"Mein Gott, look at how many people there are. More than a thousand! Und, there is my favorite pair, Petey and Shawn. Too bad those boys are touched with the lavender, I might enjoy a three-way yoga session with them." Jitka, stuffed with kebabs and armed with the knowledge that she could now exit Varanasi, was in a positively scary mood.

"Sure, after a visit to the barber, bath house, tailor, and perfumery, they might be ready for you," I quipped.

"No tailors, I like their loincloths."

The three of us stood at the top of the embankment surveying the crowd, and Jitka had it right, there were easily more than a thousand people--probably twice that--stretched across the steps, up to the temples, and down to the water's edge. Except for cremations, the rituals at this part of the river had halted; it was too crowded for waders or boat passengers to get to the water's edge. Flocks of barefoot children still scurried about, widows begged with tin cups, and purveyors with baskets of food balanced on their heads still called to the crowd, but it had changed dramatically.

I smiled when I saw the battery-cooled hat of Marley Chapin bobbing through the sea of dark heads.

The crowd was noticeably segregated. Large contingents of college students and intellectuals, many dressed in Western clothes, gathered on the south edge below us. A few carried hand-painted banners. 'Believe The Simple Plan.' 'Compassion, Science, and Common Sense.' 'Let the Energy In and Hatred Out.' To the north, there was a small but powerful assembly of Brahmin and Christian priests. Behind them the complacent followers of Imam Nomani stood next to the very unpredictable disciples of Qereshy. It was a fleeting alignment of different faiths. Unusual to say the least. Actually, it was unheard of. Qereshy's group waved signs scrawled in Urdu. "Butcher infidels that mock Islam. Death to Non-Believers--Allah's retribution is swift.

Above the Scindia Ghat, a less ideological group had assembled--a large cadre of police with bamboo lathis and holstered sidearms. The scene felt more like a Napoleonic battlefield than a place of sanctity, and it chilled me enough to suggest the three of us withdraw to the safety of the villa. A part of me wanted to hear Adam's words, another said, "Leave Bhim. Now!" Uli, however, was adamant about staying, so we formed a compromise.

"Listen," I had to speak loudly. "We are not venturing into that mess. As tour guide, advisor, and general knucklehead, I'm not allowing it." I think both of them liked my tough guy role, either that or they'd assessed the scene well enough themselves.

Uli placed a hand on my arm. "But we can listen from up there, yes Bhim? Maybe in the shade of those buildings?" She pointed to a ledge thirty meters to our right at the top of a high retaining wall.

Relieved that I wasn't being pressured to take our customary seats next to Adam, I said, "Perfect. You can take turns sitting on my shoulders." In the noise of the crowd I only half heard Jitka's crude comment at that suggestion. We picked our way across to the mantel and sat with our feet dangling over a fifteen-foot drop.

The river flowed languidly in front of us, reflecting sunlight and streaks of clouds, and had it not been for the crush of humanity below, I would have thought the scene worthy of a few lines of poetry.

Uli whispered, "It's like that Bhagavad Gita painting where Arjuna and Krishna are standing in the chariot between two armies and everybody is ready to go to war."

"Let's hope the police will keep any war from happening," I whispered back.

A microphone crackled and Adam's voice hushed the crowd. He look up at us and smiled with a small nod of understanding.

Microphone in hand, barefoot, and dressed in a white kurta and white pajama pants, he looked like a nouveau poet or a musician. I had come to regard him more like some tailor weaving a broadcloth of truth. He paused and closed his eyes for three breaths, then began, "Brothers and Sisters, Welcome." There was a pause while translators rendered the greeting into Hindi, Urdu, Punjabi, and Bengali. I marveled at the organization—sound systems, translators, and four tables stacked with booklets set for distribution.

"Gott, he is handsome," Jitka whispered.

"My name is Adam, and I stand before you this afternoon a single man, a Benarsi like yourselves. I was born eighty-four paces from the ancient flame at the top of these steps, and like all my brothers and sisters, I was born to a mother." He paused again for the translation.

"At my birth that woman gave me the name Sharmalal Mehdu Dijna. Sharmalal, as is true of every infant, was a marvel of the great energy, an intricate formation of proteins, amino acids, cells and incomprehensibly complex systems. His blood pulsed through arteries like the rivers of our land. His breath flowed like wind to his lungs. His tears, lymph, saliva, digestive juices all sung in perfect harmony. He arrived as a miracle of nature's processes and entered our city as an innocent.

With his first lungful he shared the same molecules every brother and sister has ever breathed. He exhaled into the atmosphere where those molecules passed throughout the world to be shared a million times over."

Adam paused to nod amiably at the congregation of priests and mullahs.

"And if, at his moment of birth, you had gathered a single cell of Sharmalal's saliva and peered into its tiniest parts, you would have seen an amazing sight, My Friends. Inside the twisted strands of his DNA, inside the mortar that created all the cells of his body, inside the very essence of Sharmlal Dijna, you would have seen the same DNA found in every living creature on earth. You would have seen the same strands of lifecode found in every living organism going back to the beginning of life four and one half billion years ago."

There was a murmur in the crowd. This had none of the flavor Adam's previous humor-filled speeches. A few shifted uneasily. To the north a grumbling rose, and a single voice shouted something incoherent.

The microphone drowned it out. "You see, Brothers and Sisters, all life is a single, coupled entity. One source, one energy, one force, not separate, not divided, but beautifully diverse in its forms. And who has discovered this unity? Who has proven this connected nature? A million great minds possessed of the best tools humans have, logic and reason. They weren't misinterpreted prophets from ancient times, or avaricious kings mocking us with promises of domination or hatred. These were the greatest thinkers we have produced. Democritus, Einstein, Kepler, Curie, and a hundred thousand others who shared their knowledge for us." His arm stretched forward toward the top of the embankment. "Like these lofty temples above, their knowledge has been built stone by stone. It has been tested time and again until we now know it as truth."

There was a quality to Adam's voice that pulled us, forced us to take account of his words—powerful and confident in its effect. I looked at Uli and Jitka. They were leaning forward, intent on every syllable.

"Imagine a pair of reading glasses with lenses so powerful they would allow us to see the smallest objects. With such glasses these men and women have peered into the core of life; they have seen its very nature and understood the simple, indisputable truth, that we are all connected. And when they looked deeper into the tiniest particles that create life, they saw the energy that shapes us all, and all of this."

He spread his hands and turned in a full circle, the motion fluid and smooth, like a planetary model.

"We are standing at the crossroads right now, My Friends, each and every one of us. And we stand at what some might say is a cheerless time, fraught with challenges and uncertainties so large we fear to confront them. We ask, 'which direction do we turn?' We ask, 'Is it possible to fix what that has been damaged?' We see climate changing, oceans warming, extinction of species, increased carbon and methane in our atmosphere, pollution, over-population, starvation, disease, bloodshed, thievery, avarice, hatred, and the annihilation of humanity." His voice rose with each word. "But it is not these things we need to fix." He stopped, and the microphone squeaked, followed by a peculiar moment of silence. "No, we must first change how we think as humans. It must be done without laws or scripture telling us to do so. It must come from within, not outside. Change by choice. The human transformation will follow, and with it the ability to solve these problems. It is that simple. We will choose to embrace universal responsibility, to accept compassion, pure science, and common sense in our actions.

"Leaders of governments and religions must also rise with this tide, but first, they must admit a few thousand years of errors. And it must be done quickly because there is no time to spare. The message that we can work together, accept the challenges, and solve them must rise like clarified butter above all else. Those who do not accept will be left behind. The time for good deeds has come. Banners are being raised. Not a time for sadness or despair, no far from it. This is a time of passion, of healing, a time when each of us will be fully engaged. Great works will be done."

Adam's voice boomed across the Ghats, and from the south side the rumble of applause and stamping of feet rose up. From the north, grumbling.

"The projects have started, and many of our true leaders are speaking. . ." He began describing projects, movements, humanitarian aid, irrigation, desalinization plants, reforestation, animal sanctuaries, hospitals, schools. The list went on.

As Adam spoke, my eyes drifted to a figure standing apart from the traditionalists on the north side. He held himself in an aloof manner, detached yet still engaged in the speech. He looked oddly familiar. I was too far away to see more than an occasional glimpse of dark beard and heavily tinted glasses on a face intermittently shielded by a large umbrella. Every a few minutes another man in similar dress approached and stood next to him. I couldn't tell if they were conversing, but after some time the second man drifted back into the crowd. At first I thought the man might be a mullah, a cleric from the mosque on the bank above that side. His beard, robe, and cap gave him some of that appearance. He also might have been a well-dressed goat herder, but two observations led me away from those conclusions. From his demeanor he appeared to find the crowd repulsive and stood to the side as if he might be sullied by contact. The other was how he moved, especially how he positioned his arms. He was, I was certain, physically trained—a professional.

Then something bizarre happened. As I was studying him, the umbrella tilted backward just enough to see a pair of dark glasses staring directly at Uli and me. Immediately the umbrella shifted back into place as if he had seen me watching him. Did he know us? It unnerved me enough to whisper, "Uli, Jitka, we need to go. Now."

Uli, entranced by the sermon and unaware of what I had just seen, pleaded, "Can we stay just a minute or two more. Please. It is amazing what he is saying, and it sounds like he may be almost done." Jitka backed her up.

I was preparing to enter into our first real argument, when I glanced behind us to check our path back out to the gullies. The hairs on my neck stood up. A crowd had quietly filled in, students, peasants, shop merchants had packed out to the ledge. Unless we were willing to scoot back on our behinds, stand, and push our way through the crowd, we would have to wait.

Adam did indeed sound like he was drawing to a close, his voice rolling powerfully across the river front. "And what of the infant, Sharmalal? What of that innocent born just a few meters from where we gather today? Sharmalal Dijna, that marvelous product of the great energy, was left to die, Friends. His mother happened to be a bhangi, a shit-sweeper by birth, the product of an archaic and evil system of hatred and separation. She cleaned excrement from the latrines behind the Golden Temple. See the irony in that. Born at the back door of a temple of gold, she died in the same place like a rat, poisoned by cholera. And Sharmalal? He was left to die there as well. But he didn't. Compassion, you see, is a marvelous endowment. The baby was lifted up by a loving couple, fed, and nurtured, and saved from the maw of cholera. He was given the gift of life and a new name, given the gift of schooling and taught the tongues of history, math, science, and the future. And from these he learned the power of compassion, science, and common sense. And he changed. Sharmalal, by his own choice ceased to exist. It is a boon we all possess, My Friends, the choice to change. Sharmalal, the harijan infant son of a bhangi shit-sweeper, died. And Adam lived."

As this was translated, the crowd erupted. A few, like me, had already known of his origins, but this admission cauterized them. From the left, where the bearded man had stood moments earlier, a single shout rose from the crowd. I leaned out to see who had yelled just in time to see a stone being hurled toward the shala. Then two more, and like a rehearsed scene in a play, a single police whistle shrieked from above.

In the seconds that followed, tranquility disintegrated into ugliness. I grabbed Uli's arm, who in turn grabbed Jitka's and together we attempted to roll and push against the legs of the mob behind us. Nothing gave way, and we were being forced closer to the ledge as those behind us pushed forward to see what was happening. I glanced down. It was a fifteen, maybe sixteen, foot drop onto broken steps.

In that moment everything changed.

The blast arrived as a flame before we felt or heard anything. It flew out in a fireball seven steps above the shala--a searing ball of orange. Milliseconds later the force struck me like a sledge, pounding my body. The impact, even from a distance, felt like a lead mask swung against my face. My head flew back and smacked sharply against someone's shin. The sound arrived last, a deafening boom that echoed across the crowd and rattled everything along the Ghats. Rock and wood blew across and ricocheted off the wall just below my feet. The explosion rumbled upward into the sky, above the city, and across the river. Then screams filled the air. Shouts and the pounding of feet followed, whistles, more screams--the screeching sounds of chaos rang out for long, painful minutes. Then, very slowly, it faded to the desperate moaning of the wounded.

Through a fog I looked at Uli and Jitka. They seemed unhurt, terrified, but not visibly injured. "All right?" was all I could murmur. Both nodded. Jitka said something in German or Danish, and I could tell by how she responded that her hearing was not what it should be.

The pressure behind us decreased the instant the explosion reached us as people fled back up the gullies. Three pairs of hands stretched down to lift us up. I grabbed one and stood face to face with Bijram Nataratri and his two engineering friends. "Oh. Sri Bhima, it is a pleasure to see you again. I'm Bijram, we met just down there. I hope you remember?" He pointed toward the palm hut that was now a mangled clutter of bamboo and smoldering fronds. I answered sluggishly that yes, I did remember him. Jitka, in the meanwhile, was still pulling at her ear and flexing her jaw. Uli lifted my arm, slid inside it, and began sobbing against my side. On the steps below us panic had taken over. People were running in all directions away from the center. Eight to ten bodies lay crumpled near the shala. Smoke and bits of paper circled like tickertape in the breeze—remnants of the booklets to be distributed. People stumbled, some wandered, some called for friends or loved ones. In the midst of the rubble I saw the crushed battery-cooled hat of Marley Chapin.

And Adam was nowhere to be seen.

Bijram was going on about how horrible it all was, and that surely it must have been another attack by Sutradharak and his band of Pakistani terrorists. I didn't hear him. With a wag of my head and a good-bye, I led Uli and Jitka unsteadily up the gully to the only place I could think to go at the moment, Haroon's.

Fifty-Three

My good friend didn't call my name as we entered. I had to pound twice before he hustled us through the door and locked it quickly behind us. It was dark inside. The metal security shades were drawn jail-like down over the windows, and only a small desk lamp behind the bar emitted any light. I could barely make out the muffled sounds of running feet, whistles and sirens shrieking outside.

"My God, Bhimaji man. Are you alright? Are you hurt?" He held my shoulders and looked from me to Uli to Jitka. We each shook our heads. "It sounded like a lorry full of dynamite went off. I heard it from inside my office. What the hell is going on?"

"It was another attack, Maumed, smaller than the others, but the crowd was bigger. I don't know if people were killed or how many were hurt, but it's bad. The three of us were almost pushed over the edge near Lalita Ghat. I had to get us off the streets, so we came here." I almost added that I hoped it was all right, but I knew it was.

Haroon hustled around and set three tall brandies and a bowl of leechees and macadamia nuts on the bar. I started to make introductions and he wagged a finger. "Bhimaji, I remember these beautiful women. They were just here last week. Uliana and Jitka, if my memory is still working properly."

A hoarse laugh escaped. "Haroon, your memory always works properly. Jitka how is your hearing?"

She screwed up her face and popped the side of her head with her palm. "Fine, Bhim. Steel casing. Everything was ringing like a Chinese New Year for a while, but it has gone now."

We sat on stools and Uliana slid close and pulled my hand around her shoulders. She was silent and trembling. I made her take sips of the brandy. I did the same, and for a while none of us spoke. One by one we washed the dust off in the Haroon's bathrooms and returned with a little less shaking.

Haroon fetched his own snifter, poured three fingers worth of Courvoisier, and set the bottle on the bar. Raising his glass, he said, "In lousy times we drink the good stuff. To better times." This brought a faint smile to Uli's lips. We took healthy gulps, noshed a bit, and felt the warmth of the liquor pulse through us.

I kissed her neck and rubbed it gently. "Little better?"

"A little. Those poor people, Bhim. Gott, it happened so fast. People start yelling, the police blow a whistle und then this explosion. Adam, do you think he is okay?"

I wasn't certain, but I knew what she had to hear. "I didn't see him afterwards, when we were standing on the ledge, so I think he must be okay. He must've gotten away before the bomb went off."

Haroon, looking thoughtful, drained his glass and said, "From what you are saying it sounds like this bomb was detonated by a remote and not by a timer. I can't be sure, but it sounds that way. No one could have known how long this Adam would be speaking, correct?"

"That makes sense," I replied. "It went off at a fairly crucial point." I remembered the man with the umbrella. "I saw someone. Strange acting. He stood away from the crowd, and another man kept approaching and talking to him. It looked like they were checking with each other. He was a goat merchant or something. Maybe it was nothing, but it looked strange." For Uli's sake I didn't describe how he had been looking at us.

Haroon pulled thoughtfully at his chin.

Over the years I'd come to respect a few aspects of my bar-owner friend. Gregarious to the extreme and comic in his way, he also kept sensitive fingers on the pulse of the city. He was shrewd, knew the system, and listened carefully to the more knowledgeable students that entered his establishment.

"It would surprise me if this fellow and Sutradharaka were the same, because it would have been such a brazen act on his part." He paused, looking thoughtful. "But not out of the question. Especially if..." He stopped and looked at me, uncertain if he should continue in front of the women.

"If what?" I prompted.

"Just a moment." He poured himself another Courvoisier and downed half of it. Setting the glass down he asked, "Bhim, have you ever considered why this fellow has not been caught? We have lived with this fear for fifteen months, and all the so-called intelligence agencies keep insisting he is the leader of the Taweel Churi. But you notice this group has never laid claim to it."

"I hadn't really thought about that, no. Up until a few days ago I hadn't paid him much attention to any of it." I glanced at Uli.

"Uh huh. Let me ask it this way then. Do you know what RAW is?"

"That would be another no."

"I shall explain. RAW is India's number one intelligence agency, the Research Analysis Wing. When they wish to be friendly, they work with the Intelligence Bureau, known as IB, and the Defense Intelligence Bureau and the Joint Cipher Bureau. That is a lot of intelligence gathering, and yet none of them appears to be able to locate this fellow. A lot of talk, a lot of media, and a lot of very bright people searching. So I think perhaps they are searching in the wrong place and for the wrong motives."

I didn't fully understand what he was inferring. "Maumed, if he has done what everyone says he's done, then he has to have some reason, no matter how crazy."

Haroon inhaled deeply. "Correct, My Friend. I'm not saying he doesn't have a reason. He has committed these crimes and sixty-nine people have died in eight months, most of them in the last three. But is it possible there are reasons other than what everyone supposes? A lot of well-connected college types drink a lot of gin at my bar. It helps them generate the occasional lucid question, and once in a while one of them will ask why the agencies cannot establish a clear pattern other than it being along the rail lines."

The light was beginning to shine under my tightly drawn shades. "They are all operating on the wrong hypothesis."

"Ah, now you are waking up to smell the coffee, my good friend. Let me ask you another question. This one historical. Do you remember what occurred five days before the temple and cantonment bombings in March?"

More and more I was being asked to recount recent history. "I'm not sure. Do you mean locally?"

"No, internationally."

"I was probably slaving away on the Bhavabuti play that afternoon, you remember, the one we're making into a movie."

He grinned at that. "Yes, well you missed some big news. The U. S. and India signed a treaty to allow India to purchase raw nuclear fuel, a few signatures erased thirty years of non-proliferation policies, and all we had to do was agree to allow inspectors into our non-military facilities. Our government got to designate which ones. That, my friend, was a good joke around these tables."

Jitka slapped her fist into her palm. "I remember that. In Tonder we wondered who in the United States understood what was actually going on. "

Haroon nodded. "Fourteen of our twenty-two plants could be inspected, but the reality was that we could use the fuel any way we wished. In other words, fifty new warheads a year."

He popped four macadamia nuts into his mouth and continued. "Between energy and weapons, India is starving for raw uranium, as is Pakistan, Iran, Libya, and others. We have mines east of here in Jharkhand, but they are being depleted quickly. India needs more. So you see, in theory this violence could generate sympathy for renegotiated contracts for fuel. I stress the word 'could.' It is all part of the grand, irrational game. Pakistan gets nuclear technology from China. A few acts of terrorism take place, we practice troop maneuvers in Kashmir. The ante goes up and more terrorism follows. In the end we get new missile guidance systems and refined fuel from France or Washington. Hypothetically, of course."

"So how does it tie in with these bombings?"

"Just that they may not be totally based in religion or secessionist movements."

At that moment his cell phone chimed from inside his kurta. Haroon held up a finger to pause his lecture and dug into his pocket. He pressed a button and turned his back to us. I reached into my own pocket and extracted my phone. It was split into four unusable pieces.

"Uh huh. Yes, I see. And where is the other? Right." Without a goodbye, he clicked off.

As Haroon talked, I wondered why it felt like I was being

drawn into class five rapids with a toothpick for a paddle, why suddenly my simple, scholarly world felt so horribly dangerous.

I hadn't given politics or governments or secessionist movements much thought since being here. Now I was in need of four aspirin for my pounding headache and wondering how it had all reached my doorstep.

He looked cheerless when he turned back. "More trouble, I'm afraid. Riots have broken out near the Alamqir mosque." Uli flinched. "And fires have been set near Aurungzeb. It is getting uglier." He sighed. "The sad part is no one is to blame but these terrorists. Hell, most of the rioters out there don't even know what they are rioting about."

Uli, who had rested quietly against me, shook her head at the news. "They must stop, Bhim. They must. It's madness."

I didn't have a response.

Then she whispered a phrase that had stayed with me also. "The seeds of hostility, the minute germs of hatred and vehemence are sown into the fertile soil of our lives." Adam. I wondered where, how he was, and if he was safe. I thought of Sahr, and Lalji, and C.G., and Sukshmi, and even Mej. I hoped all the people in my undersized circle were tucked safely in their homes.

Beyond the shuttered windows the streets were deceptively quiet. In other parts of the city, pandemonium reigned. It would be dangerous moving about, especially for foreigners. But I also knew we had to leave. It was dark now and if we were to make it back to the villa, it had to be soon. "Haroon," I asked, "is there a back way out of here."

"Of course, over there." He waved an arm towards one of the side rooms and a locked, heavily-barred door. "You may stay here if you wish, Bhim, but I must be going myself. I have to feed my cats or they will conspire to mutiny." That image made me smile.

"Thank you, Maumed, but we will stay off the main streets and work our way through the gullies, maybe even be lucky enough to find a deaf taxi driver who hasn't heard about any of this."

"Deaf is fine, but make certain he sees well enough to take the back streets. Taxis are prime targets."

We stood, and Haroon came from behind the bar. "A final toast: to the world becoming a more peaceful place." The four of us clinked glasses and drank. The heat of the brandy drop into our bellies. In typical gentlemanly style, he kissed Jitka's hand, and I was certain, even in the poor light, that she flushed from something more than Courvoisier.

Then he handed me an envelope. "The information you requested."

I folded it and slid it into by pocket. "That was fast."

"I have my sources, and, as you will see, the facts are minimal at best."

Uli kissed his cheek and as he held the door for us he said, "Haroon's will always be open for you, my friends, and I will always be here to greet you."

Like too many promises uttered in moments of urgency, that one would not hold true. We thanked him and stepped silently into the blackness of the gullies.

Fifty-Four

My best skills as a guide were tested that night. The moment Haroon closed the door behind us, a band of six men sprinted across the opening of the alleyway. I couldn't tell what religion they were, just that they seemed to have plenty of faith in the clubs they carried. Fortunately, the shadows concealed us. At first I lead us on shallow switchbacks through the black lanes. We passed a few people, as terrified as we were, but no one spoke to us. A young Hindu couple, the man holding a blood-soaked kerchief below his chin, passed us on the run. Reasoning that they were likely being chased, I took us on a more southerly course along back streets. Slowly, with the utmost care, we passed from the center of the city. We pressed against the walls, inside shadows, and moved in silence. We walked rapidly, and at times ran, especially when we saw groups larger than two moving about. Twice we heard shouting and a horrible screaming, and with every step we smelled smoke. The orange glow of flames painted the belly of clouds in the north. Jitka looked grim and tired, but both of them amazed me with their composure and stamina. Eventually we stole our way to Sonapura Avenue. I kept us on parallel lanes in and out of the shadows to the crossing at the Asi Bridge. We halted and I motioned us to press against the wall.

A dozen young men in tattered shirts and loongis had just crossed the bridge south, looking for something to beat, or burn, or worse. They appeared to have no other purpose than to cause havoc. Two sputtering torches waved and illuminated them. I peeked out and pulled quickly back just as the blast of another police whistle rang out. I hoped this one would have a better result than the one sounded at the Ghats.

The police were quite protective of the wealthier homes on that side of the river--my side--and I guessed that the thugs would be routed before they could do any damage. I guessed correctly. The constable guard swept in from three directions, lathis whipping shoulder to shoulder. From across the river we could hear the cracking of ribs and thighs, and within seconds the scuffle disintegrated into a full retreat.

Torches fell and the better part of the mob fled back across the bridge holding up their wounded. Three, who limped too slowly, were roped together and pushed roughly across the span.

I still didn't like the option of crossing by foot to negotiate with the officers standing guard. I trusted no one but the three of us that evening. "I want us to move up river and find another place to cross." My voice shook with uncertainty.

Uli squeezed my elbow and whispered, "You're the guide, Mein Shatzki." That helped.

Fortunately, we didn't have to search long. Two hundred meters up the river, a small dinghy was tied high up on the bank, and after a few slippery moments, we were all gliding silently away from the north shore. I tore off the bottom of my kurta and wrapped mufflers around the oars and drew gently on the blades. Midway across, Uli pointed east where the stream flowed sleepily into the Ganga. An ember of silver moon was just rising above the fort on the far side. The scene was breathtaking—the ancient ramparts of the palace under a halo of silver on a ribbon of glittering water. Any other evening and it would be a beautiful dream, I thought. Let the sun rise on a peaceful city tomorrow.

Uli looked at me and mouthed, "I love you." My heart sang, and then, with a soft whoosh, we reached the other bank.

Lalji astounded me that night. The front gate was not only secured with a second chain, but three of his card-playing partners were stationed inside on the patio. They held kitchen knives and four wooden clubs that I hoped hadn't been fashioned from the legs of my chair. They jumped officiously to their feet as we arrived, and for a moment I thought they were going to salute.

"Saab, Maam and I have been so frightened. She has shredded her sari down to the chola worrying for your safety, but as you can see, I have been standing guard vagilantly."

"Vigilantly, Lalji." I tried to maintain a serious face, but couldn't help but laugh. He looked a tad let down that I was finding humor in his intrepid watchfulness until I patted his shoulder and said in front of everyone, "You are the best watchman in all of Varanasi, Lalji. None better, and you gentlemen as well. I am in your debt." I namasted deeply to each of them.

With a lot of wagging of heads and thank-yous, they relinquished their weapons and filed out the gate. I told each of them to return the following day for some payment for their night's work. That brought another round of head wagging.

Wrapping my arm around his slender shoulders, I said, "Lalji, you did well tonight. Thank you. Lock everything up and sleep in the hammock. But sleep easily; there will be no more trouble. And let's wrap that finger again tomorrow, shall we."

Genuine fear born of disaster often propels us into acts of greatness, more often into acts of compassion. It is something felt in battle-scarred trenches, burning buildings, flooded

neighborhoods, and riot torn cities. There is an invisible entity, a
bond of humanness that draws us to a deeper understanding of
ourselves, our companions, and the ones we love. As I sat with
Uli, Jitka, and Sahr, sharing steaming bowls of saag paneer, rice,
and dal around a familiar kitchen table, I realized that small
thought. Maybe it was a big thought, but we had, that day, been
terrified, numbed to the core, and here we sat, all of us trying to
comfort each other. We spent the entire dinner reassuring each
other that tomorrow would be brighter.

I also realized something else that evening. Varanasi would
not feel the same for me ever again.

After we made a bed on the sofa for Jitka, and Uli went to
shower off the smoke and fear, Sahr motioned me back into the
kitchen.

"Masterji's daughter came to see you this evening, Saab."
Her swan's wing was buried to near invisibility in a frown.

"Sukshmi?"

"Yes, Saab. In the big car of Master Chandragupta, she came
and left quite quickly."

"Sahr, you can stop with the frowning and calling me Saab.
She is Devamukti's daughter, not my premika. My premika is in
the bathroom. I'm pretty certain your bhuta and deva cards
have pointed that out."

"Well, this cheeky Brahmin girl with the fancy tinted glasses
and orange lipstick asked me to give you this." A small pink
envelope appeared from behind her back. I opened it.

"Would you like me to read it out loud?" I asked.

Though I was certain her curiosity was bubbling like a geyser,
she said, "No . . . not really."

I read it anyway. "Friends in hiding wish to speak with you.

The arrangements have been made. And, My Boy, please bring your new friend. I would like to meet her." It was signed in a weak spidery script, C.G.

Sahr harrumphed.

Below, in Sukshmi's exact cursive, her own message read, "Bhimaji, C.G. asked me to deliver this to you. Can you come to his house tomorrow at 8:30 AM. It is urgent. There is good news--and sad. By the by, who is your new friend? S."

I didn't read that aloud.

Fifty-Five

Mistakes were unacceptable to Sutradharak, but they were far worse when committed by himself. In the early days he had set his standards with gruesome examples, cutting out tongues or castrating those who crossed him or made errors. The idea of doing that to himself merely brought a sneer.

His identity had been breeched two days ago—an unfortunate mess he'd been forced to resolve in a very unpleasant manner. The widow girl had recognized him as he moved through the alley in his other persona. That had necessitated slicing her throat. But then there was the incident at the harijan's speech. He was nearly recognized again, and it bothered him that both of those had come from his own foolishness.

Analysis told him that he was committing too many errors, and he knew why, the desire to be close to the flames. Vanity, inquisitiveness, ego, they had resulted in foolish mistakes. *Over-confidence leads to quick death,* he chided himself. *Get back to pulling strings, PuppetMaster.* This thought brought him to another conclusion--he needed a rest, a long one, perhaps even permanent. Retirement. He had been pondering it since the bombing at the temple back in March. Finances were certainly in order. Every euro, dollar, and yen was accessible, and with half a dozen passports, he could travel wherever he wished. He could be anyone.

More importantly, his work for his current employers was nearly done. Their primary goals would reached within days.

The decision was made. Retirement would come after this next event, and then a vanishing act. Go out with a bang, disappear into the great cities of the world to become a hazy legend, an episode on Unsolved Mysteries.

His only concern was that his employers might decide he was a risk, a liability to be dealt with. That would not be good, because he knew how difficult it was to conceal onesself from some of the most powerful, best-financed people in the world.

I'm still a chameleon, though, and the best at what I do. Take for example how I ripped apart a city with the simple press of two cell phone buttons.

Fifty-Six

The chaos of the previous night had settled like a passing thunderstorm outside the walls of my villa.

Inside, Uli and I lay curled like spoons, the sounds of breath and heart composing our sonata of love. I remembered dreamily that it had rained in the wee hours. The breeze was cooler, and for long moments I let all my senses open to the woman in my arms. I smelled her fragrance, tasted her shoulder, felt the warmth of her thighs, and gazed at her auric beauty, and asked again, how could I be so fortunate?

With a soft moan she rolled over, eyes still closed, hair drawn in soft curtains across one cheek. My hand slipped across her stomach and around to the small of her back. Her smile lengthened, one eye fluttered open, then closed contentedly again. "Hello, Lover," she whispered. I pulled her flat against me and kissed her neck and the underside of her chin down to the top of her breast. She moaned softly, and at that splendid moment I remembered two things that I wish my memory hadn't been so willing to recall. A pink note was summoning me to be somewhere in two hours, and I wasn't positive, but I thought I had told Mej I would play Frisbee with him that morning.

"Uli?" Her hips wiggled against me. "Uli?"

"Do I have to open my eyes to answer?"

"Not really, no. You can keep them closed, but I believe I have to get up."

"Like get up, go to the bathroom and come back to bed, get up?" Her accent was thicker when she wasn't fully awake.

"Er, no. Like get up, brew some coffee, and cancel a Frisbee game with Mej. Not that I believe he's actually going to show up after the events of last night . . . but he can be pretty committed when it comes to these things."

"Oh." Disappointment. "Well, you do need to keep those legs in shape, but you cannot go if it is dangerous. My orders. Go make us a cup and I'll be right there."

Throwing back the sheet and setting my feet on the floor was the last thing I really wanted to do.

I set two cups of hot coffee, warm nan, butter and marmalade on the table, and turned as she stepped into the kitchen. Her hair was pulled back by a cobalt hair band that matched her eyes. I assumed it came from another one of those pockets in her handbag. She had one of my white kurtas on, and the same purple skirt from the day before. It was torn at the hem, and smelled of smoke.

I didn't wait for my sip of coffee, I pulled her close, kissed her, and said, "Listen, I want to promise you that it's going to be safe now and that it will all settle down. But I can't. To be truthful, I'm worried. There are too many ugly things happening right now, and I don't have answers." I paused and took a breath. "So, what do you think about going up to Nepal for a couple of weeks, maybe a month, that is unless..." The thought had come to me in the blackness of the night before as we avoided a gang of thugs. It was simple thought. I didn't want to lose her to anything. "Unless, you think you want to fly home with Jitka. I don't want you to, but I also don't want you to stay here just for..."

I didn't get to finish. While still holding herself flat against my body, she sucker-punched my middle just hard enough to hurt.

"Don't say that. Don't ever say it, Bhim. Never. I'm not

going anywhere. Not to Denmark, not to Paris, or the moon without you. I'm here, right where I want to be und where I'm going to stay." She looked hurt and angry, and that was a first.

Taking another breath and rubbing my abdominals, I whispered, "I had to ask, Uli. It's gotten too crazy and dangerous, and I don't want you hurt. I just thought it might be good to give you the option."

"Well, I don't want the option." She rubbed my stomach and then brought both of her hands to the sides of my face. "I am home, Bhim, inside these arms, and I don't want to be more than this far away from you ever. Okay?"

"Okay. I'll make you an agreement. I'll never ask that question again, and you let me know next time you feel like punching me in the stomach. Sound like something we can agree to?"

"Maybe."

"Maybe? That's not particularly fair."

"I'm reserving my woman's right to punch you whenever your eyes wonder too far from mine."

"Umm, then I guess I'd better tell you where we're going this morning, and who you are going to meet."

Her hands slid around my back. "Let me guess, the beauty from Haroon's?"

I nibbled her ear, felt her quiver, "You are so amazingly clairvoyant. Adam will be there also."

She beamed. "He is okay, unhurt?"

"I don't know that, but he's alive. A message came through Sahr last night. We're meeting them at Professor Chandragupta's house inside the university."

"One of the pundits you worked with, yes?"

At that moment Sahr walked through the back door with Meghaduta chattering happily on her shoulder. The kitchen melted instantly into a noisy exchange of squawks, good mornings, and kisses.

It took about three seconds before I started becoming jealous of the parrot. Uli stroked its head and wings, cooed over it, and gave it all the attention I had just been receiving. I did have to admit he was cute—little green suit with a flashing red waistcoat. Noble features, too. He chirped and hopped about the counters while Sahr added to my trifling attempt at breakfast.

"I have three readings today, Bhimaji," she announced as fritters and pakoras settled onto the table. "I thought to postpone them, but with all the uncertainty of last night, my clients want more certainty in their future."

"Not a problem. Uli and I will be gone most of the day anyway and won't be back until the afternoon. What have you heard of the city? Has it quieted?"

"The gossipers say it has, but you should go carefully. So, how many should I count for dinner?"

"Three, I suppose. Plan for that."

Jitka came in, freshly showered, and showing a long purple bruise on her jaw. I pulled out a chair for her. "Sahr's very traditional Indian breakfast is designed to chase away all memories of sneaking through an Indian city in the dark."

She gave a small shudder. "Ach, what a night. I woke up thinking it must have been a dream."

"It was a dream, a bad one, but these are guaranteed to help." I pushed spicy pakoras and yogurt cucumber sauce in her direction.

Sahr explained all of Meghaduta's clairevoyant talents while the sisters ate. With the parrot hopping across all the counters, and everyone comfortable, I went to the courtyard.

The morning sky was clear, the air washed clean of smoke by the rains during the night. Lalji, looking as if he hadn't slept, squatted on his heels outside the gate with two of my three erstwhile guards. I was pleased to see them. I needed information.

"No, Sahib, this bad business has stopped," the shorter one replied to my question.

"So you think it is safe to move about then? Even for a ferenghi."

The taller one wagged his head assuredly. "Indeed, Sahib. This town lives on tourists and dying people. The tourists spend more money, so the police and district bosses have plenty of patrols out. They want every foreigner who spends rupees to feel safe doing that. There is even talk of the army sending soldiers to make sure there is no more trouble." That was exactly what I needed to hear.

I handed out two hundred rupees each and the same for their missing friend. They saluted me and sauntered off. I had the comforting feeling that my house would remain under watchful eyes in days to come.

Lalji and I went back to the courtyard, where I unwrapped his grimy bandage. Coconut oil, soot, and an inexplicable sticky goo wound away like a kite tail. "It's still a bit swollen, but I think you can manage without the tape now." I patted his shoulder. "Lalji, I have a small errand for you, and then I think it might be good for you to take the day off afterwards." He started to protest, and I began to wonder if he had hit his head on something during the night. "Are you okay?"

"Yes, Sahib, I am well. I just want to be sure our house is safe."

I took his palm and placed a week's wages and a folded paper inside it. "I want you to go to the cantonment and purchase three tickets. Here is the route. First class all the way. Then I want you to get cleaned up, get a fresh shirt and a new loongi, and I want you to go to Ramuna, the tailor's daughter, and tell her that you would like to take her to the cinema this afternoon. Ask her nicely and have the film picked out before you get to her door. Tell her you wish to buy her lunch at Vikandi's ice cream café afterwards. And Lalji,"

"Yes, Sahib?" He looked like he was going to cry.

"Bring her carnations from the shop on the corner. The small ones that smell like cinnamon."

As I reached the top step of the veranda, a Frisbee struck me on my hamstring. "Bugger me twice, must be getting old. Didn't miss like that when I was twenty. 'angovers are a foockin' bitch."

I spun with a grin as he approached the gate "Hello, Mejanand. You are out of practice."

"Shite, I wouldn't be so bloody off if you'd get your arse out 'ere." His thumb hooked towards the fields.

"Seriously? You still want to play after last night? I mean, I'd understand if you wanted to miss it." I hoped he would.

He cleared the steps in one leap and popped the Frisbee with his toe, sending it like a flipped coin back into his hand. "No way, Bhimster. Got to stay sharp. Both of us do, Mate. Bunch of foocking loonies aren't keeping me from the dance. I'm up for busting a right good sweat this morning. What do you say?"

In many ways, a good run was just what I needed. Clear

away the leavings of the night.

Mej glanced beyond my shoulder toward the salon, assuming, I guessed, that I was going invite him in for coffee. I wasn't. Too many questions in there. "Okay, Sir Whiton. Three minutes. Keep the discs spinning and I'll be right out."

Sahr and Jitka were still in the kitchen getting acquainted in a new common language, food. Cookbooks and spice jars were spread out across the table. Sahr was pointing to a page and enthusiastically stirring and mixing invisible ingredients with her hands. A culinary project was brewing, and I was told that no one would need me or miss me for an hour. After her readings, Sahr would take Jitka to the market with her.

Uli, however, wasn't letting me off so easily.

"This is something you love to do, ya?"

"Actually, yes. It's kind of a passion with me."

"Then I'm coming with you. I want to learn all the things you are passionate about." I started to object and she sort of growled and made the cutest little fist. "Woman's right, Mein Schatzki."

"Right, got it. Then, if I may suggest, let's get a thick blanket. The ground is a little bumpy. And you might want to wear my sunglasses. It gets bright on the river."

"I have my own, thank you very much."

I thought of asking how many compartments were actually in her magical handbag, but went to slip on my scruffy tennies instead.

As I was lacing up, I remembered the envelope Haroon had handed me as we were leaving the bar the night before. I tore it open and the two pages quickly told me that Imperial Holding

International was a ghost. There were records of tax filings for the past two years, corporate officers listed, annual P and L statements, and all of it under another name, Maharashtra Mining. And Mahrashtra Mining was held by a foreign holding company Titan World Ore. It was a shell game, all legal, all in order, and with absolutely no substantial information at all.

Moments later Uli and I stepped into the pale morning light. Pastels and oyster-shell blushed the east, and cooler drafts than I had felt in months kissed our cheeks. The back of my hand touched hers, and suddenly, I was elated to be alive. It felt perfect to be doing something so simple. Walking with this woman to the river to throw a Frisbee with a companion. It was an odd, but totally correct action in a world gone crazy. I looked at her and her smile told me that she understood.

Mej immediately began with an obnoxious fawning that irritated me considerably. "Whoa, knock me down. Uliana with the sapphire eyes is joining us boys?" His thumb flipped my way. "Not that Bhimer 'ere is such a 'orrible date, but you are 'elluva lot cuter to catch the sunrise with. You don't happen to play Frisbee do you?"

Uli reacted with the same coolness as two days ago. "No, Mejanand. I just came to watch." The sunglasses masked the frost in her eyes that I knew was there.

The three of us strolled toward the river as rose and magenta dissolved in the east. The mood was strained. At least for me. Uli clearly found Mej's extroverted manner abrasive, but I sensed there was something deeper. A mistrust of sorts. She tolerated his humor with a tight smile and responded to his questions with curt monosyllables. I let it all go in anticipation of a good run,

and as we approached the flat brownness of the marigold
grounds, I sprinted ahead.

True, spontaneous exercise has the favorable quality of
keeping the mind keenly focused. There is no ruminating, no
weighing decisions, no politics or question of faith. It just is. The
players are suspended in the moment, wrapped in the clarity of
seeking perfect motion, which convinces me that Zen Buddhists
would have loved Freestyle Frisbee. The disc arrived at the
precise moment I turned. Without contemplation, I tapped it
ten feet straight up and let it settle onto my index finger for a
clean three seconds of spin before I flipped it back. Pure Zen.

Our times in the marigold fields always had a surreal feel to
it, an out-of-place, modern dance in an ancient setting. I suppose
that was part of the reason we loved it. Women and girls, bent
to the picking blossoms in nearby fields would always straighten
for a moment to watch the crazy ferenghis with the flying discs.
The Bernoulli Effect can be explained by physicists, but it is still
magic to anyone witnessing it.

Mej and I began unhurriedly, in a relaxed manner, the discs
drifting smoothly on light winds. It was a warm-up. But then,
little by little, Mej started shooting the discs lower and faster,
just outside my reach so that I needed to sprint, stretch, and
jump faster than in any previous runs. I returned the
compliment. It had the odd sensation of a high school
competition, a battle of machismo pettiness, and all the while,
Uliana sat on her folded cloth and watched from behind dark
lenses.

As we were nearing the end of an hour, Mej snapped both
discs in succession, two or three seconds apart and twenty feet of

lateral space between them--a near impossible feat to catch
both, especially with fatiguing muscles. He meant for me to miss
at least one.

But I was on top of my game that morning, one hundred
percent.

I didn't catch the first disc; I stretched and popped it straight
up twenty feet with my knuckles. Then, with a single step in the
other direction, leaped and kicked the second with my toes in a
flawless roundhouse. It angled up just enough for me to step
back and catch the first one and then jump over to snatch the
second in a Nuryev leap behind my back. I couldn't have
repeated it in a hundred years--the grand finale of the fireworks
display, a dramatic finish where the crowd roars with approval.

I looked first to Uli, who was rocking up and down lightly on
the balls of her feet in some sort of dance of adulation. I cocked
an eyebrow at her and shrugged with a look that indicated I
made catches like that every day. Maybe she believed me.

Then I looked at Mej. He had donned a mask of non-emotion.
The entire morning had felt strained with him, and his reaction
to my catch was the oddest. It wasn't like him to lose humor or
be aggressive to that degree.

Then, as if a switch was flipped, he started clapping and
pumping his fist into the air like a prizefighter. "Foocking
incredible, Mate. Play of the week material. Where, I mean
where, did you learn to do that shite? Never seen noothin' like
it."

I shrugged. "Just sort of happened, Mej. Didn't really plan
it." *Pure Zen*, I thought.

"Right-o, well you should 'ave seen it from this side. Michael
Foocking Jordan, it was. Ain't that right, Uliana? The dogs

bollocks, eh?"

Uli kept her gaze on me and answered flatly, "Yes, it was amazing. I didn't understand why you enjoyed this game. Now I do."

We started walking hastily back along the road to the villa, overtaking sari-clad women returning from the river with water pots balanced on their heads. The sun was above the horizon now, the pulse of the city growing in the north. Even from that distance, I noticed the odor of smoke and charred wood from the riots.

I looked at my watch and started walking faster. There was barely enough time to shower before getting a taxi to Chandragupta's.

As we turned towards the villa, Uli slipped her hand around my elbow--a tender reminder that she was there. I slowed and touched her fingers with my hand.

Mej strolled in front and cracked a few one-liners that were intended to be humorous but didn't have the usual timing. No one laughed. I snapped the blue disc fifteen feet up. It flattened against the breeze and drifted back to his index finger. With his back to us he spun it with his other hand, rotating it like a plate on a stick. In a show-off move, he shifted it deftly to his middle finger, then to his ring finger, and finally to his baby finger. We watched the smooth whirring in silence.

Morning sunlight refracted off a band of silver on his baby finger.

Tossing me the disc, he twirled his ring habitually with the fingers of his other hand, and at the same time Uli dug her fingers into my skin like pincers. I almost froze. We had both noticed Mej's ring. A small owl, its wings spread and talons

curved, screeched from the sky on his baby finger. We saw it
clearly.

He spun on his heel and grinned at us.

"Foockin' good sweat today, Bheemer, even though you
showed me up right fookin' good in front of Uliana 'ere. I'll 'ave
to repay that one sometime."

No expression, I thought. *No emotion.* I grinned sloppily.
"Look forward to it, Mej. Give me call when you're up for
another one." I had the absurd realization that my cell phone
was lying in four pieces on my desk.

"Yeah . . . definitely." Hollow insincerity in his voice.

God, tell me he didn't see my eyes. Tell me he was still
looking ahead when I noticed the ring. He was, wasn't he?

I nudged Uli towards the gate as Mej added, "but it may not
be for a week or so. I've got some business to attend to."

"Import/export," I uttered automatically.

"Yea, something like that." He tossed me the second disc.
"Hold onto these 'til I'm back, Bhimer" But I had the distinct
impression that he wasn't planning on returning anytime soon.

Fifty-Seven

I understood all too well how changes popped into a person's life. The abrupt ones. They came with my fiancé's last breath. They came with the murder of my adopted sister, and with shrapnel exploding against a river wall, and with finding love again. They entered whenever they wished, however they wanted, suddenly, violently, or tenderly. I understood all that, but this change was incomprehensible.

Uli spun before we were half way across the salon, anger smoldering in her eyes. "It's him. I know it. I knew it when I first met him. I could feel it. Ist like the nord vind freezing the trees in vinter, Bhim." Apparently it wasn't just sleep that brought on her accent. "My heart felt cold when he touched my hand. He is . . . evil." Her speech slowed, and without speaking I pulled her into my arms.

It's a ring, Bhim, *just a ring, not a proof of terrorism. A Shivdas witch's twisted words about a piece of silver. That's all it is, nothing more.* The voice was trying to convince me Mej was just a lousy comedienne with good muscle tone. Uli was clearly convinced otherwise.

"You talked about the goat herder you saw in the crowd yesterday, is it him?"

I closed my eyes, forcing the memory to return. There had been a familiarity to the figure on the Ghats, a lightness in his step that seemed somehow familiar. The man had looked directly at us, but could I be certain that he, the PuppetMaster, and Mej were the same person? "I don't know, Uli. I don't. God, I've played Frisbee with Mej fifty times at least. He's just not . . ." Had he so completely fooled me, the unsuspecting, reclusive ferenghi? Was he that good? His Hindi was excellent, his physique suggested a lot more than weekly exercise, his appearance . . . then it struck me. He had features that could be molded into anything, a face that could melt into a crowd and be transformed--American, French, Saudi, or an NRI that cranked out tasteless jokes in Cockney. There was another detail, one I had forgotten until that moment because it had seemed insignificant at the time. On one of his higher leaps, on a morning right after we had started playing together, I had noticed a piece of leather on the inside of his left calf. It was worn from use, and I supposed it to be a sheathe. Now I couldn't stop wondering if it held the knife that killed Soma.

I shook my head. "I just don't know," I said again.

"Well, I do," she replied emphatically.

Fifty-Eight

"We need better proof, Uli. I can't go stirring up a wasp's nest accusing some NRI of killing sixty-nine people. I don't think the police are apt to believe a foreign Sanskrit student who marches in and claims he knows the identity of the most wanted terrorist in the country. Yes sir, it's based my theory of an owl ring that I heard about in a séance in the red light."

"Okay, I get your point. But maybe they would listen or at least investigate. You can't just ignore it, Bhim."

"I'm not going to ignore it. I'm going try to find something using other methods. There are ways to get information in this city that even the police can't tap into" I kissed her neck. "I am going to try to find out who he is. Okay?"

She nodded, a bit reluctantly, but it was in agreement.

"And remember, we have a huge advantage right now," I said.

A smile danced on her lips. "That you are a strong, handsome, intelligent lover who is better at Indian espionage than he thinks?"

"No. Mr. Mej Whiton doesn't know that we suspect him. That is an advantage."

Her arms slid around my waist. "Okay, but however you do it, you do it carefully."

"Promise. Now, go get your magic handbag. We need to be at the professor's in twenty minutes and I need to call a taxi without the use of my phone. Mine, as you notice, seems to be malfunctioning right now." I pointed to the shattered chunks on my desk.

She went into the bedroom, while I went to the kitchen.

Sahr was just lifting two cheese-filled nans from the oven

while Jitka peered over her shoulder. The entire back of the house was filled with the delicious odor of flatbread and paneer. "Are those for lunch? Or a post-breakfast treat?"

Sahr straightened and turned to set them on racks on the counter. "Neither, Rajah Bhim. These are gifts for Miss Jitka, who not only appreciates all of my cooking, but has memorized my best nan recipe."

"But there are two of them," I pleaded.

"Ya, und maybe if you are respectful, Mr. Knucklehead, you vill get a small taste of one."

With that, I motioned Sahr to the back courtyard where I asked her to tap very discreetly into every source she had. Gather anything on Mejanand Whiton. She promised that it would not take long, and I knew it wouldn't.

Fifty-Nine

We drove through the outer sections of the city and most
appeared unscathed, like a man-o-war that had seen its battle
fractures on the opposite side. The neighborhoods felt peaceful,
like washed air after a mountain storm, but I sensed it was
illusory. Sections to the north had been shattered. Shops had
been burned, some to the ground, and the façade of the Alamqir
Mosque had been the target of fusillades of rock and bottles.
Most of the damage had been inflicted without reason, as I
supposed was normally the case with senseless violence. Young
Hindus had seized the occasion to vent their frustration in
Muslim neighborhoods; fundamentalists had urged them on,
inciting them to strike at any prominent targets. Few seemed to
remember that it started with a blast directed at every faith.

One target had been more visible and symbolic to the Hindu
youths, because it represented all things decadent and
contemptibly Muslim. Haroon's. Three of his back rooms had
been torched and badly damaged.

It jolted us to think that it had happened moments after we
slipped out his back door.

A mob had tried unsuccessfully to crash through the front
and burn the bar to the dance floor. Frustrated by the steel
shutters, they made their way to the back and set fire to the
rear. The police routed them, and fortunately my friend, who
was really Muslim in name only, had left right after us to feed
his cats. I knew Haroon well enough to know that he would have
it all rebuilt with better wood and, regrettably, larger speakers.

The beauty of the morning couldn't prevent this news from
saddening us. Uli showed amazing composure, but I knew she
was imagining what would have happened had we lingered over

another glass of Courvoisier.

The explosion at the Manikarnika had killed three people. In a sad twist of irony it was later discovered they were of Hindu, Muslim, and Christian--a surprisingly small number considering the size of the crowd. Fourteen more has been injured, six critically. According to our driver, a small charge of plastique had been detonated beneath a wooden box on a step ten feet above the shala. Fortunately, there was enough hardwood and concrete to limit the damage. I was also thankful to hear that no ferenghi had been hurt. Marley Chapin's refrigeration hat, however, would be laid to rest with all due respect.

Uli and I taxied to the main gates of Benares Hindu University--the Central Park of Varanasi--a disproportionately large, open space in the middle of a very dense city. Thirteen hundred acres spread out in an enormous fan of roads and pathways from the entrance. The gates themselves rose like the portals of Mogul fort, twenty meters, and on the other side the greatest collections of Hindustani studies were housed in some of the most exquisite buildings in the city.

With a few extra minutes, I lead us along a gravel lane past the main library. Unknown by most visitors to the city, it is one of the most stunning structures in Northern India. Uli, as I knew she would, was enchanted the instant it came into view. "Mein Gott, it's amazing. Und you have spent time inside?"

"A few hundred hours, here and there," I replied.

"Is it as pretty on the inside as the outside?" She asked this as we strolled through the hedged gardens paralleling the facade.

"Some might not say so, but I'm partial to musty, old books with squiggles on the spines. It could probably use better air quality, but you can get lost in stacks and not be found for weeks."

"That sounds like your kind of place, Lover. Can we sneak in and get lost together sometime?" Her sly grin had returned and I was suddenly glad I had taken us down that path. We came to the front steps and she read the wooden sign, "Maharaja Sayajirao Gaekwad of Baroda Library. That really is just too big a title for any building."

"The students call it The Main Library."

"Well, they're smart. I guess that's why they go to the university."

A few of those students went jogging past us, though no classes were in session on Sunday morning. The riots had kept anyone else at home. A bicyclist wheeled by and glanced back at the tall ferenghi couple holding hands. We picked up our pace, my Casio reminding me that we were now a minute behind schedule, but unlike my teacher; C.G. never seemed to mind if I was tardy, early, or punctual. I had visited his house twice before and remembered that it was nestled in a quiet, wooded area between the cricket fields and one of the massive lecture halls.

I asked her about her university in Denmark and added, "Ms. Hadersen, have I told you how stunning you look in my kurta this morning?"

She smoothed a few wrinkles along the torn hem and replied, "You realize that you are taking me to meet one of your famous pundits und the Queen of Haroon's, und I am wearing one of *your* shirts, which is torn, und a rather smelly skirt."

"And you still look more beautiful than anyone on earth. Anyone."

She stopped, her face and hair bathed in splintered sunlight.

We stood on the path near a copse of betel palm and sandalwood. She touched my lips with the tips of her fingers and said in a low voice, "How do you manage to say such perfect things to me, always make me feel like I do right now? Do you know how incredible that makes me feel as a woman?"

"It's because you *are* the most beautiful woman in the world. Five days and I know it. All this craziness keeps spinning around us, and I look at you and it stops. I want to spend the rest of my life learning how to say the right things you."

"You see," she whispered, "that is exactly what I mean, Mein Schatzki, you always make the perfect words." She smiled and turned down the path again. "Geology," she said after a moment.

"What?"

"Geology. You asked what I studied at university. I told you on our first date. I studied earth science. Rocks. Boring old rocks."

I kicked a piece of gravel. "I love boring old rocks. They're like boring old languages. You study them long enough and you find a universe inside them."

"You see," she laughed.

Sixty

The door flew open before we had finished climbing the four steps to the porch. Sukshmi, in a rust-colored sari, motioned us quickly into the front parlor. The sari was traditional, but little else was. Her nouveau hairstyle was uncovered and radically cropped, lipstick and fingernails blazed in bright shades of peach, and her rose-tinted sunglasses were still perched like a canary on her head. She wore the same sad smile I'd become accustomed to, but behind it was an expression of puzzling vitality.

I stood for a moment not knowing what to do or expect. The note of the previous evening hadn't provided much. Sukshmi placed her palms together and with a little bow said, "Namaskara, and you must be Uliana. Now I see why Bhimaji has been smiling so much lately. A beautiful woman has filled his heart with peace and joy, what a blessing." She took Uli's hand in both of hers.

Uli, with the poise of a duchess, replied, "Bhim has filled my own heart with joy, and told me often how beautiful and kind his teacher's daughter is. I see for myself that both are true." I suppose it shouldn't have surprised me, but each seemed completely sincere.

Then Sukshmi, with a sweep of her hand toward the inner rooms, said something that truly surprised me. "Welcome to my godfather's home. Follow me."

"Your godfather?" I asked in amazement.

She glanced at me, puzzled. "That's right. Of course, you didn't know. C.G., as Father's oldest friend, was asked to be my spiritual guardian." She aimed her teasing smile at us and added, "Father just didn't guess what kind of guardian C.G.

would turn out to be. Come, come, there is little time. And Bhim?"

I stopped behind her in the arched entry. "Yes?"

"Two things. Do not be alarmed by what you see. Or sad. They are not."

"And?"

Her eyes sparkled. "I am in love and engaged."

"The boring bank clerk from Delhi?"

"Not a chance," she snapped.

Oh God, I thought the battle has escalated now. I motioned for Uli to go in front of me, and as we walked down the hallway to a room on the right, I pondered how so much had changed in such a short a time. That is India, I thought to myself.

It was a fair-sized space, books, desks, and pillowed divans, wrapped around the walls. Long windows hid behind thick curtains. In the center, two beds were set a few meters apart, a chair and table between them. C.G. was propped up in one and Adam in the other. C.G.'s private study was now converted into a type of hospital ward. Satnam Kangri leaned forward in a high-back chair between the beds, his fingers on the professor's wrist. And as soon as I saw the old pundit, I knew he was dying. The eyes were dim, the light fading like late evening in his pupils. It was a good-bye, and Uli and I had, for unknown reasons, been asked to put in an appearance.

What ultimately convinced me of C.G. passing was Satnam. He looked drained, as if the power of his skills had been tested and were no longer proficient.

We stepped forward and all three men spoke at the same time.

Satnam--"Ah, my boy welcome. This beautiful woman must be the same who has restored your heart to such fine health."

Adam--"Bhim, Uli, how marvelous that you have arrived. Please, sit." I watched as he pushed himself up against the headboard, wincing slightly with pain. An unseen stanchion buoyed the sheet around his knee and lower leg.

But it was Chandragupta's words, barely audible, that caught my ear and brought me habitually to my knee to touch his feet. "My boy, come let me see you and this beautiful light in your life." He reached weakly for my hand.

"Professor..." My voice caught. I took his hand and touched my forehead to it.

His breathing was labored and soggy.

Uli moved to the opposite side of the bed.

"Have you brought it?" He whispered. "I would like to see it just once more. That is my only regret, you know, that it will enter the world as I leave. It was a fine time with our project, was it not?"

I raised my head to look at him. "One of the greatest privileges of my life, Punditji"

"And you will see that it is done correctly? Devi will need your help. He doesn't see the ways of the world like us."

"I know, Professor."

"Satnam and Adam will help. My boy has finances and knows many very important people. Use his help."

From Adam I heard a familiar chuckle. "Ah yes, another unmentioned detail. We really have not had enough time to talk about these things, have we? Chamuk, whom you call C.G., and Mundika are my parents. They are the loving people that saved me from the cholera of the gullies."

It astounded me momentarily, then it all fit. The professor from BHU. Chandragupta and his wife had raised the infant boy. Mundika had died six years earlier, after Sharmalal had been sent away to England.

C.G. smiled and lapsed into a nasty coughing spell, and when it passed, he said, "After we scrubbed him off he turned about to be quite a curious gift, a prodigy for two old Benarsis who couldn't have children. He sucked the world in like a sponge, our Adam did. A gifted learner with far too much aptitude for this place. I sent him to Mundika's sister's in London for a proper education." He smiled weakly. "My friends in the physics department at Oxford still tell me how he taught them a thing or two when he was seventeen." I guessed at some of the parts C.G. wasn't telling me. Sooner or later someone had discovered that Adam was a harijan. It would have been difficult for all of them had he stayed. In England his origins could be obscured, but not in the holy city.

I opened the files on the laptop while Uli took Satnam's chair next to Adam. Laying her hand lightly on his arm she asked, "Are you badly hurt?"

He chuckled, "Scratches, Dear Uli, just scratches. The good doctor has removed a few splinters from my leg and one of his disgusting pastes is seeing to it that infection will not set in. I seem to have a remarkable capacity for survival, known otherwise as good luck."

Satnam chided, "That paste comes from a recipe a thousand years old, and those weren't splinters." He looked at us seriously. "The explosion sent two sticks the size of my fist into his right leg, one in the back of his thigh, the other in the calf. Fortunately for the world, they didn't sever any major arteries.

He was moving away from the hut when the bomb went off above."

"Actually," Adam corrected, "I was being pulled quite forcefully towards a river barge by some compassionate young followers. They saw to it that I was brought here unnoticed."

I adjusted the laptop and set it gently on C.G.'s stomach. I wanted to lift him higher against the headboard, but he looked too fragile. His attention went immediately to the screen, and I turned to Adam whose eyes seemed changed now, serene and filled with confidence. Seeing him that way prompted me to ask, "Why would someone want to set off a bomb at your sermon?"

He lifted a glass of water from the bedside table and gazed intently at it before answering. "Too many reasons, Bhim. Anarchy, hatred, violence; they were likely all at the heart of it. It is likely someone wanted the city set upon itself for a time, or perhaps they really do detest the words I speak. Whatever their reasons, they wanted the result to be chaos."

I thought of what Haroon had said and tried to place Mej in that role. Like a misshaped puzzle piece, he still refused to fit.

Adam continued as if he were sitting in the shade of his shala, "We are entering desperate struggles, Bhim, large and small, but with each battle, the ripples will spread. At the center of it, there is still love. Christians call it agape. Hindus, bhakti, but it is the same. Love for the energy. Love for creation and everything in it. Those who have understood this have merged with it. But, it is always done through love. And that is why hatred can never be a part of any truly righteous belief system. It has no place." He still held the glass. "Look here; a plain glass of water. But is that it? Is it all we see? If we choose, we can see more. See its shape, its color, the refracted light on its surface, the bubbles that cling to the edge." I looked at the glass, momentarily absorbed by his voice. My breath slowed, eyes closed halfway. Relaxed, Adam's voice guided me. "See its smaller parts— connected, spinning orbs circling at speeds beyond imagination. But is it beyond our imagination? Choose to imagine it. Go deeper. The suns of the universe spin inside. See them, fly within them, and let go. Feel the light, the infinite speed. Nothing remains but that light, Bhim And that light is you. It is Lilia, and Soma, and Uli, Sahr, your parents, and all the galaxies of the universe. It loves you, and it is all that you should love. Now see the glass of water again." I came drifting back, feeling like a hypnotist's subject. "Now, when you look upon anything, see this. Know that center. Continue to love it and you will become one with it. And remember, from that, good deeds will be done." I looked into his eyes. His face shone like the sunrise over the river.

In that moment I saw Adam as he truly was, a man young in years, and ancient in wisdom. A prophetic leader capable of mending. A healer. "The good has arrived," he continued. "More comes each day, and it will not, cannot be stopped. Our battles are waged without violence, and the ripples are spreading " He lifted a large sheaf of bound pages from the table and set it on his lap. "You know what the most powerful instrument of change is, don't you?"

I answered without hesitation, "Language, spoken or written."

He smiled. "Precisely so, as Devamukti would say. Take this. Read what you wish. I think you will find some of it technical, some inspirational, and some downright boring. But I will ask you to consider doing an important favor for me."

I was puzzled, but more so, questioning my confidence.

"It is because you understand the power of language that I ask this."

Editing? Proofing? My mind jumped from lily pad to lily pad.

"Write the forward. An introduction in your own words." Four plus inches of bound document was handed to me. "Neither long nor complex, Bhim. Employ your poetic conciseness, and when you are done with it, deliver it to Britland Press on Connaught Circle in New Delhi. They will know what to do."

I immediately asked myself, why me? Adam seemed to think I was proficient. Am I?

My thoughts were cut short by C.G.'s voice, stronger now, "I knew it! Bhimaji, come and look at this." I stood and came to his bed. "This corner, where it disappears under the rock, can you read the first line?" He pointed to a faint string of angular lines magnified on the screen. I studied it, but it was too difficult to read. Magnifying it created a distortion and the resolution was too choppy.

"I need to reduce it to normal size and use a magnifying glass," I said.

Satnam pointed to the desk below the window. "Bottom left drawer."

Uli went and returned with a large, black-handled lens. She peered through it at the screen to focus it for C.G. and then lifted his hand to the handle. I came to the other side of the bed and the three of us peered at the script along the base of the wall.

"Asvini twins," he whispered, and I understood immediately what it implied. It was another salutation.

With the same awe I felt standing in the cave itself, I said,

"My god, it's the beginning of another shastram."

C.G.'s head drooped, his chin settling into his chest. "There are others," was all he could manage. With a smile his eyes closed.

Uli gently took the lens from his hand and quickly studied the screen again.

Satnam stepped to the professor's side to take his pulse, and nodded to all of us.

Sukshmi began weeping softly behind me, but Adam, sounding almost elated, said, "Bhim, help Satnam pull mm close to Father's bed, please. Take these, and make certain Devamukti gets this letter." He handed me the manuscript and an envelope addressed, To Jatanaka Devamukti, The Best Friend I Had. "Read them, if you wish, but the book will be better for the long hours on the train." He smiled at my bewilderment of how he knew of our travel plans. "And these you may use as long as you need them." He handed me a set of car keys and a cell phone. I went to protest but he hushed me. "Understand that we have resources and I am much more affluent than you might imagine. Use them. Dispose of the phone when you are done, or continue to use it; it will not be needed again. Now, shift my bed and go."

Uli stood next to Sukshmi, offering soothing words. Satnam and I lifted and pulled the bed until it was parallel to C.G.'s and as we moved toward the door, I looked back. Adam was sitting upright holding his father's hand, the hand of the man who had lifted him from the gutters, loved him, and given him life. He was gazing at C.G.'s face in the same way as he had the glass of water minutes earlier—seeing the energy. Both seemed bathed in a soft, pulsing light, and I watched him kiss his father's hand

and begin whispering, "The light is great, Father. Look into it without fear. Feel the center with love and feel its love for you. Like a river, flow into it. It is you and you are it." Adam's voice followed us as we exited out into the hall. A final spasm of coughing ended in silence, and I leaned against the wall and said a silent good-bye to my friend.

In the parlor Satnam turned to me. "It was the explosion. He was convinced that Adam had died. It drained what little was left in his heart. News didn't reach us for many hours, and when it did, C.G.'s energy knew it was time to let go. He called for me and then asked to see you."

Seeing the sadness in my eyes, Satnam placed a hand on my shoulder. "Do not be grieved; it is good and proper this way. He was with the people he loved most at the end. You were one of them. And the deeds of his life were brought to fruition. How many can say that? His love for Adam was so strong that it created . . . well it created Adam."

"I should tell you that I took the liberty of talking, before all this evil erupted yesterday, with a few of my Ayurvedic friends—a council that represents the best traditional medical knowledge around here. Do not fear though, they are discreet to the point of being cabalistic. A great deal of excitement followed my little announcement, as you might imagine. I hope you don't mind, but I gave a few of them permission to begin studying the shastram as soon as you are willing to provide me the notes. They are incredibly excited about the method you discovered for proportioning the plants; it will likely open up reviews of some the old recipes. A lot of volunteers will want to take part in this. It is still early, but it looks so hopeful." He paused and tapped my chest. "But, it is up to you to decide if you want them to continue."

I reached into my backpack. "I'm not sure if I am the sole person to make that decision, Satnam. But I know what the pundits would say, 'precisely so, keep going forward." I removed the memory stick from my pack and handed it to him.

"Excellent. Perhaps we can announce the medical news at the same time Devi's releases his letters to the Sanskrit societies." He looked at Uli and his dimples deepened. Laying his hand on my chest again, he said, "And as your physician in the partial healing of your heart, I proclaim you healed. Fully so."

I nodded with gratitude and a small smile, then hoisted the manuscript and envelope; heavy in more ways than one. Sukshmi tapped the envelope with lacquered nails. "Do be careful with this one, Bhim. It is the key to my freedom."

"I won't ask what that means, Jatana."

"You'll understand soon enough. Read it when Father is done and you will see. By the way, my fiancée told me he thinks the name Sukshmi fits me better. I have decided to drop Jatana as my Nom d'Soir."

"Good, You can tell that very fortunate man that I always thought Sukshmi fit you better, too. With long hair and a sari, but that is just my humble opinion. Is he Benarsi?"

"No, but he is quite the handsomest graduate student at the university in Delhi."

I asked an all-important question. "Brahmin?"

"Of course, political science major with a good brain, lots of wit, and beautiful eyes. He even likes to dance on occasion." She slid an arm through Uli's, and looking a bit conspiratorial, whispered, "Your Bhim is good man, Uliana, but you already know that, don't you? "

Uli kissed her cheek and replied, "Yes, I do, Sukshmi." With a promise that we would safeguard the mysterious envelope, Uli and I stepped back onto the graveled paths of the University.

****

Living in Varanasi had been a flight from my former life, and in some ways, a husking of my accountabilities. I had taken shelter in the reclusiveness and taken on a smaller set of obligations. There were disciplines, studies, and exercise, of course, but few true commitments beyond that. Now, as the morning sun pressed down upon my shoulders, I felt the enormity of what I carried. It didn't take long for that weight to increase.

As soon as we were on the path towards the library, Uli turned to me with an unusually serious expression. "You remember, I told you I studied a lot about boring old rocks?"

"Yes, that would be one of those beautiful secrets about you I will not forget twice."

She tugged on my arm and stopped me cold. "There is something in the cave photograph that is more significant than you know."

I thought she was referring to the script. "You mean more words?"

"No, the rock."

"What rock? What do you mean?"

"I can't be sure until I look closer and have a sample, but I'm pretty sure the floor of your cave may be covered with uraninite."

***

The hairs on the back of my neck rose into an uneasy tingle. "I'm assuming from the first three syllables that its something I don't want to hear, like uranium?"

She nodded. "Uranium oxide, raw ore before any refinement, und if it is high grade as I think this is, it is dangerous."

As I pictured picking my way across the oily chunks with Devamukti, the tingling increased. "Do you mean like radioactive dangerous?"

"No, there is little radiation. The danger is what it can be made into, yellowcake."

"Yellowcake? " I resisted a small itch to be comic.

She turned onto the path again. "Ya, it's the first step in nuclear fuel process. It looks like yellow cake crumbs. Well, it used to look that way, now it is made better and looks more like brown or black cake. I had two courses at university with a lot of reading about it. There were films and learned how much is mined, und how much is sold on the black markets. It is a lot more than you would think, und the more refined it becomes, the more valuable und more tempting it is to smuggle."

My mind reeled. "Uranium. Yellowcake? Is it really that prevalent?"

Her eyes blazed. "The entire nuclear program of Pakistan came from smuggled materials. Abdul Khan, the head of the program, then sold his knowledge *and* the critical materials to Libya and Iran. So yes, it is prevalent. Everything from gas centrifuges to high-grade fuel moves to countries that can't purchase it on the open market because of the non-proliferation treaties. Or sanctions. You remember what Haroon said about India's need it? And Pakistan's? Refined, it can be used in reactors, warheads, dirty bombs, und that, Mein Schatzki, is why it is so valuable und dangerous."

That phrase kept coming back. Suddenly, I understood. "My God, that would explain the actions at the mine. And why nobody wanted us near it."

The phone in my pocket bumped against the keys, reminding me that I was in possession of both. "I forgot about our car."

"What car?"

"Adam gave us C.G.'s car and a phone to use."

"That's fortunate, because we need to take a drive."

"A drive? Now? Where?"

She tugged sweetly on my sleeve to get us moving again. "Not now, tonight. We have to go out there and collect a sample."

"What! You're kidding, right? You want me to drive out there in the middle of the night and sneak around like a peeping . . . rock collector?" The hairs on my neck now felt like pins.

She kissed my cheek and whispered, "I'll be right there to protect you."

"I may need it." The idea of driving to the cave at night was appalling, but another part of me knew that it was necessary. "Wasn't it you who said I needed to do all this carefully? This morning, if I remember correctly."

"It is the only way we can know, Lover."

I shook my head and blew out a long breath. "Okay, but right now we need to go to a place I meant to visit yesterday, an internet café."

Taking my hand and turning me back towards the cottage and the car, she said, "You're our guide, Lover."

Sixty-One

Sutradharak was quite pleased with himself again. In opposition to the harsh self-censure of earlier, he was now patting himself on the back. The outcome of the explosion at Manikarnika had been much better than planned. With the smallest amount of HBX-3, not enough to make a difference to his other design, he had set the city upon itself. Chaos, always his intention. In addition, his team had assembled at the location an hour after sunset. Two cars, under a moonless sky, and with exacting touch, had placed six charges. The HBX-3 was taped in carefully assessed locations and wired to cell phones with the vibration mode set to on. Those were the receivers. The transmitters were now in his possession. They had tested the signal three times and, just before they left, inserted the cap wires into the plastique.

The four men left in pairs in opposite directions, registered at mid-fare hotels, dined on rice and dal, and engaged in indifferent conversation. Then they showered, slept, and settled down for the wait.

Sutradharak was now standing in the central-city loft, staring absently at yet another funeral to the Ghats. *Two days, no more, and the biggest event I have ever planned will take place. A crowning achievement of diversion. A coup de gras before the disappearing act. Then I can be rid of this filthy place.*

He looked across the roofline and admitted stingily that it wasn't all bad. A few pleasant moments, a few good meals, some good distractions, and of course, the challenge of different personalities. Now? Perhaps Europe for a spell. Or back to the Americas. Suddenly, it all felt proper, and for a brief moment he allowed his ego to rise. Really, he decided. I am the master of this competition, the teacher. Success through the planning, leave no trail, and set no patterns. He twisted the owl ring on his finger and slowly closed the slats across the window.

Sixty-Two

"Under no circumstances are you allowed to make fun of my driving," I pronounced as I lifted her up to the passenger seat. "This monster is more truck than car, and I haven't sat behind a steering wheel for a few years now."

"Would you like me to do it?"

"The first thing that we be dented if that happened would be my male ego. Besides, I think men *have* to drive their women in this town. Some sort of law."

"You're our guide. Lover. Besides, you know where we are going." She slid in close and kissed my neck.

I shifted into first gear and rolled forward with the caution of teen taking a first license test. I knew of three Internet cafes on this side of town, all wisely placed close to the university. If the first didn't suit our needs, the next one would.

Rolling through the university gates in a dawdling second gear, I asked, "So, if you put all of the pieces together in this puzzle, what do you come up with." I had begun to form my own theory, but wanted to hear hers.

She thought for a moment and frowned. "Well, this Mejanand is in the center of everything, I am certain of that. He is vicious. Und somehow I think he has local police in his pocket."

"Like Madru Ralki?"

Uli was heating up. "Ya, this Ralki you talked about. He tried to find out from Soma what you were doing in the cave. I think he was trying to scare you und Devi because it was so close to the mine. When that didn't work and the guard came, they collapsed the entrance."

"And you really think the mine has something that goes on

the black market?"

"Ya, und I bet they are turning the ore into yellowcake there. It would be risky, but very smart because of the weight. The ore is heavy, but the yellowcake is light und worth much more. It would mean bringing in very special apparatus und chemicals, but it would be smarter."

I thought about the machinery I had seen at the entrance-- ordinary mining equipment to my unqualified eye. "But what would they do with it then? How would they move it?"

She slid her fingers to the side of my face to tuck strands of hair behind my ear, the motion triggering the painful memory of sitting on the bed in the foulness of the Riverview where she had done the same thing. It had all felt so raw then, new and uncertain. But now, still facing uncertainty, I felt sure of myself.

Uli was answering my question. "Probably shift it to another place where it can be sold to the best buyer. Und this is where it gets frightening. That could be anyone, a terrorist group, though they usually don't have equipment to complete the refinement. But a rogue country? Iran, North Korea. They might even sell it back to India."

That seemed preposterous. "You mean to smuggle it outside the country and then sell it back?"

"You would be surprised how often that happens. Remember what Haroon said? The biggest uraninite mines in India are in the next province. Smuggling und re-selling is common. Last year a shipment made its way to Nepal and was sold to Libya or Pakistan. The International Atomic Energy Agency has new cases every week, but think of getting four thousand dollars a kilogram or more on the black market und you see the motivation."

"Almost four million dollars a ton?"

"Good money, ya?"

"And you remember all this from university?"

She smiled sweetly. "My mind is good for what I read, und I read a lot"

I maneuvered around a pack of unpredictable bicyclists and pulled up in front of Rayan's Highspeed Internet Café. Some curious university types watched as it took me three minutes to figure out how to lock the doors and set the alarm.

Rayan was good to his word in regards to high speed. What weren't so up to date were the computers themselves. A bank of machines on the left looked like Tandy 1000s with five and a quarter inch floppy drives. Green screens glowed below woven tapestries. I groaned and asked the bookish-looking associate if there was something a little closer to the current decade.

"By all means, Brother, we've got some Dells in the back corner," He glanced at a crowd of young males huddled around them, a few now gawking at Uli. "But my guess is it's forty minutes before they become available. They came in just before you."

I was considering driving to another café, when Uli nudged my backpack. "Aren't you forgetting something, Lover?" I looked at her. She pointed merrily at the Acer inside.

Three minutes later, with the help of Rayan's helpful employee, the Acer was connected and open to the desktop. It wasn't blazingly fast, but it would suit my purposes.

I started where everyone starts. Google. Imperial Holding International. I expected a few hits and got half a million, but none with the name in a single string. In an advanced search I connected them and also got nothing. I added Lucknow to the search. Nothing. Businesses, corporations, LLCs, and every financial entity in existence with the name Imperial Holding. Nothing that even remotely resembled it. After ten minutes of mega searches and Boolean selections, I admitted failure and came to the ugly conclusion that IHI of Lucknow didn't exist. Or it existed only in the Uttar Pradesh, way the hell out in the middle of nowhere next to our cave. It was just as Haroon's report had indicated. A ghost. Strike two.

Before leaving I read three articles on black market uranium and scared the hell out of myself. Uli was right, it was far too prevalent. After a small payment to Rayan's, we left.

I started the engine and said, "I suppose I should have expected it."

She didn't comment, and after a deep, hesitant breath asked, "Bhim?"

I glanced at her for as long as the traffic would allow. Intense longing stared back. "Yes?"

"Do you think we could go to Devamukti's, and then to the villa to make sure Jitka is alright, and then someplace . . . to be alone? Just for an hour? You and me? Would that be alright, just for an hour?" She was almost pleading.

I had obligations to consider, which I did for about a microsecond. The world could wait. Right now my pledge was to Uli and me, and I told her as much. "The universe has turned inside out in the last ten days, and in the middle of it, the only thing that really makes any sense is you. Being next to you. I want years of it, and right now an hour . . . would be paradise. I know a hotel, and if it stretches into a second hour, what the hell...the world can wait sixty more minutes."

Her arms wrapped awkwardly around my shoulders and the headrest. Her mouth found the side of my mouth. In a throaty voice, she whispered, "Thank you."

"By the way," I whispered back. "I wrote . . . a little something for you." I fumbled my way into a side pocket of my backpack and pulled out a single sheet folded twice.

She didn't say anything, just unfolded the paper and read. She studied the Sanskrit first and then read the English twice. A tear slid slowly down her cheek to the corner of her mouth.

"Mein Gott, it's beautiful."

"Probably because it's true."

"Say it in the Sanskrit, out loud" I took a breath and recited the original. She folded the paper and closed her eyes to recite the lines of English she had just read.

"Like warming lips of spring kissing frozen mountain rains
Unfurling wetted leaves and drying wings of bees
Like shameless rays of moonlight pushing blackness from the night
And sighs of gentle breezes tossing chaff into the air
You release me

Like evening birds of love trilling nightly to the stars
And drops of silver dew moisten parched and sleepy seeds
Like eaglets winging upward at dawn into the sky
Your touch has freed my captive heart to let me live again
You release me."

As she spoke the final line I realized it was true, she had an amazing memory for what she read.

Sixty-Three

Devamukti was perched in his rocker staring silently out the window at the gate. He peered in expectation, as if his old friend might shuffle through at any moment to take tea and enter into a cordial squabble. The rocker pitched rhythmically, mechanically, his thin frame rolling it barely enough to creak on the floorboards. Standing in the kitchen, I watched as he checked his timepiece and then begin to quietly weep. His friend of sixty-seven years would not be coming to visit this morning.

I lead Uli into the parlor and without a word touched my hands to Master's feet and sat on the mat next to the rocker. Uli sat on a cushion. Seeing her for the first time, he wiped away a tear and whispered coarsely, "Would you like some tea, My Dear?"

I took his hand and offered the simplest of introductions, "Punditji, this is Uliana Hadersen. Uli, this is Sri Jatanaka Devamukti, the greatest pundit in the world, and my teacher."

Uli, as always, knew what to say. "It is an honor to meet you, Master. Bhim has told me so many beautiful things about you, especially your skills in the great language."

For three breaths Devamukti did not utter a word, he simply looked at her. Then the pain in his face seemed to ease a fraction and he reached for her hand. "You bless my home, Uliana Hadersen. Your light shines like the goddess Saraswati into the darkest corners. You are most welcome here."

He looked at me, and the sadness settled about him again. "So, My Boy, C.G. has left us. Did I ever tell you that we knew each other since we were four and five years old? We met in the school in Bhelpur."

"Yes, Masterji. I remember you telling me that."

"He was a friend to me even when I didn't deserve one.
Sometimes I think he was the only friend I've really had . . .
besides Mirabai."

I interrupted. "Master, You have a world of friends right here
in this city. If I may be permitted to say, having a few come to
tea on the occasional afternoon might be a good idea."

He nodded vaguely at that, and then, as if the memory
returned to him unexpectedly, said, "Soma will be cremated
tomorrow, Bhim. Sunrise at Manikarnika. I had . . . C.G. and I
had to quarrel with the priests over the arrangements. They
didn't think giving a low caste widow dahakarana at that
auspicious hour was right. Oldfangled imbeciles. I demanded to
preside and they relented when we teamed up on them." That
brought a faint smile.

A lot of changes had come to my teacher in recent days, and I
hoped the letter that I was about to hand him would ease them
somehow. "I brought this for you, Master. C.G. gave it to me to
me just before he died." Without anything else I placed it on his
lap.

Master studied the spidery script, and it seemed to bring a
flood of memories. He skimmed his fingers along the border, felt
the texture and departing touch of his friend. Gently he pried
the seal and removed two sheets. I took Uli into the kitchen to
introduce her to Mirabai and brew us a pot of tea.

Mirabai emerged from one of the inner rooms and pulled both
of us into warm embraces. She had chai already mulling in a
small kettle on the stove and poured three cups. I carried one
back to the parlor and found Devamukti weeping, but smiling.
He took the cup and laughed sadly. "Even from death he chides
me. Even now. I should have known he wouldn't let me off

without a last tickle of my old ribs. Couldn't pass into Vishnu's arms without a last frolic at my expense." He handed me the two sheets. "Read."

I took a sip and read.

My Eternal Friend, Jatanaka,

I hope, as you begin reading, that you are smiling and laughing at some amusing memory. I hope you are recalling a few of the twenty-three thousand days of our friendship, so many of them brought to my own mind as I pen this. I drift in and out now, and know my time has come. As I do so I think of our mischief together, like the day we swam up beneath the bottom and tipped the finance minister's boat just enough so everyone tumbled into the river. We caught it for that one, eh Devi? It has been a good, long life of such memories and sometime, not too soon, I pray, we shall create more mischief and merriment together in the world beyond.

It is important for you to know how proud I was to call you my friend, to share cups of chai and plates of iddly, and test each others knowledge in lifelong contest of minds. Fine competitions we had, and like far too many things at the end, I wish I had told you more often how brilliant you really are. How good to me you were. I wish I had told you how much I cherished our friendship. We wait too long to say what is in our hearts, and then the chances disappear and we wallow in regret. But always remember that you gave me so much.

Unquestionably, the greatest gift I received from you was the honor of being a godfather to your only child. It was a responsibility I took more seriously than you might know, one I relished every day of my life. Sukshmi has been a jewel the rajah's would have coveted. She sparkled the moment she emerged from your beautiful Mirabai, and it made my responsibility that much easier.

Her light fills many dark spaces, Jatanaka.

But, my dear friend, I fear you have not looked carefully at that light of late. It is, I suppose, one of the great afflictions of fatherhood. We draft so many aspirations for our children, and too often those aspirations cloud our vision and prevent us from seeing what is true and right in their lives.

I am certain you remember the oath I took as her godfather, her Dharmapita. I believe I have fulfilled that oath quite satisfactorily. Well enough, in fact, to now call upon the old custom-- my final request of you. And being the brilliant pundit and keen traditionalist that you are, I know you remember the observance. I call upon you now to honor it.

Allow Sukshmi to marry whomever her light-filled heart desires. Let her marry for love, Jatanaka. In a world where hatred rises in every shadow, love is a far better reason to wed than ties to traditions. And that, my dear, wise, venerated, old friend, is my request. I deem it undeniable and expect you to honor it. Though it is difficult to make too many demands from where I now walk, it is our tradition to honor such things, is it not?

Be kind to yourself, Jatanaka. Cherish the gifts in your life. You have many.

Perhaps we shall soon share idly and chai once more.

With all my respect and love,

Your friend,

Chamuk G. Chandragupta

Tears streamed down my cheeks now. The professor was gone. His laugh was gone. His petition was not. I wished Uli and he could have known each other longer. They would have laughed well together.

In due course, Mirabai entered and the four of us passed a pleasant, though expectedly solemn, half hour together.

Before we left, Devamukti told us what had been arranged in regards to the translation; a traditional announcement to all the major Sanskrit societies in the country was going out. It included four tantalizing couplets and a full description of our findings. To ensure every group took it seriously, his name, Chandragupta's, and mine appeared on B. H. University letterhead. Dozens of mailings were being prepared by two of C.G.'s former students, and it would all be finished that afternoon. He had also concurred with Satnam Kangri's idea of announcing it to the Ayurvedic societies first.

It was beginning.

Sixty-Four

An hour later I checked us into the Clarks Tower Hotel--a deluxe, white layer cake of modern air-conditioning, wrapped hand soaps, soft pillows, lotions, and cream rinse. Before we took to the elevator to our room, I took us through a richly-tiled lobby to an over-priced boutique. Together, Uli and I chose a pair of silk pajama pants for her. They were green and gathered at the ankles. We also found a rose and peach-colored blouse that set her lapis eyes ablaze in contrast.

We both knew the reasons we were there, had to be there. It wasn't the clothes, or soft pillows, or scented linen. It was the need to slow it all down and shut it out for a while, to offer a sense of sanity midst the lunacy that swirled like gust about us. And that is why we didn't rush to shed our clothes. We went slowly, deliberately. Buttons, straps, and clasps became ribboned bows of Christmas silk tugging us soothingly to mutual nakedness. We touched each others cheeks with patient fingers, letting our eyes and lips speak of love, nothing else.

Our kisses began tenderly, tentatively, and came to place where our only desire was to give totally of our selves, one to the other. And at the pinnacle of our passion, in the center of a powerful climax, Uli began sobbing. She turned her face into my neck and wept hard. Nothing else mattered. Nothing. We were escapees. Nothing else mattered. Just that moment in time, and just our union.

We slept dreamless and calm. I awoke first and gazed at her face until her eyes opened. Then I dialed room service-- something I hadn't done for a half a decade--and ordered fruit compotes, Gouda cheese, cashews, and lassis. Uli brushed her hair, which I believe was one of the most sensual things I had seen in my entire life. Then she brushed mine and fluffed our pillows so that we could lie on our sides like spoons.

As I settled my arm around her, she asked, "Do you know why I was crying?" It was a simple question but deep as a kettle lake.

"Maybe. I hope it was for good reasons and not . . ."

She ignored me. "At that second, with you inside me and me around you und all that shivering love, I felt more happy und. . . alive than I have ever been, und it just. . . made me cry."

I kissed her shoulder and drew my finger along the underside of her breast. "I understand that. I feel it just when I look at you."

She rolled over so our faces were close, her eyes studying mine, palm caressing my cheek. "You know, I like it that you weep sometimes. It is a good thing when we do, it makes us stronger." She inhaled and exhaled--almost a sigh, but more like a release. "I came here looking for answers for a feeling I thought was guilt. I now know it wasn't guilt; it was emptiness. What I did with my father wasn't wrong, Bhim. You were right about that, but it left me empty. You took that place and filled it. Maybe that's why I needed to cry, because you filled me."

I licked her eyebrow. "We filled each other. Seven days ago I was on my way to the cave and still having nightmares. Then I meet you, and now all I feel is completeness."

Our lunch arrived on a rolling cart and we ate in bed. The lassis were cold and frothy, and as we were nearing our last bites she kissed me and said, "Thank you for this."

"The lunch?"

"No, for this." Her hand swept about the room and settled on my chest. "Just to be alone for an hour, it makes it possible to do what is necessary." I knew what she meant. It was possible to go on. "Do you want to talk about Mej?" she asked. "Or do you want to keep this time to ourselves?"

"Let's talk about it tonight. Right now, this is ours." She smiled and kissed me because I had answered how she wanted me to.

Leaving the Clarks Tower wasn't exactly easy. The desire to cuddle naked was pronounced for both of us, but it was made palatable by how Uli looked in her new blouse and pants. Her smile was quicker and surer now and filled with love. Mine was, I'm certain, made of the same ingredients.

****

I drove around the outskirts of the southern part of the city. The streets were wider, with fewer people, and more conducive for maneuvering a Grand Cherokee. I parked in front of my villa, noticing immediately that the gate was unlocked and Lalji not to be seen. I was glad. It meant Sahr was home and Lalji was on the first real date of his life.

I set Adam's manuscript on the desk and went to the kitchen.

Sahr had completed her morning readings, and she and Jitka were back to stirring up culinary magic. Jitka seemed comfortable, really having fun for the first time since she had left Tonder. It pleased Uli to see her laughing and not grumbling or cleaning or standing guard for both of them. She and Sahr were disappointed when I confessed that all we wanted was some of the baked nan. As we explained that we had already taken lunch in a hotel room, a rosy smile crossed Jitka's face. She had seen Uli's eyes.

After lunch the sisters sat in the parlor and chatted about

Tonder. It was a peaceful hour, sibling memories of youth. They decided to take a rickshaw to the flat to pack their belongings. I knew they needed alone time with each other.

I took the opportunity to hear what Sahr had discovered about Mejanand Whiton.

We sat in our customary places in the kitchen—the same chairs where we had shared so much of our lives. She shook her head. "Honestly, Bhimaji, there is little that people know of him. Most say, just as you said, that he is an Indian from London. He owns some type of import export business and travels to Delhi a lot, always on the train, though he has a fine car."

"Really, what kind?" That was a detail Mej had certainly not shared.

"A Mercedes. Black, fancy thing, and fairly new."

I took this in, deciding that it didn't sound particularly clandestine or heinous. "Did your good spies tell you where he lives?"

"Uhmm, a small cottage to the north in a nice part of the city. There is a garage, some rich neighbors nearby that he never speaks with. No gardeners, no cleaners, dhobi, or cook. That would be unusual except that he travels so much he isn't home enough to need anyone." She stopped.

"And nothing else? Does he have any unusual habits, go anywhere in the city regularly."

"Oh yes." I waited. "He goes on foot to South Nagpur every few days to play with the flying discs with Bhimaji. Everyone knows that." Of course they did.

"And this information is from reliable gossips and customers?"

She grinned. "More or less, oh, he also goes to visit a man on Lahurabir Road sometimes, very rarely."

"What man?" My curiosity was rekindled.

"No one knows who he is, but they say he is in some kind of dairy business."

"Dairy. What kind?" I felt my neck hairs rising again.

Sahr shook her head. "They don't know, but from the way the man dresses, they think he may be a merchant of goat products."

I thought carefully about my final question. "Sahr, has anyone ever seen these two standing together?"

Her head tilted thoughtfully. "That I do not know, Bhimaji."

****

I was asking a lot of questions none of the answers were coming, so I retreated to my best brooding spot--the wobbly chair in front of my desk. A glass of cold lager usually helped with puzzle-solving. I leaned back, drifted into the aroma of sandalwood drifting out from the mats over the window, and flowed into a string of what-ifs. What if Mej and the goat merchant were the same person, and both happened to be Sutradharak? What if--as the cobra's voice had inferred—he was involved somehow with the mining operation? Smuggling processed uranium? So why was he setting off explosions from Delhi to Varanasi? For what purpose? I paraphrased what Haroon had said as we sat at his bar. India and Pakistan were starving for fuel. 'A few acts of terrorism, people get angry, so we practice troop maneuvers and launch rockets in Kashmir. The ante goes up, more follows and we get new missile guidance systems and fuel from France or Washington, all an intricate, dangerous game.' Haroon just hadn't considered that some of those materials might come from the black market.

Had the terrorism been created--as Haroon had speculated--for ulterior reasons, something totally unrelated to what the agencies and media were saying? If the two countries were at each other's throats, the need for processed and raw materials would rise, and the demand for black market goods would rise.

As I drained the last of my lager, an uncanny 'what if' struck me. Every available agency was being used to search for Islamic fundamentalists or ultra-nationalists--house-to-house searches, warrants, detainment, and interrogation. Radicals groups were under scrutiny and being infiltrated at every opportunity. And none of it producing results. Yet seventeen miles away, in the bleakness of the plains, an ordinary mine was mining ordinary bauxite. Or so it seemed. What if, I asked myself, the bombings had been a ruse, a well designed, perfectly executed, and frighteningly deadly diversion?

Possibly. Perhaps. Maybe.

I pondered my limited options. If the mine was extracting uraninite and processing it, whom could I alert? More importantly, how was I going to keep us from getting sucked into a vortex of exposure? Figuring that out was at the top of my to do list, because fingering a mafia capo or other such nasty guys assured you of a one thing, a quick death. I needed a plan. I just couldn't do it by myself the moment.

Adam's binder sat like the boulder of Sisyphus on the desk. From curiosity I untied the string and turned to the final sheet. Seven-hundred and eighty-two pages, single spaced, ten point Palatino. A tome. Back to the first page, I read two quotes below the title. The first one I recognized from one of Adam's lectures.

Ideas of great merit, pure thoughts and plans,
Move effortlessly about the world.
They hasten without swords or armies to enforce them.
They spread with the grace and simplicity of the power of
truth.

The second quote was more ominous.
Since the world points up beauty as such
There is evilness too.
If goodness is taken as goodness,
Wickedness enters as well.
The Way of Life by Lao Tzu

Sixty-Five

Adam had entitled his opus, not surprisingly, The Simple Plan. I smiled, thinking he could have titled it A Thousand Incredible but Plausible Resolutions for Damned-Near Everything. It began simply. "Change is constant, essential, and elemental to humankind." And from that short declaration, his statements expanded into a full blueprint for world change. The language was clean and concise, which as a wordsmith I appreciated greatly. It branched into divisions and subdivisions outlining hundreds of advancements similar to the ones he had described at the river. I skimmed the titles: Resolutions for Open-Ocean Aquaculture, Distillation and Water-Reclamation, Reforestation for Climate Change Reversal, Coral Reef Rehabilitation. It went on, and at the core, inside each idea, metaphors for the great energy were woven like fine thread. Nothing was undertaken without embracing the three tenets, compassion, common sense, and pure science. I spent twenty minutes reading excerpts here and there and came to the conclusion that it was a work of genius. Should that have surprised me? A world-changing, magnum opus of hope, just like Adam himself. Yet, there was something else concealed, unmentioned, but palpable. There was the distinct impression that battles were looming. I inhaled deeply. I was supposed to write a forward for this?

****

For obvious reasons, I wasn't particularly keen on venturing to the cave after dark, and for a moment considered asking Sahr to fetch Megadhuta for a quick check on my short-term future. Cave and nighttime were words I did not like to combine, but

Uli had been resolute--it was the only way we could determine the truth. Besides, she said, we actually weren't going inside anything. Camera images weren't enough, she said. I thought they were more than adequate and attempted to make my point. The argument was lost before it began, so I spent nervous time checking bulbs and batteries in the flashlight.

Around four in the afternoon, I heard an off-key voice drifting up the street. "Lage Raho Munna Bhai." I recognized the newest movie theme that had been blasting from radios most of the summer. From my chair I saw the front gate swing open and Lalji—looking almost dapper in new loongi and fresh shirt--come skipping into the courtyard. I assumed from all this that his date with Ramuna the Tailor's Daughter had gone well. Indeed, as soon as he saw my face in the window, he started telling me all about it--the movie, the lunch menu, the waiter's haughty attitude, and all the details of his conversation with Ramuna. The flowers had been a grand success, and Lalji seemed happier than I had ever seen him. He was so affected by the events of the afternoon that he didn't even notice the Grand Cherokee parked in front.

Minutes later, Uli and Jitka sashayed arm-in-arm through the gate, laughing and toting sacks of gifts for the family in Tonder. I marveled at Uli and pictured her face as she had slept in my arms that afternoon. She looked at me and knew precisely what I was thinking.

As we re-packed fabrics and brassware and sandalwood figurines, she handed me a flat bundle wrapped in thin paper. Folded neatly inside was a black kurta with gold embroidery stitched into the neck and cuffs. "It's beautiful," I cooed. "You get too many gifts for me, you know."

"No, I don't, und I didn't know the correct color for a Hindu cremation. The tailor didn't speak much English either, so I guessed. And you're worth every thread, thank you very much."

"The traditional color is actually white, but no matter. Soma would have loved it. I'm amazed the tailor could finish it so quickly."

"His English was good enough to understand a hundred extra rupees if he finished it in two hours."

I was going to ask how she got the size matched so well, but then remembered she had been wearing one of mine all morning.

****

At times Sahr managed to combine cooking skills with clairvoyance. Somehow she knew Uli and I were intending something dangerous, or stupid, depending on how you looked at it. On some metaphysical level she knew the puissant nature of food. She understood that if the ingredients were proportioned exactly, everything handled and combined with care, the energy and purpose imparted to the eater would be magnified. She had dishes that eased one to sleep, invigorated the mind or body, or encouraged one to be more loquacious or even amorous. She handled chilies with a profound reverence, talked to the seeds and nuts like small companions as she ground them unmercifully--always by hand--and tossed spices with the precision of an alchemist. Dinner was designed to put all worries to rest.

For Jitka, all this had come in a single afternoon lesson.

While Uli and I had been out, the two of them made Murg Noorjehani, and like many such creations, it began with garlic. That was followed by ginger, green chilies, cloves, cardamom, cinnamon, and anise seed, all ground by mortar and pestle. Fresh curds, saffron, and salt added, and all of it layered thickly on chicken that had been clucking that very morning. And then it rested as patiently as a cask of brandy, and only when we were ready, was it fried in hot ghee and topped with boiled egg and sliced almonds. Lalji, still in his most dapperness, brought it to the table with Basmati rice, pooris, mango chutney, and cucumber salad. Cold ale and cabernet flowed, and for a long time no conversation took place. Sahr came out to announce that the dinner was in Jitka's honor. She was asking her devas to see to it that her apprentice arrived home safely, but that she also returned to her kitchen quickly.

The feel-at-ease magic in the food worked right up to dessert.

As we dug into mango pie, I asked about the afternoon shopping adventures.

"It vas a gut time. I learned much from my svester," Jitka replied. Uli looked mildly embarrassed.

"About how to purchase gifts and not pay too much?" I asked.

"No, about you and her and all this business that has been going on," she replied.

"You mean between us?" I was starting to feel mildly uncomfortable. "How we feel about each other? Because…"

She shot me a look that told me I was Mr. Knucklehead again. "Gut Gott, no. We already know what is going between you. Sex, sex, and more sex. No, I forced her to tell me about this business that takes you to a cave in the middle of the night. Und why you went to the red light district, and who is this terrorist that is a friend of yours."

I sat looking bowled over, if you can do that. "First, he's not a friend, not really, and . . . things have gotten very complicated, things I don't understand. But they're too important to ignore, if you know what I mean. And if it is any consolation, I did ask Uli if she wanted to fly home with you."

Jitka grinned. "Ya, I heard about that one. I guess your ribs found out she doesn't."

I nodded and glanced sheepishly at Uli.

"Und you have decided what you will do if this mine is processing this ore und your friend is involved?"

I stared at her. "I thought I stated pretty clearly that he isn't my friend, and no, I haven't thought any of it through. Since this afternoon I've been trying to come up with a plan to alert the media and intelligence agencies. Anonymously, because I do not want any of us speaking directly to anyone."

"Well, good thinking. Und you think they will actually stop this skidt?"

Uli looked at me and mouthed, "Shit."

"I hope so. Reporters here tend to be dogged, though not always accurate. But yes, I think they will, especially if they hear the Sutradharak might be involved. The Hindustani Times, The Statesman, and Times of India would be first on the list. Then, All India Radio, and the intelligence bureaus last."

"Und you will call them if you are sure this mine is digging uranium?"

"Even more quickly if we find it is being refined."

Uli chimed in, "The group that really needs to be called in is the IAEA. They can investigate things internationally and find out who is really behind it. Tell the papers to contact them."

"Right," I agreed. "But it's got to be without *anyone* knowing who's calling. You have no idea how much people get paid off. And, we need to protect the cave."

By the end of dessert, we had a decent plan.

Lalji, looking quite ebullient, entered to remove dessert plates and refill glasses. As he was stacking the dishes, he asked, "Would Saab like me to fetch the train tickets?"

It had slipped my mind. "Yes please, Lalji, and ask Sahr to come out in a few minutes."

He wagged and left.

When he returned I opened the envelope and showed everyone our itinerary. "The first part is air-conditioned first class from Varanasi to Jaunpur then on to Sultanpur and Lucknow. That's where we have dinner. That leg is in reclining chairs. In Lucknow we switch to first class sleepers, two bunks on one side and a single on the other. We can pull curtains across, making them almost like private rooms. It's not exactly the Orient Express, but it will be a lot more comfortable than second class. From Lucknow, we roll north into the foothills. It will be cooler, more scenic, and unfortunately, traveled mostly at night." They looked a little disappointed at that.

"And when do we get to your favorite city and bridge?" Uli was looking impish and thoroughly desirable.

I pointed to Bareilly on our itinerary. "According to this, sometime near dawn. We'll breakfast there, then make the final run into New Delhi, maybe three and a half hours. It should put us there just after ten."

"Und what time do we leave?" Jitka asked.

"Two-twenty, but we should be at the station by one-forty-five."

They nodded and Uli expressed what I had been thinking; after Soma's cremation, there would be plenty of time to place the calls.

As Sahr came in, Jitka asked, "So, Bhim, how can I help?" Without hesitation I gave her an assignment--finding the correct phone numbers of the newspapers and agencies. Then I told Sahr about our schedule. Her expression, when I told her, frightened me. I assumed her cards were to blame again, but fortunately or unfortunately, I didn't get to ask. It was time for Uli and me to leave.

Sixty-Six

Night had descended across a docile city. The clouds had thickened again and a light rain had begun to fall. It would grow stronger. A few patrols and perfunctory checkpoints had been set up in the central sections, more for show than efficacy. The city dozed in tranquility. We motored south around the outskirts of the University. Uli wanted to talk, which was fine, as I didn't want to drive seventeen miles thinking about the end. But I was surprised by what she wanted to discuss.

"Bhim?"

"Yes?"

"What was it like for you when you first came here?"

"The city itself? Or for me personally?"

"For you. Don't tell me anything you don't want to. I just want to know who you were back then, how you came to be this man I adore so much. It is like your Frisbee game, if it makes you happy or sad, I want to know why."

I took a breath. "Well, in the beginning I was, excuse my language, a fucking shipwreck on a reef of pain. Mornings came when I didn't think I could go from my bed to the kitchen because it hurt so much. I convinced myself I would fail at the smallest tasks. Some days I was angry, others just incredibly sad. But then a little group took to watching after me, Sahr, Satnam, and Masterji. I wondered every once in a while if they snuck around having secret meetings about me. Anyway, they waited and then began to talk to me. After a while, I talked back."

She nodded once and I knew she actually understood.

"What made it get better?"

I had to think about that. "Mostly what they had me doing,

talking, writing, handling the day-to-day chores of living here. I needed to learn a lot of things, everything from phrases to buying groceries. But it kept me active. Eventually, I began to really live here, but even after three years I wasn't whole. I had nightmares and the shakes, and it wasn't until you decided to shampoo your way my heart that I truly got better."

She ignored that. "What about helping others? Did that help?"

I knew where this was coming from, and maybe where it was going. It was what she had told me in the restaurant after the séance. Her part in the Muslim riots had created a compelling need to help.

"I don't know. Maybe I gave of myself to Soma, maybe Lalji at times, but I think I was imploding too much. I was trying to help myself more than anything and not doing a particularly good job."

"But helping other people made the pain better, ya?"

"I suppose. I still don't feel like I did much."

Her other hand slapped her thigh hard. "But, look how you are helping now."

Along with the slapping sound came the impact of her statement. I hadn't considered the personal reimbursement of from doing something good, because I had been thinking about bombs, script, and keeping us safe. And sex, admittedly I'd been thinking about that a lot more recently. "I guess I haven't figured out my role in it yet."

Again she surprised me. "Adam has. He saw it immediately, Bhim, the moment you entered the city, because he knew you had something wonderful to give. It's why he wants you to write his introduction. He knows what you can accomplish. "

"Maybe . . . I don't know."

We motored along in silence for a few minutes, the intermittent wipers sweeping back and forth the way they were supposed to, intermittently. She seemed lost in thought. Trying not to think of our imminent trek in the dark, I tried humor. "So, do all Danish women get so incredibly beautiful when they are pensive?"

Being clearly in too serious a mood for that one, she said, "I was thinking of how . . . all those people want to take away sins, go to confession, pray, wash in the river. And the only to way to really wash them away is by taking away the pain of others."

It took a moment for that to sink in, or rise to the surface, or make sense. But it did.

"Bhim, how long has it been since you have seen your mother und father?"

"Nothing like changing subjects on me. Okay, thirty-nine months. Two weeks ago I couldn't have said it, but I believe I'm ready to see them again. Even a few of the others."

She turned in her seat to stare at me. "You would be comfortable being Martin again?"

"I don't think Martin ever really left. He just got sad and angry and ducked out for a while."

She kissed my cheek. "I'm glad he's back."

The lights of the city slid behind us and the front beams of the Cherokee cut through blackness as we sped along the Azamgarh Highway. It felt as if the earth had fallen away and we were two gypsies on an black strip floating in space. I peered through the smeared windshield and shuddered. The secondary road that led to the mine was less than a kilometer away.

Uli slid close and put her hand on the birthstone she had

given me. "Will you take me to meet them?"

At that, I pulled to the side and looked at her. "How could I not take you? I mean really, you're my breath and blood, my beautiful premika with the golden hair all rolled into one. My parents would adore every piece of you. So would my older brother who locked me in a closet when I was a kid and gave me all this stupid fear of dark places. I did tell you about that, didn't I?"

"Und you are ready to leave here?"

I thought for a moment and slid my fingers through her hair and along her jaw. "Emotionally, yes. The reasons for coming here are gone now. I've changed, and the city has changed for me. There would be things to tidy up and attend to, like making sure Sahr and Lalji have employment with the right people. But for the first time since I came, yes, I'm ready to leave."

She looked at the rain without saying a word.

I pulled back onto the highway just in time to see two enormous lorries, filled with creamy orange rock crushed to the size of lemons, turn onto the road leading to the mine. I dimmed the lights and waited until they were enough distance ahead and followed. As soon as their giant tires hit the rubble, a thick haze of wet dust swirled into their tail streams. Even the light rain couldn't remove it. I dimmed the lights, set the air to circulate inside, and kept a discreet distance. We were camouflaged inside a cloud of powder and exhaust in a black car at night, so I felt reasonably certain we weren't being noticed. Occasionally, I had to clear the grime from windshield with the blades and fluid. It was like smearing mud until the spray got the upper hand.

Unlike me, Uli seemed at ease. I asked, "Can you tell what that rock is?"

"What rock?" she giggled.

"The creamy looking stuff in the trucks up ahead of us."

"What trucks? You see trucks, Lover?"

"Now you're joking and I'm trying to get serious here. We are on a mission." It felt better now that she was teasing, because I was growing more nervous, probably because I had actually seen the well-armed assholes behind the barbwire.

"I'm pretty sure it's basalt, ores they use to make aluminum."

"Okay, so here is the important question. Why are they taking two loads of basalt toward a mine that is supposed to be sending it in the other direction?"

"You see, you are better at this than you thought. My guess is they are going to use it to cover what they bring out, like drugs in a load of pineapples. You don't dig too far in the prickles before you get tired of being poked and quit."

"You make a good detective yourself, Ms. Hadersen. That would lead me to think they're getting ready to transport something soon."

As we motored at a faster pace than I had anticipated on the secondary road, I was trying to solve a dilemma. The darkness and dust would conceal us until we were close to the fence and the frontage road. But we couldn't just make a casual turn at the guardhouse and meander down to the cave. Security would be tight, especially if they were preparing to move goods. I had to avoid the gate and cut across open country on an angle to meet the road further down. The problem was two-fold. I had no idea at what point to turn, especially since I couldn't see five feet in front of the Cherokee's bumper. I also had no idea what the terrain would be like. Without lights we could easily crack into a boulder or a slide into a ravine, neither with pleasant consequences. I needed to be as close as possible to the fence without being visible to anyone inside.

I explained all this to Uli, and, as usual she a solution.

We decided that my two previous visits weren't enough to gauge it from memory. Uli said, "If you drop back enough, maybe we can see the fence from the lights of the trucks." I cleared the windshield and slowed, and sure enough, splintered light reflected off the spirals of razor wire. And we were closer than I had estimated, less than a third of a mile away. Gripping the wheel with both fists, I veered right, off the road and was immediately forced to creep along in the ink. We bounced over and around objects that I could barely see through the side window--small boulders, brush, stunted trees, and logs. Six times we stopped to get out and check for imagined obstructions that were always there. We zigzagged, crept like robbers, and an hour later completed the hypotenuse of our triangle. I hoped with all my might that no one had spotted us. Looking toward the gates, I saw only the guardhouse security lights illuminating the front compound. The trucks we had tailed were now backed against the opening of the shaft. I rolled across the grassy lot, up to our picnic spot, and shut down the engine. For a few moments we sat without moving. The rain and a rising wind tossed the leaves of the betel tree. Drops splattered rhythmically on the roof. I rolled down my window and listened. The moment had arrived when I knew we had to act, when I had to kick fear out the window. My legs, unfortunately, were mutinying. The rain came harder and I rolled the window shut.

"Listen, Sweet Premika of Mine, I know where a good sample is. Ralki picked it up when we were here, and I remember exactly where he dropped it. Take me less than a minute to find it."

She grabbed my hand and whispered, "Remember our first date and the sketch of the lovers wrapped like forest vines? Inseparable? That's us."

Her grip told me it was moot to argue. "Okay, but . . .."

"You lead, Lover. I'll follow stille som en mus"

"I hope that means quiet as a mouse."

With a quick nod, she blew me a kiss, opened the door, and stepped into the downpour. I pulled the flashlight from my bag and kicked my reluctant legs out the door.

What path there was felt soggy but reasonably familiar. We stepped across to the foot of the spur, where I listened again for shouts or sirens or racing motors, but there was only the wind and rain and an incredibly raucous pounding in my chest. I switched on the flashlight and filtered the beam through my fingers. We were beyond the line of vision of the guardhouse, so I pulled them away and focused the beam in a tight circle on the ground.

"We'll need to climb over," I whispered. "The entrance is just on the other side, or used to be, anyway." I reached to take her hand, but she had already started up, which was better because I needed to have at least one hand to climb. The rocks were cool and slippery with rain, and when we came to the top, I angled the beam downhill. Raindrops fell like tiny jewels through the light. To the right, the channel leading the cave had been cleared. Almost.

The slag had been back-dragged from the entrance, clearing the opening, but five boulders had been re-set to close off the crevice. Small tread marks scarred the dirt, dashing my original hopes of quickly grabbing Ralki's providential rock and dashing back.

Uli crawled down into the ravine and I followed.

"They've cleared it. It looks like someone's opened it up to get inside." My distress was audible.

"That's where the front was?" She pointed to the boulders.

"Yes, Master and I entered there, and Ralki and I stood here." I spun the beam in a slow arc along the wall. And there, waiting patiently against a vertical slab, was the same innocuous chunk Ralki had selected. Perhaps it was irony or pure luck, but at the moment all I could think was, the damn thing just wanted to be found. I jumped across and scooped it up, seeing Ralki's sneer dissolve into disbelief. I laughed aloud, and in the echo I was sure I heard four-thousand year-old voices laughing with me.

"A gift, My Love." I turned and handed her the flashlight and the baseball-sized chunk. She immediately studied it in the beam. The rain was coming in sheets now, drenching us, and making vision difficult. I was quite prepared to pop our prize into my pocket and scramble back to the Cherokee.

"Color, size, shape, und texture." She was talking to herself. "All match. Definitely uraninite, and by the look of it, high grade. A drop of nitric acid would help."

With a sloppy grin I said, "I think I left mine at the villa. Can we go now?"

She was about to reply when we both heard a metallic hiss, muffled and distant, but clearly mechanical. A low rumble followed, as if a large machine was coughing to life. It was coming from beyond the crest of the hill directly in front of us, from somewhere between the cave and the guard gate.

"Uli, let's go back," I whispered, but she was already clambering up the slope. With a sigh I followed.

At the crest, the ridge ran in shallow cambers in the direction of the mine, the cave behind us at one end, and the gate a half a mile away on the other. And somewhere in the middle, machinery was hissing to life. Uli stopped to catch her breath and I grabbed her hand and tried to picture the ridgeline through the rain. Blackness.

"We don't have to do this, Uli. We have what we came for."

Her voice came in an urgent whisper. "We need to find out what they are doing. If they're processing it, we need to know. It can't be that far. Let's find where the sound is und then leave. Please."

Rain streamed into my eyes. I wanted desperately to be in the Cherokee motoring away, but I knew she was right. I hadn't won one of these discussions yet anyway. I pulled the flashlight back out.

We scrambled, with more noise than I would have liked, up and over broken shard. The mechanical sound increased, and after a few hundred meters, and an achingly long time, I saw a faint glow low to the ground. We moved on all fours until we were near enough to see what it was--three vent caps protruded from the rock like toadstools. Light glowed in muted circles below them, and the sound of hissing liquid and pumps rippled towards us.

I took a step toward it, and was ready to drop to my knees and crawl, when Uli grabbed my wrist.

"Stop."

What?" I whispered against the rain.

She pulled on my arm. "They're leaching it."

"What?" I asked again.

'They're leaching it into yellowcake right here."

I wasn't altogether sure what that meant and asked, "How do you know?"

She sniffed. "You can smell it?"

We were fifty feet away, downwind, and close enough for me to smell an acrid, alkaline odor on the wetness of the air.

"Ammonia. They're processing it. Don't go any closer."

I not only didn't want to go any closer, I wanted to high-tail it in the other direction as soon as I could turn my ugly tennies around. With a little tug, I convinced her of the same idea. We scrambled back along the ridgeline to the ravine, across the cave entrance, and back to the car.

She glanced back. "They must be crushing and leaching the ore below. That means technicians, machinery, und a lot of money. Very complicated, but the return, Gott, it could be huge."

I didn't want to think about any of it at the moment.

We were soaked and exhausted when we climbed into the car. I was just getting ready to turn the ignition key when I saw two lights moving along the road from the other direction. Uli saw it also, and we both froze. A small jeep was moving slowly south toward the gate, passing the grassy parking space at that moment. The bright beam of a spotlight bounced across the boulder field on the opposite side, exactly where we had driven thirty minutes earlier. Neither of us breathed.

Three fortuitous things saved us from being discovered that night. The increasing rain erased all signs of our trail, the spotlight shone away from where we sat, and C.G. had taken black as his color of choice. All of those, and the luck I was thinking just might be from Sahr's constellations, kept us from being caught.

The outside air had cooled enough to open the windows slightly and turn the heat on low inside. I maneuvered the Cherokee around and for a moment pondered ripping straight down the access road with the high beams lit and all four tires spinning. The anger and frustration of the last nine days was spilling out like the fumes in those vents. For the first time since seeing my adversaries behind the concertina wire, I felt prepared. I knew what they were up to and why, and now, I was ready to send a blow to their solar plexus.

We made a long, slow arc back across the exposed field and an hour later were rolling down the Azamgarh Highway once more. Deep relief flooded me and then, remembering it, reached into the back and handed Uli the small bag Sahr had given me. She opened it onto her lap, and two pieces of nan, cucumber and yogurt dip, cheese, and a small bottle tumbled out. As we neared the outskirts of Varanasi, I pulled off the road, into a spot hidden from the highway. We dipped the bread, munched contentedly, and sipped on a surprise-- brandy. "I'll be goddamned. I don't think she's ever put alcohol in a picnic before. Her birthmark scrunches if I have a second lager. Unless I'm dining with my premika."

"Maybe she knew you needed to have a little something extra to calm you."

I turned in my seat and fluttered my eyelashes. "And you don't, Ms. Hadersen? Probably not. Nothing was going to stop you back there, was it?"

She leaned over and kissed my cheek. "No. This afternoon when you were inside me and I was crying, I knew I could do it.

Your poem helped, too." She bit my lobe. "Now let's go kick them in their schlangers."

I hoped our aim was good. The thought was delightful.

I started the engine. The rain had slackened now, replaced by a floating mist and a spray of stars in the east above the river. The blush of shop lights and thrumming of the city had receded. Varanasi was drifting to sleep, without riots, without drought, preparing once again for sunrise and burning corpses.

Sixty-Seven

Emotions in the villa the next morning were diverse and peculiar. I was moving about well before sunrise immersed in the sadness that I would be seeing Soma's ashes mix into the wind. Then there was the tension we all felt of sending media and intelligence agents on the trail of people that could only be described as evil. There was the combined excitement and melancholy of a train ride to Delhi to say good-bye to Jitka. The worst, however, was Sahr's agitation. It could be felt like a high-voltage wire popping throughout the villa.

She set a bowl of pakoras on the table with a force that almost cracked the ceramic. "Bhimaji, Durgubal came un-summoned last night. He has *never* done that before."

I was trying to rush through a cup of coffee and make notes at the same time. I wasn't quite ready for Sahr's turbulence. "Right, well, I have quite enough to think about this morning. His advice will have to wait."

"It cannot wait, Saab. There is danger in the hours ahead. Grave danger. He warned me."

I popped a pakora into my mouth and mumbled, "Of course there is, and we're two steps ahead of it."

"It is even more serious than the last time he came. Look what happened then." I felt the sting of that one.

I was preparing to argue that everything not only seemed more dangerous, but was, when the sisters entered. They wore traditional saris, light blue and green, and the transformation of Jitka was astounding; she looked more feminine than I'd ever seen her. Sahr immediately helped rearrange the pleats and the length of the shawl. I poured coffee and set dahi out for the pakoras. We barely had time to eat before rushing through the door and onto Shivanan Avenue.

And there, waiting like a patient doorman, was Vinduram Singh.

The turban bobbed. "At your service, Sahib and Memsahibs. The shiniest taxi in all of Varanasi awaits to carry you in total air-conditioned comfort to Manikarnika." Doors flew open.

I looked at Sahr, whose look explained that she had arranged for Vin to pick us up the previous evening. "To Manikarnika," I repeated.

As I helped the sisters into the back--Sahr was already in the front--I saw Lalji's friends taking up posts inside my gate. "Where's Lalji," I asked suspiciously.

"Already left for the cremation, Bhimaji," Sahr replied. "He begged me yesterday, and I gave him permission. It is alright?"

"Yes. It is alright." My watchman hadn't the courage to mumble a hello to the Widow Soma while she lived, he should at least be able to say good-bye at her death. "Yes, it is fine," I repeated.

****

Two things struck me as we stepped from the gulley onto the steps of Manikarnika--the amount of mourners already gathered, and the blast crater. It was still unfilled, ringed only by a tripod of sticks and yellow tape. Master, quite conspicuous, stood in white dhoti and kurta beside the tirtha, the eternal flame. I didn't approach. Soma's preta, her encased soul, rested on a small cot-like scaffold behind him. She had been cleansed with water from the river and wrapped in white, a color she had stubbornly refused to wear when alive. The color was a symbolic stripping, a societal punishment for an undefined crime. Soma, with shy obstinacy, stuck to faded green. Uli's orange scarf still hung in stark contrast about her shoulders, though.

Her body looked so tiny to me.

Further back Mirabai, Sukshmi, and others stood quietly. Satnam Kangri sat on a stool beside them. I nodded to each with a heavy smile and led Uli and Jitka upwind of the pyre. Sahr followed, and from out of nowhere, Lalji appeared to station himself next to his mother.

Standing apart and silent were four men I didn't recognize-- young student-looking types in black trousers and white shirts. Behind them were three women, also unknown to me, two young and one older. The head of the youngest was shorn to stubble, her white sari tattered and soiled. Another widow. I wondered who they were. Even one of the police who had carried Soma's body from the river was there. Rajneesh Sukkha, his wife, three daughters and a young son arrived. That puzzled me until I remembered that Soma had delivered the money to his family after his brother Jotilal had died.

Most of the people Soma had encountered--even peripherally- -had come to bid her farewell. Everyone but her mother-in-law.

A group of beggars were assembled at the top, waiting for the traditional food and alms gifted at the end of the ceremony.

Then, with the ringing of finger bells it began. Wood was ladled with oil. Devamukti began intoning sutras from the Rig Veda and Puranas, while four doms emerged from a hut near the temple. They lifted the body onto the pyre, and I half expected Adam to appear. Nothing surprised me anymore.

With a stave from the temple flame, the head priest lit the base and flames slithered like eels through the timbers. Traditionally the eldest son performed this rite, but that was not to happen this morning.

The air was thick with smoke. Funeral fires had been smoldering throughout the night and the morning fires of the boroughs, kindled in alleys and courtyards mixed in. It was dense, biting at our nostrils, and I couldn't see two hundred meters down the shoreline. Uli touched my arm and nodded across the river--the first rays of sun were trying to pierce the haze.

Behind me, the three women and the four students sang a short mantra, a request to Lord Shiva to release this child into enlightenment.

From ignorance, lead her to truth;
From darkness, lead her to light;
From death, lead her to immortality.
Aum, peace, peace, Aum

Flames rolled about the body. I began to weep and asked that Soma's soul not be released from the great wheel quite yet. We still need her. Let her return, stronger, surer, with the same sweetness that drew all those people to the Ghat. Sparks rose into the fumes, and I watched an ember, larger and easier to follow, drop and float for a brief, orange moment on the currents of the Ganges. Then it was gone.

The flames, like life itself, swelled and subsided and slowly flickered out.

Suddenly, without reasoning why, I had to know who the three women were who had sung the mantra. I trotted up the steps, but they began moving hastily toward the street. "Wait, please," I called, but the young men kept moving. I called again and the oldest of the three women stopped. Her companions halted one step above her. I hurried. "Wait. How . . . how did you know her? How did you know Soma? Please . . . she was my friend."

They looked with uncertainty at me. It was clear I wasn't to be trusted—a pale ferenghi in the wrong colored kurta. I was male, and that distrust glared even more in the younger women's eyes. The one with the shaved head looked away, but the eldest, seeing the tears on my cheeks, softened.

"Your friend?" she asked.

"She was. My Master's servant and my friend. I called her Sister. Please." I set my fingers together in a hasty namaskar.

That seemed to further soften the oldest. "Ah, Devamukti's student." And with that universal acknowledgment, she smiled. "When Soma the Timid spoke, which was rare, she spoke kindly of one she called Bhim."

I namasted again. "I am Bhim,"

"Mata," was her reply. No handshake or namaskar.

The women looked to each other and Mata made a decision of some kind. "Come." With nothing more, she spun and marched up the gully towards Aurangbad Road. I waved for Uli and Jitka to follow and hurried to catch up. The trio came to the rear of Vishvanath temple and waited. Uli and Jitka came and the three of us ran to join the others.

"Mata, these are friends. They will do you no harm," I said.

Without a word, she nodded an assent and continued up the lane, turned right and went nearly to the gap at Aurangbad Road. At the alley before the main road the group turned again and stopped in front of a narrow, thick gate. Mata pulled out a ring of keys and pushed open the door. We followed into a courtyard full of women--dozens, young, middle-aged, and old. The entire space was filled with white saris. And every face had the tired, creased looks of pain, some appeared sick and weak, others had shaved heads. And all bore the look of the wretched-- soiled and tattered, barefoot, wrinkled, and emaciated. They avoided our eyes, and I realized instantly where we stood, in the inner refuge of the shunned. The hand-carved sign above the door of the only building announced, Ashraya, The Haven.

"This is a home for widows?" My voice was hushed with the respect for what was being done in that small space.

Uli stepped from behind me to squat next to a child-girl who couldn't have been more than twelve. Within the minute her smile had woven its magic. The young girl began chattering in Bhojpuri about something, her hands flitting about. Uli couldn't have understood a word, but it didn't matter. The child drew Picasso art in the dust and they conversed in other ways.

"Yes, it is." Mata answered. Her hand waved in an arc. "We have the roof, a few beds, and some food. Not enough, but we keep them from the death of the streets."

I looked around. Here and there were tiny sparks, signs of something not seen in the world of widows, hope. On the wooden entry to the rear of the building, I saw two of the four men who'd been at the cremation tending to a woman lying curled up on the boards.

"Soma was one of our fortunate ones. She had a few decent people around her, unlike these poor souls." She waved her again. "Devamukti and his family treated her well. She had hope and some trust. She trusted you. I would not have let you in if I didn't also." She motioned me toward the building.

"I am grateful you did," I replied" . . . How many live here?"

"Thirty-two permanents and ten or so who drift in when they need safety or nourishment."

A choking feeling rose in my throat. "And Soma? Why did she come?"

Mata's eyes pierced me, tender and tenacious in equal measures. "I believe she was lonely for the companionship of other women like her. She talked little and never asked for food."

"What about the last time, four days ago?" I asked.

Mata smiled sadly. "I thought you might ask that." We went up the three steps to the porch. "She was terrified of something or someone, and as much as we tried, none of us could get her to speak of it. She only asked to remain in the courtyard for a time." Ralki! I knew it in my heart. It explained her disappearance and the missing Wednesday I'd been trying to account for. This was her place of hiding.

Our hostess led me through a small kitchen and into an infirmary—rudimentary rooms of rough wood and austere furniture. Basics were sparse, but it was plain to see small miracles were happening there. The shelves boasted medicine, salves, liniment, gauze, and improbably, three bottles of Flintstone vitamins. White-saried women squatted before piles of thread and cloth, stitching pillowcases to be sold in the market. Others strung tiny spheres of bright plastic and laminated wood, beaded curtains. But, as Mata explained, the profit was small. It wasn't enough and food was always exiguous.

Uli and Jitka entered with their young companion, Abha, she, holding each of their hands like rope swings. Mata told us how the The Haven accepted donations from the big international charities.

"But they don't see us as a priority," she sighed, "with so many more visible problems in the city, AIDS, malaria, the sex trade, even the pollution in the river. Destitute widows? We are not deemed worthy of such large donations. The smaller foundations provide some, groups of women with open hearts and enough courage to come here and fight for us. But, always we need more." Her finger pointed at the circles of working women on the floor. "They come abused, beaten, malnourished, dehydrated, and diseased. Most would die out there, or suffer so horribly they wished they had. We take them in and do what we can. I just . . . wish we had more." She closed her eyes and touched folded hands to her forehead. "It is my great prayer, because too many nights that pot isn't deep enough." I looked at the large kettle over the wood fire.

I needed to get back to Manikarnika, but a larger part of me didn't want to leave; I wanted to be where Soma had spent her last hours, just sit and absorb her energy. But . . . there were people to talk to, and Sahr would be waiting with Vin to take us home. "Mata," I breathed. "Soma was. . ." I struggled to find the words. "special in my life. You helped her, and I will return that somehow."

Uli looked at me and smiled in that Uli-knowing way. She knew how hard it was for me to say that, and with a quick step came and slipped her hands around my neck. "May I?" I smiled and nodded. The silver chain and fire opal came off my neck with the same words that fastened it there. "For passion, Bhim. Only that." Then she turned to hand it to Mata. "Take this to the jewel merchant near the coffee stands in the market. He knows its value und should give you a fair price. It can fill that pot for a few more weeks."

With Mata's gratitudes trailing us through the gate, we trotted back to a pyre now reduced to ash and embers. Alms were being divided amongst the poor. I found Sahr and asked her to give me two more minutes, then went to where Devamukti and Sukshmi stood. She was holding her father by the arm, supporting him. Satnam and Mirabai stood to the side.

I touched his feet. "You honored her in life and death, Master. It was a beautiful dahakarana."

"She was old on the great wheel, but young in years. Just a child. We did the best for her in death because she deserved better in life." He looked at Sukshmi, eyes brimming, and she kissed his hand. Father and daughter, it appeared, were reconciled. He heaved a sigh. "And next, we must bid good-bye to my daughter's godfather."

I felt uncomfortable with what I had to say. "Master, I will be gone for a time. I don't know how long, but there are some personal matters I must take care of. I cannot be here for Sri Chandragupta's cremation." I wanted to tell him that I had paid my respects at his deathbed, but his smile told me he knew.

In typical fashion he patted my arm and wagged his head. "I understand, My Boy. Sukshmi has explained it, you see. But do not be troubled. He will have the most festive celebration this Ghat has seen in a decade. Hundreds will gather to send him on." He reached across and patted Uli's hand, and I took the opportunity to introduce Jitka. There were flurries of namastes and little bows before Master drew me to the side.

"There is good news. The notice of our work has been mailed. The world will soon read about the new samhitas. Satnam also assures me some good friends are studying very carefully the prescription. Then I'm sure there will be a hundred thousand interested. All those scientists that C.G. talked about will be coming to our little cave like a herd of buffalo." He grinned. "Let them come."

I turned to Satnam, whose dimples were imploding in a grin. "It is incredible, Bhim. Things still to be worked out, of course, trials to be employed, but my colleagues have forwarded it to the other Ayurvedic societies, along with the story of how it was discovered. It will be done informally at first, but in large numbers, and then the world can apply all its empirical judgments. We shall see what we shall see." He grinned again.

We chatted about the prospects, which countries would be in denial, which would receive it openly. "Eventually," he said, "they will all have to consider it." I took that opportunity to tell him of our travel plans and ask about Adam.

"He heals quickly, Bhim, more so than the rest of us, even claims he will be dancing within the week."

That image was amusing. "But not lecturing?" I asked.

He answered, "Not for the moment, and not here. The shala was a source of strength for him. Now his words will go with the book." His eyes sparkled at me. "As well as yours."

People were migrating to cars and taxis. Thoughts of death were over, the work of the living continued. The morning haze was starting to rise and the mist burning off. I looked at Uli and Jitka. They nodded. The hour of anonymous cold-calling was upon us.

We hustled up to Aurangbad Road, where Vinduram and Sahr stood in front the purring taxi. Sahr opened her own door and settled with an interesting familiarity into the front seat. Uli and Jitka slid into the back. I looked over the roof, down the long avenue towards the center of the city. And blinked. Something there made my skin prickle. I wasn't certain, but just before the curve in the road I thought I saw a flash of folding umbrella and a familiar turn of arms and leg slide into a black Mercedes. But like a ghost, it disappeared into the haze.

Sixty-Eight

Three factors made the calls proceed without incident. First, I made certain my Hindi was indistinguishable from that of any common citizen in Northern India—standard, non-vernacular without accent. Knowing that my voice was likely to be recorded every time I read it, I spoke quickly and didn't answer a single question. Shipments of illegal uranium are being smuggled from Imperial Holding near Sarnath. Corrupt police, especially one Assistant Inspector Madru Ralki, were involved in cover-up of activities—I particularly enjoyed that one—and possibly Cabinet Minister Qereshy. Trucks are moving today. Click. Repeat. Click.

Second, the phone we used was untraceable and throwaway. Adam gave it to me with the understanding that it would end up in the deepest latrine in the gullies. In addition, any brave soul willing to dig it out would find the man whose name it was registered to was beyond reproach and now beyond anyone's reach.

Finally, Jitka had done commendable research. Not only had she located the phone numbers we needed, but she demanded the names of the superiors, the ones who wouldn't hesitate to act on the information.

But I still didn't stop shaking until I pressed the end button on the last call. We had just inflicted heavy damage on some extremely powerful people, not something they would quickly forget or forgive. I prayed we had protected our anonymity.

"Okay, it's done," I breathed. "Let's hope it works."

"It will, Lover. Four newspapers und three intelligence groups won't ignore it. They will climb over each other to be first out there."

"I hope so, and I hope they do it with some serious backup."

****

I was the only one of us not packed, so as Jitka went to find a bigger breakfast than the abbreviated one we'd had earlier, Uli and I went to my room.

I pulled two small duffles from the bottom of the closet and began folding clothes. There wasn't much. The laptop, camera, my manuscript, and Adam's, fit into one. Uli, refolding a shirt tossed in a bit too sloppily, looked up. "You really didn't mind that I gave your opal away, Mein Schatzki?"

"No. Not that I didn't adore it, but you could probably ask me to give away everything I own," I pulled her hand to my heart. "except this, because you already have it."

"Und I'm keeping it right here with mine." She giggled and pulled mine onto her breast and held it there.

This was followed by excited questions. Did I wish to return to America soon? Yes, as soon as we returned from traveling and affairs were settled. Will we take time together after Jitka goes? Yes, to the mountains for weeks of lovemaking and climbing and more lovemaking. Would I miss the city? Yes, acquaintances definitely, but it was time to leave. Would I continue my studies? Of course, maybe at the university in Berkeley, if they would have me. I had answers to all but one. What was to be done about Mej?

"I don't know," I answered truthfully. "I actually thought I saw him this morning, or the goatskin guy, right after the cremation. It was too hazy to tell for certain, but he drove away in a Mercedes exactly like the one Sahr described. Speculation again. This morning I had the crazy idea that he's been using his bombs as some kind of diversion—a plan to keep the authorities looking everywhere but the mine."

She considered this for a moment and then began nodding rapidly. "Trickery, like the magician with the handkerchief? The words in the vision, do you remember, 'Master of diversion. Sutradharak, The PuppetMaster.' It makes sense, Bhim. He's not Islamic, he just wants everyone to think he is." Her eyes met mine with a new look of worry. "Mein Gott, what if he's timing them with the shipments?" I stared back, suddenly realizing what that meant. According to what we had seen the previous night, a shipment could be leaving soon. Now I really hoped our calls spurred some action.

As we finished packing my duffles, an infuriating truth came to me. Mej had not only used Islam as a deceptive instrument, he had used me as well. I had been a selected pawn in his game.

****

Sahr would not relent. She was going to tell me what her bhuta had told her, and I was going to listen. She dragged me to the front parlor, away from the sisters, and set me in my chair. The stance was struck—hands on hips, bosom straining against her chola, and swan's wing crushed into a frown.

"He is not wrong, Saab. Believe me. There is danger with the rising of the next sun. He warned me of flames and death at dawn. Many times over."

I was confused about what she meant. "He said it many times over, or did he mean it would happen many times over?"

"The second. He speaks his words only once, never twice. I am expected to pay attention the first time."

The entire morning had been filled with images of funerals

death, and now this. It made me anxious to have us on our way to Delhi. In addition to feeling the need to appease her, I now placed enough faith in such messages to ask, "What else did Durgubal say?"

"He said there will be death from flames, from steel and water. All coming at dawn" I felt a shiver ripple down my back.

"Another attack on the city?"

She shrugged. "Nothing else was said, Bhimaji."

"Then," I replied. "There is nothing more we can do than be more watchful and more careful."

Sixty-Nine

Sutradharak closed the door to his cottage and locked it. He tucked the keys into a pocket, thinking to himself, *departing this place will be like leaving a theater with a second-rate production under way—find the side door, erase the memories, and breathe better air.* He had witnessed his last cremation that morning, eaten his last meal in the Chowk, returned to the cottage and packed new belongings. Then he closed the door. Every vestige of the Ahkmed Jamil, the goat merchant of Varanasi, and Mejanand Whiton, the NRI of East London, disappeared with the turn of the key. His new persona, Remo Marselinni, an investment banker from Naples, Italy, was born easily, without a shred of contrition.

The Italian sat behind the steering wheel of the black Mercedes and drove at moderate speed confidently northwest on NH56. He moved unobtrusively and drew no attention to himself.

All connections to the two aforementioned men—beard, clothes, umbrella, goatskin bag, documents, and even the computer—had been reduced to ash in an incinerator two blocks from the loft. In the boot of his car a valise was packed with fashionable Neopolitan shirts, three trousers, two pairs of slightly worn Caponi shoes, a pair of scuffed cross-trainers and a used squash racket. His toiletry bag contained expensive colognes and a gold-plated manicure set—all purchased in Naples. His wallet and multi-national bank accounts were bulging, his sunglasses perfectly coordinated to a new ascot and crew cut hairstyle. The Anza fixed-blade hunting knife was still strapped to his calf and three additional passports were taped in a hidden compartment in the boot of the car—instruments of last resort. His most valued items, for the next twenty-four hours at least, were just within arm's reach. Inside the dash of the Mercedes were two fully charged mobile phones. The final and most lethal event he had ever designed would commence with the touch of two buttons. Then Remo Marselinni would board a late evening flight to Rome. And disappear.

He eased the seat back to settle into the drive, just over four hundred kilometers west by northwest. Traffic, he knew, would be moderately heavy at the onset, less so as he veered northward. The five hours would give him ample time to polish his new accent. Details. Success depended upon them. The PuppetMaster will also be incinerated, tomorrow, he mused. And Remo Marselinni will rise like the winged Phoenix from his ashes.

Seventy

At 1:30 Vinduram dropped us at the entrance to the Varanasi Cantonment Station—a massive cream and rouge bulkhead of faux temple domes, a hundred windows, and a grand rectangular clock that managed to show the correct time twice daily. Inside, concrete stretched almost a kilometer in both directions, and almost every square meter was covered with people, napping, sitting, eating, or squatting in conversation. It was denser to the left where second-class passengers waited to elbow their way on in fifteen minutes. I had braved second class a few times before, and it wasn't how I wanted us to reach Delhi this trip. We stood at the other end, waiting to board one of two air-conditioned first-class cars.

The two diesel engines, in front of our first class compartments, emitted low growls, and behind them a long string of second-class cars stretch down the station. All of them, in a display of egalitarianism, had beige, iron bars covering the windows. This deterred illegitimate entry, and easy exit for that matter.

Hawkers circulated. I bought choley bhatur, samosas, and spicy peanuts in paper cones. Bottled water topped off our menu. We sat on our bags against a column and passed the snacks back and forth, sampling flavors.

"Are you all right?" Uli asked. In truth, I was exhausted and ready to fold into a soft seat, rocking to the rhythms of the rails. The commotion of the station, the mechanics of it all used to fascinate me, the assortment of human shape and movement feeling like an impressionist oil painting. Right now, I wanted only to put it away and feel nothing but Uli's head on my shoulder, or vice versa.

"It will be good to be on board," I answered. A whistle shrieked down the line, causing me to flinch. Conductors downfolded metal steps, redcaps jockeyed for position, and passengers completely ignored the suggestion of a queue. I motioned to an industrious looking teen, a barefoot boy with shredded blue shirt and a scarlet rag about his head—the only indicators that he was a porter. He grinned—with less teeth than most—snatched up our bags, and squeezed through the door between the cars. Within the minute we were settled into our seats, bags stowed, and snacks floating again between us. Uli was next to me on the window side, Jitka to my left, across the aisle. I breathed in the oily perfume of the engine, closed my eyes, and slipped into the symphony of departure.

A hiss of the brakes was followed by Jitka's voice, throaty with melancholy. "I vill miss a few things here, you know."

I popped open an eye to look at her skeptically. "Really?"

"Not a long list, mind you, but after you, Uli, and Sahr, Johnny Chang's stir fry comes to mind. The kebobs at the Afghan café, they were gut, too. But Adam's sermons I vill miss them the most. The ones without explosions were more to my liking, but I did enjoy his ideas."

"You will be able to read more of them soon enough." I told her about the manuscript in my duffle.

"Und you write the forward? What an honor, Bhim."

I looked at Uli. She was just gazing out the window, smiling in her knowing way.

With a groan of hydraulics and a series of small lurches, we left Varanasi.

Seventy-One

Lucknow by sunset. Uli said little as we the passed hours rolling over flooded fields of rice, yoked oxen, and barefoot women. The rains had brought life back to it all. I said less and less, eventually drifting into an erratic sleep with my head in her lap. Even her caress couldn't assuage my uneasiness. Until we heard good news concerning the events we had set in motion, we would probably all feel some level of apprehension.

I bounced through kaleidoscopic dreams--dashes of conversation, images of corpses and flying sparks.

What if he is timing them to match the shipments, Bhim?

Who? Sutradharak, Yes, the master of diversion. Who? Sutradharak.

Flame and death at dawn. Little Sister, where are you?

Death from steel and water. Durgubal told me.

Flames and death at dawn. Who? The Sutradharak.

I woke with the slowing of axles and the mantras of food merchants floating through our window. Uli was smoothing my hair and looking down at me with deep-water eyes. My nightmares floated away like charred embers in the river. "Hello, Lover," she whispered.

"Hello, Uliana Hadersen. . . have I told you today how much I love every delicious piece of you?"

"No, I don't believe you have. You should tell me now, twice I think."

I sat up and kissed her. "Every exquisite, beautiful, curvaceous piece," I whispered. "Are you hungry?"

"Ravenous."

Across the aisle Jitka echoed, "Ravenous."

We knew how the meals would arrive—large circular trays of

rice, saag paneer, puris, and five condiments in small cups, all of it steaming hot. It was undoubtedly the largest, most efficient catering service in the world.

I needed to stretch, and clear my head, so I set off to fetch us drinks from the platform and check on our sleeping accommodations. I stepped into a scene of organized chaos-- passengers, porters, vendors, and hustlers all jostling and all knowing exactly where they were going. I weaved through to the station wall and found a row of food carts. Fresh, iced pineapple juice would do. Balancing three cups, I returned to find the sisters standing outside, with four libidinous young Sikhs hovering nearby looking optimistic. I approached with a gruff voice and fierce stare. "Fresh juice for my both wives. Is my dinner ready?"

Uli started giggling. I thought Jitka was going to swear, but smiled sweetly and replied, "We have just set it out, Most Honorable Knucklehead."

They carried our drinks to our seats while I set off to locate our names on the manifest posted outside the sleeper cars on the next track. Fortunately, Mr. Martin Scott's party was typed correctly with three berth assignments. Ten, eleven, and twelve weren't in the center of the car, but far enough away from the toilets to afford us quiet during the night.

Dinners always tasted delicious to me on trains; the hours of rocking seemed to make the spices come to life. That evening's meal was no exception. We dipped into rich sauces and sweet pastes and revisited the pastoral sights of the afternoon. As we neared our last bites, I explained the next stage of the itinerary, and signaled through the window for a redcap. Our bags were shifted to the southern end of the terminal, across the Y where sidetracks split from the main line. Two yellow and green sleepers, idle, were linked to two freight cars.

"We won't go very far if they're not connected to engines." Jitka stated the obvious.

"Give it ten minutes," I said. "The second class cars will be backed down and coupled to these four. Then the two locomotives will be attached to the front of the baggage cars. We'll be on our merry way right after that."

The air-conditioned compartment was already full. Passengers were stretched out on bunks and bedding provided by the rail company. Curtains were drawn across three of the alcoves. In others, wealthy-looking men sat cross-legged in pajamas, playing cards or reading. Unfortunately, bunk ten, mine, had nice bedding with a snoring body curled face-inward in it. I showed Jitka to number twelve across the aisle and shook the shoulder of the man appropriating my upper berth. I received a sharp, "Go away!" in Urdu.

I shook him again and shot back, "You are in the wrong sleeping place, Bai." I wasn't in the mood for grumpy attitudes or travel glitches. He rolled over and came more fully awake when he saw Uli and me with tickets and bags in our hand. Fortyish, with puffy jowls and too much oil in his hair, some of which had already splotched my mattress I noticed. His scowl was beginning to irritate me.

"This is my bunk, Sir. Number ten," he snapped, head wagging like a tent flap.

"May I see your ticket please, Bai," My eyes narrowed. I was doing a fairly poor job of attempting politeness. Uli smiled, pushed our bags under the bottom tier, and started unrolling her mattress onto the lower bunk.

"Here, here it is. You see, this is my ticket, Man. Number ten. My bunk." His voice was dripping with arrogance. I examined the stub thrust at my face.

"You are right, My Friend. This is a ticket for bunk ten." I held it next to my head for him to see. "But it happens to be for bunk ten in Sleeper B, the next car." I pointed with a forced smile to the letter on the stub and then the letter A at the rear of our car. "And as repayment for your error, I would like you to exchange the bedding you have slept in with a fresh one." I was not sleeping on his oil spot.

Horror filled his expression as he leapt up to make the exchange. Where the mattress had been, I found a newspaper folded in the corner-- his evening read before he fell asleep in number ten. When he returned--with no less than eight apologies--I asked him if I might keep the paper. It was the evening edition of The India Daily.

"By all means, by all means, My Good Man. And as a favor, please allow me the honor of purchasing breakfast for you and your beautiful wives tomorrow in Bareilly Junction."

From across the aisle Jitka grumbled, "As Knucklehead's head wife, I accept, now go away."

The man backed down the compartment with little bows and a promise to see us bright and early. I unfolded the paper.

The headline was large enough for a billboard. Illegal Uranium Seized Near Gardens of Buddha.

****

I sat on the lower berth nest to Uli and read aloud. Sealed containers had been discovered beneath loads of bauxite in four cargo lorries. The drivers, sixteen mine employees, and two guards were being held for questioning. Agents of the Indian

Intelligence Bureau had also detained three local police and a vice commissioner of agricultural affairs. "Four trucks at nine tons each." I did some calculating. "That's almost fifty million dollars on the black market, not including future shipments."

Uli, who had been reading next to me, replied, "It depends on where it was going and who was paying for it." I hadn't thought much about who the purchasers might be. I did know one thing. The people named in the article were going to prison for a long time. I smiled at the thought of Madru Ralki meeting his cellmate for the first time.

The true operators might never be known, but they had been stung, and fifty million was a lot of money no matter how much you had.

The only disappointment was not seeing Yakoob Qereshy's name anywhere in print.

****

Despite the fitful nap of the afternoon, my night was peaceful. The long line of cars swayed like conga dancers as we clicked along the tracks, and with each roll of the wheels we felt the frost of fear melting away.

The track through the darkness was straight, with few curves, interspersed only by subtle changes of velocity, odors, and sounds. We slid in and out of sleepy stations—Sitapur, Shahjahanpur, Madadiri. A light at each end of the compartment gave off just enough glow for passengers to find the toilets. Outside, the pitch felt like tunnel of ink. Occasionally, a far-off flicker of a hut illuminated, by a fire or solitary bulb, would slide by.

When it felt as if the entire car was asleep and snoring, I felt

Uli climb silently into my bunk. The curtain was drawn across our bay and when she slipped below the sheet and nudged me over to the window, I felt nakedness from toes to lips. I whispered, "We'll wake the car."

"Umm. Und that would be bad?" Mild disappointment.

"I think the penalty is that they tear up your ticket and leave you sitting on your bags at the next station."

"Ohhh..." More disappointment. "Okay, maybe you should just hold me then." Without a sound I lifted her and settled her in delicious nakedness on top of me. I drew my hands from her thighs and buttocks to her shoulders and down again--the undulating train, my metronome—softly and slowly. Just like that we fell asleep.

Sometime later I felt her lips on mine, a sweet touch of tongue, and she left.

Perhaps it was that kiss. Perhaps it was the silky moistness of her skin on mine or the scent of her hair, but I slept without the turbulence of nightmares. There were no visions of fire, screams, or floods to haunt my night.

Seventy-Two

The cry of a drawn-out whistle woke me, and the slow clacking of the wheels told me we were coming into the station at Bareilly. I turned to the window and opened my eyes. The lights inside the sleeper were off. Outside, a faint glow of indigo announced the arrival of dawn. I rolled onto my back and listened. Gentle rain was falling, and for a short time I lay without moving, just feeling and hearing and smelling it all. The sweetness of Uli's body stretched naked on top of me returned, every blissful follicle. A cool breeze from the foothills touched my face. The world was alive and rich with love, and in that moment I wanted to thank someone, or some thing, for that gift--for bringing so much back into my life. God? Fate? Sahr's constellations? The Good People? I wanted to shout thank you. But I didn't know how, to whom, or to what, my thanks should be given. But it was okay. At least the belief was there again.

The cries of vendors floated along the tracks. My eyes closed and I felt that belief glowing brighter. Uli had helped me find it. And Adam. And Sahr, and Kangri, and Devi and all the good people that had helped me. Love is our gift. It is the blessing we are given--each and every one of us--love, as limitless as the stars. With that thought I whispered a thank you for everything I had.

I peeked over the edge of my bed, wanting to watch her sleep, but the bunk was empty. I presumed she had made her way to the toilet and wash-basin before other passengers made the same decision. I wanted the train to reach the station before she returned so I could have coffee and treats waiting, but as I swung my legs over the edge, I saw her coming down the aisle. I knew nothing of Danish royalty, but I was certain some of their blood flowed in my Uliana. She had washed and changed into the pale green kurta she had worn on our first date, and the blue skirt with printed green sea-horses and eel grass.

I swung my legs out and dropped to the floor, then yanked one of my duffles from below the bunk for a fresh kurta and pants. With clothes and travel kit, I stood in front of my bunk. "You look ravishing," I said.

The impish smile. "A shower with my lover, und sweet soap und shampoo would make me ravishinger. But I have gotten quite good at . . . how do you call them? Kitten baths?"

"Cat baths. Good skill to have when traveling in this part of the world. Listen. We're coming into Bareilly." The concrete platform slid under the right side of the train, inches from the frame, compressing the air below and flushing it through the bars of our windows. Instantly, a potpourri of odors filled in— fragrant spices, cooked rice, breads, and the ever-present aroma of human existence.

"What time is breakfast," Jitka snarled from behind her curtain.

"And good morning to you too," I answered mirthfully. "Trays should be coming around in a few minutes, Dear. Just enough time to wash your beautiful face and brush your teeth." She bolted past me with a low growl and a bundle of clothes. I turned to Uli. "The railway tries, rather successfully, to keep to schedule, especially the dining stops. Once we have our food, the train can go on and we can eat as leisurely as we like . . . which reminds me; we need coffee and a newspaper." She stared hard at me. "And a kiss, a kiss." I added quickly.

I felt the scratchiness of my beard and a film of detritus from the previous day, but Uli kissed me as if it didn't exist. Then she gave me a gentle push toward the washroom. "Cat bath for you, Lover."

"Right," I said and moved into the line of yawning, scratching bodies at the end of the aisle.

It took some time to scrub the residue, to shave and brush and dab cologne on my cheeks, but once done, I felt presentable. Fresh clothes and some muscle stretches and I was ready for the day.

Exiting the washroom, I saw the cantankerous Urdu-speaking fellow who had usurped my bunk. He stood in a white dhoti and shirt with a black vest, conversing animatedly with Jitka. From their body language I could tell that the subject was food. Nearing, I saw two trays of pakoras, idly, and other delights on Uli's bunk. Another rested patiently in Jitka's lap. The Muslim gentleman--I had to assume he was Muslim--had been good to his word and purchased all our breakfasts. Fortunately it appeared he wasn't intending to eat with us.

Seeing me approach, he waved enthusiastically. "Ah, my friend, as you see I have taken the liberty of ordering the breakfasts I promised last evening. An unfortunate and ignorant mistake upon my part to be sleeping in your berth."

I waved it off with, "A simple mistake, Friend, and well repaid. Thank you for your kindness."

His head bobbed and wagged. "Yes, yes, quite, and I am told by the railway personnel that your meals will be tops, number one fare. First class." He pumped my hand a dozen times, as if that action sealed our agreement and freed him of an eternity of obligations to me. With mutual wishes for comfortable travel to New Delhi, I sat and he departed for the forward car.

I kissed Uli with fresh zeal.

She grinned. "Und cologne, too? Must be a special day, Mein Schatzki?"

"Most special." I tossed a few pakoras onto a napkin, while they took bites of the the idly cakes. "And when I return with the best coffee in Bareilly, I'm going to tell you why. I had the most amazing dream last night. A goddess visited me right here in my bunk." I popped a pakora in mouth and smiled at Jitka. "And damned if she wasn't totally naked. Not a stitch on." With a wave of my fingers I left.

The sun had just cleared the horizon and the platform was bustling. Women in saris were hand-feeding toddlers or nursing babies against the back wall. Men in loongis and dhotis squatted, broad leaves of rice and dal on the ground before them. Dogs nosed in, only to scurry away from kicks or raised hands. Handcarts rolled by and merchants called out their wares to any and all. Hindus, Muslims, Christians, Parsis, and Sikhs--people of every faith--bustled about or squatted on the concrete. And they all shared a common interest. Breakfast.

Beyond the eastern boundary of the station, a field of stalks pushed through the earth, seedlings of a plant I didn't recognize, and beyond the pasture, the land sloped sharply into a wide riverbed that rose to a plateau a quarter mile beyond. Then, a sight I hadn't seen for a few years, foothills and noble trees.

The spidery bridge of Bareilly spanned the ravine of the Ramganga River. It was long and narrow, supported by spindly columns of steel and concrete. A series of bolted-pocked arches leap-frogged across the top. I could only see the far side, but it was obvious the recent rains had swelled the river. Swirling eddies of brown silt chewed into the bank on the far side, pulling off chunks of grass and loam to send them tumbling like barrels downstream.

I searched the station. Near the end of the platform, at the edge of the field, I saw what I wanted, a pleasant looking coffee-walla with a cart. His sign said it all. "The Best Blends of the Northeastern Mountains." I trotted over.

"Yes Sahib, the very best from Assam and Manipur. All roasted twice and not ground until I woke this very morning before the sunrise."

Knowledge of coffees was a hobby, so as he ladled three steaming portions--creamed and sweetened--into unglazed earthenware cups, we discussed beans. "Bah," he spat. "The Nilgiri Hills in the south have their reputation, but the smart buyer knows where the number one beans come from." A finger pointed towards the sun on the eastern horizon. "Right there, in the mountains of The Seven Sisters, and the sweetest of the sisters is Nagaland." Agreeing wholeheartedly with his assessment, I paid and tipped him and hustled back. Our train would be rolling across the bridge in ten minutes, then make the long westerly curve towards Delhi.

****

I almost dropped the cups coming into the car. Crowds were jostling back into second-class compartments, and a small boy trying to catch up to his father ran across my foot, tripped, and nearly sent us both sprawling. I just managed to keep the front cup from dropping and exploding on the platform.

Then the heat from the liquid began to seep through the clay and sear my fingers. Ignoring the pain, I mounted the lowest of the steps and turned to look over my shoulder. Vendors, hoping for a final sale before the train's departure, hawked goods below the windows. Cloth merchants fanned silks and cottons for women to appraise. Brass-smiths rang small bells and held up engraved candlesticks. A jeweler, with a flat box suspended from his neck, lifted gems and necklaces that flashed like mirrors in the morning light. I looked beyond the crowd. The field was like splintered emeralds, and further on, the river moved like dark tea through the gorge. I remembered then why I loved Bareilly at sunrise so much.

Inside, Jitka had just finished breakfast and sat on her bunk contentedly reading a recipe book. Uli had taken a few bites of iddly cake and was waiting for my return.

"Take these please before they completely melt my fingers." Uli took two of the cups and I set the last one down with a groan. Shaking the sting from my fingers, I said, "Well, I can safely say they haven't cooled much . . . probably a bad idea to carry them barehanded."

Uli began soothing the ends of my fingers with her lips and tongue, stopping long enough to say, "Bad is never good until worse happens." She smiled at my questioning look. "Another of those Danish proverbs, My Sweet."

"Sounds too ominous," I replied. She was still kissing my fingers as if they were covered with almond kheer, and I really didn't want to move, but beyond the window I saw the last item on my small list, a newspaper. A gnome-like man was pushing his cart of periodicals toward the station overhang. I wanted to finish breakfast, sip Nagaland coffee, and read about the entrails of Imperial Holding being torn out. "Keep the cups and those lips warm, Ms. Hadersen," I grinned, "I'll be right back." I scrambled from the car and bolted across the platform just as a long blast signaled three minutes to departure.

The newspaper cart and its pocket-sized owner had rounded

the station corner on the north side. Second-class passengers were still pressing aboard cars in the rear. A knot of people formed unexpectedly in front of me, and I needed to wade through them and sprint across. Rounding the corner of the station-house at full speed I nearly tumbled over the cart. It was parked at a peculiar angle, abandoned while its weak-bladdered owner scurried off in the direction of the men's latrine.

I scanned the selections and snatched up a copy of The Times of India, then dug through my pockets for some rupees to place on the cart. Overhead a small flock of white herons swooped in a low arc as they descended towards the river. I watched their flight, momentarily hypnotized by the grace and fluidity of their movement. They rose into an unseen draft, winged across the breadth of the ravine and settled into the pasture on the far bank. And there, beyond the flock, in the shade of a wide acacia tree, beside a tin-roofed warehouse, was a sight that chilled every fiber of my heart. A black Mercedes Benz CLS crouched motionless like a lioness. Its hood ornament faced the bridge and a lone silhouette sat in the driver's seat. For a full breath my mind tumbled impotently and my feet wouldn't move. I stood frozen. Then every harbinger and warning of the past days flashed through my mind. Mein Gott, Bhim, what if he's timing them to match the shipments? The shipment wasn't meant to leave the mining compound yesterday, it was meant for today. Flame and death at dawn. Steel and water. Flame and death at dawn. Who Bhim? The Sutradharak. With a far-off pressing of cell phone buttons, The PuppetMaster was going to destroy the bridge at Bareilly and plunge the train with thousands of caged passengers into the swollen waters of the Ramganga river-- murder on an unthinkable scale.

The shriek of the final whistle jolted me like a starter's pistol, and a single thought flashed into my mind--the train could not reach the bridge, it must be stopped. I pictured Uli waiting patiently to have coffee with me, Jitka finishing breakfast, and a thousand others resettled in their places, and I jumped.

The locomotives, coupled back to back, were a hundred and fifty meters from the edge of the divide and nearly the same distance from me. It was an angled race between a hundred thousand tons of steel and me—speed versus mass. I had to alert the engineers before the train began moving too fast to brake.

Impatient milliseconds later and my feet were churning across earth and grass. Twenty yards into my sprint the driving wheels of the engines lurched forward with a mechanical hiss. I waved an arm, frantically screaming in English, "Stop! Stop the train. There's a bomb!" The wheels jerked forward a second time with sluggish but obstinate force. No engineer's face appeared at the window. I screamed in Hindi this time.

To my left, along the line of the tracks, I saw three figures, a conductor with a rolled up signal flag swinging into the doorframe between two cars, and further down, two members of the RPF, the Railway Protection Force, walking with all casualness in the same direction as the departing train. One of the officers either heard my screams or saw me running insanely toward the locomotives. He motioned to his partner, and they both began jogging towards me, their rifles swinging in bouncing motions from behind their shoulders around to the front. I was forty meters from the front engine when a rifle shot cracked across the field. I looked left, without slowing. The policeman closest to the train had fired a warning round above my head.

Instantly, I understood, and in that same fractioned second, knew I had a choice. The policeman, in ironic misconception, had decided I was attacking the train, now thirty meters from my pounding legs. Perhaps he had heard the word 'bomb' above the rumbling of the machinery and had reacted the only way he knew how, reflexively with his rifle. My decision was instantaneous. I didn't stop. I kept running directly toward the locomotives, jabbing my fingers toward the river. I screamed in Hindi again, "There's a bomb on the bridge." In my peripheral vision I saw the policeman lowering the muzzle of his rifle, but only enough to aim directly at my chest.

I crouched, sheered right, and anticipated the bullet smashing into some place in my torso. Then, with a whisk of breeze, I felt it pass by me, a nugget of lead inches from my waist. The delayed sound cracked a second later. With a turn of my eyes I saw both rifle barrels now taking a bead on me. The engines and cars were gaining momentum, no longer jerking spasmodically. I was eight meters from the front engine, with nothing between me and two trained riflemen.

My mind didn't process. There was no decision, no deliberation, only reaction that comes from hours and weeks and years of training. I dove forward into a low summersault, head and right arm tucking loosely into my chest. Two shots, so close together they sounded as one, ripped the air above the back of my neck. My right shoulder and upper back hit the ground lightly as I tucked and rolled forward and up onto my feet in single, oiled motion. I took a step and a half and leapt up to the curve of a handle on the cab door. It represented every commonplace object I had ever caught in the casual games of my life—a Frisbee, softball, a hoop, a tossed orange. My right arm stretched out, and out further, muscles, tendons, every sinew seeking the centimeters of steel. Then, my fingers wrapped around it like a gymnast's ring, and at the same time my left side smashed sharply against the side of the door.

My feet peddled across the empty air above the gravel of the tracks until one of them kicked onto the top step below the half door of the cab. The window had been lowered into the frame to let the cool air in, and inside the cab two engineers stood in distracted concentration, unaware of anything but pressure dials and the rhythm of the engines. Sucking a lungful of air, and thrusting my chin toward the bridge, I screamed four words, "brake, there's a bomb."

The train was less than sixty meters from the incline and the foot of the bridge and it was now rolling at mid speed. Both engineers stood like statues, startled by the monkey-ferenghi hanging outside the engine compartment screaming like a lunatic. I dove through the window, fell onto the metal plates of the cab floor, and pulled myself to my knees. The man closest to me was readying to throw punches or kick at me, when I yelled in gasps, "The bridge is wired. Sutradharak, the PuppetMaster." I pointed to the sinister looking Mercedes parked beneath the acacia on the opposite side of the river. That got their attention. They knew the name well, and what came with it. One of them instantly yanked back on two long handles rising up from the floor. A mass of engines, cars, and people jerked and shuddered in deceleration, wheels screeched desperately on the rails. But even I could tell it wasn't enough. The engines, forced by the tons of weight behind them, were sliding helplessly onto the bridge. How many passenger cars would follow? It was anyone's guess.

I pulled on the door handle, but it didn't budge. The man

next to me, with total panic in his eyes, leaned across to push the latch forward and lift the handle. Below us, wheels slid in a long, rabid shriek down the tracks toward the bridge. It felt like skiing on crystal ice. I stepped onto the outer tread and leapt from the cab, my momentum pitching me into a sideways roll that twisted my ankle as soon as my foot touched the dirt. The first engineer tumbled half on top of me as he fell. The second managed to land running and remain on his feet.

Then, at that very instant, the center of the bridge erupted in a volcanic cone, its spine curling skyward like a bristling cat. The explosion thundered across the plateau, shattering glass in the station windows. Three-fourths of the span lifted upward, hung as if held by strings, and then dropped in a single heap of bolts, girders, rail, and planking into the churning water below.

My ankle was sprained, but not badly enough to keep me from running desperately toward the first class compartments. Uli and Jitka, I hoped with all hope, had gotten to the door and were getting out. I ran alongside the engines, and two freight cars, toward one of the policemen who had moments earlier been trying to blow part of my body into the dirt. This time he heard every word I screamed. "Get the people off!" He turned and jogged along the containers of human cargo, smacking the barred windows with the butt of his gun. Used to giving orders, he wasted no breath on words. "Out, now,' he shouted, and inside, the cry was taken up like a litany by the passengers. Ever sort of rider, Hindus, Muslims, and Sikhs began jumping in pressed trousers, saris, and loongis from the only available exits, the doors between the cars. It all moved like a sluggish dream.

The train was slowing, but the front engine was still being pushed liked a reluctant child toward the severed end of the bridge. With a horrific crunch it broke through the girders and rail twisted like a turnstile above the river. There was a grinding, screeching of metal on jagged metal and for an eerie second it grew quiet.

Down the line people were leaping frantically from doorways. A few canvass bags and suitcases flew out, but mostly a frenzied stream of bodies tumbled onto the seedlings of the newly planted field. Mothers yelled for children, husbands for wives, and then an explosion of water erupted like a geyser behind me. Echoes rumbled through the ravine. The lead engine and its companion had dropped like enormous toys and jack-knifed into the water. But they weren't toys, they were masses of iron and alloy with a single purpose—to pull themselves and the humans behind them smoothly along the track, and as if that was a fixed task, a mission they couldn't ignore, they tugged just enough in their fall for the two baggage cars to come to the edge . . . and tumble into the gorge. But like rigid sticks, the freight cars didn't drop onto the engines now filling with river water; they dropped into the mud at the edge of the current. Fortune, or fate, or maybe one of Sahr's constellations, snapped the coupling between the freight cars and the first-class passenger cars. They were tumbling in twos. The momentum drew the first-class cars past me and out onto the bridge. In an act of futile instinct, I reached out a hand to try to stop thousands of tons of steel. Inside the second car I saw figures piled in the rear—human silhouettes against the windows. Then Jitka rolled out the door with her backpack onto the field. Uli will be next, I thought with relief. But she wasn't. A Hindu in black slacks and blue shirt stepped of the top step and fell like a sack of rice. The cars slid past me like unstoppable beasts.

She must have jumped out the opposite door. I ran to Jitka and lifted to her feet by the frame of her pack. She was shaking visibly.

"Where is she?" I screamed.

"I don't know, Bhim." She slumped to her knees. "She didn't come back."

I started to ask what she meant, but the front compartment rolled persistently to the edge, and with a deafening screech, the front wheels clicked off the tracks into empty space. For an instant, I thought it would come to rest on that flimsy fulcrum. Inside the compartment someone screamed, and as if the mere vibration of that sound tilted the weight, the box twisted slowly and dropped over the precipice. The shift jerked the second car and the entire length of the train slid forward again. Uli! My mind screamed frantically. It was our first-class compartment, and it slid across the jagged edge, twisted on the same slow axis, and snapped away from the others with a crack of splintered steel. It fell forty feet, slid down the embankment to crush the corner of one of the cars below. It spun a hundred and eighty degrees and came to rest in the water at the river's edge. The current swirled angrily through the barred windows of the lower half.

Directly in front of me the two second-class cars had derailed, the right wheels resting on the ties, the left wheels mired deep into the earth. Three more cars slid off and tilted precariously to one side. I lifted Jitka and held her at arm's length. She stood on her own weight and seemed unhurt other than a dirty scrape on her elbow from the jump. "Where is she?" I asked again.

She stared back disoriented, bewildered. "She didn't come back when the train began to leave, Bhim. Oh Gott, I thought she was with you. It all happened so fast."

"What do you mean she didn't come back? Where did she go?"

Jitka squeezed her eyes shut and then looked at me more clearly. "She left right after you went for the paper. I thought she was going to find you."

I looked at the mayhem--behemoths of twisted steel and the tons of scattered debris of terrified travelers. To my left, along the platform, dazed Hindus, Muslims, Sikhs, and a few disparate ferenghis huddled in ragged groups. Families, couples, and lone passengers searched for bags or relatives, looking to reorganize something, anything. Luggage flew from doorways and railway officials began running and shouting, and no one understood at all what had really happened. Except me. To my right, near the foot of the bridge, people were sobbing or staring over the precipice. She got off before it left the station, Bhim. She got off. She's safe. She's here in the crowd. Just need to find her. "I just need to find her," I heard myself whispering. But she wasn't there. I searched the faces, the hair, clothes, but none of Uli's features came back to take away my growing fear.

The other side, she must have gone out the other side.

I scrambled to the opening between the slanted cars and leapt to the top step in one stride. Through the space I could see figures on the opposite side, bodies crawling on the earth, people wandering, moving numbly in the direction of the bridge and incline. She's here, I know it. She is. But she wasn't. I jumped to the other side and saw only the trousers and silks of Indian first-class. My brain screamed. I looked into the second-class car, but knew she wouldn't be there, and the ache that had left, the one that had wrapped itself so coldly around my heart for so long

flooded back in. I tripped, fell to my knees, and then to all fours.
No, no, no. That one word, the one that denied she was gone,
railed against my fear. It repeated and repeated in my head,
cried out, then slowly, gradually, it grew quieter. And fell silent.
Then, there was no voice, no scream, nothing but emptiness. My
head sank until my forehead touched the ground. I clawed at the
dirt of the field. With a faint perseverance the voice whispered.
No. The wreckage below, maybe she's alive. No, it whispered. I
raised myself and dragged myself towards the edge. She's gone.

The engineer who had fallen on top of me when we tumbled
from the cab, trotted towards me, waving his hand in the
direction of the warehouse across the river. "He's getting away."
I looked into the distance to see the black Mercedes turning onto
a frontage road that paralleled NH 24, the east-west highway.
Sutradharak was slithering into obscurity. He had been forced to
demolish the bridge before he had intended, perhaps when he
saw the train slowing or me running like a madman across the
field. He hadn't succeeded; he had failed to murder the grand
number he had wished for.

But he has destroyed me, I thought. I stared at the receding
bumper and felt only the total despair that comes from losing
love. I had felt it before, and it hurt no less now. Uli had been
right. Mej was pure evil and I had been too naive to see it. My
hands dropped; my head sank to my chest. The victory of
yesterday, the discovered cure, it was all erased. Adam was
wrong. It wasn't the light of a million suns growing brighter; it
was only darkness. And it was closing over me. I walked silently
past the engineer to the edge of the slope and stared down at the
mass of twisted engines and cars.

Seventy-Three

The vagaries of memory are mysterious and indefinable. Critical elements, like the scent of perfumed hair, a hummed melody, the color of an iris, the touch of a moist lip, or the curve a smile, can all be triggered to return in finely wrapped packages. They burst in complete recollection into the mind with the insertion of a just single key. The totality of a person, a lover, returns fully, and all it takes is a key, a catalyst, or a spark. For me that spark was a wisp of cloth.

The engineer was rambling diffusively about the escaping Sutradharak, when a ripple of pale-blue reached my eye, and for a moment, my mind didn't comprehend the source. Then a mud-stained sea horse emerged and fluttered in eel grass. I blinked. It was coming from the partially submerged first-class compartment at the edge of the river. Her backside appeared first, then the tail of her kurta, and then all of Uliana Hadersen stood. She was straining to pull a small man up through the front door--which was now angled upward to the sky. Her skirt and kurta were torn and drenched. Her hair was smeared with grime and muck of the river, but she was alive . . . and saving people's lives. Helping. Every recollection of Uli came back, every kiss, caress, and sweet consummation.

I leapt down the incline in incredibly long bounds, my ankle ignoring the swelling pain, my feet slurping in mud, my eyes blinded with tears. I sprinted past the toppled freight cars on the lower slope and into the deep mud of the riverbed. My shoes sank into ooze that clawed and pulled at them like tentacles. I struggled across the flats to the first class cars, lying on their sides twelve meters apart, perpendicular to each other. The furthest, with my Uli somewhere inside it, lay with its lower half

sunk deep into the water. A group of Hindus, dazed and
bleeding, crouched below the protruding wheels. Two women
were cleaning blood from a man's face with the ends of their
saris. A young Muslim man climbed down the undercarriage,
which was now an eleven-foot wall up to a single exit at the top.
I stepped onto an axle assembly, then onto broken hydraulics,
springs, and shafts. As I reached the wheels near the top, I heard
her voice. "Hello Mein Schatztki." I looked into her face, eyes
like sapphires and marigolds. Her look told me she knew that I
had thought she had died. It showed in my eyes.

Her hand stretched out for mine. "I could use you help."

Fingers slipped around mine and that touch, the electricity of
it, woke me from the nightmare of pain I had been in a minute
before. I climbed onto the side of the car and stood. "Uli, what
happened? Where…"

She touched my cheek with wet fingers and pulled me toward
the opening that led down into the passenger car. Sideways
"Later, Sweets. Right now we need those strong arms and legs of
yours." Then she disappeared through the doorframe.

I lowered myself into the space and peered into shadows.
Above, the barred windows provided a muted light onto a ruin
of luggage, breakfast trays, bedding, and three desperate people.
Half way down the compartment a young woman in drenched
silk was struggling with a sobbing boy in her arms. She was
trying desperately to climb over the jumble of twisted bunks to
the freedom of the door. Behind her a familiar figure lay trapped
in eddying, black water. The gentleman who had purchased our
breakfast was pinned at the chest by the metal bars of a sleeping
berth, his left side and shoulder held tightly below the surface.
He sputtered and gasped, his body contorting against the bar

like a pinned serpent. Uli was trying unsuccessfully to lift the frame. It flexed in begrudging centimeters. I reached out and pulled the woman by the elbow, lifting her and the child past me toward the skylight door. Then I threaded my way further into the gloom. Halfway down, on the left side, amidst a crush of sleeping berths, two bodies--an older man and woman--were wrapped in each other's arms. Their eyes stared sightless at each other.

Scrambling over a mound of suitcases and debris, I saw more reason for concern—the incline was slippery, and gaining a foothold to pry the metal upward would be difficult. Uli had just pulled against the slats again and slipped. Her leg skewed sideways into the water that now swirled to the side of the man's nostrils. He couldn't draw a full breath, his eyes pleaded frantically at me. I seized the frame opposite Uli and tried to find footing. My left heel wedged against a hinge of some sort, but my right kept sliding frustratingly across something below the surface. It felt like the bars of one of a submerged window, but I couldn't be certain.

The water I was standing in filled the man's mouth, choking him.

Knowing we had only one chance, and that it would squeeze all the remaining air from his lungs, I set my right foot directly on his chest. He looked up at me with terrified eyes as his face sank below the surface from my weight. Uli on the other hand, understood, and said one word "Now!" We both lifted with all the strength we had. The berth rose six inches, no more. The man was still pinned under my foot, so I lifted onto my toes, pivoted until my heel was above his shoulder and stepped down. He twisted from the pain, and I felt his body spasm and writhe as water entered his lungs. I pivoted again until my foot was on his upper arm. Uli let go, and for three seconds I held the entire load while she reached across and yanked the man's collar away from the bar. My foot slid off his arm, the metal snapped down with a watery twang. But with gasping breaths and spewing water, our man came to the surface and rolled to his knees. He vomited a mass of brown water and idly cake and then groaned, "Christ in Heaven!" Christian, I thought, not Muslim. My earlier assessment had been wrong. Then he groaned again, "Please, can you help me from this foulness?" I lifted beneath his armpits and pulled him upright onto the tilted floor.

"Are you hurt?" I asked.

He needed to ponder that for a moment, then smiled broadly and in a booming voice said, "My arm hurts like hell, my good man, but," he patted his chest, "nothing seems to be otherwise broken."

Uli helped him over the pile of suitcases and up the incline, and as he reached the door he called back in a quieter voice, "I seem to be in your debt again, my friend." With a drawn smile he climbed into the light of the morning.

I stayed behind to complete a last chore; one that I decided was mine alone. It was, I believed, a small absolution for my earlier moment of doubt. All the lessons and gifts I had received over the last ten days had slipped away when I thought Uli was gone. I had doubted. That would never happen again.

Lfting of the dead is not such a vile task as we might imagine--another lesson Adam taught me. I didn't know their names. I didn't know their faith. I only knew that they had died in each other's arms in love together. With a serene mind and caring touch, I closed their eyes and lifted them one at a time through the door to waiting hands.

Seventy-Four

Ascending from the intestines of that car into the Bareilly sunlight was like stepping from the cave at Sarnath. Or stepping into the dazzling courtyard of my villa after a night's rain. It was the pure exhilaration of reaching the shoulder of a perfectly formed wave after being deep inside the pipe. It was liberation from all the dark closets of my life. Every muscle ached with fatigue, bruises were swelling and purpling over my body. I felt none of it. Uli was alive. That was all I knew. All I wanted.

I climbed down the undercarriage and stood in mud up to my ankles. She turned and came to me, wrapped her arms under mine, and pressed her head against my chest. We remained that way for what seemed to be a long time, tears blending with the salts of our bodies. Her fingers touched my lips and we kissed, deeply and passionately, right there in front all the staring eyes.

The huddled crowd behind us clapped.

"I thought you were gone," I whispered.

She smiled and set a hand on my heart in her usual way. "I see that, Lover. But I am right here." A little tap.

"But you weren't inside...?"

"Shh," she whispered. "Not now. A story for later."

I kissed her eyes, her hair and neck, and would have stood that way longer, but the railway police had different ideas. As we stood in each other's arms, a lone officer descended the hillside with his rifle leveled at me. In Bengali he bellowed, "Get down! On your knees, now, hands on your head!" It seemed I was still a suspect of some sort, but I was not willing to lower myself into the muck at my feet.

"I beg your pardon?" I asked as I let go of Uli and stepped away. I raised my hands, but didn't kneel. His rifle came to eye-level.

Behind me voices began rising at once, one rose above the others. "What in Christ's holy name are you doing, man?"

The policeman scowled and barked, "This fellow is a terrorist," He glanced from the small group to me and with a shade of uncertainty, added, "He attempted to blow up the train."

The engineer who stood with me at the edge and followed the policeman down the slope, now stepped between us. "He did not," he yelled. "He kept it from being destroyed entirely. This man warned us and kept all of us from going into the river." He pointed in the general direction of the highway above us. "The man you want is at this moment driving west on the NH 24 in a black Mercedes." The policeman hesitated and, then far too slowly, lowered his rifle. I exhaled.

A typhoon of noise washed over us, people shouting, whistles shrieking, sirens and horns moaning like gale winds. Uli and I stood at the center and heard only each other.

"I thought I had lost you," I said again.

"I know," she said. "It was in your eyes when you climbed up to help me. I knew you thought I had died." Her eyes twinkled. "But I didn't, you see."

"So, where did you go? Jitka told me you left the compartment."

"You want me to tell you the story right now? In this mud? You don't wish to lift me up like a shining knight and carry me away to take a hot shower with me first?" A blend of mischief and exhaustion filled her smile.

I looked over her shoulder. A growing current of people was moving in both directions on the hillside. I saw Jitka jumping up and down near the foot of the shattered bridge--a dance of joy--and I knew that it was going to be okay for all of us. We had survived, and other than an assortment of ugly contusions, scrapes, and one badly sprained ankle, we were uninjured. "Yes," I laughed. "I want to know where you went. Then I will lift you up and carry you to all the soap and water we can find."

She looked at me with a touch of embarrassment. "I went for this." From a pocket of her muddied kurta, she drew out a pouch no larger than a silver dollar and placed it in my palm. I looked at my hand. A slash of dried blood split the base of my thumb, black grease and caked mud stained my fingers, and in the center the small purse sat like a purple monarch. I opened it and the fiery glitter of an opal and chain blazed before I even pulled them out.

"You bought it from the jeweler at the station? The one with the box around his neck?"

"Yes, Love. I saw it from the window and it called to me, 'Uliana,you are his fair premika. You had better come and fetch me to him me straight away.' So, I got off to buy it. But then everything happened. I was trying to pay the jeweler, and I saw you running, and the train was starting to leave. And then . . . I got onto the wrong car."

"You what?"

"I got onto the wrong car. I jumped on the front one, and it started moving, and I saw you running and heard you yelling in English, and I understood what was happening. I told everyone to get off, but some of them were stubborn and refused, until the car braked so sharply they fell."

I thought of the bullheaded chap whose life we had just saved.

Uli lifted the opal from the pouch, kissed it, and set the clasp around my neck. The stone, lit by the sun, blazed like a thousand embers.

"It's perfect," I said. Then I remembered Adam's manuscript. "My bags," I cried.

****

We didn't make it to the airport as planned that afternoon, but I did get to finally have my coffee. And, I had plenty of time to read newspapers, eat breakfast, have snacks, and even lunch. This was all done between interrogations by very thorough officials from six intelligence agencies with lots of initials. I also got my duffles back. They were delivered to me by a railway policeman as I sat talking with a Mr. Vajpayati Panchu Rumir, a young and sad-looking anti-terrorism expert from Delhi.

He was flipping through my passport with weary eyes and sighing. "I see from your visas that you have lived in Varanasi for more than three years. You like that city?"

I nodded.

"And you have no desire to travel to others?"

"Not really. Not until now, actually. I'm a linguist and have been involved in some Sanskrit studies with a pundit there." I was beyond weary of answering questions.

He looked at me oddly. "Sanskrit? So, you like our poet Kalidasa then?" A brief smile and I perked up.

"Honestly, his poems are the most beautiful I have ever read. They're my favorites in any language."

"Yes, mine too. They still bring pleasure in an otherwise cheerless world. I also lived in Varanasi for many years. It is an incomprehensible place, even for those who have lived there for decades." He handed me back my passport. "I hope to God we catch this Sutradharak, Mr. Scott. He is a pestilent murderer who has taken the lives of many innocent people. His tongue should be cut out and he should be tied to a post for the rats to eat." He sighed more deeply. "But, as you know, ours is a large country and he seems to have both money and a unique talent for disguise. He also has a network of connections and resources to draw upon. This makes it quite difficult for us, as you can imagine. There is a forensics team searching his cottage in Varanasi as we speak." He pulled at his earlobe. "But I do not expect much to come of it."

I studied him as he scribbled notes in a thick binder. He was meticulous in his notation, but thin and somewhat unkempt in appearance. His fingernails were split and uncut, the back of his hair flowed over his shirt collar as if he had no desire to manage it. He was the last official to question me that afternoon and wanted only to hear the fine points of Mejanand Whiton, nothing else. He asked me to describe details, every one. And then he asked me to do it again. His questions probed my memory like surgical instruments. I ended up recalling Mej's habits, voice inflections, right-handedness, manner of gait, how he took his coffee, and what kind of women he talked about or preferred.

After some time, Inspector Rumir said, "I believe he may have been American, or at least lived in that country for awhile."

The thought surprised me. "What brings you to that conclusion?"

Rumir's thin smile hung briefly on his lips. "His jokes, Mr. Scott, all of them that you have told me sound American. It isn't English humor at all."

He was right, and as he seemed to be nearing the end of his questions, I asked, "Mr. Rumir, may I make a frank observation?"

"By all means, Mr. Scott. How could I deny a request from the hero of the hour?" I smiled faintly at that.

"You seem to be incredibly determined, almost dogged with your questions. You've asked me details I doubt I would have thought to ask myself, and yet you seem quite convinced Sutradharak will avoid capture. Why?"

He closed the binder, blinked at me with wistful eyes, and pushed an expensive-looking pen deep into his breast pocket. "Mr. Scott, I have been pursuing The PuppetMaster seven days a week for four months straight. I have written high-level opinions on reports about him. I have not slept or eaten well during that time. I have followed leads like a tracking dog, memorized the ideologies, writings, and methods of every schismatic, sectarian, or militant faction in this entire fucking country, and in this last hour I have learned that I have been searching down all the wrong trails. Sutradharak's motives have been one-hundred and eighty degrees opposite of what I expected. All my theories have been wrong. Everyone's has. His motives, I have believed almost religiously, would lead me to him. I hoped eventually to be given the opportunity to mete out my vengeance, and now I doubt that I shall have that opportunity. Excuse my language, Mr. Scott, but it is one big, fucking shame."

"He played on all our assumptions. Me, as much as any."

"And killed a lot of innocent people in the process."

There was something in the way he looked at me, an

overture to ask. "Did you lose someone to him?"

The sad eyes closed for a moment and when they opened again he replied, "My wife died in the blast at Sankat Mochan. My infant daughter lives with my mother and will never know her own."

I suddenly felt a compelling need to say something, anything that would ease this man's grief. My attempt was clumsy. "I have also lost loved ones, Mr. Rumir. The losses left me dead in my heart for a long time. But . . . love has come back into my life. It will for you. Write one more report, Mr. Rumir, then go to your daughter and wrap her in your arms. Show her a world of love. Show her the good, and she in turn will make a difference."

With a nod, he said, "Always listen to the advice of a poet. When this is done, I will dedicate myself to raising her well."

I rose and we shook his hands. He gave me his card and I wished him luck and left.

Outside, I looked across the aftermath of the explosions, tilted compartments, the severed bridge, and the debris of countless lives. Five humans died at Bareilly that morning, twenty-six more were injured enough for hospitalization, but I knew that we had been more fortunate than not. Much more. The disaster had been derailed, and the objectives of Imperial Holding and its invisible architects had been halted forever in India. Good had triumphed--at a price.

But Mejanand Whiton, The PuppetMaster of Uttar Pradesh was not apprehended that day. His Mercedes was found north of Delhi in Haryana, but he was not.

Uli and Jitka found me sitting on a bench outside the offices of the Railway Protection Force. A young woman was binding my ankle as a small crowd stared. The three of us were minor celebrities, especially Uli and me. They helped me to a taxi, and without saying much, we headed for two rooms in the best hotel in the city. Exhaustion permeated every muscle, dirt covered us from head to foot, Jitka was hungry, and we were saturated in bliss. The driver fawned over us, lifted the women's backpacks and set them like prizes into the trunk. I let him handle one of my duffles; the other held Adam's manuscript, and all the way through the city I held it against my chest and drifted into Uliana's warmth. She leaned into me and gently nibbled my earlobe. I exhaled. Finding the words to the forward of Adam's book would be a simpler task now.

Seventy-Five

Long, hot showers work magic on deep bruises and rejoined lovers. Uli and I had been separated for less time than it takes to dress for dinner, but they were minutes that felt like eons to me. Agony. So, we washed it away together, let the sweet soaps and shampoos of the Hotel Swarn Towers strip away our pain and send it spinning down the drain. Sadness was supplanted with love, bruises by wet kisses. Our bodies once again entwined like wisteria vines, just like the painting. And afterwards the three of us dined at the Twenty-Four Carats Restaurant, which boasted fine Indian and Chinese cuisine. With quiet laughter we let the fatigue settle further. None of us spoke of the events of the day; we talked of our childhoods, and I listened dreamily as the sisters recalled school games and the Tonder hearths at Christmastime.

Green tea ice-cream, I discovered, is also an elixir for some forms of pain. As we were savoring our last bites, a man in a well-tailored suit approached. "Mr. Scott?" I was slowly getting used to that name again.

"Yes?"

"I am Mr. Baj Dengal, manager of the Swarns Tower, The owners have informed me that they wish to provide your rooms and meals free of charge. The people of our city and are in your debt." He bowed deeply at the waist.

Uliana immediately said the correct thing. "It would be our pleasure to accept your generosity, Mr. Dengal. The rooms are perfect und the food is exceptional. Please thank the owners und staff for us." I smiled and nodded as he backed away, thanking us for gracing his establishment. Then he straightened up.

"Ah, Mr. Scott, I almost forgot. A package was delivered for you this evening. Shall I have it sent around to your room?"

Curious, I answered, "No, I will fetch it. Thank you"

"Very good, Sir. It will be at reception. The lad who brought it said it should be delivered to you before seven." He bowed and was gone.

Uli frowned. "A package? Who would send you a package here? And why before seven?" The crease deepened. "Who even knows you're here?"

"Most of Bareilly, I expect."

"Maybe it's candy or pastries from someone who wants to thank you," Jitka added. "Or a note from Adam." Uli looked unsure.

"I don't know how he would know where we are," I said. "But then again, it is Adam we are talking about."

At the reception desk a young man handed me a box six inches by three, wrapped in brown paper with nothing more than my name printed on a label. It felt neither heavy nor light when I shook it, and the contents didn't shift, but I wasn't going to risk that it might create some danger when I opened it. "I'll meet you upstairs," I said trying to look casual.

Uli looked at the rectangle as if it were poison. "Bhim, call the police and have them look at it first."

I shook my head. "It needs to be done now. I'll be fine. Besides, I've got too much to share with you to be delayed by a tiny box." My expression told her that this was not going to be one of those shared moments.

With a small knife from the bartender, I took the package to the parking lot and set in on the pavement between two cars, that way if it exploded no one would be hurt but me. Not a comfortable conclusion, exactly. I slit the ends and carefully drew out the box. Beneath the cover, a new phone was nestled inside molded Styrofoam. It was turned on and a text message stared implausibly at me from the green screen. "Call me at 7?" I lifted it and pressed the Contacts button to bring up the list of names in memory.

There was no need to scroll. M.W. was the only entry. "Son of a bitch," I whispered.

****

"It's from him, then?" Uli grimaced.

Jitka had come across the hall from her room to stay with Uli while I had been outside. She asked to see the phone, turned it over, and remarked, "This is a global model. Iridium 9505A. Very expensive, Bhim, but you could call from the North Pole and talk to a person in New Zealand with this."

"How expensive?"

"In Denmark this would probably cost you about fifteen hundred American dollars. It has some latency because the signal travels through a satnet."

I translated that mentally. "So there's some lag time from the satellite, but the callers can be anywhere in the world? Untraceable?'

"Right."

I stood at the window next to a table and chairs and made the call punctually at seven. Almost immediately a voice with no discernible accent said, "I'm glad you called, Marty." No one in India had ever called me that. Even officials called me by the printed name on my passport, Martin. He was playing games.

"You seem to have lost your accent, Mejanand, though I

don't suppose that is your real name."

"I don't have a real name, Marty."

"Of course you don't. Nothing is real about you, is it?" I wanted to shriek into the phone, but knew it would do no good.

"Not much, you're correct."

"But it's true that you're a cold-hearted murderer of innocent people."

"Another correct assessment, Marty," he answered. "But they weren't people to me, you see, just numeric objectives." His voice was flat, no inflection or emotion.

"It must have greatly disappointed you today then."

"Yes it did. You did play it well, Marty, beat me at my own game. I realize now I should never have let you in."

"You mean let me so close to you. Why did you do that?"

There was a pause not due to the satellite. "I liked the dance, my friend. I really did."

"I'm not your friend. Honestly, I don't think I ever liked you. I just enjoyed the Frisbee. You don't have a single person in your world you can call a friend, do you?"

For the first time in the conversation there was a sigh. "Correct again, Marty."

"So, why did you send me a fancy phone and have me call you? Trying to impress me? Because I'm pretty certain it wasn't to apologize."

A longer pause followed. "There were three things I thought you should know, and a question I would like answered." I waited. "First, they won't find me, Marty. Ever. You should know that."

I was pretty certain he was right. As Inspector Rumir had admitted, he was too well moneyed and too damned smart.

"Maybe, but maybe the others will find you, the bad boys you pissed off when Imperial Holding went down. They might know better where to come looking. Am I right?"

From a small, sharp inhale, and I knew I had hit a nerve. "That is a possibility, something I may have to deal with," he admitted quietly.

"So what's the second thing, Mej?" My voice had risen a notch in anger.

"I have an apology. The sweeper girl, she wasn't part of my plan, she recognized me from an error I committed."

That one stung. The cords tightened around my chest and I could tell he knew it. "And the third?" I asked quietly.

"You shouldn't take the Hadersen woman back to Varanasi, Marty."

I tried to control my breathing, but my pulse was flooding into my temples. "Why not?"

"The Imams at Alamqir Mosque know who she is and who her father is. Qereshy knows, and by tomorrow night every Muslim in the city will know. The excitable ones, well you know how they can be."

My palm was slippery around the phone, and the room spun like a carousel. My God! The risk will be everywhere. She can't stay in the country. "Was this one of your arrangements?"

"Not at all," he sighed. "A nasty little informant in Shivdaspur discovered it, and he or she decided to make some profit from it." The transvestite that had argued with us.

"So that one is sort of a gift then?"

"You might call it that."

"That's three, what's your question?" My legs were sagging. I sat in the chair and pushed the hair and sweat from my forehead.

"What was in the cave that was so important to you? The excavators from the mine got inside, and I was told it was just scratches all over the walls. Stick letters. Nobody could figure any of it out, so they made certain it was covered up again."

I shut my eyes tightly. We were at the end. The dance was nearly over, and I wanted a final spin of the disc that would leave him hurting. "Something very important was in there. Something I hope you think about as you are running like a rat to the next hiding hole, wondering if the waiter who's bringing your beer is going to shove an ice-pick into your neck. Those little stick letters? They're a cure for diabetes. They are going to spread more good in the world, and make more money for the right people than all the weapons-grade uranium your asshole friends ever sold. And there's more. Buried below, there may be more. Who knows? But we're going to find out. And right now that cure is being securely wrapped and given freely to the world. This is one time when the good guys win, Mej. Can you understand what that means?"

There was a long pause and then, in pure cockney, he replied, "It was a foocking good session, Mate. You're the best."

Then the phone went dead.

Seventy-Six

Rawalpindi—Female suicide bomber kills 21 and wounds 74.

Malé—Terror bomb explodes in the Maldivian capital injuring 12 foreign tourists.

Ludhiana---Bomb explodes in the Shingar Cinema, killing 7 and wounding 20.

Blasts in Varanasi, Faizabad, and Lucknow kill 15 and injures more than 80.

Amarah--Three car bombs detonate killing at least 40 and wounding 125.

Six months of headlines leading up to the explosion at Bareilly glowed on my laptop. I was waiting for Uli and Jitka, and the list was a simple exercise I was performing, research of some personal significance. With time, I knew I could probably find enough entries to fill a medium-sized book. My half-year's worth was still growing. Twenty perished when a female assassin blew herself up—a girl. Another female, wearing a vest of explosives, killed nine in Diyala. Most would have needed Google just know where that was. The targets? Innocents in cities around the world--cafes, malls, movie theaters, parks, and consulates, any place with a crowd. They were the Somas and Mina Rumirs of the world. The headlines, with thinly detailed stories, gave the feeling that they were merely numbers. Numeric objectives, as Mej had said.

The wreckage of the explosions at the Ghat and bridge would stay with me--scenes I would never forget. The people who had fallen that day were not numeric objectives. They were humans. They were brothers, and mothers, and sisters, and fathers. They were children all. As I sat in Indira Gandhi International

Airport, pulling up story after story, I thought very carefully about that and vowed never to forget or let it go. I thought about the murderers, The Sutradharaks, the fanatics, the ultra-one-side-or-the-others, the misled martyrs of false causes. They had all been duped.

And I thought about Uliana and me.

After Mejanand had hung up, I had made three calls on the global satphone in the hotel Bareilly. The first to Panchu Rumir to tell him of the call. He asked me some questions forgotten during the afternoon session. He then promised to send an officer around to retrieve the phone in the morning; the phone and billing account would be investigated. The second was to SAS, the Scandinavian Airlines. One ticket added, one modified. And the last was to Sahr.

"Bhimaji! You are safe? The radio has been saying hundreds were sent to the hospitals."

"I am fine, Sahr. Three dozen were injured, no more. I'm a little bruised up, but nothing that your saag paneer and puris won't fix. And please ignore the news on the radio; it will be weeks before they get it straight. Okay?"

"And the Memsahibs? Jitka and Uliana? They are also unhurt?" There was so much concern in her question.

"They are also unhurt." I echoed. "I will be back in a few days, maybe less."

"But, I thought Bhimaji was going to the Mountains of Himachal on a vacation with his beautiful premika."

"I will be returning alone, Sahr, very soon."

"Alone? But…"

"It is a long story, one I don't have time for right now. Tell Lalji to lock everything well and continue to guard our gate."

My eyes closed. "There is still some chance of danger."

She was quiet for a moment. "Bhimaji, there have been rumors, very ugly gupchup, coming out of the Muslim neighborhoods."

"That is exactly what it is, Sahr, ugly gupchup. Ignore that too. I will see you in a few days and call you from Lucknow when I know my arrival time."

Sahr always knew when to cease questioning. "Chicken bhiryani, your favorite, will be waiting, Saab."

We easily found a ride into Delhi the following morning. A guest of the Swarns Tower, whose mother had been on the train the day before, was more than happy to chauffer 'his mother's saviors' to the capital. He chatted loquaciously as we started out on NH24, but then fell silent for the next four hours in deference to our own quiet moods. Eventually, he dropped us at his office at Connaught Place in the center of the city. We took an even quieter taxi ride to the airport. And that is where I now sat with the Chandragupta's computer in my lap, trying to keep my thoughts occupied with something other than Uliana Hadersen going in another direction. Copying headlines of bomb blasts was probably not the best activity.

The sisters, sans backpacks, walked slowly through the bustling corridor towards me. Jitka's elbows were bandaged and both of Uli knees were taped with gauze. I set the computer to the side and stood with the help of a rather ugly aluminum cane. The only ache I really felt was in my chest. "So, it is set, then?" I asked miserably.

Uli slipped into my arms. "Yes, My Love. In ninety minutes, and you are not allowed to be so sad. It will not be that much time apart." She pulled her head back to look at me. "Will it?"

I touched her cheek. "I don't know. It depends on how much Master Devi needs me. Undoubtedly, he will say he doesn't need me at all, but he does. I can't leave him to fend for himself with this unfinished business. Without C.G., and the possibility of more translations."

She looked wistful. "I wish I could have seen it, you know, the inside of your mysterious cave. Perhaps when it is safer we can go?" It was a question whose answer was held in a nebulous future.

"Perhaps," I answered, "But not now."

She smiled sadly. "Und my handsome tour guide never got to take me to Sarnath to walk on the paths of the Buddha." A caress on my cheek.

"Maybe . . . maybe someday we can go there, too."

At that, Jitka actually started weeping. In a raw voice, she whispered, "I vill take good care of her, Martin. No harm will come. And when you come to Tonder we will celebrate in a big party with flaekesteg und kransekage and ten barrels of wine und beer."

I looked to Uli who mouthed, "pork roast and almond cake."

Jitka slapped a hand on my shoulder. "Und I will show you how gut is Denmark, and when you gut and ready, you will take my sister to see your home by the ocean, ya?"

I smiled and replied in what was undoubtedly the worst accent ever, "Ya, kan du hjaelpe mig? Hvor er toilletet?" 'Can you help me? Where is the bathroom?' I'd found it hastily online.

Jitka laughed and elbowed my ribs. "Those will be very gut to remember when we drink beer." She kissed Uli on the cheek and gave me a crushing hug. "I am going now. You remember our gate, Uli?"

"I remember, Svester."

With a wave, she was gone, and Uli and I once again stood alone in the middle of a stream of people. We wrapped like lovers being torn apart by winds. She kissed my neck. "I will be only half a woman until I am with you again. Less than that I think. 'Ever has it been that love knows not its own depth until the hour of separation."

"Khalil Gibran?"

"You are so good," she smiled.

"How about this one, then? Blow O wind to where my loved one is. Touch her and come to touch me soon."

"Ach, too easy, Sita talking to the wind in the Ramayana. I read it, remember? But I believe she says she wants to touch him, not her."

"A little change on my part."

Her eyes were filling with tears, which started mine to fill. "I will hurry Uli. Thinking of you every waking minute, waiting like a frozen tree for the warmth of Spring."

She kissed me like she did on our first date in Varanasi, not too long, but with such sweetness. "Always my poet," she whispered.

I handed her the single, folded sheet. "My last lines for a while. Read it now or wait."

She opened it and read aloud, as I knew she would.

We are forged in the chest of a star, you and I,
In the beating heart of the universe,
Unbroken, constant and endless light.

We are fashioned like orbs in the center,
Our eye, the suns and spinning moons.
Yet in the silent void of untold space,

When all has fled back to nothingness
And the dust of eons is all that remains,
Blackness will not draw across our light
For we will shine ever and ever and ever on.

Our tears were coming without restraint as crowds hurried by. "And the Sanskrit version?"

"I'm still working on that part."

"Good," she said. "I will wait for it. Look for the good things, Marty." She kissed me again and turned to walk towards security. My only thought was when I would see her again.

The rains fell as if they wanted to prevent me from completing my task in New Delhi. It drove in angled sheets that soaked me as I attempted to keep my duffles dry and hail a taxi to Connaught Circle. My driver asked permission to pull over twice from inability to see the road. I commended his prudence and then fell fast asleep, only to wake when we arrived at Britland Press. I had my driver wait while I went inside. It was as Adam stated; they knew exactly what to do. I was mildly surprised at how the small, erudite octogenarian publisher handled the pages. He carried them immediately to a back office and secured them in a safe like prized art. Perhaps it would be received that way in broader terms. I hoped so.

"I'll be sending you the forward by courier in a few days," I explained.

"I shall be honored to add it to such an opus, Sir."

I was surprised. "You've read this already?" I asked.

"Only the first three divisions, Sir, but such a magnificent compendium. Such language and vision, we see once in a millennium if we are fortunate."

I bid the old man well and laughed as I made my way back to the taxi. Look for the good things, Marty.

Sixteen hours, two sweltering bus rides, and a forlorn journey by taxi later, and I was in the maze of Varanasi again. Outwardly, the city appeared as I had left it, overflowing avenues, Ghats layered in gauzy haze, spires jutting into the sky, but below the familiarity there were profound transformations. The crowds in the Chowk district walked lighter. Heads were held higher and eyes looked into others' without suspicion. The monsoon rains were steady now, and Sutradharak, though not apprehended, was running. Away from the city. The coils of fear were unwinding, the air cooler, the burdens less heavy. In that respect it felt better, but I found out quickly that there was another tension brewing. Small groups of Muslims had clashed with police outside Alamqir Mosque, and a car bomb had killed six and injured thirty outside the Danish Embassy in Pakistan. Presenting a Danish passport in any café or hotel was not safe.

My taxi driver provided a few pertinent details about this, and then dropped me outside the locked gate of my villa. Standing in the courtyard was another change, Lalji. He was decked out in cream-colored trousers and fitted cotton shirt. His hair was clipped, clean, and combed, with no evidence of coconut oil to be seen or smelled. I suspected my weary eyes were playing tricks on me.

He drew back the gate with a gentlemanly flourish and lifted my bags in each arm. "Welcome home, Master Bhim. My prayers for your safety have been answered. Does your leg pain you much?" I quickly understood--the effects of Ramuna, the tailor's daughter. What I had tried for three years to do, she had accomplished in three days.

"Thank you, Lalji. A sore ankle, nothing serious. How are you and Sahr? You look rather . . . pakka, quite polished."

"Thank you, Saab. Maam and I are well, and all is safe here, although we did have some unwanted visitors last night that I had to chase off."

"By yourself?"

"Oh no, Saab. My partners were with me. We charged from the gate like tigers from the mountains."

I patted him warmly on the shoulder, the cleanliness of the cloth feeling quite odd to my touch. "Partners?" I asked with a growing smile.

"Yes, Saab. The brave men who guarded your house during the riots last week are my partners now."

"Ah . . . I see," I said, trying to guess what form of partnership this might be. It would undoubtedly be detailed later, but right now I needed food and my bed beneath the fan. "You may tell me tomorrow, now please set my bags in the bedroom." He took the steps by twos.

Sahr, true to her word, had made my favorite dish and set the table with china, silverware, and an iced tumbler. One setting. I sighed and took my place, while she came out to silently place a steaming plate in front of me and pour the ale. She paused to study me, look at my eyes and the lines of my face, to see where

I had gone. She saw the cane in the corner and then I held out my hand to her. We hugged and I felt her sobbing. "I was sure you were with the spirits, Bhimaji." She shook her head. "Durgubal was right; death came at dawn and I thought . . . " She left it unsaid.

"He was right, Sahr. You were right, but I didn't die, and neither did Uli or Jitka. Innocent people did, and the fiend responsible for all of it has escaped the country." I took a bite and savored the chicken and vegetables and the peace of a quiet meal in the villa.

"Sutradharak?" she asked.

"Yes," I answered wearily. "The same one I played Frisbee with twice a week, it would seem."

"You look exhausted, Saab. I will not ask more questions."

I smiled to myself. She was right, I was bone weary, but her questions were simmering more than the bhiryani. A few more wouldn't add to my fatigue. "What do you want to know, Oh Curious one?" That brought a smile.

"The Memsahib, did she do what the Imams say?"

I took another bite and thought about it. "That depends on what they say she did, I suppose. She did help her father with an idea for the cartoons they hate so much. She also saved five people in the explosion at Bareilly."

Sahr nodded. "They say that also."

That stunned me. "Who says that?"

"Most of the city. Even the Imam Nomani acknowledges that she saved Muslim lives. Qereshy is unnaturally silent on these matters, and some say he is being questioned by the authorities from Delhi."

"Intelligence agencies?"

"Yes, about his connection to Madru Ralki." She changed the subject. "The radio says Miss Uliana saved sixteen people from drowning. Is it true?"

I took a long draught of the ale, almost draining the glass. "That's exaggerating it about threefold."

"And they say you saved them also?"

"I did. It was only what I had to do, and it probably wouldn't have turned out so well if your warning hadn't come back to me at the right time." That brought another smile. "Okay, one more question before I fall face-first into the bhyriani."

She topped off the tumbler with more ale. "When will you leave us?" This question didn't surprise me.

"It's that obvious?"

"You forget too often that I am a nabi. Even without my cards it would be clear. You must go to your premika as soon as you can."

"I know," I sighed, "but I will bee here long enough to see to your well-being and finish my work here. It's very important to me, Sahr."

She patted my hand. "My well-being is already seen to, Bhimaji. Mr. Vinduram Singh has…"

"Asked you to marry him?" I interrupted.

She thrust her shoulders back in mock indignation, refocusing me of the enormity of her bosom, and laughed. "No, he wishes that we go steady for now, I think that is how the young people call it. But he is calling every hour and making excuses to drive by a dozen time a day. We went to the cinema last night, and now he is more nervous and more respectful." She squeezed my wrist. "He will ask me soon. It is in my cards. He has also asked me if I wish to take a job in a restaurant in Bhelpura."

"Really? Let me guess, cooking?"

She nodded. "It is a very popular place, quite modern, and they want new dishes for their menu."

"That's perfect, Sahr, your talents will fit in perfectly. What about Lalji? What will he do?"

"Did he not tell you? He and his friends are starting a security company to guard the houses of the wealthy. One of them actually seems to know what he is doing, and my boy is motivated." She made a fleeting attempt to look motherly. "And he has a girlfriend."

"Yes," I replied. "I noticed."

I dined on the last of the meal, indulged myself with a second lager, and then crawled beneath the fan and a single sheet to sleep without dreams.

The swelling in my ankle had relocated to my head the following morning. It ached more from the effects of three days of travel and my empty bed than the previous night's lager. A long, tepid shower, pakoras, fresh fruit, and two cups of Nilgiri coffee had me reasonably recuperated by nine. I selected light cotton trousers and a favorite kurta, then phoned Devamukti's house on Chandragupta's cell phone.

Sukshmi answered. "And how is my number one dancing partner and hero of the decade?"

"Feeling very fortunate to be alive," I laughed. "I assume you have heard the newest gossip?"

"I have, and so have mother and father. Father wishes to see you about two minutes ago."

"His watch is still functioning correctly?"

I heard her smiling through the phone. "Even less so now. By the way I have a large bone to pick with you."

I winced. "You really must stop using those types of phrases, Sukshmi. Your own are much prettier than your modern friends who use that stuff. So, what have I done wrong now?"

She laughed breezely. "Now I wonder who kidnapped the shy Bhimaji I once knew, the one who always mumbled namaste with his eyes dropping nervously to his feet."

"Still here, Sukshmi, along with the old Martin Scott and the new one. All here, just grown together now."

A quiet followed and in a husky voice she said, "I shall miss them, BhimajiMartinScott, all of them. But I am still displeased that you didn't ask me to dance one last time. I am to be married next month, you know, a big fancy affair that father has taken over all the plans for. Dipak and I would have had a small ceremony, you know, just friends and family. But father has invited every Brahmin in the province and most other castes as well. So . . . enough of that. Uliana is safely away, and rumor tells me that you will follow her?"

"Yes," I admitted quietly, "How could I not, Sukshmi? I came here running away. What I run to now is everything to do with love. It is a good place to be running to. Listen, I have some place I must be this morning. Can you tell Devamukti that I will come to the house at two?"

I felt her smiling. "Your Uli is a fortunate woman, Bhim. You run to her as fast as you can. I will tell father that you will be here. He will be tapping his cane until you arrive."

"Undoubtedly," I sighed.

We hung up and I hailed a taxi to Benares Hindu University.

Seventy-Seven

Adam was also walking with a cane when I found him, hobbling along the walkway near the great library. Even that he did with grace. An entourage of students and disciples moved about him like magnetized metal shavings. As usual, he didn't seem surprised to see my approach, and hailed me from a good distance away. "Martin, my good friend. We wear our battle wounds proudly, do we not? Come, let us retell our tales and share a Fanta in the shade." With that, a bottle of the orange soda materialized from an unseen cooler within the crowd. He whispered something to one of the followers, who in turn spoke to the others, and the group moved off and melted into the gardens beside the path. Almost instantly Adam and I were alone with nothing but the cold drink between us.

I went to fold my hands, but he reached out and took one in his.

"You referred to me as Martin," I said with a laugh, "but you realized that, of course,"

He offered me the bottle, and I took it, feeling the cold against my palm, the moisture on the cracked lettering, and the release of carbonation and sweet flavor into the air. "Of course,' he replied, "there is little that I don't pay attention to in my actions and thoughts these days. It comes with practice."

I nodded. "I've come to understand that about you. You're aware of all of it, aren't you? From your words and movements to your breath and beating of your heart. It's as if you're measuring each one."

He smiled and led us through the arched walkway that ran the length of the library. "Yes, I do. I feel it, my respiration, my blood, digestive juices, the synapses of my brain. It is all rather fascinating and it takes practice, of course, but I feel life inside me and out. There is no difference between, just space and the great energy."

He stopped at a stone seat underneath one of the arches and lowered himself slowly, his healing leg stretched out in front of him. I took the space next to him, and for a few moments we sat listening to the far off lowing of cows and the melody of the city. When eventually I spoke, it was from a place of sadness. "He nearly succeeded, Adam. I keep thinking about that, the thousands that would have died."

He turned to face me. "But he didn't succeed, did he? He has come and passed, and now it is time for the good people to focus on the good things."

I let out a small laugh. "You sounded like Uliana just then. She says the exact same words to me."

"That's because she knows it in her heart, Martin, and the faster you go to her, the faster you will do greater things together." He tapped the ground lightly with his cane. "You have your entire lives to accomplish it together. Already you have done so much."

I looked at our legs wrapped in bandages and thought of the other scars we bore. "You really do see it as a battle don't you?"

He didn't answer immediately, instead he ran his hand across the surface of the bench where we sat. "You know," he said finally, "right here is where I had my first revelation, Adam's epiphany, if you will. It was right on this bench in the exact place where you are sitting."

I looked at him, puzzled.

"It was my twelfth birthday and C.G. brought me to this spot. I remember the detail as if it were yesterday. It was evening, and we had been to the cinema and the park, and it was winter and cold, and no students were about. He was my father to me and Mundika was my mother, the only parents I had ever known. But twelve is the proper age to know the truth, so C.G. made certain I understood exactly who my birth mother was, where I came from. Right where you are sitting I learned about the evil of hatred, about my caste, my supposed place in life. It was then that I chose to fight against it. I have seen it as a battle since. Not too long afterwards they sent me to England."

"He was trying to protect you, wasn't he?"

"And to give me a chance to use my gift." He reached down to scratch his calf. "There is so much to learn, Martin, so much to teach."

I asked the question that had twisted inside me for more than a week. "Adam, why do you take the duties of a dom? Why lift corpses at Manikarnika?"

He laughed gently and tapped my hand with his. "Lifting corpses is not such an awful task when it is done with respect and love. You learned that. But truthfully, it was a vow I took to honor my birth mother. I did it to honor all the harijans of this ancient, but often regressive, city. It was a simple way to demonstrate good. And now, if I can change the subject, I need you to know a few things that will be of importance to you. The cave was re-opened yesterday and there is, as C.G. anticipated, an entirely new room to be translated. But do not be concerned with a need to stay here to help. Devamukti will have all the assistance he could ever desire. It will be given to younger minds, and Devi will oversee it. These students who were with me earlier are some of the brightest Sanskrit students in BHU. And there is a young woman who is the best among them.

Coincidentally, she is harijan." He clapped his hands together with a laugh. "I do love irony when it slaps ugliness right in the chops like that, don't you?"

I smiled. I liked irony when it did that too. "What about the medical parts, the clinical trials, and double blind tests, and all that? Devi knows nothing about it."

"Satnam's charge. His Ayurvedic committees have begun preparing reports for the medical journals. It will be delightful to see what comes from it, and it will certainly shed some needed light on alternative medicine."

"And on Sanskrit," I added absently.

"Ah yes, your beloved language. It will become front page news again, just like it was three thousand years ago." He patted my hand again. "I suppose there is another little secret I should share with you."

"And what is that?"

"You have wondered over the years how I knew you were arriving at the train station the evening I named you Bhim, the time I gave you your namaghanda, have you not?"

I nodded. "About once a week, sometimes a few times a day. You seemed to somehow know I was leaving my old life in search of a new one."

The enigmatic smiled played across his lips and into his eyes. "I was with you, Martin, on the train that same afternoon. I was returning to Varanasi after thirteen years of being away, coming home to C.G. and Mundika, and I watched you. I saw a very sad man indeed, one who needed a new name in his search for a new life. It wasn't difficult to see, and you were so strong in body that the name Bhim came to me."

I started chuckling, slowly at first and it built and rolled into a deep belly laugh that shook me to my swollen ankle. "On the train with me? Excuse me, but shit, I've been wondering for three years how you knew of my my arrival. I mean, you were waiting for me to step onto the platform."

"I was waiting for you, Martin. I knew you had arrived to do good things. That light was in your eyes, even when they were dark and filled with sadness. It still is."

I sighed. "I hope so. It's odd, but since returning from Delhi, I've felt everyone is releasing me, moving on and letting me know it's okay for me to leave."

"They are telling you that, Martin. Now . . . turn and look all the way down the walkway to the left."

I turned my back to him and looked through the arches with climbing vines wrapped like lovers. I thought of Uli and our new life. Adam untied my namaghanda and placed it in my hands.

"Keep this. You will always be Bhimaji of Varanasi, but now you may leave and go home again, Martin Chandler Scott." Adam hugged me warmly and after a few minutes we turned to hobble off in our different directions. As I settled myself into an autorick to travel to Master's, it occurred to me that I had never mentioned my middle name to anyone during my travels.

When I arrived at Devi's I saw that the herd of buffalo had finally arrived. The compound was teeming and had none of the tranquility of previous months. Two distinct groups stood in the parlor, strangers in prickly foreign dress with officious looking satchels hovered on the inside near Master. Some wore media ID, and they were all scribbling on legal pads. A few were observing the protocols of a Brahmin's home. Too few. Around them were the Hindus and Muslims who stood quietly in the presence of the respected pundit who was just then answering a question, "Yes, the cave has been re-opened, and excavation is taking place at this moment." Another question came from the audience and Devi answered, "No, it is being done by hand, very carefully."

With a few bows and namastes, Mirabai ushered me through, and Masterji, seeing me, rose from his seat and with a wag of his head called to the room, "Very well, we will pause for refreshments. I will continue in twenty minutes. I have a previous engagement, you see, with this young man, Bhimaji Scott, who is the third member of our research team, our Keeper of Notes and Records. He is also the brilliant hero who just two days ago saved the lives of many thousands of people at the train station at Bareilly Junction." I wish he had omitted that extremely large exaggeration. The entire room turned and began applauding and bowing and sticking hands out for me to shake. As my back was being patted for the seventh or seventeenth time, Master called out in a more commanding tone, "Juice, sandwiches, and fresh fruit in the courtyard. My colleague and I need some privacy, please." The room emptied and he turned to me.

"You have come in the nick of time, Bhim. I was trying to explain how the cave was discovered, and some history of the Samhitas, and what it means to the societies, and how old we think might be, and who was part of our team." He made a gesture of frustration. "but too many questions were asked all at once, and I couldn't remember." He sighed and lowered himself into his chair. Through the windows I saw Mirabai passing sandwiches, and Sukshmi moving with a tray of glass cups. "The water buffalo have finally arrived to trample our cave, but they stopped here to trample my parlor first." He patted a chair for me next to him. "How am I supposed to explain it correctly?"

"Who are they," I asked.

"Most are medical people, some are Ayurvedic specialists Satnam invited. Those are the ones standing nicely in the back. He wants them to begin 'authenticated clinical trials,' as he calls them, as soon as possible. The others are Sanskrit scholars from different parts of the country. The rest are journalists with no manners. I'm in room full of people, completely alone. But, by Vishnu's graces, you have come to save me in the nick of time."

I couldn't contain a small grin. "You're sure I wasn't a little late by your Timex?"

He smiled, a true smile, not like the one he had been wearing for the guests sipping juice in his courtyard. "Well, perhaps a few minutes tardy, a day or two, but you are forgiven because you do not have such an accurate watch, my boy." He patted my knee with a condor smile. "So, tell me this heroic story the entire city is talking about. And the your Uliana Hadersen, where is she?"

Over the next ten minutes I explained it all, and when I came to the reason Uli was not with me, he snapped, "Utter nonsense. Look on every corner in our city and you find paintings of our gods. Some are better than others, and some are more colorful, but what difference does it matter to the gods. None, I would say!"

I was about to agree, when I saw Sukshmi open the front gate to let someone in. For the briefest moment I pictured Soma walking through with a faded sari and a shy smile. But four of the students that had been walking with Adam entered instead. A young woman with intelligent eyes and folded palms whispered to Sukshmi and then looked our way. Reinforcements had arrived.

"Master, I forgot. Adam has some people to help you with...all of this." I waved my arm toward the courtyard.

He frowned, and I thought he was going to object, but the smile returned. "That is good, Bhim. Quite so. Time for us to give up the reins, as they say."

"I'm glad you agree. I wasn't looking forward to trying to convince you otherwise."

He patted my knee again. "And you? Will you leave us soon?"

I looked out the windows, beyond the faces, beyond the ficus and hedges and walls of the yard. Varanasi was flowing by. To the east somewhere, the Mother Ganga was making its way through the plains to the Bay of Bengal. "Yes, fairly soon I would imagine. There are people to visit with and say good-bye to, and small affairs to take care of, but as soon as they are done, I will go."

"To Denmark? And then home?"

I nodded. "Quite so, Master. Quite so." I handed him a small package wrapped in bright paper and curled ribbon. I had a short speech prepared. "A small gift for you. I had a teacher I when I was young..."

"You are still young, my boy, and will have many more teachers in your life."

"That's another lesson I have learned, but this teacher taught me mathematics when I was twelve. She taught me about time. The way she explained it, calendars are different all around the world, and seconds and minutes and hours are used only because someone made a decision some time in the past. Babylonians thought sixty was sacred, Christians saw the birth of Christ as a line in history, the Chinese created a different day to start the new year, and so on. It all depends on how you decide to measure it. She called them points of reference. Her lesson sort of stuck with me."

Master removed the gift, which, of course was a watch--Swiss, shiny with gold expandable bands, and no leather straps, and it was set precisely to Varanasi time according to the International Atomic Time clock. He looked, just for a moment, wistfully at his scarred Timex and then unfastened the synthetic blue straps and tossed it on the tea table. The new one fairly blazed on his wrist. "It is the finest gift, except my impertinent daughter and all the people I have loved my in life, that I have ever received." He clapped his hands. "And I will wear it every moment of the day to remind me that you are far too late in returning to my parlor for chai and iddly and afternoon lessons."

"In that case, I will be back before you know it."

"Exactly, my boy. Quite so." He looked from the watch to me. "And what of the Bhavabuti play? It seems I have all the help I need. What about you? You will finish the last scene on your own? You're more than capable, you know, always have been. You could have translated the entire thing by yourself. Never really needed me, you see. I just asked you to come to the parlor because I liked your company."

I grinned. "Master, I needed you for so much more than grammar lessons." I looked around the parlor, the tea table, the woven mat. "I will miss all of it, especially you, more than I thought possible. And I intend to complete the last scene before I reach Denmark."

"I thought as much, my boy. It is time for you to attend to other matters." His expression turned serious. "And what about the money?"

I didn't know what he meant and probably looked perplexed.

"The money. Satnam tells me there will be money coming to us. You, C.G. and I are the authors of three publications that the Sanskrit world is snapping at like hungry fish. A few crore people want to read it."

Having not thought about that at all, I was dumbfounded. It didn't take long for me to decide what to do, though. I wrote it down and handed the paper to him. When he read it, a broad smile appeared and he patted my knee once more. "Brilliant decision, my boy. Brilliant."

Mirabai interrupted us with cucumber and paneer sandwiches, mango and pineapple juice, and three kisses for my forehead. Then she introduced each of the students from BHU. They touched Master's feet and mine—that was a first. The young woman with the intelligent eyes sat next to us on the woven mat where I had sat for so long. Amapani was her name. Her shyness and plastic bangles reminded me of Soma. I agreed to come mornings for as long as it would take to teach her my methods of notation. It wouldn't take long. As the scholars and the media re-entered, I heard her asking Master the source of an obscure complexity in Sanskrit conjugations. It was asked politely, from curiosity, and not from a desire to flaunt her knowledge. As the room began to refill with people, I knew I could leave.

There were still surprises and discoveries for me in Varanasi. I discovered, for instance, that entering a city with a wounded heart is far easier than leaving it with cherished friendships. There would be many that I would miss. I was surprised by how much I suddenly wanted to talk to my mother and father, even my brother. With a stack of long distance phone cards I talked with them for an hour. It wasn't nearly long enough. Other surprises followed.

For ten days I settled affairs and made my rounds throughout the city. I did it with ease, chatting casually with merchants and friends and children, eating in familiar cafes, and saying good-bye to people I suddenly wished I had spent more time with. Sitting and talking without an agenda felt good. I spent an afternoon listening to Petey and Shawn describe how they had come from Blackpool to Varanasi, and I realized that they would probably be released from the great wheel right there in Varanasi. Good for them. I went to Haroon's and marveled at the renovation after the riots--the expansion was continuing. I sipped a mango smoothie contentedly, but the time had a sad edge to it for both of us. It was lightened only by the promises that we would explore the resorts of Cancun and Turks and Caicos at some future date. Knowing Haroon, I was certain that I would receive a letter confirming an arrival in my hometown within the year. I spent the first few days going to Master's to assist him, but Adam had selected well. Each day Amapani accepted more responsibility, and by the end of the week, I stopped coming.

I wrote the forward to Adam's opus. My premise was simple, that good would triumph over its nasty opposite. I thought of Uli as I typed, and the words flowed through the keyboard in liquid ease. I sent it to Britland Press by courier without showing it to Adam, because I already knew he would approve. Then I packed my bags, closed my bank account, and checked off items from my list.

Two evenings before I was to leave, Sahr, Lalji, and I had

dinner together at the dining table. There were candles, flowers, and good china. We had never eaten together that way before, but it seemed so appropriate to share our final meal together. Their futures were, as futures always are, uncertain, but they had good opportunities out there. I gifted them each a fat envelope of rupees, which none of us referred to as severance pay. Lalji and his partners already had clients in our neighborhood, and Sahr was to begin cooking for The Red Palace within the week. Moving on with their lives.

Lalji bussed our dishes to the kitchen and left for his duty as night watchman. Sahr and I sat watching the flickering of the candles for a few minutes. Then we talked about love, the kind you feel when you look for a long time at the stars and are lying next to the only person in the world you should be with. We talked about the light at death and how it probably felt exactly the same, just bigger. The candles burned down, and we kept talking.

With a laugh, I took her hand. "They didn't teach you this in Jesuit School, did they?"

"No Bhimaji, such lessons no teacher can give, I think."

I squeezed her hand and let it go. "I don't think so; you taught me a few, O Great One."

She laughed. "If I did, it was my responsibility; I was told to."

"You were told to? By whom?"

The elephant's trunk scrunched. "Durgubal. He commanded me to take care of you."

The words of river spirit had been rather instrumental in my keeping the bridge at Bareilly intact, so I listened. "When was that," I asked.

"The month before you came to the villa. He told me that you would come, and he told me to take care of you. No harm should come to you, he said, because good would come of it."

"He was right, Sahr. Good did come of it."

Our yawns were coming with more frequency when she asked, "Bhimaji, the gossips of Nagpur say the man-whore in Shivdaspur is to blame for telling the Imams about your Uliana. Is this true?" Her expression had shifted—a sharp stone-etched look. I had only seen it once or twice over the years. One of those had been when she had slapped the transvestite we were just then talking about.

"Yes, it is true. The most reliable source of all confirmed it." The thought of Sutradharak made my stomach churn.

Sahr looked at me and nodded. "I didn't like that lizard." She said nothing more, but in her eyes I saw the same look that had set the whore back on his heels. That look didn't bode well for him.

Seventy-Eight

The train to Delhi was scheduled to depart at midday. Devamukti asked me to come a final time to his house at eight. It gave me the opportunity to finish one more item on my list before I left. I swung my legs over Surya's leathery saddle and pedaled down Shivanan Avenue, across the bridge at the Asi, and along the hidden curve of the Ganges. Carts and rickshaws crowded the street. The smoke of the Ghats hung in the air to the east. Temple bells tolled, and the holymen called from the river's edge. The sacraments of five thousands years continued. I left Nagpur and pedaled along Sonapura Road and then turned right down the lane that fed into gulley to Master's. Charup was squatting idly next to his tire pump, beneath his makeshift lean-to, his eyes scanning every two-wheeled conveyance on the road. As soon as he saw the sparkling rims of Surya, he jumped to his feet yelling, "Sahib, you have returned to my servicing station. Do you wish me to polish the steering bars? Oil the going chain or clean the gears? I am at your bidding."

I let him take the handlebars, while I held the seat with one hand. Suddenly I felt like I was entering an adoption agency with a small child in tow. "Charup, she needs none of these things, unless you wish to do them for yourself. I am leaving Varanasi in a few hours time and Surya, alas, must remain. But I believe she needs to stay with a person who will take good care of her. The best. And the best person to do that is you. She is yours." I let go of the saddle and Charup, whose feet still had no shoes, beamed and laughed like a child.

"Indeed Sahib Bhim, I will be honored to keep her shining like the rani of bicycles that she is. She will be the fairest of the city, waiting only for you to return."

"That may not be for some time, Charup. You take good care of her." With a final ring of her bell with my thumb, I turned and strolled with lighter steps towards Master's.

Mirabai, Sukshmi, Devi, and I sat in the parlor and talked about family, theirs and the one I would be seeing again. I listened to the wedding plans. Devi had definitely taken over.

As the time for leaving drew near, Devi took my hand and walked me to the gardens in the courtyard. The air was warm with the portents of afternoon rain. The melodies of the city tumbled small waves, and it smelled of spices and fresh tar on the road. We didn't sit. He just turned and looked at me--the old condor with his student.

"Three years and three months is a fair amount of time even for one as old as I am, Bhim. That time has been as precious as all rubies of the world. It will be carried with me here always." He tapped his heart and with his other hand, long and delicate fingers stroked the side of my head. "You really were my boy, you know, the son that the old books all tell us we should have. Seeing you in happiness now brings me contentment. Go into your future with good memories. You have a life of bliss before you, and I know you will live it with compassion."

It was the last ritual, our final sacrament, and I knew what to ask. "And I go with your blessing, Master?'

He smiled and kissed my forehead. "A blessing for you, your future wife and children, and theirs. May it all be abundant for you, Bhimaji."

I bent forward, touched his feet with folded hands, and whispered, "Some evening I would like to return to sit on the mat in your parlor, if I may."

"I will be waiting for that moment, but please, when you

return, enter through the front gate."

With a smile, I bowed and walked out that gate.

The final surprise came just before Vinduram Singh's black and yellow taxi arrived to take me to the station. Chandragupta's phone rang. I had only given the number to a few people who might need to contact me in an emergency, so the ring surprised me.

I recognized the subdued voice on the other end immediately. "Mr. Martin Scott, please."

"Inspector Rumir, this is Martin. I am leaving in two minutes for the train station, so I hope this is either very good news, or very short."

He released the usual weary sigh. "I believe it is both, I hope so anyway. I've just had a long conversation with Italian Interpol who informed me that a man has been found in a pensione in Rome, one of the nice, expensive ones near The Spanish Steps. We are not completely certain it is The Sutradharak, or Mejanand Whiton, or Blake McDunough, or Umberto Herrera. You may take your choice. He had a dozen aliases and passports to match them all."

I took a deep breath. "Found, you said?"

"Yes, there was a small gas explosion. A badly burned body was discovered."

I let the irony of that dance momentarily in my brain. "And why does Interpol suspect it's the Sutradharak, if I may ask?"

He sighed again. "Small details were brought to my attention, and I went back through my notes to verify. The body was burned and cut very badly, but a finger was found near it."

"Near it?"

"Yes, it was severed and had a ring like you described."

"An owl?"

"Exactly. There was also an unusual callous."

I felt the one on my own hand and interrupted, "The middle finger, inside the vee, near the knuckle?"

I heard him smiling through the receiver. "Precisely. I observed that you also had a callous in this same place."

I laughed, not deeply, because it wasn't from humor. "Indeed, Inspector, keen observation. It comes from throwing Frisbees. The edge of the disc wears on the middle finger."

"I suspected so."

"There was no other identifying evidence? Just the finger and ring."

"Yes, the were found together. At any rate, I thought you should know that the file will be closed, and the actions of the PuppetMaster will be, like my pursuit of him, relegated to the history books."

"There will be other opportunities, Inspector. Unfortunately for all of us, there are too many of his kind still out there. In the meantime, you have a daughter . . ." I thanked him and hung up. Rumir could be a father now, but he was wrong. Mej always wore the owl on his baby finger.

In the courtyard, Lalji, Sahr, and I cried as we said our good-byes. None of us tried prevent it or wanted to. I started to remind Lalji to take good care of his mother, but held myself. It was clear that he would, and besides, Vinduram was there.

With a last hug and more tears, I took a seat in the front of the taxi. Vin drove, I listened. The turban wagged as he chatted, and the city passed by, and as we neared the station, he told me two more things that altogether didn't surprise me. He was going to ask Sahr to be his wife soon, and the transvestite of Shivdaspur had walked into the wrong section and been given additional alterations during the previous night. Vinduram smiled and added that he doubted anyone would ever seek out his--or her--favors again.

> Black madness flies;
> Comes memory;
> And before my eyes
> My love I see.
> Kalidasa from Sakuntala

Linguists often take note of changes that others might fail to observe. I noticed that in less than twenty hours I went from a place where the villages had suffixes of pura and das to lands where everything ended in burg and dorf—an etymologist's puzzle. From Hamburg I took a commuter flight to Freisburg, feeling the entire time as if I were in a dream, a sweet one where I knew where I was headed. Pictures of Uli rose and sharpened in my mind. I saw her face in the Chowk marketplace. I pictured her arm sparkling through a dozen bracelets on our first date. I felt her wrapped naked about me, and I tasted honeyed almond keer on her lips and patchouli in her hair. The lapis in her eyes caressed my soul. Soon, very soon.

The wheels of the plane bounced and rolled too damned slowly to the gate. I passed immigration and customs, recovered my duffles, and was mildly disappointed that I wasn't pounced upon by my premika as I left the terminal. I stood like a tourist in front. I was a tourist in front. The air felt refrigerated, but to the natives it must have felt balmy—a warm July evening perfect for pastries and ice-cream. I searched the sidewalk. I peered like Devamukti into each car as it pulled to the curb or passed by, and still she wasn't there. A small tic of nervous energy originated in my left foot and began tapping into my ankle all on its own. I inhaled deeply and thought of going back inside to call, when behind me I heard, "How could a woman not at least say hello to cute und fascinating? Und Gott, this one is both."

I spun, and she stood three meters away in burnt orange pajama pants and a white kurta--one that used to be mine--and it was as if the eons of being apart melted away in one vision. "Hello Lover," she said, and we fell into each other's arms to wrap like forest vines.

"Hello, Uliana Hadersen," I replied. With a shy touch, I kissed her lips, and then like incoming waves, her neck, and eyes, and brow. "You look more beautiful than all the flowers of spring. Did I ever tell you how much I love my shirts on you?"

She lay her head against the opal on my chest. "I think so, uhmm . . . yes you have told me. I am only feeling pretty because you are here and my hands can touch you again." She started crying, which of course started me doing the same.

I pulled her head back and kissed the salted moistness on her lips. "There is so much to tell you," I whispered.

"And so much time to do it, Bhim."

I laughed. "It may take a little getting used to, but I think you could begin calling me Marty. No one but you and Jitka know Bhim outside of Varanasi. How is she, by the way?"

"Gut, Mr. Marty, delighted to be in her own feather bed with our mother's cooking on the table, though I think she secretly misses Johnny Chang's und our Afghan café. She told me she is searching Internet recipes for masala dosas. Speaking of that, Mein Schatzki, are you hungry?" Her hand slid beneath the buttons of my shirt and along my stomach, and I wanted to shout with the happiness that boiled inside me.

"Yes, I'm starved."

"Gut," she replied. "I happen to know a small hotel with huge beds, big windows, and a small restaurant across the street."

"The amenities sound perfect. And, My Lovely Premika, I am now passing the torch, you are the guide, so lead on, McDuff."

"Oooh...I like that," she giggled.

We didn't undress slowly like the last time we made love. We tore at each other's clothes, though I did keep in mind how much I liked seeing my kurta on her shoulders and breasts. That was laid across the back of a chair. The pants were yanked off, hers and mine. Mixtures of hunger, greed, generosity, passion and love reunited. In our climax, both of us started weeping again. Afterwards, as we lay stretched sideways on the bed, I pulled her on top of me. "Like that night on the train," she whispered.

"Umm," I answered, "the only part of that journey I wish to remember."

"Ach, The food wasn't bad, the coffee was good, and you did save a lot of people."

"We saved a lot of people, but I don't want to think about it. All I want to think about is you lying on top of me just like this."

She giggled and wriggled and slipped me inside her. "Or like this," she giggled again."

We spent July and August in Tonder, but took five excursions to the coast to traipse about an island called Kongsmark. She was our guide to small hotels with quaint eateries. We savored the solitude we had wished for of in India, but found so rarely. What seemed a dream before became more so. In Tonder I fell in love with her parents, both fluent in English, and each evening at the dinner table I learned more about Uli, how she came to be the woman she was. Her father, Lars, was talented in a hundred ways, had a wry sense of humor and a goatee that reminded me more of a Burger than a political cartoonist from Denmark. He didn't broach the subject of the riots or cartoons until three evenings into my stay. As we dined on broiled trout in mousseline sauce and mustard green salad, he spoke openly of it. There was no shame in the telling, only what he saw as his right to state an opinion through his political sketches. Ingrid, Uli's mother, concurred. She had the equivalent of a P.H.D. in hydrology and glaciology, and referred to herself as modern, open-minded, but with traditional Danish views in regards to raising daughters. She had sculpted cheeks and blue eyes she had obviously gifted to her eldest daughter. The books of their library fascinated me—four languages were represented, and laid end to end would likely have stretched into Norway. I spent time every morning engrossed in a small primer on the Danish language, and in the evening helped in the kitchen—my specialty was salads. Intellectualism was high on the list in the Hadersen household, and Uli and I were expected to sleep in the same bed as long as we didn't slack on chores. I loved my chores.

Each day became the opening of another window into Uliana for me.

One night, a week after I had arrived, we sat in a small cafe on the coast. She had driven us across during that morning to hike the hillsides above the shore. That evening, over chardonnay and lager I told her, "I forgot a small, but important, detail. The publications that Devi, C.G. and I published are making money."

She squinted at me. "Und you are just remembering this detail? Gott, Sahr was right, you could forget your pen is when it is tucked behind your ear. It is gut that I am here to have such a razor sharp memory for you."

I laughed, "Ya, ya. It is gut that you are here, Ms. Hadersen. Gut that I am, too. Your accent is thicker here, you know. And Sahr might have been right about that pen thing, she usually was. But listen, I had Devamukti set things up for the money to go somewhere special."

The smile that slid slowly onto on her lips told me she knew. "You are having it sent to Mata and the Haven for widows, the place near Manikarnika?"

I nodded. "The Soma Tarahansa Trust for Widowed Women. I thought it would do more good than in my pocket. Besides," I smiled, "I have money and I really don't need it."

She kissed my thumb. "A perfect name, and it will be like seeds in a rich soil." She reached for my other hand. "And have you thought about what you will do now?"

I pulled my chair around the arc of the table and slipped my hand into the smoothness at the nape of her neck. "I have thought it all out, and not all of it is related to me. I've decided that you should become a famous geologist and live, at least part-time, in California and teach bright young students all about boring old rocks with entire universes inside them. If that suits you and feels good. Then I though you could upgrade from fair premika to stunningly beautiful wife of a slightly famous linguist and Sanskrit dude."

"Oooh . . . one who does heroic deeds und gives great gifts to the world?"

"Uh huh, the same guy who couldn't do a thing without you by his side."

She kissed me for three breaths and said, "In that case, I would be ecstatic to be his stunning wife."

Uliana made our announcement two days later and we decided upon small ceremonies in two countries. That prompted Ingrid and Jitka to begin planning immediately.

Seventy-Nine

We departed in early September, on an afternoon when the skies were cloudy and a chill mist had settled across the valley. It seemed as if the entire town gathered to wish us safe travels and bid us a quick return.

Jitka made us sandwiches with sausage and olives, strawberry pastries, and mugs of cold beer for our drive to Freisburg. As all of us hugged with promises of our return, I realized that my circles were drawing closed. In twenty hours I would return to San Diego and the arc of my travels would close. I would enter another life in an old setting, and the arc would come back to its origin. Home.

Somewhere over the Atlantic, I read four newspaper articles in different periodicals. They were the beginning of many to come, and the headlines were much more pleasant, more gratifying, than the ones I had read in the airport in New Delhi.

The first came from The Times of India.

Bangalore—New Hope for Diabetic Women. The Women's Clinic of Ulsoor Tank announced yesterday that it will be providing low cost treatments for women suffering from early onset Type II diabetes. Clinic founder, Saraswati Venkateswar, explained to a meeting of financial supporters yesterday that a series of new treatments has been tested and proven 'extremely effective' in a variety of trials. Mrs. Venkateswar added, 'The costs of the medicines and nerve stimulus treatments will be so minimal as to be offered at almost no cost to our patients.'

Durban, South Africa—Indian Treatment for Diabetes Proves Reliable. Chem-Science Laboratories, C.C. released the results of a two-month trial of treatment for diabetes. The results of the trials show 'excellent promise for a full cure of this devastating disease,' said Marcus Rosen, head pathologist for the laboratory and director of the study. 'The original prescription came out of India, and we are, quite honestly, surprised at the effectiveness of the combination of accupressure and common plant ingredients...

Paris, France—Securite Social announced today that it will be providing new programs for diabetic patients under its national health care coverage. The treatments, originating in India, will be fully covered and are designed to provide a complete cure for the disease...

Washington D. C.—The FDA announced this week that it will be delaying the release of its own trial results on a revolutionary new treatment for diabetes. "We need a few more months possibly longer, to properly study the effects of these treatments,' explained Dr. Thomas Ralston, chairman of the drug code directory committee. 'We are not about ready to fast track this just because it has been showing promise in other parts of the world. We have a lot of companies lining up to submit applications, hoping to push their version of this product onto markets in the United States, and we are in the process of determining whether these applications need CFR 314.50s or not. We're certainly not going to be pressured to move too quickly on this.' Asked whether the results of the recent in-house trials showed any promise for a cure, Mr. Ralston declined comment.

The Santa Ana winds were blowing in from the Mojave when Uli and I landed at Lindbergh Field in San Diego. The air was hot and dry and reminded me that it had been four years, nearly to the day, that Lilia had died. Those memories, and all others in of my life, were welcome; they came without pain, or remorse, or fear. They were now bright threads in my tapestry.

After a week of celebration and festivities with my family and friends, and scores of introductions and tours, Uli and I slipped away on a Sunday morning by ourselves. We drove along the La Jolla coastline and watched diamond-filled waves rise and tumble across the reefs and point breaks. We watched agile surfers perform their magic, and ate a fine breakfast of chili rellenos in the park where Lilia and I were to be married. We played Frisbee—a game where I ran and sweat through every pore of my body chasing Uli's slightly wild throws. In time, with a few pointers, the tosses evened out in the gentle winds. And then we swam in cool waves and kissed salty moisture from each other's lips.

"Is this the place?" she asked.

"Yes," I replied. "I spread her ashes from the rocks at the end of the beach."

"And you will teach me how to bodysurf here?"

"Of course," I smiled. "She would have liked that, you riding waves with me. She would have liked you so much."

"Then I will learn how to do it well." She wrapped her arms around my neck and kissed me deeply. "It is all good, Marty. All good."

www.ingramcontent.com/pod-product-compliance
Lightning Source LLC
Chambersburg PA
CBHW051531250626
47157CB00001B/6